Executive Privilege

FORGE BOOKS BY JAY BRANDON

AfterImage

Angel of Death

Executive Privilege

JAY BRANDON

Executive Privilege

A TOM DOHERTY ASSOCIATES BOOK

NEW YORK

EXECUTIVE PRIVILEGE

Copyright © 2001 by Jay Brandon

This book is printed on acid-free paper.

A Forge Book
Published by Tom Doherty Associates, LLC
175 Fifth Avenue
New York, NY 10010

www.tor.com

Forge® is a registered trademark of Tom Doherty Associates, LLC.

Library of Congress Cataloging-in-Publication Data

Brandon, Jay.
    Executive privilege / Jay Brandon.—1st ed.
      p. cm.
    "A Tom Doherty Associates book."
    ISBN 0-312-87425-1 (acid-free paper)
      1. First ladies—Fiction. 2. Marital conflict—Fiction.
    3. Washington (D.C.)—Fiction. 4. San Antonio (Tex.)—Fiction. I. Title.

    PS3552.R315 E88 2001
    815'.54—dc21   2001037134

First Edition: October 2001

Printed in the United States of America

0 9 8 7 6 5 4 3 2 1

★

This is dedicated
to my friends, and colleagues
in writerly struggles,
Robert Flynn
and
Michael Martone.

acknowledgments

Thank you again to my editor, Andy Zack, who suggested, among other things, that I cut my favorite scenes. But he was right, the book was better afterwards. I am also grateful to my agent, Jimmy Vines, for his watchfulness on my behalf, and to Erik Rigler for helping me find (anonymous) sources for information about First Family Secret Service details.

And, though she would not want to be held responsible for anything that follows, if it were not for Sue Hall I would never have written this book.

Thank you all.

Executive Privilege

one

★ The Bexar County Courthouse in San Antonio is more than a hundred years old, the oldest working courthouse among the two hundred fifty-four counties of Texas. The red stone building had played host to thousands and thousands of trials over the years, most with little fanfare. On this particular May afternoon, though, the trial going on in the grand courtroom at the south end of the fourth floor drew more attention than any civil trial in a long time. Hearing that the week-long trial was nearing conclusion, courthouse employees, idle lawyers, reporters, and even a few honest citizens had trickled into the audience seats to hear the final arguments.

Usually only a high-profile criminal case, perhaps a capital murder trial, drew this kind of notoriety. But in the old civil district courtroom much more was at stake than a prison sentence. This was a divorce trial.

David Owens stood at the spacious front of the courtroom, facing the jury across an old-fashioned railing supported by carved wooden posts. To his right Judge Louise Shahan sat attentively, her eyes shifting from David to the opposing lawyer to the gallery of spectators. The twelve jurors seemed to be paying careful attention to David, as much attention to his pauses to collect his thoughts as to his arguments themselves.

David Owens looked very young during those pauses. He was thirty-two but didn't look it. His blue suit fit him a bit loosely; he had lost weight lately. David had black hair, intense blue eyes, and too pale skin, given the ample sunshine San Antonio provided in the late springtime. This case had aged him, but finally in the courtroom he had found fresh supplies of energy.

Out in the spectator area the wooden pews were filled with silent watchers, shoulders touching. The spectators, many of them lawyers, also watched David Owens carefully, not only to judge his speechmaking ability, but for signs that the young lawyer knew how over his head he'd wandered in taking on this case.

At the other counsel table sat the highest-priced divorce lawyer in San Antonio, Ellen Bonham. Her client had chosen her not just for her experience and her reputation, but for her gender. In divorcing his wife of twenty-two years, the client, Rod Smathers, wanted not only to win but not to look like a bad guy. He wanted every minute of the trial to demonstrate that women shouldn't recoil from him in distaste. He was only doing his best for everyone. Hence the woman lawyer, who sat close to him and conferred with him head to head once in a while.

Smathers was the CEO of the only Fortune 100 corporation in San Antonio, the town's most important employer and corporate citizen. He must also have been one of the two or three richest men in town, and intended to remain so after this divorce became final.

David Owens had never done anything in his life that had drawn this much absorbed attention. But as he presented his case to the jury the weight of those stares didn't disturb him. He felt only one gaze on him, that of his client. He also felt the weight of three people who weren't in the courthouse, and his heart beat heavily.

To the jurors David said, "My opposing counsel has asked you whether Mr. Smathers should be punished for having made such a good life for his family. Should he be punished for his hard work, for providing his wife and children a beautiful home and lifestyle? Should he be punished for that by having his children taken from him now?

"Of course the answer is no." David saw the jurors' eyes widen, and heard a small gasp from his client. He went quickly on. "Mr. Smathers and my client Mary Smathers came to an agreement years ago, when their first child was born. He would work and provide income. She would take care of the children. That was the deal, and it worked well.

"But somewhere over the years their arrangement became more than a way to share responsibilities. Their roles took them over. Mr. Smathers's business began to consume his life. He became obsessed with rising to the absolute top of his company. He made it. But family life had to give way to his quest."

"Objection," Ellen Bonham said loudly. "There was testimony that my client spent lots of time with—"

Judge Shahan quickly cut her off. "The jury will remember the evidence as they heard it," she instructed, adding quietly. "Pay attention to your own memories, not to what the lawyers say."

"You heard the testimony," David said to the jury. "Not just of working long hours during the week, but of spending weekends on business trips or playing golf with important clients. That's what you have to do to get to the top of the business world, and Mr. Smathers did it."

David turned from the jury toward his client, and walked slowly toward her. "Meanwhile, something similar happened to Mary Smathers. She played her assigned role in the family, she stayed home with the children, but just as with her husband, her role took her over. Mary became a full-time mother in every sense. When a child woke up scared in the middle of the night, he called for Mom. And she came. When a child skinned her knee in the backyard, it was Mom who doctored it. For driving the car pool and chaperoning field trips and attending music recitals, the Smathers children have had only one parent."

David stood between the counsel tables, letting the jury look at the opponents who had once been lovers. Rod Smathers in his early fifties looked younger. He had kept in good shape, his jawline didn't sag, his dark suit fit him well. He looked authoritative and decisive. His wife across the aisle in her pale peach jacket and skirt didn't seem to belong with him. Mary Smathers had been very pretty when they had married, but frankly nowhere near beautiful enough to be the wife of one of the most important business leaders in Texas. In her mid-forties now, she seemed headed briskly for matronhood. She remained pretty, but in a mature way for which a different word was needed. Mary had become attractive in an almost middle-aged, lightly tended way. Trial had not brought out the best in her appearance. Her cheeks had red splotches and her eyes showed traces of those interrupted nights of motherhood and of tears recently shed. She gazed at her lawyer with obvious fright.

David asked, "Should either of them be punished for the roles they assumed? No. This isn't about punishment. This is about what's best for the children. The judge's instructions and your own good sense tell you that you have to look at your decision from the point of view of the children. If you award primary custody of these three children to their father, they'll have every material thing they could ever want: horses on the family ranch, private schools, cars when they're old enough, trips all over the world with Dad . . . once a year or so.

"But who's going to doctor their scraped knees every day? The maid. A housekeeper, a nanny. Or nobody.

"Giving this mother primary custody of the children won't hurt Mr. Smathers one bit. You've seen the standard possession order for the noncustodial parent. If Mr. Smathers exercises those times of possession—one evening a week and the entire weekend every other week, plus a month in the summer—it will be more time than he's spent with his children in their lives. He's never wanted that much time with them before. And now he says he wants even more. He wants primary custody. He wants to be the one to tuck his three children in every night."

David surveyed the jury, eight men and four women. Ellen Bonham had gotten her way there, using nearly all her strikes on women, who would be presumed more sympathetic toward David's client. But looking at the jurors, David had begun to feel a rapport with them. He wondered if trial lawyers always developed that feeling. David wouldn't know. This was only the fifth jury trial of his career, his second as lead counsel.

"It's Rod Smathers who thinks in terms of punishing people. That's what this trial is all about. That's the only reason he's asked for custody: to hurt his wife. To punish her for daring to ask for more of *his* money than he's—"

"Objection!" the other lawyer almost shouted, rising to her feet. "There is absolutely no evidence to support this argument of counsel's. Furthermore he knows very well that the division of property is no concern of this jury's. The only issue before them is custody."

Judge Shahan sat in thoughtful silence, casting back her memory over the whole four-day trial. "That's sustained. Move on to another topic, Mr. Owens."

David didn't. "I think you can figure it out for yourselves," David said to the jury. "You can see from Mary's testimony, from her very anxiety about this case, why she wants primary custody of these children. Because that's what's best for them, that they stay with the mother who's raised them. What's Mr. Smathers's reason for asking for primary custody? So that his children can be baby-sat by nannies and maids while he works late and jets around the country.

"Think about those motivations. Then you decide which of these parents has the best interests of these children at heart."

He didn't realize until he'd said it that that would be his closing sentence, but David at least recognized an end line when he heard one. He turned rather abruptly and resumed his seat beside his client. Under the table she took his hand and squeezed it so tightly the tips of his fingers turned instantly white.

Judge Shahan quickly dismissed the jury to their deliberations, but didn't leave the bench. Leaning casually in her high-backed black chair, she asked, "Ready for my part of the decision?"

Before the jury portion of the trial had begun, the parties had presented evidence concerning the Smatherses' community property to the judge. In Texas, juries have very narrow powers to decide issues in divorce trials, primarily custody of the children. Judges decide how to divide the property.

Ellen Bonham rose quickly to her feet. "If you are, Your Honor. Of course I'd like to present argument on the property division first."

The judge paused a beat, then said, "Of course, Counsel. Take as long as you like."

Uh oh. David recognized that the judge's order didn't free Bonham in the way it sounded. It was an offer of ample rope. Judge Shahan had probably already made up her mind, or almost. Overlong or overly intense argument would only raise her hostility. Bonham wouldn't be doing her client any favors by talking too much.

Just on the near side of fifty, Ellen Bonham had been practicing family law in San Antonio for twenty-five years. Always soft-spoken and cordial in negotiation, she changed in appearances before a judge or jury. She focused fiercely, never letting a point pass without putting her own spin on it. She knew the judges intimately and held their respect.

"I just want to remind the court of a couple of points. First, there's Mr. Smathers's personal property that isn't included in the community estate. The house at the coast that he inherited from his aunt, and the block of Travis Investments stock left him by his father, which has appreciated in value but only due to dividends and rise in stock prices, not because Mr. Smathers invested community time in the stock. I'm sure the court is aware—"

"I don't plan to take anything of his from him, Counselor," the judge said quietly.

Bonham hurried smoothly on. "As for the rest of the community property, we are only asking for an equal division. I do think it's appropriate that Mr. Smathers be awarded the stock options in the company he heads, since those are incentives for his performance as CEO and closely caught up in the company itself. The house should be sold and the proceeds divided equally, after Mr. Smathers is compensated for his separate property that was used for down payment eight years ago. That's all, Your Honor."

With a slight movement of her head the judge turned her attention to the other lawyer. Ellen Bonham also watched David Owens attentively, hoping he would talk the judge into boredom and his case down the tubes.

From his seat at counsel table David said, "We don't care about the property division, Your Honor."

This announcement caused a stir among the spectators, but drew no reaction from David's client. Seeming to affirm what her lawyer had said, Mary Smathers sat staring at the closed door through which the jurors had departed.

David rose to his feet. "But for the sake of the children we have to argue about money. Because Mr. Smathers hasn't offered them enough to support those children in the way—"

"Objection, Your Honor! Settlement negotiations are inadmissible, and there's been no evidence—"

"She's right, Mr. Owens. Move on," the judge ruled.

"Your Honor, I suggest you order that the bulk of the community estate follow the children. The community estate is valued at approximately eighty-two or -three million dollars. If Mary Smathers doesn't get custody of her children, a tenth of that will sustain her comfortably. It won't matter to her how much money she has in the bank if she doesn't have her children with her.

"But if the jury awards her primary custody, she should have the bulk of the community estate. Those four people will be on their own financially, with no hope of the kind of income they've enjoyed as Rod Smathers's family. Mary will need to provide schooling, travel, college educations, everything those children deserve. Everything they'd be assured of having if only their parents had managed to stay together."

Abruptly David sat down, looking weary. Ellen Bonham stared at him, looking for cunning strategy in the nonsense he'd just spouted.

But Judge Shahan nodded thoughtfully. She too looked appraisingly at the young lawyer. "So you want to roll the dice with your client's money, eh, Counselor? I find that an excellent suggestion."

"What?!" Bonham said, echoed by so many lawyers in the audience who thought they were speaking quietly that they made a ghostly chorus from all parts of the courtroom.

"Yes," the judge said. "It's the children who should have the money. Mr. Smathers, if you are given custody of the children I'm going to award a disproportionate share of the community estate to you. But I'm going to award it to you as trustee for your children. If this happens, within sixty days of the date of my ruling I want you to show me proof that the money has gone into irrevocable trusts with your three children as the beneficiaries."

Rod Smathers had looked momentarily pleased, then puzzled. He recovered quickly, half rose, and said, "Uh, that's fine, Your Honor."

"I'm not asking for your approval. On the other hand, if Mrs. Smathers is awarded primary custody, I'm going to award her ninety percent of the community estate."

"What?!!" This time it was Rod Smathers who shouted the question.

"Sit down. Yes, of the community estate of eighty-three million dollars—a figure I find remarkably low, by the way, for an executive as well compensated as you are—"

"I've only been CEO for two years, Your Honor. Before that I was simply an employee with a salary."

"Save it, Mr. Smathers. I'm only saying that if it turns out in the next few years that you receive a hefty deferred compensation package, I'd be willing to entertain a bill of review for fraud on the community." That comment was directed at David Owens, who caught it. The judge continued. "I will award Mrs. Smathers the house, and award you the mortgage debt on it. You wouldn't want to put your children out of their home, would you? Also I will award Mrs. Smathers ninety percent of the remaining assets. I can do that, Mr. Smathers, because I find that you are at fault in the breakup of this marriage. There was no testimony that your wife did anything wrong except devote too much of her time to the children. You're the one who changed, working longer and longer hours and being gone from home more and more frequently. I wouldn't be surprised if your emotional life had left your family behind as well.

"The community should be reimbursed for that lost time, and all I can award them is money."

Smathers looked confused and short of breath. "You'll be award-ing it to her in trust, Your Honor, like with me?"

"No. I trust her to use the money for the benefit of the children. That's been the whole pattern of her life. And of course I'll also be ordering child support and spousal support. But we'll get to those after we hear from the jury."

"Funny, Mr. Smathers," Judge Shahan concluded ironically, "for the first time you look concerned about the jury's verdict. Your wife has looked pretty anxious about it all along."

The judge rose casually and strolled down the courtroom aisle, waving a hand to tell the spectators not to rise on her behalf. But the audience members stood up anyway, some walking out into the hall, others standing in clumps discussing the interesting spectacle they'd just witnessed. A newspaper reporter circulated, asking lawyers if the proceeding had been as unorthodox as it seemed. Most assured him that it had indeed been unusual, starting with the fact that David Owens had presented at least as good a final argument as Ellen Bonham and concluding with the judge's odd ruling on the community property division. All in all it had been a highly enter-taining morning in court.

As the courtroom emptied out Mary Smathers slumped in her chair. Her head close to her lawyer's, she said quietly but in a heart-felt tone, "If that jury gives him custody I'll kill myself. Or him."

Her words chilled the air, not just because of the threat itself, but because Mary Smathers sounded so downcast that she must have thought about this idea very seriously.

But David Owens didn't sound worried. "No you won't," he said firmly, not an order but a prediction. "Because your children will still need you no matter what happens. You couldn't do that to them."

Mrs. Smathers raised her head. Her features grew more serene as she thought about her children, and David knew she was remem-bering something one of them had done or said.

An hour passed. Ellen Bonham and her glowering client returned to her office a few blocks away. David suggested that he and Mrs.

Smathers do the same, but she wanted to stay. At three-thirty she called to make sure her children were safely home from school. She talked to each of them in turn, and that was the first time that day she smiled, though her eyes glistened. After the call she went off to the ladies' room for some time.

David phoned his office. There had been no calls of consequence. His secretary sounded bored. With the preparations for this trial done, David's office produced very little activity. Since he'd gone into private practice this had been his only case.

At four-fifteen, after two hours and a quarter of deliberations, the jurors rang their buzzer. Judge Shahan emerged from her chambers saying, "So soon?" and shot a glance at David as if she wanted to tell him something, but refrained.

It hadn't seemed like a short time to Mary Smathers. They had to wait another twenty minutes for Mr. Smathers and his lawyer to return, and Mrs. Smathers vibrated like crystal the whole time. Her life's fate rested on a piece of paper behind that closed jury-room door. That twenty-minute delay was one of the cruelest things her husband had ever done to her.

The room gradually filled as word that the verdict was in spread through the courthouse. Even the judge took the unusual step of sitting behind the bench waiting, along with everyone else.

At least when he arrived Smathers looked grim. David would have wanted to punch him if the executive had looked unconcerned about this verdict. It wasn't about money. The judge could award Mary Smathers the whole community estate, and Rod Smathers would make it back in a couple of years. What bothered him was the judge's public ruling that he hadn't been a good husband. Smathers treasured his public image, serving on charitable boards and making enough corporate donations to have his name on public projects all over town. It was good for business, good for his ego. The only way to redeem himself in this trial was for the jury to find him a good father by awarding him custody of his children. Smathers didn't look at his soon-to-be ex-wife at all. But he glared at David Owens, the lawyer who had cost him part of his good name.

The jurors filed into the jury box. A few of them looked sheepish and shy as jurors often do during their time in the public spotlight. But most of them held their heads high, looking directly at the two parties. Two women and one man smiled reassuringly at Mrs. Smathers. David's heart began to unclench, but sometimes jurors gave those sympathetic looks to the losing party, to say, *We don't think you're a bad person even though we just screwed you with our verdict.*

"Have you reached a decision?" the judge asked.

A juror on the front row stood up, a man with a bland expression but alert eyes. He wore a checked shirt and solid blue tie, which made him look like a professor or engineer. His quiet manner had marked him as a follower in the eyes of the lawyers who'd left him on the jury, but now he displayed a quiet authority. "Yes, Your Honor."

The judge nodded and the foreman continued, "We find that the best interests of the children would be served by awarding primary custody to their mother, Mary Smathers."

Mrs. Smathers gave a long, shuddering sigh, sinking back into her chair as if suddenly boneless. David squeezed her hand, got no response, and turned toward her, afraid she'd had a heart attack. But his client sat with eyes uplifted and an enormous smile beginning to shape her mouth.

Past Mrs. Smathers David saw her husband. Mary hadn't glanced at him at all. This wasn't a triumphant moment for her, it was just a relief. But Rod Smathers watched his wife questioningly, as if asking himself if he'd been wrong to oppose her for custody at all. Then the executive's eyes lifted to David and his expression changed to one of pure hatred.

There had been a rather noisy reaction from the audience, but it died down quickly as the jury foreman remained standing. In a voice that carried, the man said to the judge, "We also have a request to make of you, Your Honor. That's what took so long, composing what we wanted to ask. Is it possible for you to order that Mr. Smathers *must* exercise all his visitation times, or be fined or sanctioned or otherwise punished if he doesn't? We think that would be in the best interests of the children."

Judge Shahan smiled at him serenely, and didn't answer the question. "Thank you for that advice, Mr. Foreman. I'll take it under consideration. Now the jury is dismissed with the heartfelt thanks of the court, and of the parties too, I'm sure. Thank you for resolving this difficult question."

"It was easy, Your Honor," the foreman said, and several jurors nodded as they made their way out of the jury box.

"Now on to my issues," Judge Shahan said, with relish in her voice. "Mr. Smathers, as promised, I'm awarding ninety percent of the community estate to Mrs. Shahan. I'm also ordering you to pay four thousand dollars a month in child support, because I find that the children have special needs of that amount. Counseling, for one thing, to get over the trauma of this breakup. I also order you to pay spousal support to Mary Smathers of two thousand five hundred dollars a month for a period of three years."

Rod Smathers looked as if he'd been struck a body blow and then slapped in the face. That amount of monthly support would mean very little to him. But the judge had just ordered the maximum of everything from him to his wife and children. He looked at his lawyer in surprise beginning to turn to anger.

"Anything else? Oh, yes, attorney's fees. Mr. Smathers, I also order you to pay your wife's attorney's fees of—what was the amount you testified to, Mr. Owens?"

"One hundred and twelve thousand dollars and change, Your Honor." David felt embarrassed at saying the amount aloud, but it was accurate: he had worked on nothing else but this case for months.

"I'm surprised your fees didn't run higher," said the judge. "But I order you to pay that amount, Mr. Smathers, directly to your wife's attorney Mr. Owens. David, will you draw up the final decree?"

"Of course, Your Honor."

"I'm sure we'll be back together on other issues, but that's all for today. Oh, except for the most important thing. I grant the divorce on the grounds that the marriage has grown insupportable. Also on the grounds of fault. Good luck to you both."

The judge left the bench quickly and disappeared into her office, not catching anyone's eye. Abruptly court was no longer in session. They all just stood in a big public room, like children finding themselves on a playground. David breathed his own sigh of relief. It seemed he'd been holding his breath for a long time.

Suddenly what little breath remained in his body whooshed out as his client clutched him tightly. Tears flowed down her cheeks onto his collar. "Thank you," she said softly, but so fervently that David felt warmed all over.

"I'm so glad," he answered.

Mary Smathers pulled back suddenly and said, "I'm going to call them."

"Don't say—" David began, but she stopped him. "I'm not going to brag to them, David, I just want to tell them I'm coming home."

Then she beamed the brightest smile he'd ever seen and left quickly, not answering or even seeming to hear the reporters who called questions at her. The bailiff let her disappear into a court office that, David knew, had a rear exit.

He lifted his own face, more in relief than joy, glad the trial was over, glad he'd won, glad mainly to have the enormous responsibility of his client's hopes off him.

"Congratulations," said a quiet voice. Ellen Bonham stood before him, holding out her hand. Her client had stalked away, talking angrily into his cell phone. A man in a black suit hurried after him.

"Thank you," David said, meaning more than thanks for her congratulations. Bonham had been a tough but fair opponent, keeping him so alert that there had been nights when he'd awakened sweating, thinking he'd missed something Bonham had put past him.

"You did a good job."

"You were awesome," David answered, then lowered his voice. "Although it seemed to me you laid back a little bit in your final argument."

She shook her head, making her brown hair swing. "Never. Once

I take on a client I do my absolute best for him." She glanced across the courtroom at the noisy Rod Smathers. "No matter what," she sighed. To David she added, "I hope this case does you some good. But you've made some powerful people very unhappy. Watch your back, kid."

David thought that a figure of speech, until seconds later when a hand grabbed his shoulder fiercely and spun him around. David found himself staring into the face of Roger Ainesworth, inches from his own. Until that moment David had also thought the phrase "breathing fire" was only an expression, but Ainesworth seemed to be doing just that. He glared so fiercely and breathed so hard that bits of the red and white peppermint he habitually sucked sprayed out of his mouth, looking like flame. A year ago, Ainesworth had been David's boss, the managing partner of Reynolds McCrory, one of the most prestigious law firms in the city. He dressed conservatively always, today in a black suit, white shirt, and crested tie. Ainesworth's dark hair had receded respectably from his forehead, leaving an arrowhead of hair pointing forward. His small dark eyes glared past his sharp nose, so that Ainesworth's whole face seemed aimed at his former colleague.

"Don't think you've won anything here today," he said angrily.

"Gosh, Roger, I think I have. Seventy-something million dollars, custody of the children, my attorney's fees . . ."

David's carefee tone calmed the angry lawyer. Ainesworth snorted a laugh and said, "You don't think you're going to see a penny of that money, do you? First it will take you months to get a decree entered. Then post-judgment discovery. Then we'll give notice of appeal. You remember how long one of our appeals can last, don't you, David? You'll be a little old lawyer before this case ends. That's right, Reynolds McCrory is taking over Rod Smathers's divorce case now. Where we should have been all along. Ellen Bonham was just for show."

David suddenly lost much of his joy, because he knew the truth of Ainesworth's claims. But he answered, "Roger, I don't think your client will be able to post a big enough bond to avoid paying that judgment. Mrs. Smathers will get her money no matter what you—"

"We don't care about that. It's your money we'll put a hold on, David. And your business. Solo practice!" Ainesworth laughed sneeringly. "Has it been fun on your own, David? You don't even have a paralegal, do you? Have you noticed how little the phone rings?"

Roger Ainesworth stopped abruptly, no doubt realizing he might be opening himself up to a lawsuit. He'd said enough to get his point across, without actually admitting anything that could be construed as evidence of retaliation.

With a confidence he didn't feel, David said, "I think this case might bring me in a little business, don't you, Roger? There's been a certain amount of publicity, or hadn't you noticed? And after this verdict—"

"Sure. Divorce clients. Housewives who want you to take on their cases for no money up front in hopes that their husbands will be ordered to pay your fees somewhere way down the line. Think that'll keep you going for a year?"

Ainesworth lowered his voice. David knew he was about to say something that he would later deny. "Rod Smathers should have been our client all along, with all his corporate business. He would've been if you hadn't insisted on representing his wife instead. But we'll get him back. Right this minute he only wants one thing in the world, and that's to see you ruined. And you remember us, don't you, David?"

Meaning Reynolds McCrory was just the firm to ruin someone. They'd had lots of practice. The brief conversation had cheered Roger Ainesworth enormously. He smiled as if offering congratulations, clapped David on the upper arm, and turned away, then hurried after his prospective client.

Meeting his former boss had had exactly the opposite effect on David. He felt hollow. He had to force himself to put on a triumphant air to accept lawyers' congratulations and answer the questions of reporters. After all, David would need the publicity.

Three weeks later David Owens sat in his small office as the work-day drew to an end. David wore a suit rumpled from a day of sitting, but might as well have been in jeans. He hadn't been back in a courtroom since the end of the Smathers trial.

The verdict for Mary Smathers had generated a good deal of local publicity, even a mention in a national newsmagazine story about the empowering of traditional women. In the first couple of days after the trial David had spent more time being interviewed than lawyering. But that soon died away, other events became newer news, and David settled down to a law practice that did not bloom spectacularly as a result of his one win. In fact, his career seemed in imminent danger of withering away.

Rod Smathers and Reynolds McCrory between them wielded an enormous amount of influence in San Antonio. If they were trying to strangle David's law practice, as Roger Ainesworth had almost announced, they were doing a good job. Most divorce cases came as referrals from lawyers who practiced other kinds of law. Those had stopped altogether, like a faucet being tightly turned off. There had been a flurry of phone calls and prospective new clients after David's triumph in court, but Ainesworth had accurately predicted the type of those clients: women who had spent their lives as homemakers and mothers, and so had no money to pay a retainer. David had taken on a few of these cases, but they'd brought in very little cash.

David felt as if he were living someone else's life, or a bad dream. This had not been his destiny: sitting lonely in a shabby little office in an old downtown building. Eight years ago he had graduated near the top of his class from the University of Texas law school, already with a job at the top-dollar, prestigious law firm of Reynolds McCrory. He'd started in litigation, where the tough guys practiced law, and proven himself a quick learner and clever strategist.

The detour in his career had come without David's realizing that there had been a fork in the road, let alone that he'd taken the turnoff. A business client had asked him to represent his son in a divorce. There were no children, little property to divide, just the formalities of paperwork. David had done it as the kind of good deed one does to hang on to good clients.

But then somehow he became known as the family lawyer at Reynolds McCrory. He handled a few other divorces for other good clients. Family law didn't become a significant part of his practice, but he gained experience at it. So when Mary Smathers called wanting to talk about a divorce matter—for a friend, she said—the firm had steered her to David. As it happened, they knew each other slightly already, from serving on a charitable foundation board together. At that first meeting in David's office Mrs. Smathers had been coy, saying she just wanted general information to pass on to her friend. David had been sympathetic and informative, not trying to prove his expertise at family law. He wasn't angling to acquire the case of her "friend."

But when Mrs. Smathers had left after that first visit, Roger Ainesworth stopped David in the hall and almost licked his lips at the thought of who David had had in his office. "Be good to her. We'd love to get her husband as a client."

"Yes, sir."

David saw Mrs. Smathers again only a few days later, at a board meeting at the downtown public library, a few blocks from David's office. During the meeting he noticed her anxious, distracted air, but he wouldn't have intruded except that she turned to him quite suddenly as the meeting broke up and began talking to him. Her conversation was inconsequential until they walked out of the library, alone by that time.

"It wasn't for a friend," Mary Smathers said. She started talking about her husband, of his drifting away not only from her but from their children as well. About her loneliness, her fears for the children, uncertainty about what to do. Within minutes she'd completely won David's sympathy. She made it sound as if her children had lost their father to a tragedy. Then she'd pulled out the divorce petition.

"This is why I came to see you."

David looked over the simple form quickly. He flipped to the last page to see the lawyer's name, whistled a low whistle at seeing the petition had been signed by Ellen Bonham, then looked again at the attached first page, which showed when the petition had been served on Mrs. Smathers. He grew a little alarmed. "How long have you been hanging on to this? You know you have to file an answer. If you don't he can get a decree entered that says whatever he wants. He can take all the money, the children . . ."

"I haven't been able to think what to do," Mary Smathers moaned.

"The answer's due to be filed today."

"I thought so. Can you—?"

Thinking quickly, David said, "I can recommend someone. Your husband has one of the best divorce lawyers in town, you need a good one too. Let's go to my office, it's right over here, I can make some phone calls."

"Can you do it?" Mary Smathers asked, with a shy, earnest expression that would have looked at home on a much younger face. "Can you represent me?"

David meant to say no. He knew he should decline for a variety of reasons, including the good of the law firm. But when Mrs. Smathers added, "I trust you," David couldn't refuse. They hurried back to his office, and David drew up the simple answer, having it filed before the courthouse closed that afternoon.

If he had known how he was changing his own future, he would certainly have hesitated longer.

Roger Ainesworth went nuclear when he heard the news. A short impromptu conference convened in David's office, the young lawyer sitting bemused behind his desk, older and more important lawyers crowding in to discuss his blunder. "Get rid of her!" Ainesworth screamed shrilly. "We can't get her husband for a client if you're representing her against him!"

"It's probably already too late," another partner pointed out. "David's already entered an appearance on her behalf. We could never—"

"No, we couldn't represent the husband in this case, the divorce case. Who cares? But we do manage to let him know that our boy David withdrew out of respect for him." Ainesworth began to smile. "This could work out well, in fact. Good thinking, David. You withdraw, we quietly help Rod Smathers with the business aspects of this case, he gets comfortable with us . . . and of course we let him meet you. This can be great. But you've got to withdraw, David. Today. We're into damage control now, we have to move quickly."

That clenched it. Because when David Owens received a direct order, he naturally resisted. When he looked into Roger Ainesworth's shiny face, the beginning of a smile stretching the managing partner's mouth unattractively, and thought of the contrast between that face and Mary Smathers's, David's decision seemed easy.

David withdrew, all right. From the firm of Reynolds McCrory. That day.

That decision landed him here, in this small office in a nondescript medium-sized old office building, a few blocks and millions of miles from the gleaming tower that housed Reynolds McCrory. It had been heady to be on his own, caught up in the intensity of the Smathers divorce case. Now, having ended that case in triumph, David's life had settled down to the reality of small-time law practice. Every day found him pondering just where his life had changed, and whether he would make the same decisions if he had the chance again. Pointless speculation. This was the life he had: locally famous divorce lawyer, headed relentlessly for bankruptcy.

He felt a shift in the building's current, or the day. Dusk growing quietly. He should let his secretary Janice go home. She just killed time during the day anyway. But just as David was about to buzz her, he heard the small chiming sound the front door of his office made when it opened. He waited expectantly, and a minute later Janice entered. His secretary was a few years older than David, slender with nervousness, given to staring at him sometimes as if she disapproved of him. But on occasion, such as now, her brown eyes grew large with anticipation or curiosity. "Someone new," she said. "She just says she wants to see you, it won't take long. Her name is Helen Wills. That's all she'll tell me."

Janice made it seem very mysterious, but David's curiosity barely stirred. Divorce clients often appeared furtive after making that decision to seek out a lawyer. For many of them it was the first time in their lives they needed a lawyer, and they didn't like the idea. David made his way down the short hallway into his reception room, which held Janice's metal desk, three straight-backed chairs for clients, and a small spindly-legged table. If a whole family came to see David, the reception room grew crowded.

The waiting woman didn't take up much space, though. A slimly elegant blonde, Helen Wills was younger than David had expected, around his own age. In a dark suit, she looked more like a businesswoman than a housewife. She wore no wedding ring or any other jewelry. As soon as David entered the reception room the woman's eyes attached to him, studying him critically. This appraising stare also set her apart from the average first-time client, who would usually spend half the time looking at the floor, embarrassed to be there. But Helen Wills looked David over quite frankly.

"Ms. Wills? Would you like to come in?"

She did. As she passed him she said, "I'm not interrupting something important, am I? I'm sorry I couldn't call for an appointment." David thought he detected irony in her voice, and wondered what she knew about him. He exchanged a glance with Janice.

Helen Wills strode ahead of David to his office, and looked around while he closed the door and circled to his desk chair. She gave his office the same knowing looks she'd given him, glancing quickly at his framed diplomas and law license on the wall, giving a little more study to his furniture: the large oak desk he'd bought secondhand, the much more modern black computer desk and bookcase, which David had put together himself after buying them at Target. In his old office the furniture had belonged to the firm. He'd had to furnish this one quickly and efficiently, and his previous client Mary Smathers hadn't paid attention to the office furnishings. Helen Wills did.

But she didn't say anything, caustic or otherwise. Nor did she take a seat, even when David waved her toward one of the client chairs. Oddly, she didn't pace or fidget, either. It's a hard trick to pull off, just standing straight. Helen did it unself-consciously.

"What can I do for you, Ms. Wills?"

"Not a thing, Mr. Owens. I think I should tell you that this isn't my idea, and I don't think it's a good one."

"You mean your husband has forced this decision on you?"

"I'm not married."

Now she had baffled him. If she didn't need a family lawyer, what was she doing here? David suddenly wondered if Roger Ainesworth from his old firm had sent her. Was she an emissary here to offer him peace, or was her job just to report back on David's circumstances? That would account for her watchfulness, as if she had to give a report on this meeting.

He tried her own approach, just sitting silently until she felt like talking. That suited Ms. Wills fine. She continued to stand and to look around, now out one of David's two windows. He had a nice view from the fourteenth floor here, although bigger windows would have done the hills in the distance more justice.

"Ms. Wills, I took it you wanted to talk to me about something. A legal situation, I presume. Are you uncomfortable? Would you like something to drink?"

"I'm fine. It is getting to the end of the workday, though. Why don't you let your secretary go for the day?"

"She works until five-thirty."

Helen Wills didn't answer. Her silence and her posture made it clear that she wouldn't say anything about the purpose of her visit until she and David were completely alone. David knew what a bad idea that was. For a variety of reasons one often wanted a witness close by in a law office. Vulnerable, emotional clients opening up about their personal lives: who knew where that might lead?

"I'm not going to hurt you," his visitor said wryly. It was the first time she'd sounded less than perfectly serious. David liked her better for it, but that didn't mean he trusted her.

Nevertheless, he picked up his phone, pressed the intercom button, and said, "Janice, you can take off now. Have a good evening."

"Yes, sir," Janice answered, a phrase she never used, the suspicion in her voice so obvious that he could feel it entering his own office. He hung up and he and Ms. Wills looked at each other for a minute or two until they heard the chime of the front door. She opened David's office door and disappeared, apparently making sure that Janice had gone. Was this the part where his visitor reentered his office suddenly naked? David pictured that, with a certain enjoyment, in fact.

Ms. Wills came back in briskly, fully clothed and still moving quickly. "Does that door open into the hall?" she asked, indicating the other door in David's office. She crossed to it before he could answer. She opened the door, looked out into the hall, and seemed satisfied. "Just a minute," she said over her shoulder, found the button that unlocked the door so it could be opened from the outside, and disappeared again.

David thought about relocking the door. He also thought he should call someone, have the phone line open as a kind of witness line. But he couldn't think whom to call. Just as he picked up his phone his hall door opened again and Helen Wills returned. She held the door open for someone coming in after her, a woman who acted much more like a typical divorce client. She ducked her head, averted her eyes, and left in place a scarf that acted almost as a veil.

David began to resent the mysteriousness. Helen Wills quickly relocked and closed the door, then gave David her most penetrating stare yet, but one with a hint of pleading in it. "This never happened," she said forcefully.

"You're right about that," David answered with equal firmness. He put down his phone and came around his desk to confront her. "Nothing has and nothing will if you don't stop behaving in this childish—"

"I'm sorry, Mr. Owens," the other lady said. She had a higher but more mature voice than Helen Wills. And her voice sounded oddly familiar, though David felt sure he'd never met the lady. "The childishness is my fault. I have to be very careful."

She removed her hat and pulled the scarf down around her neck, and turned to face David fully for the first time. He stopped dead, his jaw hanging. That was a good thing, because if he had spoken at that moment he would probably have said something foolish. Of course, this lady had probably grown accustomed to people stammering when first meeting her. Her weeks were filled with such meetings, as a matter of fact.

"I'm Myra McPherson," the lady said, extending her hand.

He knew that. Anyone would recognize McPherson, the wife of the President of the United States.

Ten minutes later the scene had gained a semblance of ordinariness. The First Lady sat in one of the client chairs, a glass of diet soda on the desk in front of her. David had resumed his normal seat at the desk, and had regained some composure as well. "I didn't even know you were in town," he said lamely.

"It's a quiet visit. We had an event in Houston, then I always try to stop by home."

David had almost forgotten, as had most people, that San Antonio was theoretically the hometown of the President and First Lady. John McPherson had lived here before being elected to the Senate and then to the presidency. The first family retained the fiction of legal residence in Texas for voting purposes, but in fact had lived in D.C. for years and had little more contact with San Antonio than any other city in America.

"Actually I'm from Baytown, near Houston?" Mrs. McPherson said, in the southern style of speech of making a statement a question. David nodded. "I never really lived here. John was already in the Senate when we married. We've been away from Texas a long time."

"That's true," David said, wondering at the purpose for this visit. The enigmatic Helen remained standing, slightly behind the First Lady. Myra McPherson seemed the most comfortable person in the room. She sat quietly, not fidgeting with her hands or crossing and recrossing her legs. But her neck showed a certain tension, and she had trouble keeping her eyes on David.

Myra McPherson was in her late thirties, very young for a First Lady, twelve years younger than her husband. In person she seemed younger still, hesitant and shy in an odd way. She had a slender face framed by straight brown hair, and clear gray eyes that seemed elongated sideways: doe's eyes. When she leaned toward David, he felt the thrill of intimacy with the famous. But Mrs. McPherson had a very human quality.

"You must be wondering why I'm here," she said suddenly. She had read David's mind—not a difficult trick under the circumstances. "I've read about you recently."

"Ah. Don't tell me you're here to ask for advice for a friend. You could have had your assistant do that." He hesitated over the word "assistant," looking at Helen Wills. She might be a Secret Service agent, a bodyguard. "Did you have some personal interest in the Smathers case? Do you know Mary Smathers?"

Mrs. McPherson glanced up at Helen, who nodded slightly. "We've met at a couple of functions. But no, I didn't have a personal interest in her case."

Now Helen Wills seemed to be playing the role of social secretary. David wondered again at her precise function in life.

"But I enjoyed reading about the Smathers case. Especially the way you represented her." The First Lady smiled, but turned quickly serious again. "I understood Mrs. Smathers's position. The way even a woman who's thought of as rich and powerful can feel helpless. It took a special person to convey that to a jury. It took nerve for her to stand up to her husband, but it took you to let her do it in a courtroom."

Finally her eyes fastened on David, studying him. He felt his face growing warm. Just as he was about to thank her for her praise, the

First Lady said quietly, "I need the same kind of help."

For a moment David didn't understand the words. Then they sank in, and his first reaction was alarm. "No."

"Yes, Mr. Owens. Trust me, I've given the matter a great deal of thought. I want a divorce."

The lady looked painfully sincere. For a moment her lip trembled. She understood very well the painful significance of what she'd just said. David cleared his throat and became lawyerlike.

"Mrs. McPherson, if we're going to have an attorney-client conversation, the first thing I have to tell you is that having a third person present voids the attorney-client privilege. Your assistant here wouldn't be bound by the confidentiality of—"

Mrs. McPherson reached back and grasped the younger woman's arm. "No need to worry about that. We can trust Helen implicitly. In fact, she's the only person I do trust. After all, she helped me get here."

David thought that explained Helen Wills's extremely watchful expression and that note of pleading he'd also seen in her gaze once. She had overstepped the bounds of her job by bringing the First Lady here.

"Do you want details?" Myra McPherson asked.

Of course he did. Hearing the intimate details of people's lives was one of the prime perks of divorce work. At the same time, David wanted to withdraw from the conversation completely. "I don't want to put myself on the Secret Service's hit list."

Mrs. McPherson reached a hand toward him comfortingly. "Why do you think we did all this silly secret agent stuff to get to you? Helen and I slipped away from my guards. Not just because of what I was coming to see you about, but to protect you. In case you decide you don't want to take the case."

"Let's make sure you really want a case," David said smoothly, sounding lawyerly and comforting. "I want to know why, and especially why *now*. Your husband has been in office three years. He's up for reelection next year. If you tell him that your marriage depends on his not running again . . ."

The First Lady laughed abruptly and harshly. "Give up the presi-dency for me? And Randy? You have no idea what an absurd sugges-tion that is, Mr. Owens. My husband—"

"Then if you could wait—"

"Another five years until he's done?" Mrs. McPherson looked fearful for the first time. "Have you ever been in a bad relationship, Mr. Owens? Do you know how long five years is when you live with that every day? But that's not the reason. My son is eight years old. Five years is a lifetime to him. He's starting to become aware of what's going on around him. I don't want him in that place for even one more year. I don't want him growing up in that atmosphere."

The presidential son had been hovering in the back of David's mind before his mother mentioned him. David drew a clean yellow legal pad from a drawer and uncapped his pen. "All right. Let's begin. Ms. Wills, will you sit down, please? I can't remain sitting any longer if you're going to keep standing, and if I stand up too I can't write. Thank you. Now, Mrs. McPherson, tell me why you want a divorce. Convince me."

The First Lady began to betray nervousness. She looked down at her hands. "I should never have married John in the first place. I realized that some time ago. He was already running for the Senate when he proposed to me. I was thrilled, of course. He was twelve years older, smart, energetic. He seemed very strong. I found his wanting to marry me very flattering. Now I realize"—she glanced at Helen, whose face had softened; the younger woman put her hand on the First Lady's clenched ones—"that I was a necessary orna-ment to John's political life. He needed a wife, and a family, to look like a normal American. Our wedding took place less than a month before the general election, and was like a campaign rally.

"After that, his career took him over."

"Everyone who holds high public office has to spend a great deal of time performing that job and keeping it. You must have known that," David said.

"I did. And I was content to be the stay-at-home wife, making a home for John and staying in the background. But I also thought there would be moments of . . . tenderness, like we had when he was courting me. Some sort of private family life. Especially after Randy was born, I thought we'd have family times at least occasionally. But there's been none of that. Once we had a son it seemed I'd served my purpose for John. He's never seemed to have any feeling for Randy, or for me. John's passions lie elsewhere."

David sat impassively, pondering her last comment. Was he being asked to out the first gay President?

He put down his pen and looked straight at his visitor. "Mrs. McPherson, I sympathize with you. Believe me, I do. But—I feel stupid even saying this, of course you must have given it a lot of thought—but do you realize the public scandal your filing for divorce would cause? On the other hand, I don't see how you'd be harmed by waiting. I doubt you're the first woman to endure a loveless marriage in the White House."

"I told you, five years would be too long to wait. Randy would be irreparably damaged by then. Besides, I *want* the threat of scandal. If I wait until John leaves office, I won't have the leverage I'll have now, to get away from him."

David didn't quite understand that. His visitor appeared to realize she hadn't made herself clear, but she didn't try to explain further. "*Can* you cause a scandal?" David asked. "Do you think your husband's having an affair, for example?"

"I know he is. But that's not the problem. Well, it's part of the problem. It's part of what I meant when I said I don't want Randy growing up in that atmosphere. The infidelity, the lies, the whole facade of family life. That's not all. There's something very dangerous going on in the White House, Mr. Owens. I want my son out of it."

David looked at Helen Wills, hoping for a dash of reality, a roll of the eyes to indicate she understood how crazy this sounded. But Helen looked downcast, as if she didn't want to be present when these things were discussed. Her eyes caught David's just for a second.

The First Lady abruptly stopped talking. Mrs. McPherson's voice and face had grown stonier as she'd talked about her marriage; obviously she had trained herself in emotional defense. But for a moment she almost broke down, looking again very young and confused. On television Myra McPherson appeared completely buttoned-up, a person placid to the point of unemotionalism. In person David saw that wasn't true at all. She had lost her youth to politics, but somehow retained it, as if those years hadn't counted. David pushed a box of tissues toward her. "All right, Mrs. McPherson, you've convinced me. I believe you need to break away. But I have a lot more questions, and more to explain. First of all, I'm not licensed to practice in the District of Columbia."

"No, I want to file here."

"I'm not sure—" David began, but Mrs. McPherson leaned toward him with renewed urgency.

"John and I have always claimed San Antonio as our legal residence. Isn't that what counts? We've come here to vote every election day. There's a small condo that's the official residence. Isn't that good enough? Doesn't an elected politician maintain legal residence in his hometown?"

"I'd have to do some research. It makes sense, but it's just a fiction. I doubt any court has ever ruled on the issue. At any rate, why . . . ?"

"I don't want to get divorced in Washington," she answered quickly. "John would have everything his own way there. The judges are all appointed, they all owe favors. John would find their strings. No. They'd crush me there. He might even be able to take Randy away from me. I want to get away from that world, don't you see? Starting with where the divorce is filed."

"Yes, I understand." Though David continued to sound placid and reassuring, his mind raced. Huge excitement grew in him, starting in the pit of his stomach and spreading outward. He felt the center of attention of a great crowd of people. Filing a divorce case against the President of the United States. The idea frightened him, yes. It was also a lawyer's wet dream.

"There are a lot of issues," he said slowly. "The community estate, separate property, reimbursement claims. The grounds for divorce, first of all. You can either allege insupportability, which is the same as irreconcilable differences, no-fault, or the traditional fault claims such as cruelty—"

"No, that first one would be all right. I don't want to hurt John, I just want to escape him."

A moment's silence embraced the three people in the small room. They had drawn closer together, like conspirators. David stared across the desk at the First Lady, who sat erect, eyes gleaming, an anxious but determined woman. The First Lady saw a young man who exuded confidence, but whose fingers tapped quickly on his desktop. David smiled briefly.

Helen Wills's expression had warmed up. She too looked at David appraisingly, but no longer hostilely. He glanced at her in a quick moment of understanding, asking her opinion of her employer's sanity. Helen raised one eyebrow and lowered it again, a facial shrug. Their eyes stayed on each other. David understood what Helen had known when she'd entered his office, that this was an historic meeting.

"I'm afraid I don't have that much time now," Mrs. McPherson said. "I'm expected somewhere. But I want you to be able to file whenever I call you and say so. What do I have to do?"

"There's just one short form you have to sign." David continued talking while he turned to his computer, called up the document in question, erased the name, typed in a new one, and printed the form. "It's an agreement that you'll go through mediation short of going to trial. I'll explain that if it becomes important, but it's a promise everyone has to make in the first pleading in a lawsuit. It's the only form you'd sign. I sign the petition for divorce itself."

He handed the sheet of paper to his visitor. She read the paragraph quickly and signed the signature line in a clear, schoolgirlish script. David took a long look at the signature when she handed the page back to him. Her name written in her own handwriting made the scene real for him.

"Now what about your fee?"

"I charge two hundred dollars an hour, and in a case that might involve child custody issues I get a retainer of ten thousand dollars." David's tongue didn't stumble as he gave himself a quick raise.

"I could raise that much, but right now—"

"It's all right, Mrs. McPherson, I trust you."

She smiled shyly and suddenly rose. David came around his desk quickly, then stopped as she held out her hand. He realized she was offering a handshake, as if concluding a formal business meeting. But when he took her hand she held his. The First Lady seemed more formidable for a moment, giving him her most penetrating stare yet. "Even without my paying you, are you my lawyer?"

"Yes, ma'am, I am. Don't worry about that."

"Thank you." She gave his hand a last tight squeeze and released it. "Then could you please call me Myra?"

David laughed, taken by surprise. "I really doubt I could. But I'd be pleased if you'll call me David. Usually when someone calls me 'Mister' it means I'm in trouble."

"All right, David." She turned away, Helen hurrying around her to the hall door.

"There's just one other thing." David's voice stopped his client and she looked back at him alertly. "I know you read about how brilliantly I handled Mary Smathers's divorce, but I have to tell you that I haven't been practicing family law all that long. There are much more experienced family lawyers in this city, people who would do a great job for you. I could give you the names of two or three. Ellen Bonham, Mike Garrells . . . I think anyone would advise you, starting with Ms. Wills there, that you need the absolute best lawyer you can find. I'm very flattered you came to me, but I have an obligation—"

Myra McPherson shook her head decisively. "No, I want you. I thought so before I came here, and now I'm sure.

"Besides, now that you know my plans, if I didn't hire you I'd have to have you killed."

He had seen the First Lady's smile. Everyone had, on television. Her smile was a demure, gracious expression, extremely suitable for formal occasions. The quick grin Myra McPherson gave him now was an altogether different animal, stretching her cheeks wide and making her eyes shine. For a fleeting moment she looked genuinely happy.

Helen watched David too, and gave him a very small nod in acknowledgment of the end of their first meeting.

Then they both turned and were gone.

★ After his visitors had left, David still didn't feel alone in his office. He felt the presence of Mrs. McPherson and Helen Wills, as if they'd left behind a spy device to observe his reactions. David continued to behave very professionally, suppressing the urge to laugh at the enormity of what had just transpired in his office.

He walked down the short hall to the reception area, carrying only the page signed by the First Lady. After giving the signature a long stare, he scanned the document into his secretary's computer. An image of the page appeared on the screen. David clicked on SAVE, then paused over giving the page a file name. FLady was too obvious, as was WHouse. After a moment his thoughts turned from his newest client to her assistant Helen. He typed in the name HWills.1. He liked the blandness of that. It looked like some probate matter that would be found in any lawyer's computer. David saved the page, cleared the screen, then placed the original signed page in a clean new file folder and put it under a stack of much fatter folders on his credenza. Quickly he made sure the doors were locked and prepared to leave the office. His belief in what had happened began to fade as he walked out of the office. David stood at the front door, hand on the light switch, and as the rooms went dark the day itself seemed to be erased. Maybe he would wake up now.

The next morning David came into his building whistling. The security guard noticed, giving him a surprised look, to which David returned a snappy salute. In the elevator he smiled at strangers. David must have been the happiest lawyer in the building. He wore his best suit, a sharp blue that brought out the color of his eyes and made his shoulders look broad. For the first time since the Smathers trial David had a sense of events pulsing, life beginning anew. Something would happen today, he felt sure, and he wanted to be dressed well for it.

In the reception area of his offices Janice, the secretary, sat stoically doing nothing, just staring straight ahead as if under arrest. Her stony look stopped David's whistling. Oh, hell, personnel problems first thing in the morning. Janice must be mad because David had made her leave yesterday just when the excitement was beginning.

"What's the matter, Janice, are you—"

Without looking at him, still staring straight ahead, Janice said one word, "Company," and inclined her head back toward his office.

David lowered his voice. "Are they back?"

Janice shook her head.

David's excitement reasserted itself. He grinned. "It's not her husband, is it?"

Janice shook her head again as David went down the short hall to his own office. As soon as he entered, the smile dropped off his face.

Three men occupied his office, seeming to take up all the space. All three wore dark suits and colorless ties. They had short, clipped hair and stern, angular faces that gave few hints about their ages. Two of the men ignored David's entrance. One sat at David's computer, calling up documents on the screen and clearing it again. The other stood at the corner of the desk, going through David's files. He had set half the stack aside, fairly neatly, but still, the sight of a stranger going through the files full of privileged information made David suddenly furious.

The third stranger, who seemed to be in charge, leaned back against the window ledge, his upper body very straight, overseeing the work of the other two intruders. The man was tall, half a head taller than David, and wore very dark sunglasses. He stared at David as if he'd been waiting a long time, as if David were unforgivably late for an appointment. "Mr. Owens?" he said, lips barely parting to admit the words.

"I don't know. Who are you?"

"Sorry for the intrusion, sir. Believe me, we'll ignore any documents we see that don't relate to our case. But we need to search for evidence."

"Of what?" Past the stranger's shoulder, David saw that someone had spread black fingerprint powder on the door frame of the door into the hall. More powder dusted the arms of David's visitors' chairs. And someone had taken away his wastebasket.

"Just let me see your search warrant and you can go on with your hunt."

"I think you'll want to hear what we have to tell you, sir. I'm afraid you've been the victim of a hoax."

The man's self-assured tone set David's teeth on edge. "How do you know?" he asked.

"We're the Secret Service, sir. It's our job to know."

David could barely resist mouthing these words in mimicry. "How do I know I'm not being hoaxed now? Can I see some ID?"

"Certainly, sir. My name is Jensen." He pushed himself straight and approached David, holding out a small flip-open wallet. Sure enough, it contained a badge and an ID card identifying Lawrence Jensen as an agent of the Treasury Department. David knew a printer in the building who could have made a card even more authentic-looking in about fifteen minutes. Lamination extra.

"All right? So? What're you looking for evidence of?" David

snapped at the guy sitting at his desk, "There's nothing in there, I promise you."

The other agent smugly turned the computer screen toward David. "Well, there's this, sir." The agent had brought up on the screen the one-page Agreement to Alternative Dispute Resolution with a signature line for Myra McPherson. It wasn't the one she'd actually signed and David had scanned into the computer, just the form he'd created, but still, there was her name. The agent's thin-lipped, ever-so-slight smile made David feel he'd been caught at something.

"So it's about her? You know, any conversation I may or may not have had with her is protected by attorney-client privilege. You cannot find a judge who'll order me to tell you anything."

Jensen resumed his agent in charge role. "That would be true, sir, if events had happened as you think they did. You had a visitor yesterday afternoon who claimed to be the First Lady of the United States . . ."

" 'Claimed'?"

"Yes, sir. That's the hoax I mentioned. The lady was not Myra McPherson. She was an imposter. We've known about her for some time. We were just down the hall during your interview last evening."

David thought an obscenity, but didn't say it. "That *was* the First Lady. She looked more like Myra McPherson than you three look like Secret Service agents. Shouldn't one of you be black and one of you be Hispanic or Asian if you're going to look authentic these days?"

"Are you sure, sir? How closely have you ever observed the real Mrs. McPherson?"

Jensen's smug tone made it sound as if he and the First Lady sat around sipping afternoon tea every day and laughing over the rubes who would claim to know a member of the first family.

"It was her," David said, but with less certainty.

Jensen sounded sympathetic. "If she weren't a good imposter, she wouldn't have us so worried. Tell me, sir, did she get any money from you?"

"No."

"That's good. But she didn't pay you any either, did she? Would you mind telling me what she talked to you about?"

"That's confidential," David said hollowly. All three agents watched him now, with similar condescending expressions. He wanted to say something that would blast them all out of the room, but couldn't think of anything. They obviously knew much more about the situation than he did.

"Complaints about the President, I'm sure," Agent Jensen said, unperturbed by David's refusal to cooperate. "Which was it this time, his secret business dealings, physical abuse of his son, or his extramarital affairs?"

David winced slightly. Jensen, sensing he'd struck a nerve, pressed on. "She's used all those lines at other times. The other lawyers she's contacted tell us—"

"Others?"

"Yes, sir. Mostly in the District and in Texas, but in a few other states as well. An attorney gets some publicity from representing someone in a high-profile divorce and the next thing he or she knows, this lady shows up, claiming to be Myra McPherson and wanting a divorce. She's got two or three dozen lawyers waiting by their phones to hear back from her."

David didn't like the image. He drew himself up. "If you were right down the hall, then why didn't you arrest her?"

"Enough rope, sir." Jensen smiled smugly. "We want to learn what she's up to. We're especially interested to know whether she's in the employ of a foreign power. With the help of cooperative citizens such as yourself, we're compiling quite a dossier on her. Speaking of that, sir, would you please contact me at once if she gets in touch with you again? Your government would appreciate it."

David had never before felt appreciated by his government. Jensen handed him a business card that again looked very official, with the United States seal embossed on it. David didn't answer.

"You probably won't," Jensen continued. "That's been her pattern. One visit and that's it. That's one reason why it's so important that you not tell anyone about what happened. We think one of her objectives is to spread these false rumors, and you'd be aiding and abetting in that. Plus you'd be interfering in an official investigation. I don't want to threaten—"

"Then don't," David snapped. "I'll keep this to myself. I would have anyway. It's not my habit to go around blabbing my clients' secrets."

Jensen grinned, as if playing along with David's joke. "Perhaps that is the best way to think of it, sir. Remember . . ." He gestured at the business card, still in David's hand.

"Let me ask you something. There was a young woman with her. She seemed very official, kind of like you guys. Are you after her too, or is she one of yours?"

Jensen's expression turned stony again. "We can't discuss details of our investigation." He jerked his head emphatically and the other two agents rose and walked out of the room.

After all three had left, David looked around his office, at the computer screen still running, the dirty doorjamb and desk, his disordered files. He felt invaded.

With a sudden thought of vindicating himself he hurried around his desk to the credenza behind it. Digging through a stack of files, he found the thin file folder where he'd saved the one page statement his visitor had signed. It carried her signature. David could have the handwriting analyzed, prove that his visitor had been the real First Lady.

He opened the file folder and found it empty. Of course. The Secret Service agents hadn't left him anything. He had no tangible proof of his extraordinary visit of the night before—only a memory, and he could no longer trust that.

Helen Wills sat in the office she shared with other people. She wore black slacks that fit her like a leotard until flaring out above her ankles to end in regular pants cuffs. Above she wore a long-sleeved white blouse. The outfit served the functional purpose of a uniform. Helen didn't have to think what to wear in the morning, just reached automatically into the closet. The clothes fit her well not because she'd taken much care in choosing them, but because she had the kind of body fashion designers had in mind when they cut clothes.

She was alone for the moment, but other employees roamed nearby, even though it was almost ten o'clock at night. In a few minutes Helen would go down to the gym and work the equipment, lifting and stretching, then swim a dozen laps before going to bed. The workout would leave her tired but honed, so she could sleep soundly all night or wake up alert at any time if necessary.

But now inertia held her at her desk, an uncluttered rectangle without photographs or other personal touches. Helen didn't live at this desk, she lived mostly on the road, or in other people's houses and offices.

She realized she continued to sit in the office because she was relishing being alone. Helen almost never enjoyed the luxury of solitude. Her job involved response, the constant reading of other people and projecting the image needed for the moment. The relief of sitting here not having to respond to another person held her motionless in her chair.

She couldn't relax, of course, even slumped in the chair. Helen wondered if she'd made a mistake. Inevitably, she must have. She'd had to do something—again, reacting to someone else—and she knew that no matter what she'd chosen she would now be sitting here invaded by regrets. They had embarked on a course, drawing Helen along, making small corrections as she could. She had never been in charge, except in small subsidiary ways. Helen had a gift for following, even for anticipating, but it had been a long time since she'd gotten to make a significant decision.

Well, that wasn't her job. Helen sat up straighter in the desk chair, and when she heard footsteps approaching the office, suddenly stood and headed for the door.

Washington, D.C., is not a city that grew gradually from a frontier town into a metropolis. It was built all at once, to be the capital city of a new nation. The streets are designed to lead a foreign visitor along broad avenues, past imposing monuments and ever-larger government buildings, to the heart of town, to the home that is much more than a residence. The White House was designed to impress and intimidate. It has always performed this job well, even sometimes exercising its power on people who live there.

The House sits on eighteen acres of grounds, a park insulating the residence from the noise of the city streets. Of course, the White House creates its own bustle. It is served by about a hundred full-time employees, some of them on duty and working at any given time.

But at night the second and third floors are reserved for the exclusive use of the first family. Even Secret Service agents are supposed to stay away from the family quarters, unless an emergency calls for them. These regulations, designed to provide the President's family as much privacy as possible, can also serve to isolate.

The First Lady of the United States, Myra McPherson, sat in her bedroom on the second floor. The President had flown to California that afternoon, to tour a slum destined for urban renewal and to meet with entertainment industry executives. Myra had stayed behind, so now she sat as alone as one could be in the White House. The house had grown very quiet as midnight approached. She had checked on her son Randy hours ago and made sure he slept. One thing she didn't have to worry about in this house was her son waking up sick in the middle of the night and finding no help at hand. If he coughed or moaned, the night Secret Service agent would be in the room a minute later.

Otherwise, though, the staff tried to provide the family with the illusion of privacy, withdrawing from the private quarters at all possible times, such as tonight. This evening Myra and Randy had talked, played chess—Randy was just learning the game, and in the process making her remember—and read together before he went to bed about nine. From then on the First Lady had been alone. She had dressed for bed but didn't feel like sleep. What she most wanted was what she couldn't have: conversation. Since Myra McPherson had come to the White House, even before, she found that longer and longer stretches of life would pass without her being able to talk to anyone. People crowded her life, nearly always, but they were all strangers, who smiled and stammered and were very flattered and pleased to meet her, but wouldn't think of using up her valuable time in chat. Myra sometimes wondered if she even still retained the power of conversation. What did people talk about?

Her marriage didn't provide an outlet for her thoughts, either. Actually it was a relief when John was gone, like tonight. Even when he spent the night in the White House he often stayed late in the Oval Office or in meetings. Certainly it had been a long time since he and she had talked about anything personal.

She made one more slow drift through the private quarters, wearing a peach-colored full-length negligee and matching "robe" that floated almost transparent, so that Myra looked and felt like a ghost passing through the White House. She seemed to herself bodiless. Walking through her "home" didn't comfort her or bring her down to earth. The rooms loomed large, so that in the dimness she couldn't see the far corners. Especially the centerpiece of the family quarters, the oval yellow room that gave onto the Truman balcony, seemed intimidatingly large, a movie set rather than a home. If the McPhersons had had a large family to invade the family rooms, strewing clothes and toys, Myra might have felt differently, or if she'd been allowed a freer hand in redecorating the residence. A few family photographs sat on bookshelves and the piano—her parents, her sisters and their children—but these few personal touches couldn't overcome the furniture, which always struck Myra as oversized and from another era. When they had first moved in, John had urged her to explore the attic and pick out pieces for their historical significance: Pat Nixon's end table, Dwight Eisenhower's easy chair. But he had strictly forbidden buying new furniture. John McPherson was a Republican, he refused to be accused of spending the people's money frivolously. Besides, what John enjoyed most about private life in the White House was sitting where his predecessors had sat, gazing on the same coffee tables and lamps, imagining himself part of that continuity of history. But in the furnishing sense, his rules resulted in a mix of furniture that to Myra's mind didn't fit together. The furniture clumped uncomfortably, as if a few of those former Presidents and their wives had been gathered against their will in this room, smiling falsely and staring into the distance, with nothing to say to each other.

That was how the First Lady lived. It could hardly be called a life at all. She shouldn't go to bed at night, she should just be put away in a closet like the other unused equipment.

Well, now it *was* time to put herself to bed, when she fell into this mopey wallow of self-pity. She would feel better in the morning, when she sat at breakfast with Randy.

She walked into the bedroom, but the tall, empty double bed didn't beckon to her at all. Instead she sat at the dressing table— Roslyn Carter's dressing table, she thought, or maybe Mamie Eisenhower's—ran a brush down her hair, and began to cry. Vaguely she saw herself in the mirror, and felt soft air currents on her skin, where the negligee left her chest and shoulders bare.

Myra cried in a soft, decorous fashion, not calling attention to herself, just quiet sighs and tears running slowly down her smooth cheeks, but her tears seemed to draw response. She heard footsteps in the outer room, where no one should have been walking.

Myra held her breath, watching the open bedroom door through her dressing-table mirror. But a single bedside lamp lit the room, so the intruder must have known she wasn't sleeping yet.

A moment later a young man in rather formal dress entered the room. He came in quietly and stopped just inside the door, as if to let her inspect him. The young man, Paul, was rather short but well proportioned, with a face that looked remarkably untouched by experience. His blue eyes danced alertly. Paul wore a white shirt and dark vest, but had loosened his tie, so he didn't appear to be on duty, but more as if he had been suddenly called to her service. But in his hands he carried a wine bottle wrapped in a white napkin.

In the dim evening light he looked very young, not quite fully formed, in fact, as if her imagination were still creating him. Myra McPherson felt young too. That was a large part of her problem, that she hadn't had a youth and now filled a role where maturity above all else was expected of her. But she didn't feel like the first matron, or certainly like Mom to a nation. She wanted to live the carefree years that had been taken from her.

"You ordered wine, ma'am?" young Paul asked without a trace of irony.

Yes, she had, though she had almost forgotten. Myra turned slowly and faced him, feeling her skin for the first time that night, feeling the small shifts and tugs of the peach-colored negligee. She didn't speak or change the expression she'd been wearing, one of regret and longing.

The young steward smiled sympathetically and walked slowly toward her, waiting for the First Lady to ask what he was doing or to order him out. When she did he would say something about letting her see the wine label.

But Myra McPherson never said a word.

★ David Owens's head snapped up quickly. He'd nodded off on his old brown sofa where he'd been reading a transcript of a hearing. The TV was on. The camera showed and briefly described four "citizen heroes" who'd done such good deeds as starting a neighborhood recycling facility, collecting toys for children at a battered women's shelter, and turning an abandoned house into a day-care center. They had come to the White House to receive presidential citations for their good works. The President spoke briefly to each, handing the proud recipient a certificate of some kind. The winners appeared proud and humbled to be there, though one woman took the occasion to speak to the President at much greater length than he or his staff had obviously allotted her. President John McPherson listened with apparent gravity, but his eyes shifted as if looking for rescue.

David studied the President, a tall, grave-looking man with rather dark skin, black hair receding from a point, and slightly sunken eyes. McPherson did not have a face suited to this kind of benevolent occasion. He had a face for announcing that the U.S. trade deficit had risen to a record high. He looked sincere, alert, and always concerned with some greater problem an average American didn't know about and had no hope of solving. The McPherson face had given a lot of voters hope of a new seriousness in the White House, a welcome respite from his perpetually smiling predecessor. But the President's face didn't inspire warmth.

After the awards ceremony the news channel gave a long minute's footage to the post-awards photo op in which some of the children from the day-care center frolicked on the White House lawn (they'd obviously been directed to frolic, and half of them didn't seem to know what the direction meant) while the awards recipients and the President smiled benevolently at them. At this point in the story the President had been joined by his wife. Quiet Myra McPherson, looking matronly in a beige suit in spite of her relative youth, stood by her husband holding his hand and beaming.

Yes, smiling broadly, looking pleased to be there. David studied her face as best he could, but the camera didn't give him a close-up. She looked so much like the woman who'd come to see him in his office. Well, a phony *would* look like the real thing, wouldn't she, or her hoax wouldn't be important enough to worry the Secret Service. More to the point, the First Lady of the United States looked happy standing with her husband, being the White House hostess. The story ended with her kneeling to hand one of the children a toy and talk to him quietly. David sat in his dimly lit living room watching her, America's Mom comforting a parentless child, doing the job very well. As Myra McPherson studied the child's face a look of wistfulness seemed to cross her countenance, but that could have been David's imagination. He could no longer trust his own observations.

He clicked off the television and looked around his house. The small living room boasted hardwood floors, the room's only distinctive feature. Under the coffee table a rag rug added some softness. But the room looked very plain. David had bought this house three years earlier when he'd seemed to be on the partnership track at Reynolds McCrory and thought he should stop throwing his money away on rent. It had also seemed that a young attorney of his rising stature should own a home suitable for entertaining, not spend any more of his adulthood in a bachelor apartment. But he never had entertained, and after three years the house retained a barely furnished appearance, as if he were waiting for the rest of his things to arrive. This front room was the largest in the house, suitable for a party or for children playing on the floor. The room boasted several windows, through one of which he could see a corner of his wide front porch, where David had planned when he first moved in to install a porch swing. He'd never gotten around to that. The house's possibilities for hominess or elegance remained largely unrealized. David seldom noticed the unfinished quality, but he did tonight, after his glimpse of White House life.

David snapped off the lights decisively and went to bed.

Unfortunately, David couldn't as easily turn off his own thoughts. In his office the next day, David caught himself listening for the sound of footsteps in the hall. For some reason, David found himself disbelieving the Secret Service agents. They seemed more like people cleaning up a mess than conducting an investigation. So David couldn't get past the fact that he had never heard from Myra McPherson again. Even if she found it impossible to contact him directly, couldn't she ask her aide, the watchful Helen Wills, to call him?

David found it harder to concentrate on his other cases while still emotionally engaged with this imaginary one. His attention span had shortened alarmingly. On this sunny early summer morning in his office, he turned from the inventory of household assets he'd been studying to his computer. Idly, just for something to do, he checked his E-mail.

His E-mail seldom carried any message of value. David used the most popular provider in America. He had the E-mail address on his business cards and letterhead, but sometimes forgot to check it for a day or two.

Of this morning's four new messages, two were advertisements, one was from another lawyer who seemed to know more about computers than about law, and one message bore a return address David didn't recognize. He clicked on that one.

The message was short and obvious: *Please help us,* it said. Nothing more. "Help who?" David said aloud. He looked more closely at the return E-mail address. *WHouseboy.* It didn't take a genius to make the connection. "White House boy." Only one boy lived in the White House, eight-year-old Randy McPherson.

"Bullshit!" David said, standing up. So the game continued. Who was playing it, trying to draw David back in? The fake Myra McPherson? The Secret Service, wanting to startle him into revealing something? If so, they would be out of luck, because David had a foolproof defense to that ploy: he didn't know anything.

"Bull," he repeated, still talking out loud and staring at his screen. Anybody could call himself WHouseboy. This could have been a brand-new account, created just to send this one message. David had no way of tracing it. An E-mail message didn't carry a postmark.

But the short message glowed on his screen with urgent sincerity. *Please help us.* David started to send a reply, but couldn't think of one. He tried to go back to work, but failed at that. Finally half an hour later he clicked on the REPLY button and sent a simple message of his own: "Are you sure you've got the right person? My name is David Owens. I'm a lawyer in San Antonio. Please send me more information."

He sent the message, feeling suddenly vulnerable as his reply sped off to an unknown destination. David waited all day for a response, but by six o'clock no reply had come.

The next day he still had no reply in his E-mail. But on that night's news he got a clear, though unintended, signal. The White House drew TV coverage again with a visit from the President of Russia. This ceremony was much more precisely orchestrated than the other, with solemn-faced staff members all around the President and his wife, who wore very formal smiles and even bowed slightly and stiffly to their visitor.

David again studied Myra McPherson, but her face didn't tell him anything. But as the presidential entourage turned to lead the Russian President inside the White House, an unwieldy clump of people all pivoting at once, like a caterpillar, David caught a glimpse of another face he recognized. On the fringe of the crowd, wearing a black suit with only a V of white blouse showing at her chest, Helen Wills looked around alertly. For a long moment she stared toward the camera, or past it. There was no chance he was mistaken. This was the First Lady's companion, the initially chilly woman who'd thawed and held her boss's hand while she explained how unhappy being married to the President of the United States made her. On television, Helen wore her alert, suspicious expression as she scanned the crowd on the White House lawn.

David sat on his couch staring sightlessly at the images that followed. The Secret Service agents who had invaded his office had lied to him. What fraudulent First Lady could have come to his office accompanied by the real Myra McPherson's staff person?

David knew the Secret Service would be able to explain this sighting. Helen Wills had been working undercover, helping them follow the phony First Lady. Now she'd returned to her regular duty accompanying the genuine Mrs. McPherson. They could come up with some such story, and there were probably even people in America who would believe the explanation. But not David. His sight of Helen Wills standing near the First Lady had brought back the meeting in his office with great vividness. He knew that had been the real Myra McPherson who had come to see him.

Something extraordinary *had* happened in David's office. Somewhere, the drama continued without him. He couldn't fall comfortably back into his ordinary life without knowing the truth.

Only one thing could convince him he was wrong: hearing the real First Lady herself deny having met him. Two days later he was on a plane for Washington.

David had an uncomfortable flight, trying to make plans but having no material to work with. He had been to Washington, D.C., only twice before, the more recent trip eight years ago, right after law school. He'd gone with a friend and classmate who'd had a job interview; David just went as a tourist. That remained his role now. David had no connections at all in the capital. His law school friend from years ago hadn't gotten the government job. David had never had business dealings in D.C. Since seeing Helen Wills on television he'd ransacked his memory and worked the phone lines hard, but hadn't been able to come up with anyone who could get him inside the workings of the nation's capital. The best he'd been able to come up with was a letter of introduction to a recently elected Congressman from San Antonio. David wished he'd contributed to the man's campaign, or ever met him. Besides, even if the Congressman wanted to help him, how much clout did a freshman Congressman have? Enough to get David into the private quarters of the White House? He doubted it.

The city confronted him as he rode in a cab from the airport. David remembered what everyone who'd been to Washington as a tourist remembered: the monuments, the mall, the Capitol dome, the view of the White House through the fence, across a wide, wide lawn. He'd forgotten how big the city was, how long it took to get to those landmarks, through streets thick with traffic, past clusters of office buildings and strip shopping centers and fast food dispensing stations. It seemed strange: people lived here, had their everyday lives in the District of Columbia.

Finally inside the Beltway, the cab deposited him at a Marriott in the northwest quadrant of downtown. David had been able to learn what part of the city to stay in, and had managed to find a hotel rate not aimed at visiting shahs or diplomatic corps. By midafternoon he'd checked in and taken another cab to the governmental heart of town. David walked, turning his head constantly like any visiting gawker. June had come, summer having made it harder for David to get in touch with people. Washington's heat wasn't oppressive, not like San Antonio's, but had the same muggy quality. David walked slowly, trying not to sweat. Nothing would give him away as a stalker of the first family like sweat running down his temples.

He took half an hour just to walk around and try to acclimate himself to the city. He walked to the Lincoln Memorial because it was the one site he remembered best from his previous visits. The size of the statue and its humanity awed him again. People stood in clusters just staring upward, struck by the burden of sadness that huge frame bore.

Then David made his way to the Rayburn Office Building next door to the Capitol. He walked slowly, deliberately postponing his meeting with the Congressman, because if that plan for access to the presidential family failed he had no other. At the entrance to the building he passed through metal detectors where security guards looked him over in a bored way. David had worn a gray lightweight suit, in the expectation that he could get away with more if he looked like a lawyer. Apparently it worked with the security guards, who waved him on. He climbed wide stairs to the third floor of the building and finally found the Congressman's office. The rows of identical doors did not impress. It looked more as if the legislators wished to be anonymous. David realized he didn't even have a very clear picture of what this Congressman Breckett looked like.

Behind the door a very small reception room made him feel immediately trapped. A fiftyish lady with heavy forearms resting on her desk stared at him as if she'd been waiting for his appearance. She wore a slight smile set in the middle of a very firm expression. "Yes, sir?"

"Hello. My name is David Owens. I'd like to see the Congressman, please, just for a minute. I have a letter—"

"Congressman Breckett is out of town, sir. He's on a fact-finding mission. He'll be back in the office on Wednesday of next week."

Today was Thursday. Wednesday was too far away to imagine. David stood in front of the receptionist feeling stupid. Her firm expression softened into sympathy. "Can I help you with anything?"

"Can you get me into the White House to meet the First Lady? I think she wants to see me."

The receptionist smiled at his jest. "I'm afraid I can't help you there. I don't think the Congressman could either."

"Is there anyone who could? There's not a certain time of day when the first family comes out and waves to the crowd, is there?"

The receptionist found David increasingly amusing. "I don't think so, sir. The Secret Service wouldn't approve at all. Here, this is the best I can do for you."

She pulled a booklet from a drawer in her desk, tore off one coupon, and stamped the back of it with a rubber stamp. "It's a pass to get in the White House gates. Just the regular tour, I'm afraid. It's at eleven A.M. and four P.M. every day."

"Thanks." David accepted the pass, thinking this was probably the biggest perk he'd ever receive from Congress.

"Maybe the President or Mrs. McPherson will drive up or walk by while you're on the tour," the receptionist offered. "It's happened before."

Yes, if he went every day for a year it might happen once. David thanked her again, then paused in the doorway before leaving. "Where's the fact-finding mission that the Congressman's on?"

The receptionist's face went all neutral again, and she hesitated before giving the answer. "Bermuda." She said it with absolute neutrality.

David nodded. "He's learning his way around fast, isn't he?"

So he walked to the White House, his pass a small limp token in his pocket. His clever lawyer's brain working in overdrive, David devised several cunning schemes as he walked, such as pretending to be Congressman Breckett, a freshman legislator so befuddled he'd left all identification behind in his office. But he *did* have an *official White House* pass from his office. Wouldn't that be good enough? Probably the guards would believe such an idiot could have gotten elected to Congress, but that didn't mean they'd let him into the White House.

When he arrived at the long fence around the mansion, the best plan David had come up with was to take the regular tour and try to slip away from it into the private quarters. Probably every tourist who'd ever taken the White House tour had had this same thought. David had no illusions this scheme would work, but he might as well get inside and reconnoiter.

He took a slow stroll along the fence, staring through at the most famous residence in America. The White House didn't look as wide across as he'd imagined, but it was taller and deeper and had more extensions. When he came to the public entrance it turned out that he'd missed the last tour of the day, so his plan would have to wait until tomorrow. David continued circling the fence, until he came to another entrance, one guarded with an electronic gate and three burly security guards wearing very visible guns. David realized that his other devious plan—yelling, "Look! Over there!" and bolting past the distracted guards—probably wouldn't fly. But he wondered suddenly if he could get a message to someone in the White House. If he left his name and the phone number of the hotel where he was staying, would someone deliver the note to Mrs. McPherson? Then it would be up to the First Lady to contact him, knowing he waited nearby and how far he'd come to see her.

Worth a try, at least. David approached the gated entrance. One guard who'd been watching David the whole time said immediately, "Name?"

The guard was an African-American in his thirties, with prominent cheeks and impossibly broad shoulders. He carried a clipboard that looked small in his hands.

"No, I was just wondering—" David stammered.

"Just tell me your name, sir."

David started to say the Congressman's name, but then gave his own. While the guard scanned a list on his clipboard, David tried to explain what he wanted.

"I didn't want to get in, I just wanted to see if there's someplace where I can leave a message, maybe a public receptionist or even just a phone number you might have . . ."

The guard showed no sign of listening. Any moment he would send David packing, possibly with drawn gun. David backed up a step in anticipation.

The guard made a mark on a list, and looked into David's eyes again. "Can you prove that?"

"I'm sorry, what?"

"Can I see some ID, sir?"

David fumbled out his wallet, thinking this was a good way to go about arresting an intruder. But after looking over his driver's license and David's face, the guard said, "All right, sir. You're late. Come in."

David knew when to stop talking. The gate opened with an electric hum, and the guard waved him through. "Up this pathway, sir. Through the ground-floor entrance, the main door. Someone else will point you the way to the reception. You should hurry a little."

"Thank you." David would have hurried even without this advice, to get out of the guard's sight before he realized his mistake. He walked quickly along a narrow asphalt path that inclined upward toward the White House, wondering how he'd gotten in. Maybe another guest with a similar name had failed to show up? That required too many coincidences. Someone obviously wanted David inside the White House.

Over a small crest of land and through a cluster of trees, the familiar front of the building appeared before him. David didn't take time to admire. He entered the house and stopped on the wide marble floor. The house was genuinely *white*; the room dazzled with white walls, columns, and reflected sunlight. To David's right a slim black butler in a tuxedo stood by another doorway. As David approached the man smiled graciously and opened the door for him. "Through to the garden, sir. You might just be able to get on the end of the receiving line."

Thanking the attendant, David hurried in the direction he'd been told. He wished he had time to stroll casually and take in his surroundings. He breathed shallowly and felt encased in tingles. David had moved too fast, couldn't take in the experience of being in the

White House. His nerves also jangled with the expectation of being confronted and ejected momentarily.

Instead he came down a short hallway to a set of French doors that opened to the outdoors. David had no idea whether this was the Rose Garden, but it was a garden. Carefully trimmed bushes surrounded a space of perhaps half an acre, with flowers growing all around, both in the ground and in large planters. About half the space comprised a flagstone patio. The guests had assembled there, perhaps fifty people. The occasion, whatever it might be, appeared less formal than the ones David had seen on television, but the guests were dressed well enough to make David conscious of his wrinkled gray suit. This could be a coffee for large contributors, or a mutual lobbying session for the executives of some industry.

David walked across the garden, trying to saunter and insinuate himself quietly into the gathering. He gave a small wave as if recognizing someone. A few people in the crowd turned toward him, most smiling, a couple of the men looking at him searchingly. Men in black suits and sunglasses took note of his appearance as well. David moved slowly and kept his hands in plain sight.

A lane opened in the crowd and David caught sight of a tall man in a navy blue suit, a man with a practiced smile but hooded eyes. The President. David walked toward him like a zombie, drawn by a strange instinct even though his fear increased as he approached. Any moment he expected to be tackled by the black-suited Secret Service agents.

He found himself at the end of a short line of people and joined it, clasping his hands in front of him and smiling at the world in general. The line moved jerkily as those meeting the President had their turns for an intimate moment and then moved on. When the couple in front of David moved up to shake the President's hand and chat, David saw for the first time that the President was not alone. His wife stood next to him, smiling and inclining her head attentively toward the lady in front of her. But the First Lady's attention strayed, her eyes moved past the visitor's shoulder, lighted on David, moved back to her guest, then jerked back to David. She stared at him, losing her plaster smile, then wrenched her attention back to the lady in front of her to say good-bye. Then it was David's turn.

He stepped up in front of her. She extended her hand automatically and he took it. A small hand, and cold, even on this warm afternoon. Her mouth opened slightly but she didn't speak.

"Hello, Mrs. McPherson. It's an honor to meet you. I'm David Owens, from San Antonio."

"A pleasure, Mr. Owens." She passed him on to her husband. "John, a visitor from home. David Owens."

The President held his hand firmly, putting his other hand on David's elbow and giving him a penetrating stare that made David sure that John McPherson knew everything about him. Then the President smiled.

"Always great to see somebody from home. How's the Alamo?"

"Still standing, sir. And fiercely guarded by the Daughters of the Republic of Texas."

The President laughed boisterously, enough so that other guests turned to look at him and smile along. But neither the President's smile nor his hearty laugh changed his dark, watchful eyes.

David moved on, but looked back over his shoulder to see Myra McPherson still watching him. Her expression broke his heart. She looked frightened but hopeful, as if David were her rescuer. Feeling her regard made David's breath deepen and his shoulders broaden. His anxiety unclenched. She wanted him here. He hadn't made a mistake.

The receiving line done, the President and First Lady separated and mingled with the guests. David expected her to approach him then, but she didn't. Even though he moved into Mrs. McPherson's line of progress, she turned aside and he lost sight of her. David frowned. He looked for the President to see if he seemed to be watching his wife, but the President's back was to him.

Ten minutes later the gathering clearly approached its ending, and David hadn't had a private moment with Mrs. McPherson. He moved through the crowd, looking for a last chance or even another glance of recognition. Turning, he bumped into a woman in a white pantsuit. She stared at him icily, not offering apology.

"Excuse me, I—" Then David smiled. "Hello, Ms. Wills."

Helen Wills didn't reciprocate the smile. "She'd like you to come to the state dinner tonight if you can."

"I'll be here."

Helen relaxed a bit, cocking a hip. She looked him over critically but with a hint of amusement. "You did bring evening clothes, didn't you?"

Why on earth would he have brought a tuxedo on this fool's errand to Washington? That is, if he had owned a tuxedo in the first place. But David proved equal to Helen Wills's challenge. He was, after all, a lawyer.

"Of course," he said.

Helen continued to regard him, crossing her arms. She seemed on the verge of asking or telling him something. David waited, but she wouldn't speak.

"Go ahead," he said, "tell me how glad you are to see me again."

Helen stood straight and began to turn away. "The dinner begins at eight. You'll be on the guest list." That reminded her of something. "By the way, how did you get into this reception?"

"I have my methods."

Helen's smile said she didn't believe him, but she softened for a moment. "Please be careful," she said quietly.

Then she turned and walked briskly away. David watched her go, wondering whom he'd just been warned against. Maybe only his own ignorance.

If David had lifted his eyes he would have seen another woman watching him from a window. The woman had long black hair, a figure like a model, and a face that would have been lovely if she smiled. The blank, watchful expression she wore now emphasized the length of her nose and how tightly she could purse her mouth. Angela Vortiz in her intense mode had a chilling concentration.

★ John McPherson paced the Oval Office. Ordinarily he liked being here alone at dusk. He would sit on a sofa or swivel his desk chair to look out the tall windows, watching night slowly erase the city. The lawn, the capital, the whole world seemed to turn imaginary, as if he could reach out and shape it.

When McPherson had become President he had waited for wisdom and a feeling of power to descend on him. The sense of power had come, but not the wisdom. Instead the presidency had taught McPherson the great reach and depth of his ignorance. Surrounded as he constantly found himself by experts who had spent their professional lives examining one particular field, he frequently felt lost. What did he know about managing a world economy, the internal politics of any number of African or Asian or European countries, or the effect of car emissions in Oakland on wheat production in Nebraska? McPherson's previous jobs as Senator and salesman and candidate had required only a thoughtful expression and a good line of bullshit. None of that had prepared him for performing as President. Even now after three years in the office, he knew the job had become undoable by one man. It needed a committee. Even if he'd possessed wisdom, it wouldn't have helped. He often thought of the "great" Presidents resentfully. What had Lincoln had to do but the obvious: try to restore the Union and find a general who could win the war? Crisis was simple; John McPherson could handle a nice crisis, where the experts presented him with one clear issue and only one decision, without breaking a sweat. Bring Lincoln back from the dead and ask him whether to slap a tariff on Japanese computer chips, tell him the dozen possible repercussions, and see what good his famous wisdom would do him.

To John McPherson's credit, he had learned to delegate and even to defer to those subordinates who had studied some dull subject more than he ever would. But he resented them. He imagined their sly looks of self-satisfaction as the President virtually admitted that they knew more than he. Partly in consequence of this discomfort, McPherson had modeled his presidency along an older line. The West Wing was not as hectic a place as it had been under his more activist predecessor. Aides didn't scurry into the Oval Office at every minute of the day asking him for a decision. The President set policies, and expected others to carry them out. President McPherson was more Eisenhower than Clinton. The nation didn't seem to have suffered.

McPherson touched an intercom button on his desk phone and ordered a martini, very cold and straight up. "Yes, sir," came the answer. "Right away, Mr. President."

That aspect of the presidency would have frightened a more introspective man than McPherson. He could equally have asked for a roomful of roses or a pony—or the ambassador from Ghana— and the answer would have come the same. "Yes sir, Mr. President. Right away." The presidency didn't teach impulse control.

Wisdom might have eluded him so far, but McPherson had felt the power of the presidency. Oh, yes. *That* had descended on him very early, in his first year on the job. That explained his satisfaction in sitting in this famous room and watching the world disappear, waiting patiently for President McPherson to re-create it in his own image.

But tonight he felt strangely restless. He couldn't settle on the sofa or at the desk. He walked around the room, standing at one window and then another, hands behind his back, staring out intently as if awaiting a signal. It was after seven o'clock, he should have been dressed for dinner, but he still wore his daytime blue suit and felt reluctant to go up to the family quarters.

He turned when the door across the room opened. Angela Vortiz entered carrying a small silver tray with his martini on it. Deftly she closed the door with her foot and walked slowly toward him, wearing a mischievous smile.

"How did you . . . ?"

"I anticipate your every desire, Mr. President."

Well, not quite, McPherson thought. He had some damned complicated desires. But Ms. Vortiz anticipated quite a few of them, and answered them. He had given her a job in the White House, in communications, that she performed well, while carrying out her other duties apparently effortlessly. There were moments when Vortiz's efficiency almost scared the President. On the other hand, any time when she entered a room to find him alone was usually the high point of McPherson's day, or led to it.

She hadn't dressed for dinner yet, either. Vortiz wore a lightweight jacket cut like a suit coat, but in a gray and white V-pattern that made the jacket more feminine and allowed her flimsy white blouse to show. He noticed that she had opened the blouse an extra button or two.

Below the jacket she wore a black skirt that ended a few inches above her knees. The outfit appeared conservative enough to do business in, but Angela Vortiz had a knack for changing both her clothes and demeanor, instantly. McPherson sat at the desk and she handed him the brimming martini, not spilling a drop. He toasted her and drank.

"Shouldn't you be dressed for dinner?" she asked.

"Shouldn't you?"

They smiled at each other.

"Anything interesting on tonight's program?" he asked, knowing she would have checked.

"Only that a name's been added to the guest list at the last minute. You met him this afternoon in the garden. Your hometown boy."

"Yes. David Owens. The lawyer from San Antonio."

The President was not remotely a stupid man. He remembered important information. "How did he get here?"

"Just on his own, apparently. Don't worry, I'll find out."

McPherson smiled. Her promise sounded like a private joke between them. "He's just a kid," McPherson said, "looking for work or publicity."

At age fifty-two, McPherson tended to dismiss anyone under the age of forty as a child. This age group included his own wife and son. It included Angela Vortiz, for that matter, though McPherson took her seriously. She made sure of that.

She stood above him, the President in his desk chair sipping the martini. "When is Mr. Boswell going to attend one of these things?" he asked idly. "I've invited him enough times."

"When he thinks the time is right, I suppose. Why ask me?"

"I thought you'd have some insight into your boss's thoughts," McPherson teased.

"He's not my boss. I work for you, Mr. President."

Her use of his title in private often served as a signal between them, so McPherson had a hint as to what she would do next. Angela leaned back against the edge of the desk, right next to him and facing him. Suddenly she lifted her right leg, raising it higher and then surprisingly even higher, like a gymnast. When she elevated her leg it looked about four feet long, the calf and thigh muscles bunching and then elongating again, with a smoothness and flexibility that spoke of long hours of training. She brought her leg over McPherson's head and down again, resting her foot on the edge of his chair.

The President had managed not to drop his martini during this rapid performance, but he did stop breathing. He set the glass aside, touching her leg in the process. With her right knee cocked higher than her waist, her black skirt slipped back. He rested his hand on her thigh, admiring again its softness and strength. She smiled down at him.

"How do you feel?" she murmured.

"Like a boy on Christmas morning looking under the Christmas tree."

She laughed as if he'd never said this before, throwing back her head, which allowed her long black hair to cascade. McPherson wet his lips. He ran his hand slowly up her left leg.

Angela bent toward him to murmur something else. But in the silence they both suddenly heard a small scraping sound.

The President stood up from the desk chair and Angela Vortiz somehow levitated to the side so that she stood nonchalantly six feet from him. Turning toward the door of the Oval Office, she deftly turned on a floor lamp. The room brightened. McPherson crossed it and opened the door. No one was there. He looked out into the hall to find it empty except for a startled Secret Service agent who stared at him. The President shook his head and went back into his office.

"I don't think it came from that door," Angela said.

There were four exits from the Oval Office, not counting one into a bathroom. McPherson didn't bother to check all of them. The moment had been lost, anyway.

Angela Vortiz came close to him and whispered, "We have to be careful. You know what's at risk."

As if he'd been the one who'd put them in a compromising position. But McPherson only nodded.

"I'll see you at the dinner," Angela said more loudly. She winked, meaning, *And afterward.*

John McPherson stood a moment after she'd gone. Living in the most public private home in America had very obvious disadvantages. When he'd become President he'd ordered all recording devices removed from this room, then he'd borrowed equipment and run a scan himself to make sure the order had been carried out. But he remained surrounded by human ears, with a variety of motives.

Suddenly disliking his office, he turned quickly and left.

"Can't I come tonight, Mommy?"

Myra McPherson, standing in the large private living room on the second floor of the White House, looked down at her son, then sat on an ottoman so she'd be at eye level with him. "Do you really want to be there, Randy?"

The boy shrugged. Randy was eight years old. The first thing one noticed about him was his thick shock of brown hair, his mother's color. His pale face made his hazel eyes prominent. He had an almost nonexistent nose, rather prominent ears, and a small mouth. Not many people had seen him break into one of his beaming smiles that made anyone in the room want to hug him.

Randy remained painfully thin, the muscles in his chest and arms clearly defined, his forearm tendons developed by thousands of hours at various keyboards and game buttons. He cocked his head, waiting for her reply.

"They're not much fun, darling," Mrs. McPherson said of state dinners, speaking quite sincerely. "You'd have to sit for hours, listening to people talk and make speeches, and you wouldn't like the food. We've never once had pizza at a state dinner."

Randy grinned, recognizing a joke. He and his mother had lots of jokes between them. Randy's father had been Senator or President or running for President all his son's life, so that Myra had become in effect his only parent. It was the role she enjoyed most in life.

"One of these days we'll plan a state dinner just for you, Randy. You can invite anyone you want, and we'll all wear shorts and T-shirts and have Game Boys at every table and we will serve pizza."

As Myra described the occasion it sounded as if it could really happen. She imagined fun in the White House and her heart lifted. She hugged Randy to her chest.

"Okay, Mommy," he said obediently.

At the age of eight he should have been getting past this "Mommy" business, but Myra loved hearing it and Randy undoubtedly sensed that. Besides, he *was* her baby, her only one. She and Randy comprised a nation of two; each was the only person to whom the other could turn for unconditional love, and be sure of receiving it.

As if to illustrate this thought of hers, John McPherson suddenly entered the room, walking briskly as always.

"Hello, my dear," he said in passing. He added, "Hey there, rascal," and tousled Randy's hair. Randy stepped away from Myra, toward his father, but the President had already hurried by. "I'll be ready in just a minute, dear," he called.

Myra and Randy looked at each other blankly, waiting for reaction. After a moment Myra said, "Yes, darling, that *was* your father."

They both broke up laughing.

"He's awfully tall, isn't he?" Randy said, leaning close to her, and they laughed again. They had many jokes between them about the hole in their lives where a husband and father should be. The first such joke had burst from Myra's mouth rather bitterly one time when she'd seen too many looks of longing on her son's face as his father hurried from a room. She'd responded with a half-funny, half-angry remark that had made Randy laugh, so she'd kept up the joking and he'd begun to join in. Probably it wasn't psychologically healthy for a boy to laugh about his father's frequent absences, but she couldn't consult a psychologist, and she greatly preferred seeing Randy laugh to watching him fight back tears.

Randy went back to playing with his new *Star Wars* toy, a spaceship that George Lucas had handed Randy personally a month ago after a private White House screening of the latest episode in the space saga. Lucas had thereby joined a very select company of people who had met the first son face to face. John and Myra McPherson didn't spend much time discussing family matters, but they'd agreed on one policy and had implemented it very well: that Randy should be kept out of the public eye as much as possible. They had tried to give the boy an ordinary life to the extent they could. Randy attended a private school, but at least it was a school with classmates, not private tutors. Often his mother dropped him off or picked him up, rather than a nanny, and the Secret Service agents dressed unobtrusively at school.

His parents also kept Randy out of White House functions. They didn't put him on display. Years ago John McPherson had insisted on including his wife and infant son in campaign photos and appearances, but Myra had begun to balk at including Randy, and McPherson's political instincts had told him that appearing to be a concerned parent would do him more good than dragging an unwilling family with him in public. After his election as President he'd begun to show even less interest in spending time with his family, publicly or privately.

So Randy had become the phantom of the White House, its most secret denizen. The press cooperated in letting him alone, and his parents had allowed him to be photographed often enough that he didn't become a sought-after target for paparazzi. The public had some idea of what the first son looked like, but Randy's appearance was little-boy generic enough that he could have walked the streets of any city unrecognized.

Not that his parents would ever allow that. But someday, his mother hoped, after this awful period of their lives had ended, Randy could be normal. She had no higher ambition for him.

"All right, Mommy, I'll be fine. I'll see if Peter can play." Peter, the six-year-old son of one of the cooks, had become Randy's best friend by default. Myra wondered if the boy played with Randy because he genuinely enjoyed it or if Peter's father thought this an additional White House duty.

She gave Randy another hug, holding him extra tightly for a moment, then stood as her husband reentered the room.

"Ready, dear?"

"Yes," she said. Randy held her hand and whispered, "You try to have fun."

Another private joke. She smiled for his benefit, even maintaining the smile as her husband came up beside her and put his arm around her waist.

"Good night, son," the President said, and the first couple went downstairs to their lovely dinner.

Arriving at the White House after dark impressed David Owens even more than his daytime visit had. The house loomed more majestically, brilliantly lighted and displayed against a black backdrop of night, so that it looked indeed the whitest house in the world. It loomed larger and larger as David walked up the same asphalt path. David felt sure someone watched him, or at least video cameras, but he also felt oddly alone. The White House lawns stretched around him. He stepped off the path and found the grass wet. Droplets fell onto his black shoes. That seemed a marvel to David too: the White House yard had ordinary grass, and they'd watered it before guests came.

He saw other guests as he approached the front door. The doors stood open, tuxedoed servants greeting the visitors and discreetly checking their names. Part of David's impression of elegance stemmed from his own increased confidence. This time he was invited, and he'd come dressed for the part. It hadn't been hard to find a tuxedo rental place in Washington, and he fancied that he looked at least as good in his rented number as these older guests did in the tuxedos they no doubt owned. David wore clothes well—even clothes other than his own. He entered the White House feeling he belonged.

The President and First Lady greeted their company in the large entryway. John McPherson looked delighted at hosting the occasion. Myra McPherson smiled graciously. David moved naturally to the side, circling the fringe of the crowd rather than immediately taking his place in the line to meet the first couple. He studied the First Lady from a small distance, not trying to catch her eye. He couldn't read anything from her expression; Mrs. McPherson was obviously well practiced at maintaining her expression of quiet enjoyment at these formal occasions.

This White House dinner didn't feature a foreign leader as guest of honor. The central guests were four "artists," and no special occasion seemed to merit this honor for them on this particular day. Insiders knew the four to be excellent fund-raisers who had served the President well in his campaign. And there would always be another political season, so the party needed to keep its special contributors happy, and the President was the head of his party.

Besides, McPherson obviously relished the occasion, standing shoulder to shoulder with the famous for photographs, receiving their homages. He bent to listen attentively to one of the guests of honor, a woman talk-show host whose television show didn't remotely rival Oprah's in popularity but was widely watched by conservative audiences. Beside the President, holding his hand, Myra McPherson also inclined toward a guest, a retired football quarterback and sports commentator. The tall blond former athlete obviously was talking about a subject of great concern to him, but Myra's expression presented a contrast to her husband's. While John McPherson seemed very intent on the talk-show hostess, Myra's expression didn't change. She maintained her gracious hostess face no matter how intent her companion grew. David would bet she couldn't pass a test on the subject of the quarterback's talk. As he watched, her hand slipped out of her husband's.

Dinner began shortly. A dapper, sixtyish African-American butler consulted a chart of seating arrangements, looking for David's place.

"I was kind of a late addition," David said. "You probably had to set up a card table in the kitchen for me."

The butler smiled graciously. "No, sir, we always make do. This way, please."

David's table was on the outer fringe of the seating, but there were only ten tables of six guests each. The room didn't feel remotely crowded. He sat close enough to the President's table to hear the laughter from it as one of the other guests of honor, a television actor of remarkable longevity, told a joke.

A large man who looked uncomfortable in his evening clothes sat to David's left and extended his hand. "Burt Briswell. Aerospace manufacturing. And what's your game?"

"David Owens. I'm a lawyer."

"I meant golf or tennis. So, a lawyer. Just what Washington needs." And Burt Briswell turned his back on David.

To David's right sat an extremely beautiful woman who must have been a model at one time. She looked to be in her thirties and seemed somehow retired. Maybe her makeup and her coiled blond hair gave David that impression, because both seemed the result of at least a day-long labor. This woman hadn't rushed home from the office, thrown herself together, and then toddled over to the White House. She sat very straight and stared ahead attentively, but her attention never fastened on her dinner partner. She looked across the room, her eyes brightened, she said, "Excuse me" to no one in particular, and got up and walked across the room. Leaning down, the beautiful woman whispered to one of the other guests, who whispered back with great apparent concern.

This went on throughout the meal. The chair to David's right spent most of the dinner empty as the lovely woman excused herself every few minutes to go and talk to a guest at another table. David never learned her name or received a comment from her at all, except her frequent "Excuse me's." She seemed to be inadvertently dieting, as her plates arrived and were taken away barely touched.

So David spent the dinner in lonely isolation, but luckily the meal didn't last long. As the very efficient White House staff served dessert more people followed the example of David's seating partner, leaving their tables and strolling about the room. David wondered if he could do so himself, perhaps getting close to the First Lady. He heard the legs of the chair to his right scrape the floor, but the woman sitting beside him now was not the blond beauty. She was instead a black-haired beauty, who disconcerted David by staring at him intently. David had spent the evening and in fact most of the last few days being ignored, and had almost begun to think of himself as invisible. Quite obviously from this woman's gaze, he had reappeared in the land of the living.

"I've been watching you," she said.

"That accounts for this burning sensation I've had on the back of my neck."

The lady smiled. She didn't insult David by laughing aloud at a joke that didn't deserve it, but she did look as if she appreciated his remark and was pleased to be in his company. She put out her hand.

"Angela Vortiz. I work in the White House communications office."

"That seems a shame."

"Why?"

"I'm sorry, never mind, I was going to say something about how you should be in front of a camera instead of arranging for the President to be, but luckily I caught myself in time and realized how stupid and sexist that would be."

Angela's smile broadened. "I don't mind sexism when it comes in a compliment. Don't you wonder why I've been watching you?"

"Since I'm about the least famous or obviously wealthy person here, yes."

"That's why. Celebrities, millionaires, you trip over them all the time around here. Somebody real like you, you must be here for something important."

"Really? What?"

She smiled. Reaching out her slender hand to touch his lapel, she said, "Besides, you looked interesting enough to come and get to know just for my own purposes."

Her own purposes sounded intriguing. Angela Vortiz had a gift for quick intimacy. Already David felt as if the rest of the crowd had receded, leaving the two of them alone.

"So what do you do, David Owens?"

He didn't ask how she had learned his name. In a room with a seating chart, in a building where she worked, that would have been easy. But the fact that she'd gone to the trouble to do so was flattering. David felt a small mental twinge warning him to be careful, but the woman's attention overwhelmed this tweak of caution. Angela wore a deep blue evening dress with just an occasional sparkle of thread in the weave, as if it were her own personality shining through. She crossed her legs, revealing them through a long slit in the skirt, and leaned her chin on her hand as if settling in for a nice cozy chat, her dark eyes never leaving David's face.

"I'm just a lawyer from the President's hometown. Now I know

I've grabbed your attention, because you so seldom have the chance to meet a real attorney."

"We have a separate entrance for them." Angela smiled.

"But I'm not here on business. Just visiting."

"Visiting whom? Do you know the President or Myra from back in Texas?"

Angela Vortiz had just struck her first false note. Her voice gave the First Lady's first name a tinny quality, as if Angela didn't deserve the intimacy implied, or as if she generally used the name in a different tone of voice. David hesitated.

"Oh, no more so than anybody from back home," he said, his voice beginning to drawl. "In San Antonio we all feel like the first family are home folks. But I'm no special friend of either one."

"Then what—"

David felt a slight breeze from his left side. For the first time, Angela's eyes left his face. A slight look of annoyance crossed her expression.

David turned and found Helen Wills sitting on his other side. She smiled at him, leaned back in the chair, and sat looking uncharacteristically comfortable.

"Don't mind me. I just wanted to meet the gentleman from San Antonio, too."

David looked back from his new visitor to his first, and found a glare just leaving Angela Vortiz's face as she felt his gaze. She smiled at him again.

David cleared his throat and said, "My, we Texans must be great rarities in the White House. I would have thought there'd be a steady stream of us."

"Don't let me interrupt your conversation," Helen Wills said languidly.

"I was just wondering what brought Mr. Owens to the White House."

"Call me David, please." David leaned forward as if about to whisper. Both women leaned flatteringly toward him. "Actually, I sneaked in. Remember that intruder who slipped into Buckingham Palace a few years ago and walked right into the queen's bedroom? I wondered if someone could do that here. And voilà! here I am. My ultimate goal is the Lincoln bedroom. You won't give me away, will you?"

He smiled at Angela. Her eyes narrowed slightly behind her own smile.

And abruptly she stood up. "You'd find the Lincoln bedroom boring these days. It's been turned into a sitting room. No bed. Well, good night, David. Another time, I hope."

On his feet, David said, "I do too, Angela. Thank you. You made the evening memorable for me."

She waved a hand around, taking in the room and the building. "It took me to do that?"

She turned and walked slowly away. Behind David's back Helen Wills said, "Think of the earning potential that would be ruined if she had a prominent facial scar."

David didn't answer, watching the supple, subtle shifting of Angela's hips as she crossed the room. If that movement wasn't for him, if she didn't feel his eyes on her, then she had an amazingly instinctive sway to her pace.

"Does she always walk like that?" he asked aloud.

In a voice that had reverted to normal from the playful tone she'd been using, Helen said, "I frankly haven't studied her from behind. The way you are."

David looked at Helen more closely. Was that jealousy in her voice? She had heard that note, too. She, like Angela, stood abruptly. All the guests in the room had left their tables now, milling around, the anonymous trying to meet the famous, the famous drawn toward each other. White House servants began trying to usher everyone into the next room. In the confusion it was easy for David to draw Helen aside. He spoke quietly and earnestly. "I know I won't be able to get close to Mrs. McPherson in this mob. Could you give her a message for me, please?"

"What is it?"

"Tell her I came here to get her instructions. I'm ready to file a petition for divorce whenever she wants. I'm also ready to go away and never bother her again. If I don't hear anything, that's what I'll do."

Helen studied him in her suspicious way. His trust that she would deliver his message was flattering, but Helen didn't show it. "You'd really love to have this case, wouldn't you? You just can't wait to get famous."

David shook his head, returning her watchful scrutiny. "Actually I don't care about the McPhersons at all. I came to Washington hoping for a date with you."

For a moment Helen had no comeback. Then she laughed. She had a startled, honest laugh that drew smiles from people nearby, including David. Her face changed wonderfully with laughter, turning younger and vulnerable. David wanted to keep her laughing.

Quickly Helen regained her composure. "Right," she said. "Well, I'm afraid this is going to be the most disappointing trip—"

"Will you give Mrs. McPherson my message?"

Suspicion returned to Helen's face. Talking softly and sincerely, David added, "I got a message in San Antonio asking me to come here and help. And when I arrived this afternoon my name was on the guest list for that reception. Someone wants me here. Who is it?"

Helen continued to look skeptical, but she couldn't deny that David had made his way into the private reception. He couldn't have done that on his own. "I don't know," she finally said. "I'll pass on your message. And you can deliver it yourself, too. Here's her phone number. No, don't write it down. Memorize it." Helen spoke seven digits, enunciating clearly. David quickly tried to assemble them into a pattern, and distracted himself for a moment by repeating the number mentally several times. "Call about ten o'clock tomorrow morning. She should be alone then."

"Thank you."

The crowd had left them behind. David continued, "You hate giving me that message, don't you? And this is probably just me being oversensitive, but you seem to hate me, too. What have I done?"

Helen crossed her arms and looked straight at him. "My job is to protect her from people like you."

"People like me?"

"People who would put her in danger."

"But I'm just helping her do what she wants to do."

"Yes!" Helen said emphatically, as if he should get it.

"She wants to put herself in danger," David said.

"Yes. And you'd help her."

"So have you."

"I know that." Helen looked ruefully across the room. The White House staff had left the two of them alone, apparently trusting the room to Helen's attention.

"So you need to protect her from people like you," David observed.

"Yes. But I trust myself. I'm not supposed to trust anyone else."

"Who said that?"

"The job, David. That's my job."

"Not to trust me?"

"Yes. Or myself."

"Or . . ." *your feelings,* he started to say, but stopped himself. He understood Helen's apparent hostility. It was half directed at herself, and the conflict in her situation. Knowing what the First Lady wanted, Helen could either help her or give her away. She'd chosen the former, but didn't like the resulting danger to her charge.

"You're putting her in my hands," David said.

"Yes. And that's exactly what I'm not supposed to do. So I'll help her and that means helping you. Just don't ask me to trust you. Okay?"

"Okay. So we've got that issue worked out. Right?"

Helen smiled wryly. They trailed the crowd into the next room, both of them instinctively dropping the subject as other people pressed closer to them. "So," David asked conversationally, "do you sleep in the White House? Which direction is your room?"

Helen chuckled, a much smaller version of her laugh. She laid her hand on his forearm as if they were a couple walking into the theater together. "Give up on that, son," she advised.

"I just hoped to offer you a walk home after the entertainment."

Helen smiled softly, looking down at the floor, and didn't answer.

At the end of the evening David had barely a moment to speak to Myra McPherson. The President and First Lady stood at the front door shaking hands with each departing guest. David couldn't avoid the meeting. "Good-bye, Mr. President," he said heartily. "Any message you want me to take home to San Antonio?"

McPherson gripped his hand strongly, holding it, and David's eye as well. The President looked into him for a long moment as if he could read David's thoughts. Then he said, "Just that I take care of my own."

David passed on, wondering if that commonplace phrase held some special message to him. Then he had his moment with Mrs. McPherson. He only murmured good night and thanks for the special evening, and she said nothing more significant, but as she held his hand her left hand passed over his wrist and hand in a caress or a plea. He nodded as if he understood, touched again by her expression of longing, and passed on. Unfamiliar night enfolded him, but he walked through it confidently, feeling competent to deal with the enormous burden about to descend on him.

At an upstairs window of the White House Angela Vortiz and Helen Wills stood together, watching David walk away. "By the way," Angela said testily, "I heard that 'facial scar' remark. You always struck me as essentially unaggressive, Helen."

Helen didn't turn to her. "You wouldn't want him to think we're on the same team, would you?"

She continued to watch the departing lawyer from San Antonio until he passed through the gate in the fence and out of sight.

David woke up smiling. But as he waited to make his call to Myra McPherson, he wondered what might be happening in the family quarters of the White House that morning. Had the President and First Lady breakfasted together? Had the President asked why that young lawyer from San Antonio had been at both receptions yesterday? David pictured Mrs. McPherson shrugging off the questions, then he imagined her answering directly: John McPherson's face darkening, his standing up, throwing down his napkin, maybe raising his voice so that a servant came in with a worried expression.

David had heard from his clients many varieties of reactions at home to the things David did in court. Spouses sometimes wanted the petition for divorce filed secretively and served on the other spouse with the utmost discretion. Others wanted to hold a press conference. One husband had wanted to accompany the process server when she served the papers on his wife at her office. He had also wanted to go in and punch his wife's boss and supposed lover at the same time, but David had dissuaded him from that.

Sometimes, weirdly, husbands and wives continued to live together all through the divorce process. Mrs. McPherson might have to do that in a way: remain the nation's hostess while divorcing its leader. Probably she needn't worry about many wives' main fear, being beaten up. After all, she had Secret Service protection. But the mere unpleasantness of remaining with the man after he knew her intentions would be a frightful emotional journey. Never having been divorced himself, David couldn't imagine, but every adult has experienced failed relationships. David began to remember the heartbreak and guilt and anger of his own worst breakup.

This is what made him a good divorce lawyer: his empathy with his client. It was the reason Myra McPherson had chosen him, and he felt determined to live up to her expectations.

When the digital clock in his hotel room turned over to ten o'clock, David reached for the phone. As he did he remembered the one factor he'd left out of his imagined White House domestic scenes, because David had never seen him: the White House son, Randy. If feeling between his parents were so bad and distant and cold, how did Randy react? In an analytical lawyer's way, David filed the thought away for his subconscious mind to work on. Another problem in the case, maybe the biggest one of all.

Contrary to Helen Wills's instruction, he'd come back to the hotel last night and written down the phone number she'd told him. He hoped he'd had it memorized correctly in the meantime. If not he'd have no way of getting the number again. David got an outside line and dialed the number. After a brief pause it rang. David held the phone tightly, going as tense as a boy calling for a first date. The phone rang twice more. He tried to picture the room where the telephone on the other end sat. A living room, a bedroom, a small home office of some kind?

The phone rang and rang. No operator answered, nor a machine. David's tension escalated, then declined as he realized nothing would happen. After ten rings he gave up. He blew out his held breath loudly, looked around the room, and felt his specialness ebbing away. Maybe he was just an idiot instead, not even a special one.

He stood and stretched, then walked downstairs to the lobby, where he bought a newspaper just to look as if he'd had a reason for getting out of his room. No one in the lobby seemed to notice him. He'd gone invisible again.

On the way back up to his room David enumerated the possibilities: Helen Wills had given him a fake phone number. He hadn't remembered it correctly. The First Lady had decided she didn't want to talk to him. She wasn't home. Her husband had murdered her overnight.

In his room he glanced through the newspaper and found nothing that remotely interested him in the stories of war threats, terrorism, or possible breakup of the European Union. Tossing it aside, he dialed the number again, this time with much less unease because he expected no answer again.

The second phone ring was cut short as someone on the other end picked up quickly. A small, breathy voice said, "Hello?"

David sat up. "Mrs. McPherson?"

Her voice grew louder and more adult, though no less breathless. "David Owens, is that you?"

"Yes, ma'am."

"I'm sorry, I heard it ringing before but I couldn't get to it in time. I was, um—"

David imagined she'd been in the bathroom but felt too embarrassed to say so. Myra McPherson seemed like that kind of lady.

"It's all right, ma'am, I—"

"Someone was here and I wanted to be alone when I talked to you. I am now. Hello. How are you?" She seemed to compose herself.

"I'm fine, Mrs. McPherson."

"I'm so glad you called. I didn't have any way to reach you, and I was afraid—"

"Your efficient staff could certainly have tracked me down," David said, thinking of Helen Wills.

The First Lady chuckled. "Thank you so much for coming to Washington. I felt so relieved somehow when I saw you. Like a visitor from home when you're in a strange place, you know?"

"You still feel that way, after the years you've lived in Washington?"

"I feel that way about my"—she hesitated—"about the White House."

"I'm happy to hear you were glad to see me," David said, feeling like a suitor. "When I didn't hear from you again I thought you had changed your mind. I almost didn't come, I thought it might seem—"

"Oh, no. Don't think that I wanted to talk to you again, I did. But when I came to see you before? That was a rare occasion, when I could slip away like that? I don't get many such opportunities."

As Myra talked, David heard her questioning, southern-lady style of speech. She finished, "I'm so glad you came."

"I don't want you to think I'm pursuing your business, Mrs. McPherson, or that I'm urging you to do anything. If you've changed your mind, or just want to wait, I understand completely. That might even be the best thing to do."

"Oh, no!" She sounded alarmed. "No, believe me, nothing's

changed. I still feel everything I said to you in your office. More so every day. I have to take Randy away from this place."

David had the confirmation he'd wanted. He stood straight beside the bed in his hotel room, his whole body clenched with attention. At his side his fist closed and tightened in anticipation.

"David, are you still there?"

"Yes, ma'am. I'll always be here for you." A little melodramatic, that, but he couldn't help himself. "I can file the petition whenever you tell me, and we'll go from there."

Now the First Lady hesitated. "I just—I want to have everything worked out as much as possible before that. As much as I can, at least? I want to be in Texas, established someplace, with Randy. Maybe even get him enrolled in school down there before the school year starts again. Can you help me with that?"

"Yes, ma'am."

"My parents are in Alabama, on the coast, so we'd be closer to them. Maybe—I don't know, I've been thinking and thinking about it. I want to come see you again in San Antonio and talk again about everything. I've been looking for a space on my calendar when I might be near there again anyway, but so far—"

"It's all right, Mrs. McPherson, whenever you can make the time I'll be available. I'll wait for you."

"No!" She sounded frightened again. "I don't want to wait. Maybe since you're here Randy and I can go back with you."

"Whatever you say." David continued to speak in the staunchly bland manner that had come over him during the call, but his excitement grew. If he were seen traveling with the First Lady, the secret would virtually be out in the open, no matter what kind of cover story they concocted. The case would have begun.

"Mrs. McPherson, have you talked to your husband about this idea at all?"

"No. Don't you understand, that's the problem, we don't talk about anything."

"Do you think maybe you should? I don't think we want to startle him."

A long pause made David wonder if she'd lost faith in him. "I don't know if I could," she finally said in a very small voice.

"All right. That's fine. Tell me what you want me to do."

"Just . . . Can you just wait here in Washington a bit longer? Let me get some things together, and talk to Helen, and Randy. I'll—I'll be ready very soon. Can you call me back this evening? After ten, after Randy's asleep. I can't remember if John is supposed to be here or not. I may not be able to talk, but I just want to hear that you're still here."

She would wait for the sound of his voice. Myra would long for that moment the whole day. David grew solemn with the realization of how much she already seemed to rely on him, a stranger. How lonely she must have been. She should have an old family retainer, a confidante, someone. She seemed to be placing David in that role.

"I will do that, Mrs. McPherson. And here's where I am if you need to reach me." He gave her his hotel and room number. She repeated them as if writing down the information. David pictured that, too: his name and phone number on a note in a White House bedroom.

"Thank you," the First Lady said, still rather breathless. "I'll talk to you soon?"

"Yes, ma'am. We certainly will."

A moment later he hung up the phone and felt a thrill run up his arm. Perhaps he'd been holding the phone too tightly and blood was now rushing back into his arm, but it felt like a volt of electricity. David suddenly felt enormously energized. He knew he couldn't stay in the hotel room. He could go look for that local law firm he was going to need, maybe do a preliminary interview. Maybe he'd walk to the Supreme Court and hear an argument. Or find a law library and do research. First of all he had to walk, feel connected to the ground. His life was becoming a fantasy.

He passed the mirror above the dresser and saw himself grinning enormously. The smile looked a little frightening. Good. He needed to be at his smartest and most ruthless now.

But he'd need a better smile to reassure Myra McPherson.

When Benjamin Larsen arrived at work that morning, he knew something was wrong. There was no receptionist, for one thing. Anyone could walk into the office building through the revolving glass doors. He heard the sound of voices, as if dozens of people went about their jobs as usual, but he didn't see anyone.

Larsen ran for the stairs, avoiding the elevator that could trap him. The stairwell seemed empty, but as he clattered up to the second floor, he heard steps behind him. Someone had followed him into the stairwell.

Larsen turned the corner at a landing and his feet continued to pound the cement stairs, filling the stairwell with echoes, but he no longer moved upward. He just ran in place, creating the illusion of climbing stairs. A few seconds later, sensing movement below, he vaulted over the handrail to the stair level just below. Leading with his feet, he landed atop a heavy, fleshy obstacle and heard the satisfying "oof" of a man going down under him. The pursuer's head hit a concrete step, and he groaned and went quiet. Larsen hit him once just to be sure. Then he quickly searched the fallen man and the area just around him. Sure enough, a Glock semiautomatic handgun had fallen from the man's hand. If Larsen had been slower or less suspicious, he'd be dead now.

Carrying the gun, Larsen ascended the stairs again. He imagined he needed to get to his own cache of weapons. He pictured floors two and three of the three-story building where he worked. His own cubicle was on the second floor, at the far end of the building from the stairs. There would be two security stands to get by before he could reach it. The third floor was quieter and less populated, but housed some very secret research and development the nature of which he didn't know. He might run into some serious obstacles there.

This time he decided not to take that risk. He emerged from the stairs on the second floor. Holding the pistol casually down beside his leg, he strolled toward the security station, lifting his other hand in a wave, calling, "Hi."

The two security guards looked up from their study of a screen. The guards were new: another sign of trouble in the workplace. One was a tall, dark man with very sharp features and a forceful stare. The other guard, Asian, might have been in training for the junior sumo wrestling championships. He was massive, with shoulders more than three feet wide, and a broad, angry face and extra chins. "How may we help you?" this one said in a deep growl.

They could have been legitimate security guards. But Larsen didn't think so. Their ponytails gave them away. Just to be certain, he brought his gun into sight. Sure enough, the guards reacted like trained killers. Immediately they jumped away from each other. The taller, thinner one leaped over the counter, while the samurai disappeared behind it. Larsen jumped, caught the leg of the first man while it was still in the air, gave a great heave, and flipped him. The guard hit the ground in a heap and Larsen shot him where he lay.

But now he didn't know where the other guard was. He leaned cautiously over the counter, and a wide samurai sword, slashing up from below, almost took his head off. Larsen screamed and jumped back. He fired a shot into the counter, but it was bulletproof. The slug came zinging back toward him. Then the fat security guard leaped up onto the counter. He wielded the sword in flashing arcs. Larsen fired at him, but the guard seemed bulletproof too. Some of that fat might have been Kevlar armor.

Larsen turned and ran, hearing the heavy pounding of feet behind him. Ahead of him the corridor ended at a window. No doors on either side, no exit from the monster chasing him. And the gun was useless against the guard. Larsen looked back over his shoulder and saw the guard coming after him in great leaps, quickly eating up the distance between them.

If the gun was no use, why did he have it? He couldn't use it against the guard. He could shoot himself, but that didn't seem to be a solution. Could he shoot the sword? Doubtful.

Suddenly Larsen understood. He looked back, saw the guard's massive legs bunching with the leap that would catch his prey. Just ahead, Larsen was about to be trapped at the window. He raised the

Glock again and fired. The window glass shattered but didn't break.

Hearing a grunt behind him, Larsen suddenly fell flat on his face on the floor. He heard a whoosh through the air above him and looked up. The guard hurtled over Larsen's prone form. He hit the glass of the window. Already shattered, the window broke completely open under the impact of the guard's massive body, and the guard sailed on through the window.

Larsen scrambled to his feet and looked down through the broken window. It had only been a one-story fall, but it had been enough. A spiked fence stood below. If Larsen had gone through that window, it would have been the end of him.

The samurai had left his sword behind. Larsen reached down for it, seeing as he did so that somewhere in the scuffle he had lost the sleeves of his shirt. His long, brawny arm easily hefted the samurai sword. "Interesting," he said aloud. Now he had a sword and a pistol, but still felt woefully underarmed for what he knew was coming. He had a lot of other employees to fight his way through before reaching that top floor.

Because now he had realized his goal. Larsen was going to see the boss.

Multibillionaire Wilson Boswell, President and CEO of the software mega-corporation TitanWorks, sat behind his black maple desk in the most private office in America. Soundproofed walls, white noise filters, electronic screening devices, and microwave scramblers guaranteed that nothing left this office or came into it except what Wilson Boswell wanted. Paranoia didn't account for this array of antispying equipment. Boswell simply operated under the assumption that some competitor out there might have the same scruples he did; that is to say, none. This philosophy had always paid off for him.

Boswell sat very straight behind his desk. He was sixty-three years old, but maintained the posture first instilled in him in military school. Boswell remained thin, he disdained activities that would produce a tan, and he had been bald for years, making him look older. But sometimes he surprised younger men with the strength of his handshake, and of his grip on life. Wilson Boswell had started his life as most people he knew had started, by inheriting a business and a small family fortune. Before he turned thirty he had started the family factory on the road to becoming a national retail chain and turned the small fortune into a large one.

If he had one gift, it was envisioning the future. The first time Boswell had seen a computer, in the 1970s, he had had a vision. If one of these could let a company work more efficiently, rival companies would have to have one too. Then every company. Boswell had moved into the computer business, where he seemed ancient and wise to the young geek geniuses who were creating the personal computing world. He found a promising company, Hardrive Inc., provided capital for the starving trio running it, then offered to handle the business aspects. About the time the company achieved its first breakthrough in a PC model small enough for home use, Boswell had stolen the company from its founder so deftly and easily that the founder remained grateful.

Soon Boswell merged the computer company with a software company, then another, and used the leverage he soon enjoyed in the marketplace to put his most threatening software rival into receivership and then take over its assets. By the late 1980s Boswell's company, now dubbed TitanWorks, dominated both the hard- and software markets, and Wilson Boswell found himself, almost inadvertently, the richest man in the world.

At the age of fifty-five he could have sat and wept because there was no more world to conquer. But Wilson Boswell was more resourceful than Alexander the Great. His acquisitiveness only fed itself, never satisfied. Boswell's interest turned naturally to politics. He became a major political contributor, then went more selective. He invested quietly but deeply in half a dozen promising political figures. Only one of them had really worked out, but that one rather well: John McPherson, now President of the United States, a President who thought of Wilson Boswell as an old friend and mentor.

Now Boswell sat behind his desk almost alone in the office. A five-foot-tall screen stood beside the desk. The screen received digital images, such that the equipment seemed to vanish when it was receiving, showing only the image projected. The effect wasn't quite three-dimensional, not yet. Still, the projection was so much better than television reception that those seeing it for the first time could be fooled into thinking they were looking through a window rather than a screen.

Angela Vortiz filled the screen. Today she wore a beige suit that didn't give her the dramatic flair of her usually favored black. But she didn't want to look like a killer every day. Standing with her hip cocked, she held up a small tape recorder.

Behind Angela, Boswell could see her small office in the White House. Idly he wondered what it would be like to live there. But Boswell didn't want to be a politician, only to own some. He'd cultivated a relationship with John McPherson years ago, before he even seemed to have presidential prospects. McPherson had found the tycoon's attention flattering, not realizing that Boswell had many such relationships. Like most of Boswell's other investments, this one had paid off, giving him a direct line into the White House and a President who wanted to be his business partner.

Angela finished playing the recording of Myra McPherson's telephone conversation with David Owens for Boswell. The tape ended with the First Lady's timid but hopeful good-bye to her lawyer. Boswell frowned in distaste. Emotion always affected him that way.

"Want to hear it again?" Angela asked.

Boswell shook his head. "This can't happen, of course," he said.

On the screen, Angela Vortiz shook her head in agreement and waited respectfully for his decision. This experimental system didn't have enough capacity yet. Every few seconds Angela's image would freeze, then jerk back into action, making her look a little robotic.

"Time to take some action." Boswell sighed, as if the thought wearied him.

Angela Vortiz nodded. "I agree."

"Thank you, Angela. We must put our heads together." Boswell sounded as if he meant it, and Angela smiled almost shyly. Boswell had always kept his relationship with Ms. Vortiz strictly businesslike. For his sexual needs he had an administrative assistant in Human Resources, a maid at home, and even, very occasionally, his wife of thirty-five years. He had decided to make himself immune to the charms of Angela Vortiz, which obviously left her baffled and very respectful.

Noise from the hallway interrupted their conversation. That shouldn't have been possible. Boswell turned toward his office door, frowning. He heard his secretary scream. The next moment the door burst open. From the screen, Angela Vortiz gasped.

Larsen stood in the doorway of his boss's office pointing a gun at him.

Larsen looked at the obviously disguised form of his apparently normal boss. He was distracted momentarily by the beautiful woman who seemed to be hovering in the air beside the boss's desk. The woman stared in horror at him. Who to shoot first? Larsen needed a hint.

Boswell stood up. "Take that damned thing off!" he snapped.

"What thing?" Larsen asked, trying not to give in to the creature's tricks. Boswell started toward him and Larsen fired. The flame gun he'd liberated from the research department sent a five-foot-long tongue of fire.

But Boswell walked through it, advancing on him relentlessly. "No!" Larsen screamed as the creature reached for his eyes.

Boswell pulled off the virtual reality helmet Larsen wore. From Larsen's perspective, his brawny arms turned skinny and his flame gun into a game controller.

"I've asked you not to roam the halls in this thing," Boswell said with remarkable patience.

"Just testing it," Larsen said rather sullenly. The helmet was of his own design. It didn't restrict the wearer's real vision entirely, but instead allowed the game running in the helmet to blend with the outside world. Within the company, only Larsen seemed to think this a good idea. The game was his, too, though most of his fellow employees thought it only represented Larsen's genuine view of the world. Larsen called the game in progress "Office Melee." Other employees, in whispered giggles, called it "Postal Worker."

Some of them had gathered now in the doorway. Larsen's progress through the building had disrupted their own work, and they didn't like being shot at, even with a game gun.

If only they knew, Wilson Boswell thought.

He made peace, ushered the others out, but Larsen remained behind. Of all the employees of TitanWorks, only this one enjoyed the freedom of the building, including Boswell's private office. As always, the young designer looked lost, as if he might have opened the boss's door while looking for the men's room. Not lost in thought, just lost. Larsen couldn't have weighed one-fifty. He had long limbs, almost skeletal fingers, and stringy blond hair. Almost no substance to the man at all. He wore glasses perpetually, with the same tortoiseshell frames he'd probably had since junior high.

Larsen didn't look at his boss, or indeed seem to focus on anything. His eyes wandered as his feet did. When Larsen left his cubicle he strolled at large through the TitanWorks complex, apparently thinking about his latest game design, and while thinking walked without apparent direction. Fellow employees had given up greeting him as a waste of breath; he never replied. Often, in fact, he would bump into someone who didn't see him and get out of the way in time. Larsen didn't seem to believe in other people's reality.

"Did you need me for something?" he asked, apparently to Boswell's office itself.

God, Boswell hated it when he did that. As if he had summoned Larsen without knowing it. Or as if the skinny bastard could read his mind from afar.

"No, thank you," Boswell said firmly. "Not yet, anyway."

Larsen shrugged and turned away again. In his wake, Wilson Boswell shuddered ever so slightly.

five ★ Having the high point of one's whole professional life come at ten o'clock in the morning can really ruin the rest of the day. After his phone conversation with the First Lady, David felt torn between staying in his room in case Mrs. McPherson called him back, and the restless urge to get out. Finally, after pacing around his room about twenty times, he called the White House back, this time the regular number, and asked for Helen Wills.

Interestingly, the operator had trouble finding her. Apparently Helen was hard to pin down. This didn't surprise David. But eventually a line rang and Helen picked it up. She sounded a little breathless. "Hello?"

"Hi, it's David Owens."

A pause, as if she didn't recognize the name. "Yes?"

At a sudden loss, David sprang his big card right away. "I talked to your boss a little while ago."

"Don't say anything," Helen said quickly.

"I wouldn't," he answered, offended. "I just wanted to talk to you."

"What about?"

"I was wondering if they ever let you out of the compound."

"What?"

"Your job there, the building, you know, do you ever get out during the day?" David still sensed puzzlement through the phone line. He sighed and said, "I was wondering if we could have lunch."

Helen laughed, surprised by the simplicity of the idea. "Gee, what a great idea," she said with genuine enthusiasm.

"You mean you can?" David sounded surprised as well.

"Oh, no, I can't actually do it. I pretty much have to be on call all the time. But it was a nice idea. Thank you, David."

"You're welcome," he said confusedly. "Okay, well, I'm sure I'll talk to you soon. Maybe, anyway . . ."

With a hasty good-bye, he hung up, sighed, and hurried out of his room.

In the First Lady's private office where the White House operator had tracked her down, Helen Wills held the phone, looking at it oddly until it began to whine to be hung up. She wore a bemused expression between a smile and a frown, trying to think how long it had been since someone had asked her for a date. When had the last opportunity come up for her to meet anyone new, for that matter? As David had suggested, she didn't get out of the compound much.

"Who was that, dear?" Myra McPherson asked, coming in from the other room. She carried a box of her private stationery, having decided to spend the day catching up on her correspondence.

"Nobody. Nothing important. Let's get started."

A few minutes later Helen got another phone call, from her supervisor telling her to return to the office. She excused herself, hurried through the White House to her little cell, and found that the director wanted her to do some paperwork. She couldn't see the urgency in it; the task only wasted an hour of her day.

When she returned to the first family's private quarters, the First Lady was gone.

David spent the day staring at his phone and taking brief, rapid walks around his hotel. Mrs. McPherson had sounded so anxious that morning he expected to hear from her again, just for reassurance. But the phone didn't ring, and when he returned from his walks he had no messages. He had two room service meals and a restless, useless day.

The boring day left him energetic at night. David stayed up past midnight, kept company by the all-news TV channel. Periodically he tried the private phone number again, even after the hour grew late. At twelve-twenty A.M. he saw a tiny news item saying the First Lady and her son had left for a summer vacation at a very exclusive island off the coast of South Carolina. A film clip that could have been stock footage showed them departing in a helicopter, turning to wave good-bye. Myra McPherson, dressed conservatively in a navy blue dress cinched tight at the waist by a broad white belt, smiled much more broadly than usual. The President would join his family in a few days, the report concluded.

David had no idea what to make of this news. Was it true? Was this Mrs. McPherson's way of getting away to a safe haven so she could begin the divorce process? Or just to think about it all? Maybe she planned to call David and ask him to join her. Maybe she had called today while he'd been out walking. Of course she wouldn't have left a message, now that he thought about it. Leave a message with a hotel operator, or even on voice mail, saying, "Please have Mr. Owens call the First Lady of the United States; he has the number"? Hardly.

He'd been an idiot. He should have sat by the phone all day, accessible to his client. Berating himself, filled with anxiety, David finally fell into a restless sleep.

In the darkness a hand covered his mouth. David's poor night's sleep had left him more alert than deep slumber would have, his eyes snapped open quickly. But that didn't help: no light illuminated the room. He thrashed, trying to get free of the covers. Instead a body landed on top of him, pinning him more firmly. David continued to struggle until a voice very close to his ear said, "Shhh."

What stopped him was that it was a woman's voice. He could feel her soft breath on his ear. David went dead still. That satisfied the intruder. She rose off him, pulling David half upright as well. He glanced at the glowing numbers of the digital clock and saw it was five o'clock in the morning.

A tiny light snapped on. In its faint glow David saw disarrayed blond hair, then focused on Helen Wills's face. She stared at him, trying to will him into wakefulness. When she had David's attention, she held up a piece of hotel notepad on which she'd written a one— word order: PACK.

David felt slow and stupid. Pack of what? What did she want from him? Why didn't she speak? Helen acted so strangely and her face remained so rigid that she could have been a robot version of herself. He continued to gape at her.

Helen gave him a clue by opening the closet door and dragging out his suitcase. She dropped it open on the bed and began removing his clothes from the closet.

Oh: pack. David stepped out of the bed, then realized as in one of those bad dreams that he was wearing only briefs. Helen glanced at him, then stopped her path from closet to suitcase to look him over appraisingly. David's eyes had grown used to the gloom. So, obviously, had Helen's. Her eyes settled on his face, she began to look impatient, and that got him moving. David hastily found his pants from the day before hanging over the back of a chair and pulled them on. He felt immediately reassured: half-dressed meant half-competent, half-awake, which was a big improvement from a minute before.

Helen herself wore black. David thought of it as a lady-spy outfit. She moved around the room sinuously and very confidently, making no sound. David let her finish his packing while he dressed, realizing in the process that he'd like to shower and shave and brush his teeth before any closer encounter with Helen.

The two of them removed every trace of David with amazing speed, turning the hotel room anonymous again. Helen jerked her head to indicate departure. David stepped very close to her and whispered, "Can I go to the bathroom first?"

She rolled her eyes and shook her head. Irritated, David followed her out into the dimly-lit corridor, which seemed very bright by comparison. He felt spotlighted. Helen contributed to the paranoia, looking both ways intently, then hurrying ahead of him, dragging his suitcase. David carried a briefcase. All the goods he had in Washington, D.C.

Helen opened a door under an EXIT sign. David followed her into a concrete, unfinished-looking stairwell. Confused by her continuing silence, he said, "Where are we going?"

Helen started down the stairs and he followed. Over her shoulder she said, "I don't know. I wanted to get you out of your room as fast as possible. They might've already had it bugged, or they might be on their way to get you."

"They who?" Helen didn't answer. "Why would anyone be after me?" David pressed.

Helen said over her shoulder, "Because you called her private phone number."

"How would anybody else know that?"

She stopped and turned to face him. "Guess what, David, the White House has Caller ID."

Oh. Right. David still didn't feel fully awake. But he made an observation. "That would only give them the hotel's phone number, wouldn't it? Not my room number."

"Right. That's why I had a head start. Or maybe they're not coming after you at all. Maybe they just want you to wait around until you get tired and go home. But I couldn't take that chance."

"You mean until Mrs. McPherson gets back from South Carolina? How long's she going to be gone?"

Scornfully, Helen said, "She's not in South Carolina. The White House put out that story."

"Then where is she?"

"I don't know."

They reached the ground floor. David caught Helen's arm. She had just scared him. "Why aren't you with her?"

"That's a good question, isn't it? Apparently I'm not trusted somewhere. Or maybe it's just a precaution, changing her protection team. I'm working on finding her. In the meantime, I don't want you to disappear too. They've found out what she was planning with you. They may—"

"Who?"

"The President. His associates. I don't think they'd do anything to you except try to scare you away, but why take a chance? But Mrs. McPherson is a much bigger problem. If—"

"You don't think . . . ?"

David looked horrified. Helen shook her head at him impatiently. "No. They just want to work on her, bring her back into line. Maybe with the help of professionals. I'm sure she's in a private hospital somewhere. There aren't that many possibilities. I think I can track her down if I just monitor communications. Meanwhile I don't want to have to worry about you."

She opened the door, a side door of the hotel that let them out to a sidewalk next to the parking lot. Night still covered Washington, but very thinly. Predawn light filtered through the darkness.

David had come fully awake. He breathed deeply of the cool air and felt more ready to take his place in events. "What about Randy? Where's her son?"

"I don't know that either." Helen stopped her rapid flight, turned to face him, and he saw how frightened she was as she crossed her arms as if cold. "This is what I was afraid of. This is why I didn't want you near her."

"I didn't do this, Helen."

"I know. But you precipitated it by coming here. Or I did by bringing her to see you. It doesn't matter. I've just got to try to fix it."

David took her arms. "I can help. I'll go to the press—"

"Who could confirm your story? You wouldn't get an inch in the *Post*. You know how many times a day somebody calls them to say there's a plot going on in the White House? No, I've got to get her free first."

"What can I do to help?"

"Just stay safe. You're my only backup. Don't get caught. Stow your bags somewhere and roam around. Don't come near the White House. Do you have a car?"

"No."

"Good. Don't do anything that will let them trace you. Don't rent a car, don't check into another hotel. Can you stay safe for a day?"

"I think so," he said, though she made that simple task sound difficult. He liked being described as her backup, though. Helen looked at him again, obviously concerned.

She reached out and raised his coat collar. "Another hour or two in those clothes and you'll look like a homeless person," she said approvingly. "Then nobody'll pay any attention to you."

"Thanks. It's my natural chameleonlike ability. Attorney to homeless guy in the blink of an eye."

Helen smiled very briefly. "Actually, you look a lot less like an attorney without your clothes on."

The remark reminded him of her staring at him in the gloom of his hotel room. "Well, thanks," he said, grinning.

She smiled wryly and shook her head. "Don't get cocky. Just stay safe, David. I've got work to do." But she had more instructions for him. "I already express-checked you out of this hotel. Don't worry about that. Stay inconspicuous. Be a tourist. Go to the Smithsonian, anybody could spend a whole day there. I'll meet you tonight. Where?" She obviously wasn't asking David. He stayed quiet and let her think. "Not too obvious a place. No monuments."

"The parking garage of the Watergate?"

She ignored him. "The National Gallery. Six o'clock. They have an Edvard Munch exhibit. I'll meet you close to *The Scream*. You know *The Scream*?

David shook his head. Briefly Helen mimicked the painting, putting her hands over her ears and opening her mouth wide.

David flinched. "Don't do that. You're too good at it. Okay: *The Scream*. But one thing. What if you need me before then?"

Helen dismissed the idea without comment. As she started to turn away David took her arm again. "Be careful."

She nodded, tight-lipped as a spy, but her hand touched his for a moment as she turned away. Quickly she crossed the parking lot, got into a nondescript gray sedan with government license plates, and drove away without a wave.

David found himself standing alone in Washington, D.C., with no destination and no plan. He wondered if he could just creep back inside and up to his nice, comfortable bed, which remained his for about seven more hours. But Helen's attitude had infected him. She seemed one of the most competent, professional people he had ever met, and she was worried to death. David looked quickly around, saw no one, and picked up his bags and began walking.

David got lucky, finding a public storage place where he rented a locker for his suitcase. Standing in front of the row of lockers, he considered keeping his briefcase with him. Being a lawyer, he felt much more confident with a briefcase in hand, but probably it would be better to try to blend into the crowds of tourists in the summertime capital, as Helen had suggested. Besides, he needed to be free to move. As soon as he thought that, David felt stupid. He had neither the training nor the instincts to be a fugitive. If any Secret Service or other police were looking for him and found him, David's best reason for having his hands free would be so that he could more quickly raise them into the air. He put the briefcase in the locker, stuck those free hands in his pockets, and walked.

By ten o'clock in the morning he was very tired of walking and of coffee, which he'd had at three different places. He found a health club where for a twenty-five-dollar guest fee he could swim and shower. He bought a swimsuit and underwear in the club's shop. Forgetting Helen's advice, he paid with a credit card.

The swim stretched muscles he hadn't been using, the shower energized him. Even though he had to put the same clothes back on, when David left the health club he felt much better, as if he actually could avoid pursuit if it came, at least for a block or two.

Finally he went to the Smithsonian Institution per Helen's instructions, and wished he'd gone sooner. He hadn't been inside the first building, the Air and Space Museum, for five minutes before realizing he could have spent a week there. The Wright Brothers' spindly-looking invention, as much bicycle as aircraft. Lindbergh's *Spirit of St. Louis*, not really all that much bigger or sturdier-looking than the Wright Brothers' plane. The damned thing appeared too tiny and cramped for a hop from here to Philadelphia; he couldn't imagine it crossing an ocean.

Later, in the American history hall, he walked very slowly through displays of presidential memorabilia. David carried a unique perspective among the tourists looking at the clothes and carriages and trinkets of past Presidents, trying to imagine those historical figures alive. David suddenly found it very easy. Perpetually solemn Abraham Lincoln, surely on occasion troubled as much by his crazy wife as by his dissolving Union. Thomas Jefferson, would-be liberator and possible father of slaves. Harding, who almost certainly fathered an illegitimate child and possibly kept a mistress in the White House itself, Franklin and Eleanor Roosevelt: please. What President had enjoyed a happy family life in the White House? Why couldn't Myra McPherson endure a few years of personal misery as well as these people had—and who the hell was David Owens to think he should help her be the first to make the White House a broken home?

In his relatively brief career as a divorce lawyer David had never faced such potential repercussions. He had obtained temporary restraining orders to keep the other spouse from taking the children out of county or cleaning out the bank accounts. That always sufficed: even if such an order tended to infuriate the one who received it, the order also put the recipient on notice that he was under the scrutiny of the court. What similar authority could David employ to tie the hands of the leader of the free world if he chose to exercise his power against his own wife?

Sobered, he retrieved his luggage from the locker and walked to the National Gallery. After five o'clock, car traffic in Washington grew so thick David felt as if he walked through a cloud of fumes. Drivers cursed and simmered and lunged for openings. David glanced over his shoulder from time to time, feeling conspicuous. The streets were so crowded even an amateur could have followed him easily.

In the National Gallery of Art he wandered slowly through the large white halls, designed like all the public buildings in D.C. for a race of Titans. That had been the idea. The founding fathers had intended to inspire veneration.

The current exhibition was entitled "Edvard Munch: Inventor of the Modern." The paintings of the Norwegian expressionist were interspersed with those of artists from the same period. Gauguin, one note read, had been a major early influence on Munch. David couldn't see it: the gap from naked Tahitian women to gaunt psychotics was too great for him to leap. Munch appeared to have invented alienation in the literal sense. The central figure in many of his paintings looked like the modern version of the legendary Roswell visitor from outer space: body slight to the point of wispiness, oversized bald head, big blank eyes. David recognized the creature from what Helen had called *The Scream*, but hadn't realized until he walked through the exhibition how hard it might be to meet her here. The same figure appeared in many of Munch's paintings. A historical note beside one such painting provided the unsurprising information that Munch had suffered a nervous breakdown in 1908. Duh. A competent alienist would have slapped this boy in a straitjacket after one look at his dark, maniacal paintings.

David began to feel creeped out. He needed a break from Munchland. David took to staring at the building itself, the cornices and rails, like a burglar casing the joint. Wandering, he turned into a narrow corridor and stopped at a locked door. A heavy hand fell on his shoulder from behind. David turned quickly to meet the blandly stern face of a heavyset, fiftyish security guard.

"Sorry, sir, this is a restricted area."

Since he'd become an adult David had always felt the urge to challenge unfounded shows of authority. Sometimes he did. But today it wasn't worth it. The encounter with the security guard set off other worries. Where was Helen, what was she doing? She had apparently been removed from her position with the First Lady. Did that mean Helen wasn't trusted? Was someone already watching her? Whatever the answer, she had to work within the organization. That would help her learn the information they needed, but it would make her vulnerable, too. She could be gotten rid of just by a supervisor deciding to transfer her.

Much worse could happen too, of course. Helen had to ask questions, and the people who'd secreted the First Lady would be very suspicious of anyone apparently trying to find her. David worried for Helen, but also for himself. If she were caught or otherwise removed, he would be the only one left on the outside who knew the truth. What could he do? He didn't delude himself for a second that he could infiltrate the ranks of presidential insiders. All he could think to do would be to cause a stink in the press, and he didn't have the evidence to do that effectively. He would only end up making himself a target as well.

Paranoid, nervous, feeling lost and alone, David became the perfect patron of the art exhibition through which he wandered. Slowly, without even intending it, he drew close to the centerpiece. Edvard Munch had painted one painting with which he would always be associated. Helen had been a little mistaken: the name of the painting was *The Cry*. It depicted the alien figure in the pose Helen had mimicked, mouth open very wide in a scream. He (it?) stood at the end of a bridge, as if afraid to cross over, or as if he had just come from the other side of town to warn against an approaching menace of insane proportions, so enormous that it could only be one thing:

the psychotic modern world. The painting was dark and hallucinatory. The buildings appeared to wave and shimmer. David came across the famous painting without much warning. *The Cry* didn't draw a large, immobile crowd. People tended to approach it eagerly, then frown, look at it from a different angle, then walk slowly away, maybe coming back a minute or two later but not lingering. David was the only one who stood and stared. He felt he understood the little figure perfectly: he was a divorce lawyer in a strange city whose client had just been kidnapped.

"Hey," said a quiet voice at his back. David turned slowly. Helen Wills stood behind him. He hadn't even sensed her presence before she'd spoken, so lost was he in the painting.

"I should have warned you not to get here early. Twenty minutes' exposure to Munch can cause clinical insanity." Helen tossed her hair back from her forehead. Sometime during the day she had changed into a white blouse and cream-colored jacket, so that she looked like a normal working woman at the end of a business day. David felt glad to see her and hear her voice. But noticing her constantly moving eyes returned him to the seriousness of their dilemma. Helen didn't look as if she carried good news.

"Have you found out anything?"

"Yes. Let's get out of here."

They had no other option there: the National Gallery was closing. David had to stand in a short line to retrieve his luggage from the cloakroom, which made him nervous. Other people no longer seemed like protective coloration. He felt nervousness emanating from Helen. By this time it had become very unlikely that anyone had followed David around D.C. all day, but Helen could well have inspired surveillance by her day's activities. David emulated her study of the crowd.

She had parked her government-issue gray sedan in a restricted parking area, the laminated card hanging from her rearview mirror apparently keeping her immune from tickets. Was that a good thing for a spy to do? David wondered. To set herself apart from the crowd like that? But Helen could carry it off. Even with her increased anxiety, she still walked confidently, chin up and with a long stride. She got behind the wheel, David stowed his bags in the backseat, and they cruised out into the diminished traffic.

Apparently Helen trusted her own car to be free from listening devices. She began talking quietly, without preamble. "Mrs. McPherson is in a private psychiatric hospital in Pennsylvania. *Very* private. Elizabeth Taylor would have to go elsewhere to have a breakdown. This place doesn't care about celebrities. You have to have connections and lots of money. No one checks in voluntarily. It's not the Betty Ford Clinic. You don't check yourself in, you don't check yourself out. It's for rebellious teenagers of the very wealthy, executive wives needing very quiet drug rehab, that kind of thing. The patients don't mingle. Each has a private cottage where they live and where treatments are performed."

Envisioning a Frankenstein-laboratory kind of place, David asked, "You mean it's so private that if things don't work out they can—"

"Yes. Though of course they can't do that with the First Lady of the United States. But they'll keep her there until the President and the others figure out what they want to do. And they might . . . change her mind."

In the most literal sense. "She might come out a Stepford Wife?"

"Let's not get too melodramatic. But still . . ." Helen made a turn and left more of the traffic behind. They drove in silence for a while. The buildings around them turned residential, narrow brownstones standing shoulder to shoulder, with elaborate pillared entryways.

"Where are we?" David asked.

"Georgetown." Helen found a parking lot, paid the attendant, and they walked. The evening air of June in Washington remained a little muggy but was turning pleasant. Helen led them to a small neighborhood café, half of the few tables on an outdoor terrace under a green and white awning. They sat inside, at a round table with a white tablecloth. The restaurant was quietly elegant, not touristy at all, with a menu consisting of continental flourishes and a couple of American standards. The waiter, a young man wearing a long white apron, gave friendly but unobtrusive service. After bringing Helen a red wine and David a draft beer, he withdrew to the far wall. Only a few couples occupied the café's tables, giving Helen and David relative privacy. Helen seemed to trust the place.

"How can we get her out?" David asked.

"Only one way," Helen answered, watching the street. "Go in and get her."

David had known she would say that as soon as he'd asked the question. It was obvious in Helen's silence and the set of her shoulders that she was preparing herself to take action. But David didn't naturally choose such a course.

"What if I go to the press? Tell them the First Lady's being held hostage? Isn't that a great story, good enough to investigate, especially if I know the place where she's being held?"

"Was being held. She'd be gone before anyone in the media could make a phone call. Besides, the first call they'd make would be to the White House, which would deny the story and that would be it. They wouldn't even—"

"But I'm not just some nut walking into their office. I'm a lawyer. I have some credibility—"

"You don't understand. The story brands the storyteller. It's a crazy claim, so you must be crazy. And being a lawyer, well . . ." She laughed, and didn't have to finish the sentence.

"The Secret Service came to my office," David said sullenly.

"Those weren't real Secret Service agents, David. I guarantee it. They don't work like that. They wouldn't be there to clean up a mess for the President. That's not their job."

"Then who were those guys?"

"There's something you don't understand. It's not just the President behind this. There are others who have a tremendous amount of resources, and a lot at stake. The President may still have some feelings for his wife, but these people, I don't know what they're capable of."

"Who are they?"

Helen shook her head. "It's not my secret to tell. I think this is what Mrs. McPherson would have told you about at your next meeting, but for now let's just deal with the immediate problems."

It sounded as if she was afraid to tell him how much they faced. David said, "All right, then, what do we do? I'll help you however I can."

"There's a problem," Helen said, and fell silent as their meal arrived. David would have predicted that Helen's dinner would consist mostly of lettuce and rice, but in fact she had ordered beef tenderloin with a twice-baked potato. Her leanness didn't come from lack of appetite. She attacked the steak in small but efficient bites.

"A problem?" David prompted her. "I'm sorry to hear there's a problem. It seemed so simple the way you put it."

Helen ignored his sarcasm. "Randy. He's gone too. Remember their fake story said he'd gone on vacation with his mother? That's because they had to account for him, too. Randy would notice his mother's being gone. They're the two closest people in the White House. Plus the President wouldn't want Randy around without Mrs. McPherson there to take care of him." Helen shrugged, aware of the coldness indicated in this statement.

"So they snatched him too?" David sounded outraged. Kidnapping a young boy seemed much more sinister. Mrs. McPherson had gotten herself into trouble, but Randy . . .

"It's not that bad. They just sent him to a boarding school in Virginia. Kind of a real fancy summer camp. Not bad people who run it. I checked them out as much as possible. I'm pretty sure they don't know they're holding the first son hostage. They just think he's a guest. So does Randy, I'm sure. This place is used to a very exclusive clientele."

"Of kids whose parents don't want them around for the summer," David said, sounding bitter. Helen shifted her attention from the street to his face.

"The kind of place where you used to spend summers?" she asked, the first time she'd shown any curiosity about him.

David shook his head and returned to the subject. "All right, so it's a double problem, but not much worse. We just have to get her and then him. In fact, once we have the First Lady, she can get Randy out of the camp, after all, she's his—" Helen was shaking her head. "Why is it that everything I say is wrong?" he said irritably.

"Sorry. It's just that I've had more time to think about this. We can't do it sequentially. If we manage to get Mrs. McPherson out, they'll be alerted, they'll move Randy someplace where we'll never find him. Where *she'll* never find him. Then they'll have a hold over her stronger than any drug. Randy means more to her than anything, he's all she cares about in the world. If they manage to get him from her, they'll be able to keep her in line forever. Just doling out little visits, with the unspoken threat that they'll take him away again. That's why she wanted to be so careful to get somewhere safe before she filed for divorce. Isn't that what she told you?"

David hadn't before heard Helen sound so emotional. He suspected she shared the First Lady's feelings about Randy. Interesting. "So we—"

"They have to be rescued simultaneously."

"Oh, shit," David said, understanding.

"That's right. Two jobs have to be done at the same time and only you and me to do them."

David sighed. He pushed aside his pasta, most of which remained on his plate. In a confessional tone, he said, "Listen, Helen, the last commando raid I pulled was when I was eight years old, and the enemy was the girl next door."

"Did she kill you?"

"She was a tough little mother, and besides, she was six months older than I was. But my point is, I mean, I'll do whatever you say, but putting blacking on my face and slipping through electronic security, I'm sorry, but I didn't take those electives in law school. There's got to be somebody else we can enlist, somebody—"

"There's not. I don't know anybody else I trust, everybody I know is on the White House payroll and their interest is in doing what the President wants. And Mrs. McPherson hasn't made any friends in Washington. Believe me, if there was anyone else I'd be on the phone with them right now."

David pushed out his chin and sat up straighter. "All right, sorry. I'll do it. Just—"

"Don't be sorry. I like this much better than if you came on with some macho bullshit about how you can go barreling in there with your six-guns blazing and snatch them out of harm's way. Nervous is good. It makes you more careful." She pushed his plate back in front of him. "Eat your dinner, you're going to need your strength."

"Yes, ma'am."

"Although I would like to have that girl from next door on our team. You still know her?"

David shook his head. "We had a brief torrid affair a few years later—three kisses—and her family moved to Ohio."

"To get her away from you?"

"That's what I've always suspected."

Helen laughed again. This was the most fun David had ever seen her have. She had finished her steak and baked potato and motioned to the waiter for coffee. In some complicated, Georgetown regular exchange of hand signals she managed to convey that she wanted the real thing, not decaf. The waiter brought it steaming, took her plate, and gave David a rather disdainful glance when he saw him still eating. Helen sat back, relaxed. Danger must have this effect on her, he thought. David had read about great athletes who had that gift, becoming relaxed to the point of sleepiness before a big game or fight. David, on the other hand, jiggled his foot under the table and wanted to get up and pace. His mind raced with abortive plans for rescuing the First Lady, most of them conjured out of juvenile adventure novels and episodes of *Mission: Impossible*. Also, most of his rapid-fire scenarios involved a team, and he would be on his own.

Helen again surveyed the street, where cars passed every few minutes. When she returned her attention to David she was glad to see that he had pulled himself together quickly and wore a look of resolve.

"Okay, tell me about this docile-wife factory in Pennsylvania. Have you learned much about it yet, or do I have to go in cold?"

Helen shook her head. "That's my problem. Your job is Randy."

"What?"

Helen leaned close to him. "Yes, David, I've thought about this all day, ever since I learned Randy was missing too. I have a much better chance of getting to the First Lady than you do. I'm her staff, remember? I might be able to bluff my way in with a show of authority if necessary. You, on the other hand, are nobody."

"I'm her lawyer."

"She probably won't be in any condition to confirm that. No, I'll take that assignment. I think you have a much better chance of getting Randy out. Like I say, I don't think they're evil people consciously holding him hostage. I may be wrong, there might be one or two of these other people on-site to keep an eye on him, but mostly it'll just be camp counselors and of course his Secret Service detail."

"Piece of cake."

"I know, I know, but I can help you there. I know the way they work, their routines. First of all, remember this about Secret Service agents: they're there to protect Randy from outside attack. Their usual posture is standing with their backs to the client, looking outward. If you can get Randy in on the deal, he might be able to get away from them while you create a distraction somewhere else. That's how Mrs. McPherson and I slipped away to come see you the first time. We've done it a few other times, too. So try to get close to Randy and then—"

"And how exactly am I going to do that, Coach? Why won't he run screaming for help? He's never even seen me before, why should he believe I'm there to rescue him?"

"I've brought you some help with that problem." She lifted her oversized purse from the floor and pulled from it a dark blue plastic aircraft of some sort.

"What's that?"

"Oh, we've got a problem if you don't recognize the XK Vibra-Wing. We'll have to get you a crash course in—"

"Oh. *Star Wars*, right. Don't you have a full-size version that I can land right next to him and pull him on board before anyone can stop me?"

"This is Randy's favorite toy. Show it to him and he'll know you came from home. They made a big mistake not taking this along with him. He's probably crying himself to sleep every night without it."

That image gave David a sense of urgency about his mission that Helen hadn't been able to impress on him before this. He took the model spaceship from her carefully.

Leaning close again, she gave him a rapid briefing on kidnap-or-rescue techniques.

"Randy's Secret Service code name is R2D2."

"Clever. How'd they come up with that?"

"Because he's short and smart. His mother's code is Lady Dove. Don't ask me, I don't know. But you might be able to use those. Don't pretend to be from the White House, though, except in an absolute crisis. I think you should pretend to be the father of one of the other boys. I found out one name, and I got you this." She handed him a laminated card.

"What's this?" David said wonderingly. "A driver's license? How'd you do this?" The name on the license said John Armstrong, but the photo was of him.

"Never mind. But they won't bear much investigation. Mostly it's up to you, David. You have to carry it off. Be offhand. Be anxious to see your son. You're a neglectful father running in for a quick visit to the camp. This is cutting into your schedule."

"I can do that." David thought of Rod Smathers, and other such fathers he'd seen in the last few years. He began to look grim.

"When you're trying to get away, back up sometimes instead of going forward. It confuses pursuit. When you get into a car drive like hell, even if you don't think you're being followed. Use public transportation. Change your appearance. Small changes make big differences, you'd be surprised."

She sat back, looked him over, and appeared resigned to failure. "Look, your bar card's going to be worth jack shit in this situation. If you have someone you think can help, call him. I can't give you any. And if either of us fails, it's all over. Just scream as loud as you can."

David took her hand and smiled slyly at her. "You'll come rescue me, won't you?"

Helen sighed. "We'll probably both need rescuing, and there

won't be anybody to do it. Let's get out of here. Pay with a credit card."

David looked surprised. "I thought you didn't want me to leave a paper trail."

"Tonight I do. If anybody's checking, it'll look like you're still in D.C."

David looked around the elegant little café as the waiter came with the check. "I'd never have found a place this nice on my own."

"I'm trying to increase your air of sophistication. We'll fool them."

Outside, they stood on the sidewalk for a moment. Helen continued her instructions. "Get as much cash as you can before you leave D.C., and don't use any credit cards once you're gone. The name of the place where Randy's staying is Lakeview Lodge, in Somerset, Virginia. Tiny little town. You'll stand out a mile. But that's okay. That's your cover story. Meet me three days from now at a mall in Rockville, Maryland. It's called Town Center Mall. Two o'clock in the afternoon, the women's shoe department at Nordstrom's. All right?"

"Three days, that's all?"

"That's too long already. If I don't get the First Lady out of that place in the next twenty-four hours or so, we might as well not bother. A day to get there, a day to reconnoiter, a day to pull it off and meet up."

David nodded, telling himself to look staunch and reassuring. He stood tall and tight-lipped, hands in his pockets. Close by, a car passed slowly down the street. Helen didn't look in the car's direction, but casually turned her back to it. She seemed assured, competent.

She drove him to a train station, Helen taking unexpected turns and watching her mirrors. She seemed satisfied that no one pursued them. David shifted uneasily in his seat, but after a few blocks settled down a bit. Near their destination, he said, "Let me give you a little advice, Helen."

She glanced at him with a raised eyebrow.

"I know," he continued. "Ridiculous. But I want to tell you how you come across, so you can use it. You need to go straight ahead, Helen. Don't try to be devious. Because here's how other people see you: you seem so focused on the essentials it's impossible to believe you'd lie about anything. You're too"—He hesitated for a word—"straightforward for that. Too uncomplicated, frankly, to be a schemer. So if you can bring yourself to lie, you'll get away with it. Trust me."

She stopped at a corner to give him a longer look. "I am trusting you, David. Think how much I'm trusting you with. But I really don't think you're in a position to analyze my character."

"I know I'm not. I don't know you, of course I don't. I know you're not uncomplicated, either. I'm just telling you how you come across. So you can use it."

She started driving again. Two blocks later she said, "Thanks."

"Sure."

Helen got him close to the train station and told him which train to take. They got out of the car to get his suitcase out of the trunk. They stood there for a moment, and Helen remembered the object of David's quest.

"Listen, about Randy. He's an unusual little boy. Grown up very isolated. I think he'll like you, though."

"Really, why?"

The question struck her. She really had no answer. "I don't know. Why do I trust you? Something about you; you come across as . . ." Trailing off, Helen smiled at him and held out her hand. "Good luck."

David shook his head. "A handshake isn't for luck."

He kissed her, not taking her entirely by surprise. It wasn't a long clench, but more than a brush of lips. He gave her a reassuring grin and walked away quickly.

Helen watched him go, feeling quite sure he'd be arrested before he reached the gates of Lakeview Lodge.

★ President John McPherson stepped down from the helicopter, stood erect for a moment to receive salutes from the commanding officer of the Air Force base and his entourage, then walked briskly toward them. Tall, composed, and steely-eyed, McPherson fit these ceremonial occasions well. As he passed the color guard he nodded to them and said, "Thank you, men." They couldn't answer, but looked pleased in a grim military way. Always good to acknowledge the peripheral players. Nearly everywhere John McPherson went, that place had its biggest day in a long time. Preparations for his arrival had made many people frantic, and at least several people had spent days trying to think of some additional ceremony that would impress the President with how glad they were to have him. All the pomp gratified a man's ego, of course, but also grew wearisome as a daily way of life. The ribbon cuttings, bands, receiving plaques from homecoming queens, nervous glances rather than honest opening welcomes. Sometime McPherson would like just to step out of his car and walk into a building.

"General Crenshaw," he greeted the short, thick commanding officer, then looked around for the colonel or major who would actually know the project he'd come to see. The President's three visible Secret Service agents stared through their dark sunglasses at the equally stiff military men who stared back. Dispensing with most of the company, four of the group and McPherson went inside the converted aircraft hangar. The interior seemed dark, and smaller than one would have expected from the outside. The walls had been very strongly reinforced, and screening equipment scanned twenty-four hours a day to detect any attempt at surveillance.

Colonel Albert Parker, a thickset African-American with a scar that went down his left cheek and neck, led the way to a corner research area that boasted very little equipment. A computer, a wooden table, some kind of radar-looking device, a telephone. The President glanced around at the people accompanying him. He'd expected more in the way of high tech.

Colonel Parker made another introduction. "This is Dr. Margaret Lew, Mr. President. Much of this technology is hers." A slim, smooth-faced woman with Asian features leaned back on the table, dressed in casual civilian clothes. She and the President shook hands.

"Well, I'm impressed, Dr. Lew. Which did you invent, the computer or the telephone?"

Everyone laughed. Presidents' jokes are always funny.

Dr. Lew laughed least, which made the President like her. "That's a good observation, Mr. President. Actually this project hardly involved developing anything new. I've just put a few things together from different fields."

"Project Needle," McPherson said. "Does that mean we're looking for something?"

"Correct again, sir. Actually the name signifies two things. Finding a needle in a haystack, as you observed. Also the needle on a compass."

She sat at the computer and with the touch of a couple of keys put a grainy photograph up on the oversized screen. The picture showed an injured-looking soldier lying prone under a bush. In the near distance, shadowy figures approached.

"It happens in every war. Sometimes just in policing actions. We lose a pilot, a foot soldier, a tank crew. If they hang on to their radios, fine, we can find them by having them describe the terrain and we send our helicopters or whatever looking for that area. That's how we rescued that downed pilot in Bosnia."

"Actually, *we* did that, Dr. Lew," said the Air Force general, drawing chuckles and a smile from the President.

"But we want to do better," the young scientist continued. "We want to pinpoint them quickly and get them out at once."

"Of course," said McPherson, watching the screen. It changed to a map.

"First of all, we've created a Web site—"

"The first solution to any problem," the President observed wryly.

"Constantly updated, it shows the positions of our troops in any given area. If the pilot has a laptop, he can get to this site and see which way he needs to head to meet his rescuers."

"The last I knew, pilots didn't carry laptops. Besides, this seems very dangerous. We're going to put our military positions on the Internet for anyone to see?"

"That's why we had to make it inaccessible to all but a few people. We have a password—"

The President made a dismissive sound.

"Yes sir, but that's not all. The site requires voice identification." She leaned down to a microphone and said distinctly, "Margaret Lew. Open sesame."

The computer developed a hum. After two or three seconds static flickered on the screen, and a blue box appeared with the words "ID Verified." The blue box disappeared and so did the map, replaced by a smaller, much more detailed map showing troop positions.

"Where is that?" the President asked, not recognizing names.

"Puerto Rico. That's the only location I have clearance to see. We don't consider it a high-risk area." Dr. Lew smiled benignly at the military men around her. "Of course, for soldiers we provide access to the area they need."

"Still seems risky. Also needs a laptop. If a pilot goes down or a tank is destroyed and the crew barely escapes . . ."

"Yes, sir. That's what we've been working on. We want to be able to rescue a man who is naked, helpless, possibly wounded. That's why we've gone to implant technology."

The telephone rang. Dr. Lew picked it up, smiled, and said, "Right on time, Sergeant." She held out the phone. "It's for you, Mr. President."

The President took it, feeling himself the butt of a joke. "Hello?"

A voice came through the line, static making it sound as if it came from a man who'd been a heavy smoker for forty years. "It's an honor, Mr. President. This is First Sergeant Bradley Jones."

"Where are you, Sergeant Jones?"

"I'm out on the confidence course, sir. About three klicks from your position."

"What are you talking into, Sergeant, a laptop microphone?"

"Nothing, sir. I'm empty-handed." And breathing heavily, from the sound of his roughened voice.

Dr. Lew had put another image up on the screen. It showed a muscular man, stripped to the waist, going up a ten foot wall. At the top, the man threw a leg over, turned toward the camera grinning, and waved.

"Hello, Mr. President," came the voice over the phone.

John McPherson began to feel a tingle. It ran up his spine and outward into his shoulder blades. Wilson Boswell had described this feeling to him before. It was the future calling.

"Keep up the good work, Sergeant," the President said, and hung up the phone. "Where's the microphone?"

"It's in his throat, sir. Surgically implanted three weeks ago. As you can see, it didn't put him out of commission for long. He doesn't even have a scar left."

"And where's the receiver?"

Colonel Parker answered. "It's on the roof of this building, sir. The sergeant's microphone broadcasts on a certain frequency that only we are equipped to pick up. We can triangulate to pinpoint his location. If he just moans or breathes, we can find him. If he can talk to give us additional information, so much the better. But we can get to him in any case."

"Very impressive," the President said, seeing the faces watching him for reaction. He kept it muted. "I see another use or two, plus some problems. If the soldier's captured, can we also hear anything his captors say to him?"

"Faintly, sir. We're working on boosting that capacity."

Think of the spying applications. Any agent could be a roving bug. He or she wouldn't have to wear a wire and risk exposure. McPherson knew the military men would have thought of these possibilities as well. He wondered suddenly if anyone in the room also carried an implant. He glanced surreptitiously at the thick throats around him, and Margaret Lew's slender, supple one. Probably not. Okay to risk a sergeant's throat, but not a general's. Not at this experimental stage. Besides, they would have thought of the other possibilities as well.

"Who turns on the microphone, the soldier or command central?"

Dr. Lew smiled slightly. She'd been waiting for this question, wondering whether the President would think of it. "We do, sir."

The small group watched the President receive this answer and instantly understand its implications. "Does the sergeant know that he may be broadcasting twenty-four hours a day?" He smiled.

General Crenshaw decided to demonstrate his sensitivity, but didn't answer the question directly. "We've grappled with the privacy considerations, sir. Of course we don't monitor all the time. Just for this demonstration purpose."

Dr. Lew flipped a switch on the console and the room grew quieter. President McPherson hadn't realized until the background noise stopped that they had continued to hear Sergeant Jones breathing.

The President pictured that near future. Once capability like this existed, it would spread. First only a few soldiers would be implanted. Then whole combat units. Commanding officers so they could stay in touch with their bases. At-risk government officials. American executives in foreign countries, subject to the possibility of kidnapping. CIA agents. Finally it would filter into the civilian world, as cell phones and computers had. Receptionists would be implanted, so they could talk into phones and still have free hands. Maybe cabinet officers. And anyone who had access to the receiver could listen in on their lives any minute of the day. Or record every minute.

Feeling the tingle of anticipation invade his body again, McPherson remained soft-spoken. The military men and scientist continued to watch him closely. They had already thought of these far-reaching implications. Now the executive decision of whether to proceed had to be made. So they had asked the President to come see their simple demonstration.

"Those problems," McPherson said, clearing his throat. "Once word of this gets out, I can imagine our captured soldiers having their throats ripped out. The enemy won't want to risk—"

"Word must not leak out," the general said. "That's why we've kept this so quiet. Sergeant Jones doesn't even know exactly what's been done to him. We told him there are hidden microphones on the confidence course. That's all he thinks."

"Bullshit," said the President. "People always figure out more than you think. He's probably already told everyone in his squad, if not his family back home."

Dr. Lew flipped the switch on her console again. Suddenly Sergeant Jones's raspy voice filled the room. "Who knows? Goddamned stupid brass just jerking my chain. If this little demonstration impressed McPherson, then he's even dumber than I thought."

People smiled surreptitiously. Dr. Lew turned off the receiver again. "I don't think he suspects," she said ironically. "In answer to your concern, Mr. President, the implants will not be detectable. The surgery is very simple and minor. It doesn't leave a scar. As for the microphone itself, you've been looking at one without noticing ever since you walked in." She picked up a small box off her desk, the size of a ring box. It didn't have a lid, and looked empty.

McPherson took the proffered box and peered inside. It still appeared empty. Margaret Lew reached into it and very carefully pulled out a translucent, almost invisible piece of plastic. It looked like a pregnant staple, that small.

"That's the microphone. Hardly any metal in it. The implantees will be able to walk through metal detectors with no problem. Even an X-ray won't pick it up. If we can keep it secret, no technology we know of now will be able to tell whether anyone's wearing one or not. Even the recipient needn't know."

McPherson held the almost weightless wire on his fingertip. The room had grown very quiet again. These people knew what they had, what they were offering him.

"All right," the President said decisively. "Dr. Lew, go ahead with trying to develop this, but don't bring anyone else in on it. How many people outside this room know about this?"

"Two, sir," the colonel answered. "Two researchers hired by Dr. Lew, one in Baltimore, the other in California. But they haven't been given all the pieces, they haven't been told exactly what they're doing."

"All right. Their work is done. Move them to other projects, keep them on the government payroll, but doing something else. Keep them busy enough that they forget their part in this project. Dr. Lew, you're on your own for the time being. Can you handle that?"

"Yes, sir. It's not that tough from here on. Just refining."

"Good. Absolute secrecy. Understood?"

Everyone nodded, and the general and colonel said, "Yes, sir," with impressive sincerity. McPherson didn't believe it. With this many people in on the secret, it couldn't stay a secret long. The President wished he could, like the Egyptian pharaohs, have all these people killed and buried with the project, while he walked away with the result.

"All right. I will be in touch. Believe me." Shaking hands all around, the President made significant eye contact with each person. They all looked very solemn, people in on a secret. Dr. Margaret Lew, though, had a gleam in her eye and a slight sardonic twist to her mouth. McPherson wondered if her soft handshake conveyed anything else. This power-aphrodisiac thing, it gave off a powerful scent to the right receptor. He would make a point of seeing Dr. Lew again.

The President walked briskly away to rejoin his Secret Service team near the door, where they'd waited out of earshot. He should get these guys implanted soon, find out what they really thought of him. McPherson cleared his throat again, feeling a slight tickle there, possibly imaginary. Someday in his lifetime, it would be possible to eavesdrop on damned near everyone in the world.

He thought about how he would tell Wilson Boswell about this project. Casually, as if he'd been on top of its development for years. For once, he would be ahead of the tycoon in technology. The President smiled.

Land of Peace Residential Treatment Center didn't have a sign anywhere along its tall brick wall announcing its name or function. The center might not go by that name anymore anyway, since its director had discovered the name's susceptibility to satire. One executive who had been told the fees for having his wife committed there for two weeks always thereafter referred to the facility as A Piece of Your Land, since he would have had to sell off part of the family ranch to afford it. "People who aren't willing to pay our fees don't really need our treatment," sniffed Dr. Tosoros.

People who had sent loved or despised ones to the center for successful therapy referred to it as "Dr. Tomoro's." Patients who had served a sentence there and been released always just called it "the place," with a shudder and a look over their shoulders. The treatment center had such a quiet but powerful reputation by now that it didn't need a name or advertisement. Word of mouth sufficed, when they were the right mouths.

The morning after leaving David in D.C., Helen Wills arrived at the center before dawn. She parked half a mile away down a dirt road that led to an abandoned farmhouse. She found the very private enclosure of Dr. Tosoros's facility and walked all the way around it, which took an hour even at Helen's brisk pace. This trek confirmed what she'd suspected. The twelve-foot brick wall completely surrounded the facility. Trees had been cut back from the fence so they couldn't be used to climb over. Helen assumed the top of the brick wall would be wide and imbedded with broken glass or nails. Not a problem, really. Helen could blow a hole in the wall if necessary. She had worked with explosives before. Such drama wasn't even called for to surmount this wall. She'd spotted several fallen branches long and sturdy enough to lean against the wall and climb over. But she hadn't decided she wanted to go in that way. Once she had sneaked in surreptitiously, she would have to remain in furtive mode. It might be best to walk boldly in the front gate, brandishing her Secret Service credentials and a haughty attitude.

But she would like to see the place first. Get some idea of the layout. She knew the facility had one central building, but the most private patients stayed in separate bungalows scattered around the grounds, and she didn't know which one held the First Lady.

So she walked around the wall, looking for an opening to peer through or a tree tall enough and close enough to the fence to climb and look over the grounds from outside. She didn't find any such visual access. But a stream flowed through the grounds of Dr. Tosoros's facility, and had to be allowed an exit. Helen found this exit at the far back side of the property, where the bottom of the brick wall raised up in a wide archway so that the stream flowed underneath. Of course the builder had spotted this weak spot in the center's defenses. Thick iron bars spaced about eight inches apart descended from the underside of the brick wall, and would undoubtedly be imbedded deeply in the streambed.

But running water is a wonderfully entropic force, urgently and constantly trying to wear away anything that impedes it. An accumulation of brush and twigs trapped against the inside of the bars by the stream told Helen that security didn't maintain this area well or often enough. This barricade formed a partial dam, forcing the stream wider where it passed under the wall. Sometimes rain would swell the creek and make it a stronger decaying force. Helen checked the edges of the brick archway and found sure enough that the water had eaten away at the brick. The stream had taken some of the wall. The remaining edges of brick, constantly immersed in running water, had grown very porous. Helen broke off pieces in her hands.

She looked up quickly, thinking she'd heard something. Undoubtedly she had. The woods like all woods were filled with noises that sounded hostile to a city dweller. Rustlings became especially noticeable as the sun came up and the day shift of squirrels and birds and lizards and snakes became active. Helen, peering around, saw none of this activity, and felt reassured by seeing nothing human. She stepped into the stream, which ran no deeper than two and a half feet, not even up to her waist. Helen wore dark jeans and a black turtleneck, an outfit that left her perfectly visible now that the sun had risen. She had her hair pinned up and carried only a flat purse that strapped to her back like a very small backpack.

For twenty minutes she worked at the wall, the water gurgling around her legs. Helen realized she had become dangerously oblivious to her surroundings, absorbed in her task and with the sound of the running water obscuring other noises. She knelt and peered through the bars. She saw a large parklike meadow with many elms and oaks. The grounds of the center didn't boast any benches or other refinements on nature. Probably the patients didn't do much strolling through the great outdoors.

Some eighty yards away she saw one cottage, but couldn't see the main building from here, which was fine with Helen. She didn't want to enter close to the heart of activity. Lowering her gaze, she gasped at the sudden sight of eyes watching her. Helen scrambled out of the stream and watched as a small watersnake swam by, wriggling for navigation. Helen watched it with distaste. "Damned nature," she muttered. Next there'd be a badger or porcupine or something coming at her. In this expedition she concentrated on human danger, men with guns. It seemed unfair to throw snakes at her as well.

Back in the stream, she crouched to see if she could slip through the space between the bar and the edge of the brick wall. The widest part, almost a foot, was down in the water itself. Helen turned sideways, wriggled low, and found that she could get her hips through. Her chest would be the hard part, but the only way to find out if she could fit through was to make the attempt. She held her breath, sank down in the stream, and tried to slither through.

One breast flattened against the iron bar and slipped by, but then the middle of her back caught on a snag of brick. Head under water, Helen tried to reach behind her back to free herself, but couldn't reach the obstruction. She wriggled fiercely without managing to break loose. So she decided to go back out and widen the spot farther. But Helen was trapped now. Her legs and most of her body had passed through to the inside. She tried to push with her right foot, push herself free, but couldn't get a good purchase on the slippery streambed. Nor could she get a good grip on the bars with either hand, to push herself free one way or the other. The space was too confined.

Her heart beat hard and fast, adrenaline pumping through, her body outraged at drowning in less than three feet of water, air only a few inches above her head. Looking up, Helen could see through the water to safety. She could get her hands up there but not her head. Damn damn damn. The little finger of brick digging into her back wouldn't let go.

Helen's left arm was already through the bars. With that hand she grabbed a bar and pushed hard. She tried to find a hold in the streambed with her right hand to help push. Her legs, already inside, remained useless to pull her through. She gave one great push, felt something give in the wall, but not enough. She remained trapped. Helen's heart slowed. She was growing weak from lack of fresh oxygen. Looking up hopelessly, she expelled her breath, unable to stop her body's reflex. The bubbles raced up to the free air. Helen lost the last of her lungs' store of oxygen.

Which freed her. With her air gone her chest shrank. She slipped through between the bar and the wall.

In her rush Helen hit her chin on the iron bar before turning her head sideways. She pushed hard with her arms, passed all the way through, and scrambled to her feet, starting to inhale even before she was out of the water, so she came up gagging and coughing. Lousy commando technique. But for long seconds Helen forgot her objective and even where she was, breathing deeply and feeling the body's rush of elation at still being alive.

She recovered. Looking around anxiously, she saw no movement. She was inside now, on the grounds of the treatment center. Helen crouched into the water again, keeping only her head above. She turned slowly, scanning. The meadowland of the treatment center remained undisturbed. Nothing human moved through the landscape. Reassured, Helen rose out of the water, slowly this time. She needed to get out of here, find the First Lady's cottage, see what transportation might be available, make further plans.

Starting to hurry away, Helen finally turned to look back at the inside of the wall she'd just managed to pass through. "Oh, shit," she said.

A small video camera mounted high on the inside of the wall stared at her.

David Owens checked his watch. Ten 'til eleven A.M. About the time a really Type A personality would be arriving at this camp in Somerset, Virginia, if he had gotten up very early and driven down from New York. David sat in the blue Lincoln town car—the kind of car such a man would drive—with his bent elbow hanging out the window. He looked over what he could see of the camp, ignoring the guard beside him who held David's fake business card while checking the name and trying to decide whether to call the camp office to verify. A busy man always ignored underlings like security guards.

"How many cabins are there?" David asked idly. He felt himself slipping into this character very easily. A man who really didn't like children, even his own, was only here out of obligation, and wanted to get the visit over with as soon as possible. Helen had given him the idea for the role, but David embraced it.

"Twelve, sir. And which one is your son in?"

"Hell if I know. His mother registered him. She and I only talk through lawyers."

The security guard had white hair, which David had been glad to see. Younger guards tended to be more officious. But this man, rumpled and grandfatherly in his light blue shirt and darker blue trousers, moved maddeningly slowly. "Well, Mr. Armbruster, I'd better—"

"Armstrong," David corrected. "John Armstrong." Hoping like hell that was what his card actually said, that he'd remembered the fake name correctly.

"Oh, right. Sorry. And your son's name is . . . ?"

"Tony."

The guard looked over the inevitable clipboard in his hand. "It says here Toby."

"Toby?" David allowed himself to begin sounding impatient. "They must've gotten that off something he wrote himself. Boy's got the worst handwriting in the world. Maybe he'll be a doctor someday. Look, do you have their schedule here, or do I just track him down myself? I'd kind of like to see him and be gone by eleven. I've got a lunch appointment in Baltimore."

David looked at his watch again, making sure the guard noticed, continuing to establish the character of a busy, impatient man.

"Yes, sir." The guard consulted another page. "They're at softball right now. That's until—"

"All the boys?" David asked. The guard glanced up at him curiously, and David quickly added, "You don't know my son Tony. If they give him a choice, he'll go for something inside every time. You don't have Nintendo here, do you?"

"No, sir. All the boys in your son's cabin are in the softball game. The rest of the boys are in various activities. Take this road, circle around the cabins to the left and you'll find the parking lot. Then you'll have to keep walking back that way about two hundred yards or so. Can't miss the softball fields."

David thanked him and drove away, sure the guard was writing down his license plate number, wondering if he was also picking up the phone to call the office, or the Secret Service.

David had gone to camp himself two times, when he was nine and ten. He hadn't liked the experience at all. Camp had made him feel like a captive, but only because the boys were held to a schedule, marched around and ordered to play games or make crafts. Too much like prison. But there hadn't been security guards. Anyone could have driven in, waved to the counselors, pretended to be a parent. In the modern world no one took chances. Every place had grown security conscious: metal detectors in courthouses and airports, armed security guards in malls and schools. This camp would have required some ingenuity and false credentials to get into even if the President's son hadn't been staying here.

The boys were engaged in "various activities," the guard had said, unhelpfully. So Randy McPherson could be anywhere, and David had very little time before more people would start questioning his presence. He drove slowly down the dirt road, looking around for men in dark sunglasses. They would have stood out. Everyone he saw wore shorts and white T-shirts. Boys walked between the cabins. A few played desultorily at volleyball; when the ball landed in the dirt everyone just stared at it. Teenage counselors walked around in the same outfits, some of them herding boys, some walking alone. David only saw one adult, a man in his forties who didn't look comfortable in his shorts and T-shirt even though he must live in such an outfit. The man ducked into the largest building as if ashamed of being seen.

David parked in a small, unpaved lot and got out, becoming at once the most conspicuous person in the camp, in his white shirt, tie, and navy slacks. He'd thought of coming dressed very casually and trying to blend in, but had thought he'd have better luck getting in the front gate if he looked like a businessman. He stood for a moment beside his car and looked around. The cabins were actually that: small, low structures built of logs. The largest building, also made of logs, looked to be more than two thousand square feet. Probably it was the dining hall. Two other buildings in the center of the grounds were stucco, added like afterthoughts. One small, one larger. The smaller one was probably the office, the larger one some kind of gathering center: library, nursing station, something. David decided to avoid both for the time being.

David had a vague idea of what his "son" looked like. The camp had a Web site on which they posted pictures of the campers so parents back home could see them on the 'net. So during the mostly sleepless night before this adventure, David had seen Tony Armstrong on screen, a blond boy with two prominent front teeth. He had a better idea of what the first son looked like. David had seen him on television, and Helen had given him a photo. As he stood in the parking lot, hands on hips, of the dozen or more boys David could see, none looked like Randy McPherson.

Besides, if the President's son were in the vicinity there would inevitably be Secret Service agents nearby. Even if they had doffed their usual dark suits, they wouldn't be so well disguised as to look like these teenage counselors. Although now that David thought about it, the graying man in shorts who'd gone into the large building was a possibility.

He walked the way the guard had indicated, a gentle downhill slope away from the cabins. David swung his arms jauntily like a former camper for whom the place brought back happy memories. Passing two counselors coming toward him, he gave them a little two-fingered wave. "Hello, sir," they said in unison, with bright smiling faces. For all they knew, he might be a parent who tipped.

David felt very comfortable in his role. Maybe he had a knack for this undercover stuff. He picked up his pace. The temperature must have been in the mid-eighties, warm but quite bearable for someone used to south Texas summers. Past a small copse of trees David saw the softball fields and turned in that direction.

"May I help you?"

David's skin jumped. The deep voice had come out of nowhere. David turned to see that a tall man had stepped out from behind a tree. The man wore crisp tan walking shorts and a white T-shirt that proclaimed the name of the camp. But the man's legs and upper arms were white, tinged with red. He didn't normally spend summer in the sun. He wore a whistle around his neck, a wide-brimmed sun hat, and carried a clipboard like a counselor, but he had refused to give up his black sunglasses. More than anything, the man's stiff attitude and unsmiling countenance gave him away. His hat might as well have proclaimed "Secret Service."

David thought his character would demand to know what business it was of this guy's what he was doing here, but decided not to create a confrontation. Looking toward the softball field, he said, "Just trying to find my son." He decided not to specify.

"Who would that be, sir?"

David took a step to continue walking, but the man touched his arm and David stopped. "Tony Armstrong," he said, and cleared his throat.

This guy didn't have to consult his clipboard as the security guard had. "Yes, sir, he's down there."

"Thanks." David gave the agent one curt nod and walked on, feeling the man's eyes on his back and on the small plastic bag in David's hand.

Well, at least now he knew the first son was nearby. David strolled on down toward the field. A typical young boys' softball game was in progress. On each team two or three boys shouted with enthusiasm, the rest wandered in circles, drew designs in the dirt with their toes, or appeared to nod off, including the fielders. In right field a boy dropped his glove and did a cartwheel. The batter swung and dribbled the ball out toward third base. The third baseman approached it cautiously, like a hand grenade, while the counselors and a few teammates yelled at him to hurry.

On the batting team's bench, boys sat shoulder to shoulder, squirming and pushing each other. One on the right end of the bench appeared to be a blond boy with large front teeth. David waved, flashing a big smile. Three boys waved back. Maybe these kids had as vague ideas of what their fathers looked like as David had of the boy he was looking for. At any rate, his cover remained intact.

He slowly circled the field, in no danger from a hard-hit ball, and approached the bench. The boys made room for him and he sat next to the one he thought was Tony. "Hi, son," he said warmly, putting his arm around the boy.

The thin boy endured the semi-embrace without responding. He twisted his neck to look up at David, squinting in the sun, and asked, "Did my father send you?"

"That's right," David said easily. "He wanted to come himself, but he couldn't get away today. Maybe tomorrow . . ."

Tony Armstrong snorted. So did two or three of the other boys, all veterans of disappointment.

"What'd you bring me?" Tony asked.

Luckily David had come prepared for that question. He handed over the small plastic bag he'd carried from the car. "Some candy. I would've gotten you a couple of comic books, that's what I liked to get when I was at camp, but I didn't know what you might like."

"This is great," the thin blond boy said, digging into the bag. Other boys leaned close to peer into it. David stood up to get out of their way. He stayed just behind the boys, hands on hips, looking at the game. All the boys looked alike, except a few were blond, a few darker, most thin, some of them chunky, but alike in age and race. Their caps hid their faces pretty well.

"Who's winning?" David asked, and got no answer. The boys on the bench continued exploring the candy bag. At least he'd done that right. "Who's on the other team?" David asked just as casually. "Anybody famous?"

One of the boys turned and peered up over his shoulder. "You want to see the President's son?"

Damn. David felt himself become much more conspicuous, felt the boy studying his face. "President of what?" he asked inanely.

The boy said, "You know. Randy McPherson." All the boys glanced up at David now. He'd managed to draw their attention from the candy. "I think he's down at the lake," one of the other boys said, and the others nodded. "He's a weirdo," one of them confided.

"Yeah. We're gonna dunk him when we go swimming." All the

boys laughed, and went back to their candy. David walked slowly away.

An older counselor coaching first base stared at him, so David stopped. "Here to see my son Tony," David said. "How's he doing?"

"Great," the counselor said enthusiastically. He looked about twenty, a college student at a summer job, tall and muscular. "He loves the game."

Even David, a father for only ten minutes, didn't buy that. He turned away. The counselor called, "Sir?" obviously concerned to see David walking away from the field. David turned back and said to him confidentially, "It makes him too nervous for me to watch him play. I'm just going to look around the facilities. I'll be back."

The counselor nodded understandingly. David walked away, looking back at the field as if still involved in the game, trying to drift as if the field were leaving him instead of the other way around. Up in those trees the Secret Service agent watched him, David felt sure, though he could no longer see the man.

He had to hurry. He'd committed himself to too many people. As soon as someone asked Tony Armstrong about his "father," David's cover would be blown. And the boys knew he'd asked about Randy McPherson. David hurried down a path that continued to slope gently downhill, until the softball field was out of sight and David felt unobserved. He slowed down and tried to look like a parent seeing if his money was well spent on this camp.

Another hundred yards brought him within sight of the lake. Large pond would have been a more accurate term, big enough for swimming and canoeing but not for sailing. Two docks close at hand thrust out into the water. A very new-looking wooden boathouse stood with its doors open, revealing racks for canoes and oars and life preservers. The small lake itself looked very well tended, no moss on it, the water deep blue.

Twenty or so boys squealed and jumped and tumbled over each other on the bank and one of the docks. Four were in canoes, two apiece, but had only made it a few feet away from shore. They used the paddles at cross-purposes, laughing and splashing each other.

David stopped, standing carefully with his arms folded. He looked out at the lake itself rather than the boys, and waited to spot the Secret Service agents. Fifty yards away, on the other side of the boys, a man who'd been sitting in a canvas deck chair rose to his feet. This one also wore a wide-brimmed hat and dark glasses, and the camp outfit, and was just as convincing in it as the man who'd come out from behind a tree and confronted David. This man was African-American, but otherwise indistinguishable from his colleague. He stared penetratingly at David. David, pretending not to notice him, put his hands on his hips and turned in a slow circle, as if surveying the lake. He hadn't worn a jacket for just this reason, so that he'd look less suspicious. The agent could see that he had no dangerous-looking bulges under his shirt in either front or back. Turning back around, David thought the agent looked more relaxed about him, but he didn't sit down again.

David walked more briskly, spotting a counselor and approaching him hand extended. "Hi! John Armstrong. I'm here visiting my son Tony and I thought I'd look the place over. Never been here before, want to see what you've got."

"Yes, sir," the teenaged boy mumbled. He must be a first-year counselor, hadn't yet learned the lesson of enthusiasm. "Well, it's all new stuff, you can see that. This place keeps everything up-to-date."

"Yeah. What's the boys' favorite thing to do down here at the lake?"

"Try to tip over the canoes and hit each other with the paddles when they come up. Ha ha. Just kidding. No, the boys love it down here."

Definitely a new boy. A veteran wouldn't have made such a joke, which had the ring of truth. Trying to make up for his gaffe, and as if remembering his training, the counselor began to talk more animatedly. David looked over the counselor's shoulder at the boys. More were piling into canoes, assisted by two other counselors. One boy remained apart, sitting on one of the posts of the dock as if he'd been put in time-out. A small, thin eight-year-old boy with thick brown hair two shades darker than his mother's. He sat staring down at some small object in his hand, ignoring the clamor around him.

David, staring covertly, knew he'd found Randy McPherson.

But he couldn't think how to put this triumph to use. Twenty yards away, Randy might as well have been inside a castle guarded by knights, for as much chance as David had of getting to him. Pretending to listen to the counselor yammer on, David decided his only option was to go back up to the softball field and wait for Randy's group to move on to their next activity. Of course, why would he have any better chance of reaching him there? Once David did get close, what was he going to do, grab the boy and run? Tell him some story? Surely the President's son had been taught to resist such overtures from strangers. David had tried to plan ahead but hadn't been able to think of anything. He had hoped an opportunity would arise once he'd found the boy, but now that he had this rescue seemed more hopeless than ever. If he took two steps in Randy's direction he'd find himself arrested.

It suddenly occurred to David that Helen Wills should have known how incompetent he'd be at this. Maybe she had intended him to get caught. What did he know about Helen or her motivations, except that she was a Secret Service agent herself? It was part of her job to uncover and destroy plots against the security of the first family. Maybe she considered David such a plotter, and she was entrapping him into getting himself arrested. This wasn't a rescue, it was a sting.

Had Helen led him into a trap? Why? Just to take him out of the picture, perhaps, put an end to all this divorce nonsense. After all, except for the First Lady herself, David was the only person who knew that Myra McPherson had contemplated leaving her husband. The only person in on the secret and still free. If David got arrested legitimately, such as for trying to kidnap the President's son, he would be buried for years. Myra McPherson would remain trapped in her role. Maybe Helen saw that as her job: protecting the first family by keeping it intact, even against the First Lady's will. Helen had seemed sincerely to want to help Mrs. McPherson, but it would be part of Helen's job description to be convincing.

David felt observed by that Secret Service agent again, and he suddenly felt very vulnerable. He needed to get away. To hell with this stupid rescue attempt. He just needed to rescue himself.

"Thanks, son," David said to the counselor, clapping him on the shoulder. "Go ahead and help the boys, don't let me keep you from your duties. I'll just . . ." He trailed off vaguely and started to turn away, taking one last surreptitious glance at the object of his quest as he did. Then David halted in his tracks. The first son was staring at him.

Randy McPherson had risen from his perch on the dock post and taken a few steps forward. He looked steadily at David as if recognizing him. How could that be? But the boy's attention obviously remained focused on David. Maybe someone had warned Randy about this man, and shown him a picture. David, feeling even more exposed, began walking away.

"Wait!" came a high-pitched cry. Tingling with alarm, David looked back and saw Randy McPherson starting to run after him. On the other side of the dock, the black Secret Service agent started hurrying too.

Shit. If David ran he'd give himself away. If he stopped and let the boy catch up to him he'd be arrested, or at least held for questioning. His fake identity would be found out easily. He was dead no matter what he did.

Randy McPherson suddenly stopped running. He glanced at his protector, the Secret Service agent. Then Randy moved again, but jerkily. His leg hit one of the supporting pillars of the dock. He fell to his knees, then all the way prone, screaming in pain. He rolled over to grab his injured knee, and rolled right off the dock, hitting the water below with a noisy splash.

The world seemed engulfed in noise, boys shouting, the sounds of their paddles in the water, the echo of the splash Randy had made entering the water. He didn't come up again. David stood stock-still, stunned by this development. He felt guilty even though he hadn't done anything. The Secret Service agent he'd seen kept running toward the water. Suddenly David was knocked aside as another man came from the side of the boathouse, bursting between David and the boy counselor. David noticed the man's thick calves, pumping furiously. As the man, obviously a second Secret Service agent, ran, he knocked off his hat and glasses and leaped into the lake in a smooth dive, like a former college competitor.

This agent must have been keeping out of sight beside the boathouse, from which he could watch the first son while remaining unobserved, in approved Secret Service fashion. When Randy screamed the agent had probably been just about to seize David. Instead, Randy's fall into the water had caused the agent to revert to his first duty, keeping the President's son safe.

The first agent splashed into the water in great strides, reaching the spot where Randy had gone under in seconds. He waited, trying to see through the water that had suddenly gone murky with all the splashing about. Then a hand came up and he seized it. Randy McPherson's small body broke the surface, and the black agent grabbed him up.

The other agent came up too, from underneath, pushing Randy up ahead of him, putting the boy's safety ahead of his own. The two of them held the boy between them for a minute, almost struggling over him, then hurried the boy to shore. Randy began coughing. He clutched his leg again and moaned. "Ow!" he shouted. "My leg, my leg!"

The noise seemed to reassure the agents. At least the boy hadn't drowned. But it also made them move even more swiftly. They got Randy to shore and the one who'd dived into the water after him took him in both hands. "I'll take him to the nurse's station," he said tersely. "You—"

He jerked his head in David's direction, which the other agent seemed to understand instantly, nodding. The one agent hurried away holding Randy, who looked back over the man's shoulder, again at David. Did he look accusing? The boy's small face struggled to convey something.

David suddenly felt his elbow seized in a firm grasp. Startled, he found the burly black Secret Service agent holding him. The man's face remained absolutely blank and unreadable. He didn't need sunglasses to hide his expression.

"Would you come with me, please, sir?" he said quietly. The grip
on David's arm told him this was not a request and was not refus-
able.

"I didn't do anything," David said, irritated to hear himself sounding like a whining child. "You saw, I was nowhere near the dock."

"Just come with me, please. It won't take long."

The agent's flat tone sounded otherwise. He released David's arm
but stayed close beside him as they hurried up the slope after the
other agent and the injured first son.

Helen Wills jogged across the grounds of the treatment center,
changing her plan as she moved. Now that she'd been caught by the
video camera sneaking into the place, she didn't have long before
she'd be discovered. The lack of response so far told her that a guard
didn't sit constantly watching all the footage from the various moni-
tors obviously scattered around the place, but the tapes would be
reviewed on fast forward periodically. Twice a day? Hourly? She
didn't know, but once they saw her on tape coming out from under
that barred exit, Helen wouldn't be able to claim she was here on
official status. Could she say she'd been testing the security measures? Would anyone in charge of security at such a place as this be
dumb enough to buy such a story? Forget them; her fellow agents
would never believe it.

So she had a very limited amount of time until her credibility
vanished, unless she could get to the security video room and erase
the tape that showed her entry. Very unlikely. She sought out the
First Lady instead. Helen expected to find her drugged, or otherwise
incapacitated in some way. Slipping her out of here seemed impossible. But Helen had to try. Soon she'd be in the biggest trouble of
her life anyway.

So, disdaining subterfuge, she walked briskly toward the first cottage she came across, and approached it boldly to stare through a

window. A teenaged boy sat watching television. He appeared unattended. The scene looked very normal until Helen sidled along the window, changing her angle of vision, and saw that the television wasn't on. When she looked at the boy again, blankly staring at that blank screen, the image chilled her. She hurried away.

Helen looked for the telltale signs of Secret Service presence that she would know better than anyone. The agents guarding the First Lady would try to make her look like an ordinary patient, meaning the agents had to stay out of sight, but they couldn't hide their traces altogether. When Helen approached the next cottage she looked for a small satellite dish on the roof, extra wiring snaking down the wall, a new black sedan parked nearby in case of the need for a quick getaway. Tire tracks in the grass where such a car had come and gone. Seeing no such signs, she went quickly to a window and glanced in. In an unoccupied living room a brown jacket lay on a sofa. Checking another window, she saw a maid making the bed in a bedroom. The cottage's tenant seemed to be elsewhere. A sudden plan forming, Helen went to the front door of the cottage, found it unlocked, and slipped inside. She could hear the maid's feet moving across the bedroom floor. Quickly Helen crossed the room, grabbed up that brown jacket, and went out the door again as a voice called questioningly from the bedroom.

Outside, Helen put on the jacket, drew a stocking cap from her back pocket, and put it on. From that point on she watched for more video cameras and made sure to pass through their fields of surveillance, but with her face averted.

But her primary objective remained Myra McPherson. She came close to the main building of the treatment center, stood behind a tree, and watched. Would the First Lady be kept in there? Helen doubted it. She wouldn't have chosen the main building if she'd been agent-in-charge. Too much traffic, too many people passing through on legitimate business who would nonetheless have to have their stories checked out. And the main building would be where the First Lady would be most likely to be seen by someone outside the secret that she was here in the first place. A logistical security nightmare. No, the agents would want to be in the most secluded cottage, and the largest one, because they would need at least one room to themselves for their own operations, and to be close to Mrs. McPherson while affording her some slight privacy.

Helen wished she had a map of the place. She thought she could pick the right cottage if she could see the layout. Sighing, she realized she had to come in out of the cold. Going cottage to cottage would take too long. She came out from behind the tree and strode to the front entrance of the main building. Just outside it she doffed the brown jacket and stocking cap and dropped them behind some bushes. Her clothes had almost dried in the warm morning and from her activity. Her hair probably looked awful, but she didn't have time to make up. Helen opened the door and walked in without any attempt at stealth.

She found herself standing at one end of a long hall that appeared to end at another outside door fifty feet away. The twelve-foot-wide hall had hardwood floors, with a long strip carpet running down the center. Down in the middle of the building the hall intersected with a similar hall that disappeared to left and right. Along the corridor in which Helen stood, large framed landscape paintings took up space on the taupe walls, interrupted at regular intervals by white office doors. Down toward that center hallway, a bulletin board hung on the wall beside one such door. The ceiling of this building was at least ten feet tall, and featured crown molding. Over all, the interior gave the effect of the administration building of an expensive private school.

Standing very tall and straight, Helen walked along the hall, her feet silent on the carpet. She approached the bulletin board, but before she reached it she came to one of those frames on the wall and saw that it didn't hold a traditional landscape. About four feet square, the frame held a print of an artist's rendering of the grounds. In white scripted letters at the bottom it proclaimed unashamedly the original name of the place: "Land of Peace Treatment Facility." Quickly Helen looked over the drawing. It gave an overhead view of the grounds, the building in which Helen stood in the center. The grounds in this artist's rendering looked very lush and contemplative. Cottages were scattered here and there, most along two angled lines that formed a **V** with this building at the apex. But the pattern wasn't rigid: other cottages were sprinkled liberally, some two dozen in all. They all looked exactly the same size. Nothing distinguished one from the others. Helen's heart sank. By the time she sought out each of these, she would surely be found out.

In fact, discovery came much, much sooner. The door of what appeared to be the main office opened almost right in front of Helen and a woman of about fifty came out. She wore a navy skirt, flowered blouse, and reading glasses on a gold chain around her neck, and was looking at some papers in her hand. But sensing the presence of another person she looked up, gasped, and her glasses fell down to her ample bosom. The woman reached a hand in that direction herself, but then her face grew stern. "How did you get in here?" She didn't step back, but remained standing only a foot in front of Helen.

Helen pulled out her flat black credential case and opened it to display her Secret Service identification. She held the case open long enough for the woman to read her name, her number, and study the photograph of Helen. The woman's sternness turned to studied patience. "Well?"

"I'm here from the White House, ma'am, sent as backup to the team already here. Tell me, please, which cottage is your, um, special guest staying in?"

The lady's administrative air grew even more formidable as she folded her arms across her chest. "I guess if the White House really sent you, they would have told you that information already."

Helen smiled. "Very good, ma'am. That's exactly the right answer."

"Oh, yes? Well, if you're so security conscious, why did you mention the White House to me without knowing if I even knew about the 'special guest'?" The lady gave a tight, triumphant smile.

"Oh, they told me about you, ma'am." Appearing more serious, Helen said, "I just wanted to check in with you so you'd know there'll be another of us here. Of course we don't want to alarm anyone."

"Oh, we're getting used to all of you," the administrator said, not sounding indulgent.

"Thank you." Helen nodded alertly, like a bright robot that didn't understand irony. She turned and walked back toward the front door.

"You're going the wrong way," came the woman's voice, sounding more ironic still than suspicious.

"Yes, ma'am. I just need to get my equipment."

When she turned back, at the front door, the administrative lady had disappeared. Possibly back into that office to call the First Lady's cottage. Nothing Helen could do about that. She hoped she had what information she needed from the artist's map.

Outside, she retrieved her jacket and stocking cap and put them on. She slipped around the opposite side of the administrative building and walked briskly up a gravel path toward the far back corner of the center's grounds.

Nothing had distinguished the cottages portrayed on the map she'd seen in the administrative building. They weren't designed for individuality. But Helen's attention had been drawn to something not on the map: an empty space behind the other cottages. In the artist's drawing of the camp, this space appeared only as a large wooded area. Helen didn't believe the legendary Dr. Tosoros, known for his avidity in seeking wealth from his "treatments," would have allowed such a large section of his grounds to sit idle. Maybe that blank area Helen had noticed really did just contain woods, through which patients were supposed to walk for therapeutic reasons. Maybe the center of the woods held a campfire around which they all gathered to sing camp songs or hymns. But Helen didn't think so.

She hurried up the path, back into a wooded area, still watching for video cameras and keeping her face averted when she saw one. There would be a lot of taped footage of the figure in the brown jacket and stocking cap. The path began to curve to the right, toward the other cottages she had seen portrayed on the map, away from the apparently unpopulated area she had noticed. But at this point tire tracks crossed the path and veered up into the woods in a twisting route. Helen bent and examined the tracks. They were narrow and not deep, small enough that nothing bigger than a golf cart could have made them. No normal car would have been able to pass between those trees anyway. The tracks could have just been made by a maintenance vehicle for the center itself. On the other hand, these impressions in the ground might confirm her theory. Agents wouldn't have walked or carried the First Lady through these woods. They would have found a way to use a vehicle.

Helen followed the tracks through the thick pine woods. Dried needles slithered under her feet, an occasional pinecone threatening to twist her ankle. Helen walked very carefully, expecting at any moment to see a broad black-jacketed back beside one of these trees. Or not to see the person, until a hand fell on her arm and a stern voice challenged her.

Helen felt ready for whatever happened. She thought she had one advantage: the Secret Service agents guarding the First Lady thought they were doing just that, not holding her hostage. They wouldn't be in on the ruse; they wouldn't stand for it. The agents would have just been told that Mrs. McPherson was disturbed and needed treatment. There might be one person, maybe two here in on the secret of the real reason for the First Lady's being whisked away to this secretive facility. But most of the agents would still have her best interests at heart. At least Helen hoped so.

Of course, that didn't mean they'd believe anything Helen told them.

Soon the trees opened out in front of her and she glimpsed a cottage, as in a fairy tale, the kind that featured a witch or monster or poisoned fruit lurking nearby. This cottage had more adornments than the others, with elaborate fish-scale shingles on the roof and a wide Victorian porch with a wicker porch swing. It was larger than the cottages Helen had seen, too. This one was definitely set apart, designed for a very special guest. And deliberately left off the center's map for even more security. A thrill of excitement raced up Helen's arms and across her shoulders. She had been right, which meant the hardest part was about to begin.

She circled around, staying in the trees, saw one agent close to the house, again passed through the range of a video camera, keeping her head down in the stocking cap. She saw no other Secret Service agents, which didn't mean they weren't there. On the bright side, none of them seemed to have spotted her, either. At the back of the cottage she saw a small, attractively designed outbuilding that probably held at least one car. A service road led out the back way. She crept up to the building, peered through a back window, and indeed saw two long black sedans inside. No one seemed to be guarding them. Helen slipped inside the garage and checked the cars. Keys not in the ignition but up over the visor. Standard Secret Service procedure. They didn't want to be trapped if the agent carrying the keys got shot or otherwise couldn't get to the car.

A few minutes later Helen slipped back out of the outbuilding and resumed her survey of the house. After circling the cottage, she dropped her jacket and stocking cap under a bush, kicking them well underneath the shrubbery out of sight. As she did so, she remembered David Owens's advice to her: *Just walk straight in, Helen. No one can believe you'd be lying.* She straightened her shoulders and walked boldly out of the trees, calling out, "No target! No target! Friendly incoming. Who's here to greet me?"

The cottage's front door, centrally located in its inviting front wall, opened almost at once. A man with a narrow brown face, slim build, and very alert black eyes stepped half out of the door and stared at Helen. She walked up the steps to him. "Hello, Roger. The deputy director sent me to give you a break. You're relieved."

"I'm not even reassured," Roger Enriquez said flatly. "What are you doing here, Helen? Nobody said anything to me."

He didn't challenge Helen's access, though. As she opened the door wider he stepped aside and let her in. Helen entered a small living room, saying casually, "Are you sure? Have you been checking your E-mail? Well, that's typical, isn't it? A secretary goes on vacation or to the bathroom and a relay gets lost and I get here faster than the message to you does. Well, she is my primary assignment after all. How's Lady Dove?"

"She's fine. Resting." Roger Enriquez glanced down the hallway that led back out of the living room. "That's all she's been doing since we got here. That doctor—" Enriquez shook his head, obviously not pleased with the situation but unwilling to comment further.

"All right. Give me the setup. How many agents do you have? Four, right? I saw Herbert in the woods. Communications center in the back room? How often are you checking in?"

Enriquez narrowed his eyes at the news that Helen had spotted one of his agents outside but the agent obviously hadn't seen her and reported it to the house. "It's about time now," he said in answer to her question about checking with his White House supervisors. "I need to find out about you, too, Helen. I can't believe they didn't inform us."

"Fine. Don't ask for the deputy director, though. He left town after assigning me. Maybe try Jensen, I think he was in the loop on my assignment."

Enriquez didn't reply, but walked away toward the back of the cottage. No one at the White House would confirm Helen's story, of course, but Enriquez might be busy for ten minutes finding that out. Helen walked quickly and quietly up the carpeted hallway. Enriquez had disappeared into a room at the far back of the cottage. Helen tried a door on the left side of the hallway. A bathroom. A lovely bathroom at that, with a maple wood washstand and elaborate re-creations of old-fashioned fixtures, even to a ball-and-foot standing bathtub. But Helen didn't stop to appreciate the decorations. She closed the door and tried the other side of the hall.

On the plus side, Enriquez obviously trusted her enough to leave her alone and unwatched in the cottage. No one had ever questioned Helen's devotion to her charge, or her duty. In the next few minutes, though, she planned to lose that trust irrevocably.

The door across the hall led to pay dirt: a bedroom. The bed was an old-fashioned, tall four-poster, in keeping with the decor of the rest of the cottage. A large armoire with mirrored doors stood in the corner to Helen's right. To her left was an interior wall with a door standing ajar. That would lead to a room where a Secret Service agent would be constantly on watch. Helen hoped that had been Enriquez, leaving his post momentarily now and counting on Helen to take over for him.

Directly across from her were two windows in the outside wall of the room. Helen saw that a thin wire mesh had been added on the insides of the windows. She knew from experience the strength of this mesh. It would secure the opening even if someone broke the glass of the window.

The bed's occupant stirred. Helen shot a glance in that direction and saw Myra McPherson raise up in the bed. She wore a pink sleeping mask but Helen recognized her at once. The First Lady sat up, putting her back against the headboard, but didn't remove the mask. She didn't appear to know it covered half her face. Helen felt a sudden chill. Mrs. McPherson looked somehow recovering, like an accident victim. The way she sat, patient and blind, looked eerie. Helen suddenly wondered if she was too late, if the First Lady had undergone some surgical procedure.

Helen walked toward her, saying in a voice she tried to keep light and normal, "Good morning, Mrs. McPherson."

The patient didn't seem to hear, but then a few seconds later turned her face toward Helen, with heartbreaking slowness. Helen recognized this delayed response time and grogginess as the symptoms of a drugged state. Gently, she removed the sleeping mask from her client's face.

Myra McPherson blinked repeatedly, as if she hadn't seen the sun for days. That might well be true. Her pupils were huge, consuming her eyes so that she looked like a frightened nocturnal creature startled into daytime wakefulness. Helen smiled, waiting for recognition, but inside she grew scared as hell. The First Lady didn't recognize her. She was far gone. Probably couldn't walk. How the hell could Helen get her out of here even if Mrs. McPherson recognized her and was willing to be led?

Suddenly Helen heard footsteps close behind her. She whirled around.

A female nurse approached. The woman was obviously a nurse

even though she didn't wear white. She wore a casual outfit of beige slacks and blue-and-yellow striped top, but she had a nurse's air of efficiency and unflappability. She had a plump, creased face that looked as if it would smile easily, but she didn't smile at sight of Helen.

"What the hell have you done to her?" Helen said accusingly.

The nurse didn't respond in kind. "She's all right. Aren't you, sweetie?" She stood beside Helen and put a hand on Mrs. McPherson's forehead. Myra smiled at her hesitantly. This nurse was probably the First Lady's most frequent visitor, but Myra's memory wasn't functioning.

The nurse turned toward Helen. She kept her voice soft, not to disturb her patient, but it had a definite edge to it as she fixed her eyes on Helen. "And who are you and what are you doing in this room?"

"It's okay," Helen said with easy authority, reaching toward her back pocket for her identification. "The White House sent me."

Across the room, the door that stood ajar opened all the way, slapping lightly back against the wall. Angela Vortiz stood there. The President's intimate assistant and conduit to Wilson Boswell lounged against the doorjamb, looking tall and shapely. In response to Helen's claim of coming from the White House, Angela said, "Like hell they did."

She smiled at Helen, who didn't smile back. She continued to feel the nurse's scrutiny. Behind Angela, Helen saw an office filled with electronic equipment. A small video monitor that Angela had obviously been watching showed the stream that flowed under the back wall of the treatment center. The stream's surface was suddenly broken by the face of an intruder coming out of the water choking and gasping. The figure stood long enough in the camera's gaze for anyone who knew her to recognize Helen Wills.

Angela's smile grew frostier. "Would you get the other agents, please?" she said to the nurse.

Helen stood there as helpless as the drugged First Lady.

★ David Owens, being led across the camp grounds to certain discovery and disgrace and probably imprisonment, gradually rose out of hopelessness back into character. Whether he resumed his own character or the one he'd adopted—busy, inattentive parent—he couldn't have said, but at any rate he ceased being the hapless prisoner.

The sight of another parent prompted this rebirth. As David and the black Secret Service agent walked up toward the camp's office area, David noticed a woman wearing a sunhat held on by a filmy scarf. The woman looked around uncertainly but impatiently, as if her waiter were too slow to bring the drinks and menus. The Secret Service agent beside David barely glanced at her.

Farther away another obvious parent, a father, wandered among the cabins, looking for his child. Again, he drew little attention from anyone. Parents were commonplace here. Parents like David.

He suddenly stopped walking and said, "Excuse me. But before I go any farther may I ask who the hell you are and what you want from me?"

The agent, wearing his camp T-shirt, walking shorts, and sneakers, looked irritated, then confused. The agent remembered that he should be role-playing himself. But he couldn't keep the authoritative edge out of his voice. "If you don't mind accompanying me to the office, sir, we'll try to—"

"I *do* mind," David snapped. He stood his ground, looking angry. "I'm here trying to see my son, for which I have very little time, I might add, and instead I get dragged across the place because some boy falls and scrapes his knee. I think your staff's response to that crisis was admirable, but I'd also think someone in your position would know that little boys fall down all the time. And I had nothing to do with it, as you very well know. So if you'll excuse me, I have a boy of my own to locate."

He turned away, expecting to be stopped. His expectation proved insightful.

"I'm sorry, sir. Please. I know it's inconvenient, but if we could just have a couple of minutes of your time . . ."

The undercover Secret Service agent wouldn't let him go, but his tone of voice had changed completely. He'd remembered his own game: letting as few people as possible know there was anything special about the camper who'd fallen off the dock.

"Why?" David snapped, standing with hands on hips. He was actually beginning to enjoy this. Sight of the other parents in the camp had reminded him that he must not look as suspicious as he'd feared. He needed to blend in with their matter-of-fact attitudes, not be herded sheepishly along like a prisoner.

"We just need to get a statement from you, sir, saying what you saw, that no one was at fault, that nothing could have been done to prevent—well, the accident."

David became gracious. "Oh, I get it. Insurance, right? Why didn't you say so? Pain in the ass, I know. I have to deal with those jerks all the time. Come on, let's get it over with."

They resumed their journey toward the office, but with their roles reversed. David walked quickly, a man with little time to spare. The agent lagged behind, apparently growing down into his role and feeling foolish in his baggy shorts and motto-stained T-shirt. "This place must pay a fortune in premiums, am I right?" David asked jovially.

They left the gravel path and walked across dark green grass on which David's dully shining black shoes looked out of place. Now he didn't mind. He thought he'd managed to extricate himself from his dilemma. He only hoped to sign some quick statement, wander around as if to say good-bye to his son, and then make his escape. He'd reconnoitered, he'd learned the situation. That was all a professional like Helen Wills should expect of an amateur like David. If Helen pulled off rescuing the First Lady, the three of them could get Randy out of here. After all, Myra McPherson was his mother. She could just come get him. If Helen failed in her own rescue attempt, well, it wouldn't matter that Randy remained here. David just had to make sure that he, at least, got away to raise trouble in case Mrs. McPherson and her son remained hostages.

The agent caught up to him, David shrugged a question, and the agent led the way up three wooden steps to the largest building in the central compound. Outside it looked rustic in keeping with the camp decor, but inside air-conditioning smacked them welcomingly in the face. They stood in a large room that seemed to serve as both office and storage area. Two metal desks, unoccupied, sat close to each other off to the right. Behind them, against the wall, tall metal storage units leaned toward each other. The double doors of one stood open, revealing badminton rackets, birdies, volleyballs, and duffel bags that probably held softballs and bats. Other sports equipment lay scattered around the office.

Across the room a door stood open into another room. Through it David saw Randy McPherson sitting in a chair, being tended by a harried-looking young woman nurse. Randy still writhed in pain, sucked in his breath hard enough for David to hear thirty feet away, and clutched his injured leg.

Also visible through the doorway was the back of the other Secret Service agent, the one who'd pulled the boy out of the lake. He turned quickly at the entrance of David and his keeper, and came out into the larger room to confer with his colleague.

"He's all right," he said in an undertone to his fellow agent, while staring at David harshly. "Just scraped his knees. Of course he's carrying on like it's a compound fracture."

"Well, he *was* outdoors for almost twenty minutes," the African-American agent said, which seemed to be a private joke between the two men, who both smiled grimly.

"Just like I said," David spoke up. "Just a scraped knee. Happens all the time. Can I get out of here now?"

The agents exchanged a glance and the one who'd brought David in said, "If you could just give us that statement, sir. Have a seat at the desk, would you?"

David complied. The agent found some lined paper on a clipboard and put it on the desk in front of David with a pen. "Just in your own words, sir. Just a brief description of what happened. Please start with your name and address. And after you're done we'll have you swear to it, if that's all right."

David looked surprised. "Sworn statement? Who am I going to swear to? You people—"

"I'm a notary public, sir." The agent had regained his unflappable tone.

David heaved a theatrical sigh and began writing. Both agents turned their backs on him. His expressed desire to leave had convinced them of his harmlessness. After a brief almost silent conference the taller agent, the one who'd pulled Randy from the lake, turned abruptly and went outside, probably to circle the building and stand watch outside the windows of the nurse's office. David's original keeper stayed behind. He walked through the door into the nurse's room. A moment later the boy inside squealed loudly, bringing David to his feet.

"OWOwowowowowow!" Randy McPherson shouted, a sound that went right through any listener's bones. In fact it drove the black Secret Service agent right back out of the room. He gestured placatingly through the doorway, saying loudly, "It's all right, son, it's all right. It'll stop in a minute."

"It's just Bactine!" came the nurse's loud voice. "Here, here, I'll blow on it."

"Just let me lie down for a few minutes," the boy's voice whined.

David found he had crept closer to the doorway. The agent

turned suddenly and looked at him in some alarm. David shrugged. The agent responded in kind.

"Could I have a little privacy, please?" the boy said shrilly, as if this were a request he had to make frequently in his beleaguered life. The nurse came hurrying out of the room, rolling her eyes. She closed the door behind her and said, "I gave him some Advil. Just let him rest for a few minutes. Maybe he'll take a nap."

"Please, God," the agent said. Both the nurse and the agent looked at David, who said, "Cheerful little soldier, isn't he?"

The agent sighed as if he'd like to share his burdens with this stranger. The nurse left the room through the outside door, saying, "I'll check on him in a few minutes." David returned to his writing.

Two or three minutes passed. The agent quietly opened the interior door and looked into the nurse's office. Under a sheet, the boy lay on a cot. David, coming up behind the agent, saw the slight mound under the cover. He also saw his opportunity. The agent's back was turned. He seemed to have forgotten David. An aluminum softball bat leaned against the wall three feet from David's hand. He only had to grab it, hit the agent over the head, and go in and pick up the sleeping boy. He should be able to get to his car before anyone raised an alarm. Then just drive out the gate. Ditch the car somewhere, lay low, get to his meeting with Helen. Suddenly he could envision the success of his mission.

The agent turned, eyes widening. David stood frozen. But the man didn't reach for a gun, and his tension abated as he saw it was only David behind him. David could still get past him. Kick him in the crotch, *then* hit him with the bat. Randy looked as if he weighed less than fifty pounds, David could carry him just as the other agent had. He might even be able to find a gun on this agent once he was unconscious. David's car sat nearby, just waiting for him.

The two men stood looking at each other for a long beat of two or three seconds. David held up his paper. "Finished my statement."

The agent relaxed further. "Very good, sir. If you'll just step over to the desk and sign it and swear to it."

David followed instructions, realizing as he did so that he had just committed perjury, by swearing that his name was John Armstrong, his cover identity. Maybe that's what the agent wanted, a genuine crime on which to arrest him. As the man bent over the desk to sign the statement as a witness, David saw the back of the man's neck, thick and brown but unprotected. There was a lamp on the desk. David's imagination revised his scenario. Grab up the lamp, hit the man over the head, snatch the boy . . .

But being a man of action requires practice, or at least training. David found he couldn't make the first move. Hitting someone over the head looked simple enough on a movie or TV screen, but taking that step in real life, actually crunching metal down on unprotected flesh and bone, seemed impossible to David at that pivotal moment. Suppose he hit the man too hard and did permanent brain damage, or even killed him? Suppose he didn't hit him hard enough? David's legal training, causing him always to imagine multiple repercussions from any action, hadn't fitted him for being an action hero.

The agent stood up, looked at David strangely for a moment, then held out his hand. "Thank you for your cooperation, sir."

David shook hands mechanically. The agent accompanied him out onto the porch. He seemed relieved to get away for a moment from his responsibility inside the nurse's office. "Would you like some help finding your son, sir? If you'll step over to the other office . . ."

David shook his head. "I'll find him. Thanks anyway."

In fact he just wanted to get away, make his escape and nurse his inadequacy. He felt secretly shamed. This job needed a real man to pull it off. Someone like Helen.

David walked slowly away. Behind him, the Secret Service agent stood on the porch stretching his back, then turned and went back inside the building. David walked down the path toward the parking lot. He imagined trying to spin this tale for Helen Wills when he saw her again, if ever: *I pulled off the secret identity, they never suspected me at all. And I managed to get close to Randy, but there were just too many of them for me to get away with him.* He could hear Helen's response, and his own, if he answered honestly: *How many agents were there that you had to get past? Well, one.* Helen would nod, confirmed in her opinion of him.

As David walked toward the parking lot he realized a young boy, one of the campers, had fallen in step just behind him. David glanced back with a kindly smile—all these boys seemed so hungry for adult attention—then stopped dead, staring.

Randy McPherson stood there.

The boy looked at him attentively, in a friendly but unsmiling way. He waited for a signal. His appearance terrified David. The boy seemed like a bad conscience following him. Somehow his imagination had kidnapped the first son after all, without David's awareness. He looked back toward the administration building, expecting to see the Secret Service agents running toward him. But the building stood silent.

Too much time had passed without verbal reaction from David. Uncertainly, Randy McPherson said, "Mr. Owens?"

"What?"

"It is you, isn't it? David Owens, the lawyer?"

So the boy *had* been warned against him. As soon as David confirmed his true identity, the boy would start screaming.

"You came," Randy said wonderingly, beginning to smile shyly. "I sent for you and you came."

"*You* sent for me?"

"Yes. By E-mail. Didn't you get it? I asked you to come help us."

The E-mail. David had almost forgotten what had brought him to Washington. "That's right, Randy. I got your message. Come on, let's—"

David heard a shout from the building they'd left. Moments later the door of the building flew open and slammed back against the wall. The burly Secret Service agent who'd released David ran out onto the porch and stared wildly around the camp. He didn't have a gun in his hand, but in his expression he'd abandoned all pretense of being a camp counselor. Every muscle in his body clenched. When his eyes fastened on David it felt like a physical grasp. David stepped back as the agent ran toward him.

"Sir!" he said, but his barking voice held no tone of respect. "Did you see the boy come out, the one who was in the nurse's office?"

David glanced behind him and saw no one. "Uh, no. Which boy? The one who fell? I was just walking away, I didn't see anybody . . ."

"Damn!" the agent burst out. He stood for a long moment staring at David, then turned and ran back toward the building. The other agent appeared from the back side. The two conferred for only a second, then separated. Both spoke into small communicators. One ran along a line that took him on a slant past David.

David turned and started walking stiffly, head barely turning. He rounded the corner of the nearest cabin and stopped to calm himself.

"Gee," said a voice at his elbow, "they don't usually figure out I'm gone that fast. Maybe I've used the pillow under the sheet trick too many times."

Randy McPherson stood beside him. David caught his breath. "My God, how did you get away?"

"Just ran. See, these cabins are kind of on ledges. There's room enough underneath for me. Just barely."

"Let's get out of here." David started walking quickly, the boy right behind him. As David turned around the next corner of the cabin someone smashed into him. David was thrown back against the wall. The Secret Service agent who'd asked him his name in the wooded area near the baseball field grabbed his arm.

"Sorry, sir. We're looking for a boy. One of the campers—"

"I know," David said, trying to sound irritable rather than frightened. Suddenly his hand shot out, going just past the agent's face. The man instinctively reached behind him, where he must be carrying a pistol. David's finger came out, pointing.

"Look! Isn't that him?"

Eighty yards away, a skinny brown-haired boy walked into one of the cabins. David and the agent had barely caught sight of him. Even the agent who guarded Randy McPherson every day couldn't be sure. Without another word he took off. So did David, in the opposite direction. He wasn't surprised this time when Randy McPherson caught up to him.

"Come on!" David said urgently. He couldn't take any more encounters. He grabbed Randy's hand and they ran. The whole tone of the camp had changed. The few urgent men scattering among the cabins seemed to create a roaring in his ears. In the distance he saw another man running toward him, and hoped the small figure of Randy was too far away for the man to recognize.

They reached the car, Randy scrambled into the backseat, and David started the engine with much too loud a roar. It sounded like a fugitive's car. He forced himself to calm down, put the car in gear, and drive slowly away. In the backseat Randy crouched down without being told.

David said, "Are you okay?"

Randy's voice came slightly muffled from behind the seat. "Sure. I wish they wouldn't go so crazy all the time. It's not like this is the first time. When you and the agent went outside for a minute I slipped out, into the next room, and out the window there."

Very resourceful. The boy was obviously much better at this than David.

"I've done it before," Randy said conversationally. "They really don't watch me very closely. They're always looking out for other people paying too much attention to me, not expecting me to take off."

This echoed something Helen had told David. He wondered if Randy had learned from her or come to the same conclusion on his own.

"Oh, here," David said, handing the toy he'd brought over the seat.

"The Vibra-Wing!" Randy shouted. "All right!" He sat up, staring joyfully at the toy spaceship as if it had been a favorite puppy licking his face. David gently pushed Randy's head down out of sight again.

"Your mom said you'd be glad to have that back. Now be very quiet."

He saw the guard shed just ahead. There didn't seem to be any alarm. But before he could reach it a long black sedan glided across the exit. A stony-faced agent wearing a suit instead of the camp garb disguise got out on the driver's side and stared at David's approaching car. David stopped. He muttered an obscenity under his breath and got out of his own car, glaring at the agent.

"Do you mind? I've got to get out of here, I've got an appointment in Baltimore."

The agent walked slowly toward him. "I'm sorry, sir. No one's allowed to leave the camp right now."

"Why the hell not? I told you, I've got a meeting." David walked toward the agent, trying to keep him away from his car. But the man brushed past David as if he weren't there and peered into the interior of David's car. David winced as the man opened one of the back doors and bent over to look inside.

A beat passed and another. David started breathing again, shallowly. He walked close behind the agent and looked over his shoulder at the empty backseat of the car. David felt hallucinatory. Then he noticed that the far door of the car wasn't quite closed all the way. He stared wildly around and saw Randy McPherson disappearing around the corner of the guard shack. Now Randy was outside the camp and David was trapped inside.

"Would you mind opening the trunk, sir?"

David did so, revealing a wide and spacious but typically nearly empty rental car trunk. But the Secret Service agent didn't take anything at face value. He leaned into the interior, trying to pull up the carpet. Standing beside him, looking over the car, David saw Randy McPherson standing in the road, making a "hurry up" gesture at David. David waved him away and Randy moved back behind some bushes on the far side of the road. But he wasn't far away and to David's eye remained visible. David gestured urgently for the boy to get away.

Back at the main cabin area of the camp, a horn like a fire alarm began to blare. The agent came out of the trunk of the car fast. He whipped out a digital phone or small walkie-talkie and made a quick call. Stepping away from David, he talked urgently into his phone. "I'm calling for backup," he concluded. He stared in the direction of the camp, obviously torn between conflicting duties.

"May I go now?" David asked politely but with impatience showing. "You've searched my car, you know I'm not taking anything out. The guard took my name and identification when I came in, you have all that."

The agent looked at David, then at the empty trunk. He seemed to want to be rid of the distraction of David's presence, but made the easy officious decision. "No, sir. I'd be grateful if you'd go back to camp and wait for just a few minutes."

David glared at the agent. Escape was just a few yards away, just past this man. The agent was distracted, now talking on his phone again. He wasn't paying attention to David, he obviously didn't take him seriously as a threat.

David slammed the trunk lid shut. "Fine," he snapped, got back in the driver's seat, and started the car. He turned in a tight circle and headed back into the camp, leaving Randy McPherson alone outside the gate.

David drove as fast as he dared back to the parking lot, thinking of the boy out there alone, wondering what he would do. Randy might just give up and come back into the camp. He might wander away into those woods and get genuinely lost. Parking the car, David got out and walked quickly away. He didn't run, that would make him a target. Quickly he walked back past the nurse's station and around it, toward the wooded area on the other side of the cabins. He went more or less the opposite direction from the camp's exit.

This camp was not a secure facility. Its grounds sprawled too extensively to be fenced or completely patrolled. David had checked the area early that morning before driving inside. He reached the woods, looked behind him, and saw no pursuit. Evidence of the agents' search for their charge was still obvious, but the boy was small and the camp contained lots and lots of places to search. An ideal place for a game of hide-and-seek, one that must be horribly frustrating for the Secret Service agents. He wondered how soon it would be before they brought in helicopters for an aerial search and scuba divers for the lake.

Once in the cover of the woods, David ran. If an agent saw him he might very well shoot the running man, but David felt relatively safe. The agents wouldn't yet have spread beyond the main grounds of the camp. They probably still thought Randy had just wandered away, because they knew they'd kept anyone from leaving the camp. At least by car and road. David ran. His breath came raggedly and his face grew very red. Back at home he jogged regularly, but this headlong flight through the woods was a different proposition, he thought stumbling over rocks and roots and occasionally being scratched by small branches. But he couldn't stop. It had been ten minutes since he'd left Randy alone. In that time the boy might have done any number of crazy things, including give himself up.

David reached the small road that circled the camp, but he was now on the far side of the guard shack, several hundred yards "upwind" of it, as he thought of it. He crossed the road cautiously, exposing himself to the view of anyone nearby, but he didn't see any traffic. In the distance, he heard the sound of at least one car motor.

Across the road he went back under cover, but the trees were much sparser on that far side, dwindling into brushy scrub near the road. David felt very visible in his businessman's suit, which had served him well for getting into the camp but now had become a liability. If he'd been prepared like a character in a movie he would now reverse the jacket revealing camouflage patterning and take up his disguise as a hunter.

But he did the best he could, crouching down and staying as much out of sight as possible. In a few minutes he came within sight of the gate. The black sedan still blocked the official exit. A second black car had joined it. Two agents stood just inside the camp in their black suits and matching sunglasses. They talked quietly, but turned at angles to each other so that they took in different areas of the landscape, and even behind their glasses David knew their eyes scanned constantly. He ducked even lower and pulled farther back, to where trees gave him more cover.

David began scanning himself, and stopping every minute or so to listen for the rustle of small feet. He even ventured two or three very soft calls of "Randy?" but got no response. Damn, what had happened to the boy?

Soon he reached the spot where he'd seen the boy slide back into these trees, but now he saw no sign of him. "Randy," he called a little more loudly, then dropped to the ground as he saw one of the Secret Service agents turn in his direction. David felt the man's gaze sweep through the woods. He *did* feel the gaze, like seeing a searchlight pass over his head. On his knees and elbows David crawled back deeper into the woods.

Stopping to catch his breath, he heard a small sound. It could have been made by an animal, a small injured one. David crept quietly back through the trees and saw a small sneakered foot behind a tall pine. Coming around the tree, David saw Randy McPherson sitting on the far side of it with his back to the trunk. He clutched the toy spaceship as if it were a stuffed animal and crooned to himself. Then he saw David's suit-clad legs and scrambled to his feet with a gasp. Even when he looked up and appeared to recognize David it took a moment for him to recover.

"I thought you'd left me. I thought you weren't coming back."

"No, Randy. This was the plan all along. I just didn't have time to tell you."

David knelt before the boy, which put their heads on an equal level, and without planning David put his arm around Randy's small shoulders. The boy stood stiffly, but after a few moments he leaned his head against David's shoulder.

"Come on," David said.

As they walked quickly through the woods away from the direction of camp, David wondered how many other Secret Service agents were in the vicinity. Probably not many. They'd all be in the camp. But he only had a very few minutes to get away from here before the place would be crawling with all kinds of cops. If anyone saw them, David might very well be shot before he had a chance to say anything. His heart raced. David still felt as if he were playing someone else's role. He would much rather have been in a courtroom.

A brisk ten minutes' walk through the woods brought them out to another road, just as narrow as the one that led past the camp and looking even less used. David stood craning his head in both directions. He thought this was the spot, but—

"What are you looking for?"

"Uh—" David finally saw a dull gleam of metal off to the left. He hurried Randy that way and found the narrow cul-de-sac where he'd stashed the other car. This car was a very different proposition from the shiny dark Lincoln David had driven into the camp. This one was a twenty-year-old Pontiac with rust spots on the hood and half the back bumper missing, bought for four hundred dollars cash at the only used-car lot in the vicinity. But it ran fine. Well, acceptably.

It had taken David much of the night to leave this car here and walk back into town to retrieve the much nicer rental car. But now the preparation had proven to be worth the trouble. David had feared getting the car trapped inside the camp once he grabbed Randy and the alarm sounded. He hadn't anticipated the rescue going just the way it had, but he had been prepared for the idea of having to leave the camp on foot.

"Get in." They opened the car's front doors with rusty squeaks. David turned the key. The old car's motor protested and coughed and died. Randy looked anxiously at David. The President's son had probably never laid eyes on a car in such a disreputable condition, let alone had to rely on one for transportation. David tried to smile reassuringly, waited a few seconds, and turned the key again. The engine caught, then abruptly cut off.

"Maybe we could go back and steal one of the agents' cars," Randy suggested. "Lots of times they leave the keys in the ignition, they don't—"

"Don't worry about it. I had a car just like this one in college. I know what it needs."

David pulled up hard on the gearshift lever on the steering wheel, holding the transmission more firmly in park. He did that with his left hand and with his right tried the key again. This time the engine started raggedly, then gained confidence as David gave it more gas.

The engine roared and David smiled at Randy, who gave him a thumbs-up sign and a brave smile.

"Now let's see if this will get us to a train station," David said. The car lurched forward. Randy grinned as he bounced on the old springs inside the seat. "I've got to get you to your mother," David added to reassure him.

But Randy didn't need reassurance. He nodded eagerly, sure it would happen. "Do they have her someplace too?"

The boy was sharp as hell, he had a good idea of what was going on, working from very little information. "Don't worry," David said obliquely, "we're getting her out too."

"I hope whoever went to do that is as good as you are."

David couldn't help smiling at the compliment. "She's much better," he said confidently. "She won't have any problems."

Then he took Helen Wills's advice and drove like hell.

Wilson Boswell quickly realized that John McPherson had a secret, one he was dying to share with the tycoon. Boswell kept steering the conversation in other directions, while covertly goading the President.

"How do you like this technology, sir? Quite on the cutting edge. In fact, my research people tell me they think it will literally be the last word in communications once it's developed fully. It's as close as two people can come to being in the same room without actually being there. I don't see how that could be improved upon."

President McPherson's image shimmered a bit on the thin, invisible screen in Boswell's office, but Boswell still saw the President's smirk. Boswell kept his own secret. He had cultivated this relationship a long time, almost ten years, since John McPherson had been a freshman Senator from Texas. McPherson had a business record that looked good on paper, but Wilson Boswell had studied that record and found a history of failure. McPherson could start a business, and find funding for it, but none of the businesses lasted long. Luckily for John McPherson, he had always been clever enough to bail out before the crash. A salesman who could sell the product but not keep an enterprise going had turned out to be a natural for politics.

Senator McPherson had been flattered when Wilson Boswell had occasionally shared with him the direction of TitanWorks's notoriously secret research. Once McPherson had become President, he had been in a position to reciprocate. He'd been sparing with details, of course, and Boswell had had to draw him out with subtle observations rather than direct questions. But John McPherson had already begun to look toward the future, and that helped immensely.

The trappings of the presidency are heady and addictive. After less than a year in office McPherson had reveled in them. How incredibly unfair to give a man all this for four years or eight and then jerk him abruptly away. Very shortsighted, Wilson Boswell had said sympathetically. But then he'd begun to show McPherson how he could achieve even greater power post-presidency in the business world. That is, if he had a partner.

They kept their friendship very, very quiet—no golf outings, no lunches in the Oval Office. John McPherson's Republican reputation for uprightness, along with the death of the independent counsel law, had deflected scrutiny. In a nation grown weary of scandal, no one really wanted to investigate a President who seemed such a staunch, secure family man. This atmosphere had allowed the exchange of secrets between Boswell and McPherson to begin.

Wouldn't it be something if one of these viruses that break into people's E-mails and eat them all could in fact be programmed not to destroy the information but to send it elsewhere?" Boswell said once, as if mulling ideas. "I offer you that one for free, Mr. President. Seems like an idea the C.I.A. might be interested in."

After a long moment McPherson answered quietly, "Actually, I think they already are."

Boswell let the subject drop, feeling McPherson's desire never to be one-upped. Months later he said, "My people are having some problems with that capturing-and-sending E-mails idea."

"Mine are too," the President said.

Boswell mused, "Wouldn't it be nice if they were different problems. If—"

McPherson had no trouble keeping up. "If my people had already solved your people's problems and vice versa."

"We can't share," Boswell said as if admonishing himself.

"No."

"Not with our people, at any rate."

The two men looked at each other through the electronic void that bound them. They understood. Teams from the government and TitanWorks could not be combined, but two men alone who shared the similar fields of knowledge would have a wonderful leverage. And the means of a flourishing business partnership.

Shortly afterward, very quietly, the sharing began. To make the exchanges easier, Angela Vortiz came to work in the White House. She had a job title and description, but most importantly served as liaison between Boswell and John McPherson.

"Of course, there are some things I can't share with you," the President said.

"I understand your position, Mr. President." Wilson Boswell spoke acquiescently, secretly amused by McPherson's transparent smugness. The jolliest part of the whole enterprise for Boswell was McPherson's lack of understanding of their relationship. Boswell didn't just have the highest source possible for governmental secrets. He had the President of the United States in his hands.

"I have something to share with you the next time we meet," Boswell said. "Something that would make a good fit with the project we've discussed."

McPherson looked curious, leaning forward at his desk. "Well, as a matter of fact . . ." he began, then stopped himself. He seemed to glance past Boswell's shoulder. Obviously an aide had entered the Oval Office. Boswell remained silent as the President listened to someone else and frowned. What was that about?

When he had McPherson's attention again, Boswell asked casually, "How's Angela working out for you?"

"Just fine," McPherson said, still distracted. "She's on a special assignment now. I'm sorry, Wilson, I've got to run."

"Of course, sir." The President's image shredded and vanished, leaving Boswell alone and pondering. What kind of special assignment would McPherson give Angela, and why hadn't Boswell already heard about it?

He heard a disturbance in the hall and frowned in irritation. Was Larsen causing trouble again?

It seemed all Wilson Boswell's employees were becoming troublesome today.

Angela Vortiz looked calmly at the First Lady in a proprietary way, as if at a painting she had painted herself. "Those Valium-Prozac-Lithium cocktails are great, aren't they? I'd almost like to try one myself. Sometimes they screw up the dosage, though, and end up doing permanent brain damage."

Myra McPherson, sitting up looking dreamy-eyed, smiled the prettiest, most relaxed smile Helen had ever seen on her face. She looked extremely pleased, as if Angela had complimented her.

The nurse, standing between Helen and Angela and looking back and forth between them, obviously decided she no longer wished to be involved. She walked out of the room, probably to call one or more of the other agents. Helen was their colleague, but they might have been warned against her. Angela certainly would warn them in a few moments.

Helen wondered what she had wondered before: how much authority did Angela Vortiz really have, and what was its source? She didn't appear in the Secret Service chain of command, but everyone knew that sometimes when she spoke it was in the President's voice. But did she really command here? Would these professional, thoroughly trained agents do what she said, even if it meant turning against one of their own?

Helen would probably find out in the next few minutes.

In a clash of credibility between Helen and Angela, the other agents might wonder why, if Helen had really been sent here by legitimate authority as she claimed, she looked as if she'd crawled through mud to reach this cottage.

There'd be no contest of credibility, not once the other agents saw the videotape of Helen's arrival, assuming they hadn't already.

She looked again at Myra McPherson and saw that she would be no help. In fact, she would be a heavy burden. The First Lady struggled to get out of the bed, reaching her toes down toward the floor as if it were far away, and giggling at her own helplessness.

These twin worries suddenly coalesced in Helen's mind. Her hands grew steady again.

With sudden speed, Helen lashed out, her left foot slamming into the side of Angela Vortiz's head. Angela's head snapped back and before she could recover Helen kicked her in the stomach. As Angela bent over, Helen brought both fists clenched together down on the back of her head.

As Angela slumped to the floor, Helen moved quickly. She pulled a knife from her pocket, slashed the thin wire screen over one window, then picked up the room's decorative, spindly desk chair, and smashed it through the window. The chair's legs broke. Helen dropped the pieces to the floor and turned toward the First Lady, who gaped at her but didn't appear unpleased by the turn of events.

Helen screamed, "Intruder! Intruder!" Before the word was out of her throat for the second time she leaped at the First Lady, first driving her back onto the bed, then down onto the floor. Helen lay full-length atop her, covering Myra McPherson's body with her own.

A moment later Roger Enriquez, the agent-in-charge, burst through the hallway door, gun drawn. He scowled fiercely as his pistol moved in a fast but deliberate half circle, looking for a target, while his eyes took in the sight of the three women down on the floor. Helen's back muscles tensed as she anticipated a shot.

It didn't come. After a moment Helen lifted her head. "Intruder," she said more quietly. "He came in from the hallway and knocked out Angela when she tried to stop him."

"And what did you do?" Roger asked angrily.

"I did my job, damn it." Helen indicated the prone First Lady. "I covered the target."

Roger's face changed. "Sorry, Helen."

A voice from the hall called, "Friendly coming," and a moment later two more agents came into the room quickly. The agent-in-charge ran to the shattered window. Cautiously, he looked out, made sure no one lurked on either side outside, then leaned farther out to call to the agent stationed in the woods. "Herbert! Come in!"

Then he snapped out, "What did he look like?"

"Slender build," Helen answered just as quickly. "Anglo man wearing a brown jacket and a black stocking cap. Young, I'd say. He moved real fast."

"Did he go out this window?"

"I think so. I was covering Lady Dove. That's when I heard the crash."

"Damn it, where's Herbert? Did he get him? Thompson, out the back way and around. Call for support. Let's move, damn it."

Helen rose slowly to her feet, remaining between the First Lady and everyone else in the room. She put a hand on Myra McPherson both to reassure her and to keep her down. The First Lady glanced up, showing some alarm but still with that relentless, eerie serenity.

"Let's go!" Roger Enriquez said again. He took a moment to stare at Helen. "This room is breached," he said. "Get her out of here."

Luckily for Helen, these agents were trained to react, not to investigate. Roger wouldn't take the time to disbelieve Helen's story, not if there was any possibility of danger to the First Lady. In crisis he reverted to procedure. Roger knew as well as anyone of Helen's loyalty to Myra McPherson.

"Yes, sir," Helen snapped out, reaching to help the First Lady to her feet. Getting her out of here was exactly what she intended to do.

The agents scattered quickly to tasks they didn't have to be assigned. Two scoured the other rooms of the cottage to make sure the intruder or a partner didn't remain hidden here. After Enriquez had thoroughly searched the room across the hall he nodded Helen into it. She guided the First Lady, covering her as well, brought her into the room, and closed the door. This was the room where they should have had her all along, an interior sitting room with no windows. At the moment it served effectively as a cell as well. The only way out was through the door they'd entered, back into the hallway. Helen heard feet moving out there. Two agents would have taken off into the woods. More would be on their way. The second shift would be awakened, agents scattered around the camp put on alert and called in closer.

Helen turned to her charge and felt discouraged. Myra McPherson stood where Helen had left her. No one had given her direction, so she remained immobile. Helen stood directly in front of her, held the First Lady by her upper arms, and stared into her eyes.

"Mrs. McPherson. Myra. Do you know where you are?"

The First Lady stared dreamily at her, waiting for a hint, or perhaps not hearing the question at all.

"We've got to get you out of here. We've got to find Randy. Remember Randy?"

Something stirred in the First Lady's eyes, the first sign that Myra McPherson might still be alive in there, trapped and struggling to rejoin humanity. She lost her dreamy smile.

"Randy," Helen repeated. "Your son. Do you remember Randy?" She felt as if she were torturing her charge, because every time she said the name, Myra McPherson winced slightly. She obviously struggled to regain comprehension.

"Randy. Can you go to him? Do you want to find Randy?"

After a long moment the First Lady nodded slowly.

Helen opened the hall door and found an agent standing just across the hallway, positioned so he could look toward the entrance of the cottage to his left and the back way out to his right, but he had to keep turning to look into the room where Helen had first found Mrs. McPherson, as well. He whirled, startled.

Helen said quickly, "That window worries me. Is it resecured?"

"Not yet, we haven't had the time." This agent was young, the newest on the team. Ordinarily he was the most human of the bunch, smiling quietly at times and even seeming to hear speeches made in his presence. His blue eyes could soften. But now he looked intensely concerned, as if he had made a mistake.

"I think the intruder may be on videotape in that next room. Maybe we can broadcast a still photo of him if you can isolate it. Did you hear the description?"

"Yes, but shouldn't—"

"Can you review the tape while keeping an eye on that window at the same time?"

"Sure. But—"

"Don't worry, I'm going to call someone else in to watch the doors. And I'm not going to leave her alone." Helen held up her phone. "Get on with it. Fast forward the tape. Find him."

The agent stopped resisting. Helen had seniority on him, he probably felt relieved to be given orders. He turned and strode into the small office off the bedroom. Helen noticed Angela Vortiz still lying on the floor. No one had had time to deal with her. Angela stirred and moaned. Another reason to hurry.

Quickly Helen went back into the room and said to the First Lady, "Just keep walking. No matter what anybody says, walk out the back door to the outside. Understand? Randy's out there. We've got to go find Randy."

"Is he . . . all right?" Myra McPherson asked slowly. The short sentence obviously required a great effort on her part. Helen knew that only the thought of her son could penetrate the fog through which the First Lady stumbled.

"I don't know," Helen said, feeling cruel. "We've got to go help him. Help Randy. Understand. You have to walk outside to help Randy."

The First Lady nodded. She had lost the dreamy look for good now. She walked slowly but with gathering sureness, behind Helen out the door of the room and down the hall toward the back of the cottage.

The agent stationed at that back door, Bob Herbert, watched them come with alarm registering clearly on his broad face. Bob, whose skin and hair both carried a reddish tinge, had played tight end for Notre Dame in college. Everything about him was broad: his twice-broken nose, his shoulders, his hands. He looked like a wall, nearly filling the doorway through which Helen needed to leave.

"What are you doing bringing her out?" he said harshly.

"This place isn't safe anymore," Helen answered. "I'm taking her away. It's okay, I've checked with Roger. He's going to cover us."

"I just talked to him, he didn't say anything."

"Plans change. Who's out there?" She gestured toward the outdoors. Bob Herbert turned quickly as if Helen had suggested invaders. Helen drew him aside as if to confer. Bob, a tall man accustomed to dealing with the shorter world, leaned down close to her, while keeping his eyes fixed through the open doorway. "I mean from our team," Helen continued. "Is it Johnson or . . . ?"

"Yeah, Johnson. He and Pinelli have the perimeter. What the hell!!"

As Helen had drawn Bob Herbert out of the open doorway, Myra McPherson had continued walking in her tottering way. She went straight out the open door. Seeing the First Lady exiting the building unprotected in that situation drove the Secret Service agent crazy with panic. He lunged after her.

Helen lunged as well. "Sorry, Bob," she muttered, and popped him just behind and above the right ear with the barrel of her pistol. She tried not to do it hard, but thoroughly. She acted in a much more restrained way than she had with Angela Vortiz, feeling terribly guilty, but she did the job. Bob Herbert fell to his hands and knees, dazed rather than completely unconscious. Quickly Helen grabbed his gun, kicked his supporting arm out from under him, and saw him topple as she hurried after the First Lady.

She heard sudden activity from the woods and the house, and sensed people converging on them, but Mrs. McPherson finally seemed to understand the urgency of the situation as well and moved faster. Only the thought of her son could have motivated her. Myra struggled in a lurching run. Helen caught her arm and hurried her along to the outbuilding she'd entered earlier. She got the First Lady into the backseat of one of the two cars inside the building, then flung open the garage door. Then she jumped into the driver's seat of the car, taking out of her pocket the keys she'd taken from this car earlier. The car, one of the best serviced in the world, started at once. Helen took off. Before she reached the road to the back way out of the treatment center, she saw five agents coming toward her from different directions. Three of them talked into their phones. Two veered off and headed back to the garage. Good. Because Helen had the keys to that car in her pocket as well.

They would have other cars nearby. Soon a fleet would be after her. Maybe there would be a roadblock up ahead. Helen's only hope was that when the agents checked with the White House, the President would want the search for the First Lady toned down and kept quiet. Having her found would require explanations of where she'd been, and why.

Helen felt like a traitor, and with good reason. Those were her colleagues she'd just duped. Only someone they trusted, like Helen, could have pulled this off. She had just smashed her career to pieces. For the rest of her life, no matter how long or short or how much of it was spent in prison or free, she would bear the awful title "rogue agent."

But she had done what she had to do. She looked in the rearview mirror at the First Lady. Mrs. McPherson peered ahead. She had regained the vertical crease between her eyes that she had perpetually worn in private life. The drugs weren't wearing off, but the First Lady fought them. Concern for her son gradually overcame her relaxed state of mind.

Helen felt guilty about that, too.

★ John McPherson, President of the United States, stood by his desk in the Oval Office talking on the phone. Subordinates knew that when McPherson stood at the desk he was both angry and anxious. Standing meant restlessness: the President wanted to bolt from the room and take some action himself, not just issue orders.

"No, I *don't* want state troopers alerted. No, I *don't* want roadblocks put up. I want them found, I want them rescued from these insane people, but I want it done quietly. Understand? Don't we have the people to do that? Well, find some!"

He slammed down the phone. "Can you believe these people? My wife and son snatched from under their noses! Are these professionals? How long have they been doing this?"

The man addressed by the President, Burton Leemis, sat on one of the sofas across the room and didn't answer. But to himself the President's lawyer thought, the "kidnappers" undoubtedly couldn't have pulled off these snatches without considerable help from the "victims" themselves.

Burton Leemis, the President's personal attorney, was one of maybe half a dozen people on earth who knew how unhappy life in the White House made Myra McPherson, and the lengths to which she might go to escape. When one spent private time with the family as Leemis occasionally did, her unhappiness was obvious. Besides, the President had confided in his attorney, seeking advice on preemptive damage control.

Leemis came from a wealthy Boston family—not on a par with the Kennedys, it was understood, but no one in the family ever needed to work again, either—who had given him an excellent education, an impenetrable self-confidence, and the deep, unspoken conviction that he was superior socially and intellectually to anyone he might meet. This attitude could make Burton Leemis intolerable at times, but it also allowed him to be exceedingly cordial to all his inferiors, including judges and Senators.

He was a man in his mid-forties, of average height and some girth, which he carried like his other birthrights, at perfect ease with himself. His head was slightly oversized, making him appear dominant and thoughtful. Leemis sat at ease on the sofa and took in the President's outburst placidly.

"Is Angela all right?" he asked.

The President's frown deepened. One reason for his grumpiness was the absence of his most valued employee. "She's fine. Just mad as hell. She asked me if she can have a few moments in private with Helen Wills once we catch her."

"In a soundproofed room, I imagine. May I make what may seem an unusual suggestion?"

The President turned toward his adviser with slight surprise, imagining that Leemis was about to comment on McPherson's private life. "Of course," he said warningly.

"Leak this story to the *Times*."

John McPherson barked out a laugh, his only answer.

"No, I'm serious," Leemis continued, rising to his feet. "On deep background, off the record, to a reporter with whom I happen to be friendly. Let him know that the First Lady has been receiving treatment at a very private facility. Treatment for depression and—well, I can drop the hint about more serious mental irregularities."

"Why?"

"Preparing them in case she does go public with her story. We'll have already planted the seeds to discredit her. Of course, I'll be saying these things out of a deep concern for Mrs. McPherson, who is obviously under an enormous strain and is not quite strong enough to handle it. It's amazing that she's done as well as she has, given her . . . background."

McPherson realized that Leemis was rehearsing his covert speech to the reporter. For the first time in two days, the President smiled. "Do what you think best, Burt."

Leemis heard dismissal and turned away. "You know I always do, Mr. President. Have a nice day."

Leemis had done his work for the day. As for the rest of what the President might do, his lawyer didn't want to know.

John McPherson stood beside the desk a few moments longer, then slumped into the chair, swiveling it to stare out the tall windows. For a few seconds he remembered the early days of his presidency, when smaller Randy had wandered at will around this office. McPherson wondered where in that wide world his son might be, and in whose care.

But he had work to do. He picked up the phone and got started.

Reality bit. For Larsen, real life had long held no savor, no surprise. Like many another geek before him, he had gotten heavily involved in games in his teens. He had conquered earth, space, hordes of alien invaders, and mystic warriors. He had turned naturally to designing games himself, which was better, but still ultimately unsatisfying. At some point you turned off the screen or put away the Game Boy and walked out into the same boring world.

So after two years at TitanWorks, he'd begun developing the blended reality helmet. Also a nightlife. The helmet made things better, placing such creatures as samurai security guards into Larsen's own world. He defeated them, his day improved in excitement, and no one was harmed. Sure, other employees complained about his games intruding into their work spaces, but it had been a long time since Larsen had worried about what other people thought—or even whether they existed.

Standing in the middle of his cubicle, he completed a game of Street Smarts, in which a typical suburban world—mall, high school, day-care center—had been turned into a death trap by invading magical forces. Larsen roamed through the day-care center trying to rescue children, which made his skin crawl. Children were the worst. Kill one by mistake and the point loss would probably be enough to kill your whole game. On the other hand, children were the same size as trolls, which could be masquerading inside any of them. You couldn't turn your back on the little bastards.

He turned a corner and suddenly a cascade of toddlers dropped atop him. Larsen screamed and tried to fend them off. He tried to be careful, but his sword knicked one of their little legs. The child didn't even cry. And the leg oozed something bright green. Ah ha. Relieved, Larsen swung the sword in a broad swath, lopping off three of their little heads. Demons emerged and died. He continued flailing away, but when his sword bit into the neck of the last kid, a sweet-faced three-year-old boy with blue eyes, red blood gushed. Gurgling, the child fell stricken.

The game went black. Larsen pulled off the helmet. "Darn," he said.

A coworker stared at him. A screen had been showing what Larsen saw through the helmet. The man looked horrified. "We can't market something like that. Killing babies, for God's sake. And the high school part of it. Have you heard of—"

"Go to hell," Larsen said. "What do you know? You're like thirty-five years old. Go to a retirement home."

The man started to answer, but Larsen looked at him speculatively, still holding the game controller, and the man changed his mind and left.

Yeah, the helmet was pretty good, but still in the end insufficient. You killed trolls or guards or dragons, then took off the helmet and the world remained unchanged. Larsen always knew, even when most involved with the games, that the danger was fake. That world had lost any excitement for him.

But he'd corrected for this, by taking things to the logical next level. He turned to his computer and began looking up airline schedules.

As soon as Dennis Brin left the tunnel leading out of his flight home, he began to feel uneasy. He looked around the airport terminal, but saw no one. Brin hurried, looking around alertly. The young software designer looked bulky in his long army field jacket, but in fact he rode an exercise bicycle every day while watching videos and was in pretty good shape under the extra flesh he carried. His oversized carry-on bag bumped against his legs. Best way to carry secrets, he'd decided. Make them look unimportant.

He passed the metal detectors, going outside them, expecting to see someone holding a hand-lettered sign with his name on it or a discreet guard who would come up and take his arm. Neither happened. Brin picked up the pace even more, bypassing baggage claim. He had all his luggage in his hand.

Outside at the curb he felt reassured by the number of people waiting at this suburban Virginia airport. Cars lined the curb, people stood next to their suitcases, passengers got out of cars saying hurried good-byes. Brin didn't immediately see his ride, but felt comfortable in the crowd. The activity was familiar even if the individual people were not.

He turned right and walked along the sidewalk. His steps slowed as he passed a white Lincoln that looked vaguely familiar. Sure enough, as he stopped the driver emerged from the car and raised a hand. Brin nodded. So cool. The young geniuses who'd taken over such a large segment of the world economy at first had disdained fashion, displays of wealth, chauffeurs and limousines, all the traditional trappings of power. But by the twenty-first century they had discovered that those trappings could be fun. They were retro-cool, which was really fun to carry off, with the right blend of contempt and savoir faire. Brin secretly grinned at the driver in his cap and uniform jacket, and waited while the driver held the back door open for him. He settled in. The driver got behind the wheel and pulled away.

"I thought there was supposed to be a guard with you," Brin said.

"I dropped him off along the way," the driver said. He had a funny, adolescent sort of voice, as if it hadn't been used much since high school. "Didn't want to be conspicuous."

Dennis Brin didn't think he would make that conspicuous a figure, with or without a guard, but felt flattered. "I'm carrying some pretty important stuff here," he said.

The Lincoln pulled over to a curb near employee parking. They hadn't even left the airport complex yet. The driver turned in his seat and said, "Yeah? Like what?"

Dennis Brin went stiff. His right hand moved slowly inside his bulky jacket. "Listen, man, I'm packing."

The driver shook his head. "No, you're not. You went through metal detectors on the other end of your flight." Dennis froze, and the driver laughed. "Relax, I'm not after your stupid little secrets." He took off his driver's cap and his long blond hair fell down. He also removed his sunglasses and weird, pale, empty eyes stared at Brin. "You ripped me off, man," Larsen said.

Brin held out his hands. "No."

Larsen nodded. "Vault Keepers? Give me a break. How many times did you play CryptLords before you came up with that one?"

Brin shook his head. "We've all played all the games, you know that. Nothing's new. Nothing's completely . . ."

Larsen sat unmoved, staring at him as if Brin were a boring TV show and he were about to change the channel. Brin switched to a firmer tone. "This is for a court to decide."

Larsen shook his head. "Maybe if you'd stolen my car. But Crypt-Lords is part of my soul, man. It's my being in a box."

This sounded very strange delivered in Larsen's soulless mono-tone, as if his human elements really had gone missing. Brin reached for the door handle.

Larsen stopped him, not with a gun, but by showing him a small plastic box. "Here," he said.

Brin took the compact disk case Larsen handed over, not noticing that Larsen held the case by a corner.

"What is it?" Brin asked wonderingly, holding the case in both hands. No lettering told him anything about the contents. He tried to turn it over, but found he couldn't let go, as if magnetism bound him to the box.

"Super glue," Larsen said conversationally. He had turned away and now turned back, again wearing the driver's cap that hid his hair and the sunglasses that covered his eyes. He also wore a thick black mustache. And he had a pistol, a shiny silver automatic with a long barrel, like a Luger.

Brin screamed and lunged for the door. He had trouble working the handle with his hands effectively bound together, and expected to be shot as he fumbled, but somehow he got it open and fell out. He picked himself up from the pavement, kicked the car door shut, and ran back toward the terminal, awkwardly because he couldn't move his arms. Fifty yards away he saw people, some of them start-ing to stare in his direction.

Larsen stood up casually from the car. He waited, giving his prey a few more panicked steps, a little hope of escape. Then Larsen sighted along the roof of the car and fired.

His target only stumbled a little, as if frightened by the sound of the shot. Larsen knew better. He hadn't fired millions of rounds of bullets and torpedoes and rockets in his lifetime for nothing. Brin turned around and Larsen saw the bright blossom of blood that had torn open the front of Brin's shirt. The exit wound was bigger than the entrance wound, and centered deadly over the left side of the software designer's chest. Brin stared with a dead man's bafflement.

Larsen could have taken a finishing shot then, a head shot, but it would have spoiled the precision of the moment. Instead he tossed his gun down a nearby drainage opening, got casually into the car, and drove away. Behind him, people were running. Some kind of alarm would go off, noisy or silent. Security might halt traffic out of the airport. They would certainly put out an alert for this car. Larsen drove not for the exit but into the parking garage. He parked carefully in the long-term area, and when he emerged he had left behind the driver's cap and uniform jacket. He wore jeans and tennis shoes and carried his virtual reality headgear. Ambling slowly along, he emerged from the garage and seemed oblivous to the excitement around him.

But inside he relished it. This was why this game was better than any one he or any other designer had invented. Because the game didn't stop. Not once he'd gotten his target, not after he got away from here, not even when he slept. The whole background level of his life had been raised a notch or two, and would stay that way.

Larsen joined a crowd saying, "What happened? What's going on? Are flights canceled?" After a while he took a cab back to his car.

On her return trip to the White House, Angela Vortiz stopped at company headquarters to meet with her real boss. In her own way Angela was a people person; she liked face-to-face meetings. Her boss Wilson Boswell did very well at pretending to like people when the occasion called for it, but he genuinely respected Angela. She had a set of qualities, including both an earthy gregariousness and a deep coldness at the core of her character, that could not be reproduced easily. Unlike a software designer, Angela couldn't be replaced.

They strolled the grounds of the TitanWorks "campus," located in semirural Maryland, thirty miles from Baltimore. The campus contained a dozen buildings, none of them taller than two stories and all designed to blend into the pastoral landscape rather than dominate it. At one point the administration had even experimented with having sheep on the grounds, but soon a majority of employees agreed that sheep were rather dirty, unpleasant animals. One designer had offered to create virtual sheep that would be clean and even-tempered, but instead they just let squirrels and sparrows suffice for livestock.

Ideal for strolling and musing, the TitanWorks grounds featured pleasant curving pathways between the buildings. The paths passed under trees where the builder had planted benches and ornamental boulders designed for sitting, to encourage employees to take breaks in their work and chat with each other, which often produced better ideas than desk-bound isolation did. Boswell and Angela took over one such shady nook. She sat, leaning back and stretching out her long legs. Boswell sat next to her. For a moment he studied Angela. She seemed none the worse for her brief fight with Helen Wills and lapse into unconsciousness. Angela looked her usual languid self, though when Boswell had asked her about the encounter with Helen, Angela's eyes had flashed in a manner that belied her apparent ease.

"What's McPherson doing about these escapes?" Boswell asked.

"Having them hunted, but as quietly as possible. He wants to avoid headlines."

"And does he know who took them?"

"Well of course, Helen and that lawyer Mrs. McPherson saw in San Antonio. We were very surprised the lawyer did it himself; we weren't prepared for that. We thought he'd hire somebody. Of course, the White House wasn't able to brief the Secret Service agents too thoroughly, because they weren't in on the secret."

Boswell nodded impatiently. Angela fell silent, after giving him one sharp sidelong glance and then a smile.

Wilson Boswell wished his own employees—no, everyone on earth, come to think of it—already had those transmitters implanted in their throats. The President had shared news of that technology with him, unable to keep it to himself any longer. Other Presidents might have shared such things with their wives or very close friends. John McPherson only had Boswell. McPherson's greatest pleasure seemed to be impressing Boswell, and Boswell let him from time to time. "Hmm," he had said. "Interesting possibilities." He had seen more of those possibilities than the President had. For example, subvocalizations, those unhearable remarks that people make to themselves, below the level of speech, even below consciousness. If Boswell could pick up those, he would almost be able to read the minds of people around him. From reading to controlling would be only a small step.

What Boswell would have liked to learn from a perusal of Angela Vortiz's mind was how genuinely attached to John McPherson Angela had become. The idea didn't worry the tycoon, though. Angela's emotions were like his own, shallow and easily subdued. Boswell didn't doubt her essential loyalty to herself, and therefore to him. Angela knew where her interests lay.

"And what does he plan to do if he does find them quietly?" Boswell asked.

"Try again. Probably send his wife back to that treatment facility, see if he can change her mind. Literally."

"That's what I thought. There is no plan. Either turn the First Lady into a zombie, which people are bound to notice, or go on living with the possibility that she'll go through with this stupid divorce business. And we can't have that."

Angela shifted on the bench, stretching her black-clad legs and then her neck. She still felt a fragility after her encounter with Helen Wills, and Angela hated feeling soft. Her turn would come. She ventured an opinion. "I don't think McPherson knows how compromised he is, or how much his wife might know. Their marriage doesn't seem like much, but they have been together quite a while. He probably still feels deep down that she'll remain loyal to him."

"But you don't?"

Angela shook her head. "Not if she needs an advantage to get away."

"If she starts talking about what she thinks is wrong in the White House . . ."

"Can she really do that much damage? She must have told people already." Angela knew a little about the technology Boswell was developing, that would give him the capacity to eavesdrop on E-mail and mobile phone conversations. She had learned much on her own just by conveying messages between the President and her real boss.

"The longer I can hold off people finding out, the better," Boswell said determinedly. "I know the secret will leak out eventually. But before that happens I can learn an enormous amount about what my competitors are up to. They put everything into internal E-mails these days, thinking they're safe. One of them has a program that erases an E-mail after it's read, even if the recipient tries to save it. But I can capture those messages, too."

And not just his own industry, Boswell thought. Why limit himself? Some of his software competitors used their own operating systems rather than his. But in the world at large, TitanWorks dominated. He should be able to have a look at detailed memos from any other industry he might choose.

"Plus, if Mr. McPherson would stop being coy and give me the right access codes, I could see my whole file at the Justice Department," he said to Angela, implicitly giving her instructions.

"Would he really do that?"

"If it comes down to it, he won't have a choice. He's already so compromised he can't stop.

"That's the last piece I'm waiting for," Boswell continued, crossing his legs. "Do you know what one moment in time like that would be worth? To know what projects everyone in the business is pursuing, and how far along they are? To know what kind of case Justice has on me, what their evidence is? That moment would give me a head start on everybody that would be worth two years. Maybe more. I can't calculate the amount of the value." The true value for Wilson Boswell lay in the power of the information. He would be able to make his competitors feel nothing they did could be kept safe from him. He would break their spirits.

Also, of course, who knew what kind of blackmail material he might learn?

Angela played the skeptic. "But then when the story leaks out that people's E-mails are going other directions than what they planned, they'll discover your software did it. People will never trust another TitanWorks product again. Wouldn't that loss offset . . . ?"

"It won't be that simple. It'll happen as part of a virus sweeping the whole world, no one knowing its source. If I do it right, no one will even know their information's been stolen, they'll just think it's been destroyed. And by then I'll have planted so many false leads no one will be able to sort out the truth. I'll make it look as if we've been victims of the same scheme. There'll be too many fingers pointing too many directions.

"No. All I need is that one moment in time. Maybe a month to myself, undisturbed, after we have everything worked out. We can stave off Myra McPherson that long. We can keep her information from spreading." Boswell shook his tidy head disgustedly. "Why can't she just live in silent suffering like other First Ladies?"

"You know why. The boy."

Boswell nodded. Though he sat almost motionless, his mind raced. Human factors barely entered into the calculations he made. "Of course he's obviously the key to controlling her. Why can't McPherson see that? It would be so easy. Well, we've just got to find them."

"I can tell you as soon as they've been found, and then you can—"

Boswell shook his head. "No, I want to get to them first. In my way. I've got some people working on it, but I think it's time—"

Angela looked past Boswell and her eyes widened. "Not him."

"Yes, I'm afraid so."

Angela leaned forward and touched her boss's arm with obvious concern, even fright. "Wils, he can't be controlled. You surely can't be thinking of killing the First Lady of the United States. Even you—"

"No. But this lawyer's a different story. And that agent." He noticed Angela staring past him. "Is he coming?"

"Yes, and I'm going." Angela rose quickly to her feet, turning away.

"It's been lovely seeing you, dear," Boswell said languidly. "Take care."

Back still turned, Angela said, "Yes, sir." Then she walked away, hurriedly but with her hips canting back and forth to her internal rhythm. No man would ever know whether that walk of Angela's was deliberate or unconscious, because if a man was observing her Angela walked that way, for one reason or another.

She turned around the corner of a building as Boswell felt another presence come up behind him. He didn't blame Angela a bit for wanting to be gone when Larsen approached. Boswell hadn't sent for him, but he did need him. How did Larsen know these things?

Boswell had inherited Larsen, the skinny, antisocial game designer, when he'd taken over TitanWorks. Gradually, like everyone else who worked there, Boswell grew used to Larsen's rambling through the compound, always silent and apparently so deep in thought he didn't notice other people. But somehow Larsen learned things. One day two years ago he appeared in Boswell's private office and said abruptly, "You want to get an early look at that graphics design system IdeaMasters is working on."

"Well, of course," Boswell replied. "Wouldn't everybody?"

Larsen nodded. "I can get it for you."

Surprised, Boswell asked, "You have a friend over there?"

Larsen shook his head. Then he disappeared. Two days later he appeared in the office again and dropped a shiny CD-ROM on his boss's desk. "Have a look," he said.

It was the software system, still months away from market. Boswell had no idea how Larsen had gotten it, and Larsen never explained. There were rumors of a break-in of the car of one of IdeaMasters's designers. Security tightened throughout the industry. Boswell paid Larsen a bonus and waited for police to arrive, but they never did. He forgot about the incident.

The next one was much worse. Boswell was trying to hire away from a rival firm a very aggressive and brilliant young chief of production. They had two furtive meetings, Boswell even gave the young man a private tour of the TitanWorks facility and shared some of his ideas for expansion. Then instead of bolting from his own company, the chief of production stayed with his original company and began incorporating some of Boswell's management ideas into his own production system. Boswell felt outraged and humiliated. But when the other company even began developing a programming system that might challenge TitanWorks's near-monopolistic hold on software, Boswell grew enraged.

His desperation apparently called to Larsen, who appeared in his office one day, drifted through, and exchanged a long look with his boss. Neither said a word. But a week later the young rival chief of production had disappeared. This time rumors said something had frightened him and he'd taken his profits and moved his family to the Caribbean. Other rumors placed him at the bottom of Chesapeake Bay.

That time Boswell grew frightened. He lived with a force that was out of his control. He gave Larsen another bonus, not a huge one—he didn't want to encourage this sort of thing—and tried to keep his thoughts to himself. Larsen had become the son Boswell never wanted. Boswell couldn't have him arrested. Police would never believe Larsen hadn't been working under Boswell's orders. Boswell didn't dare fire Larsen, either, and risk his talking to people, or even coming after Boswell himself. Larsen didn't look dangerous, but his single-mindedness frightened even his formidable boss. The two were yoked together.

Larsen had midlevel skills as a game designer, he'd made some money for the company. His MonoMania game and the CryptLords series sold well, on the far fringe of the game business. Before his games could be released, other designers had to tone down the violence of Larsen's content and boost the reality level to make them marketable, though Boswell felt sure that these worlds of snarling demons and heads cut off over small insults *did* represent reality to Larsen. Boswell didn't like to use him, didn't even like having him around, but desperate times called for desperate measures, and there was no one else to whom he could give this particular assignment.

Larsen drifted up to the shady alcove where his boss waited.

Larsen looked like an overaged teenager, with his long arms, stringy blond hair, and bad complexion. He slumped like a teenaged boy, too, putting his hands in his pockets.

"You know the First Lady and her son are missing?"

"Mm huh," Larsen mumbled.

"I want to find them. At once. I don't want them hurt—understand that? that's very important—but I want to have them."

" 'Kay."

"There are two other people with them. I don't care about them." Boswell refused to be more explicit, but knew Larsen would take his point.

"Whatever," Larsen said, then grew, for him, very animated and chatty. "But I ain't no detective. How'm I supposed to find 'em?"

Boswell smiled confidentially. "The boy has a Lodestone in his pocket."

Larsen smiled too, which made his boss look away. "I guess that means you've heard of the Lodestone technology," Boswell said.

Larsen nodded. "The lab—" Boswell began, but Larsen was already walking away. He must know what to do. Wilson Boswell sat quietly. The older Boswell had grown, the fewer people he found worthy of being alive. But he still had some feelings, and the sense to mask his essential coldness. Larsen was from a similar mold, but the next version. He even frightened his boss.

David Owens arrived early at the mall in Rockville, Maryland, acutely aware of the fact that he had the kidnapped son of the President of the United States with him. David had had almost no sleep and no relaxation in the day since he'd rescued Randy. They'd managed to get away from the camp area, then onto a train, and in that way made their way close to the mall. But they could hardly sit in the ice cream store and wait for Helen Wills to come strolling up to them, First Lady in tow. David hated even driving this car in public. He'd used the majority of his remaining cash to buy another clunker.

Randy seemed blissfully unconcerned. He played with his Vibra-Wing, talked about how much he'd disliked the camp, and looked forward to seeing his mom. David had the feeling the boy would have prattled on in this same way whether anyone was with him or not. Randy seemed unconcerned about pursuit and could no longer be interested in the fugitive game, which left David to worry about what Randy might do as much as he worried about who might be getting close to finding them. Children were so damned needy and unpredictable.

Once on the train platform he had turned his back on Randy for a few seconds and almost lost him for good. He'd caught the boy just about to board the wrong train. Randy was, unfortunately, fearless. David feared he wouldn't stay put no matter how forcefully David warned him.

Nonetheless, he had to try. "Randy, I have to leave you in the car for a few minutes, all right? All right?"

"Okay," the boy said, not looking up.

"Listen, Randy, I have to go find the lady who knows where your mother is. Helen Wills, do you remember Helen?"

"Uh huh."

"Randy, you have to stay here. If you leave the car the bad men will find you and take you back to that camp or someplace worse and you won't get to see your mother."

"Couldn't you just come get me again?"

"Randy! Listen. We're almost there, give me a little cooperation, please. No, I couldn't come get you again, this time they'd guard you a lot better, they'd be ready for me."

"Yeah, but you'd have Mom with you. She could just say she'd come to pick me up."

Like all bright children, Randy was a master of logic. But his solutions didn't take into account information that David didn't want to share with him, such as that both Randy and his mother were fugitives from his father, among others. David started to describe the type of dungeon or fortress into which the bad guys would hurl Randy if they got him again, but David realized that Randy might find that prospect intriguing.

"Just stay here, Randy, please. Five minutes, okay? No more. Please. For your mother."

David got quickly out of the car, parked in the underground garage at one end of the mall. "Duck down," he said, and not receiving a reply just locked the doors and hurried away, muttering to himself.

His instructions from Helen had been very specific. He needed to find the women's shoe department in Nordstrom's. She'd picked a good time, after lunch and before the late afternoon after-work crowd. But the store was lightly populated at this time of day. That meant the salesclerks stood around bored, and all of them seemed to stare at him. He hunched his shoulders and looked downward, which made him appear even more suspicious. He needed instruction in this spy business. Helen would have told him to saunter and look people in the eyes. Then they'd pay no attention to him.

He headed up the escalator toward the women's shoe department, where he'd look like a bored husband waiting for his wife. That destination took him up two floors, making him aware of how far behind he'd left the first son. Randy would have grown bored by this time, be looking out the car window. The mall had a security patrol, in a car and on bicycles, and they wouldn't like seeing a child left alone in a car even if they didn't think him a kidnap victim. David's imagination painted all sorts of disastrous scenarios as he headed upstairs, making him walk faster up the moving stairs.

As David explored the store, he began to relax a little. The familiar surroundings comforted him. David had never been in this city before, and he was two thousand miles from home, but he knew this place: Mall-land. Anyone in America could find his way around here, even if everything outside was alien. It was as if David were a foreign visitor who had made his way to one of his nation's embassies, where everyone spoke his language and he knew the customs. He felt sure he could find a men's room or customer service blindfolded.

He could not, however, find Helen Wills. He looked at his watch. Two o'clock: he had come right on time. But Helen had probably expected to have some leeway in the time department, and David didn't feel he did, not with restless Randy waiting down in the parking garage.

He strolled over to men's wear, in sight of women's shoes, but where he would look less conspicuous, and browsed until he'd seen every item and been offered help by two different salespeople, but when he looked at his watch again ten minutes had passed and he'd seen no sign of a slender blond woman looking as if she'd recently kidnapped the First Lady of the United States.

It occurred to David that maybe she hadn't. He had been assuming that if he'd been successful at snatching Randy then surely Helen with her inside connections and superior abilities had been able to rescue Myra McPherson, but maybe he had had too much faith in Helen's powers. After all, it wouldn't be an easy rescue. Maybe the Secret Service had even moved the First Lady to a different location, maybe Helen's intelligence hadn't been so good after all. Maybe the fact that he'd seen no news coverage of a kidnapping of Myra McPherson meant there hadn't been one. Helen had tried and failed and the White House had quashed news of the attempt. Or Helen hadn't even gotten close enough to try.

If the latter had been the case Helen would probably have come here to meet David anyway and devise a new plan, but she might just as easily be in custody. In fact, under who knew what kind of pressure, she might have told authorities about her fellow conspirator.

David began to panic again. He shot glances at the salesclerks, an athletic-looking African-American man and a lithe, sharp-eyed Asian woman, and realized how inappropriate they looked to their supposed jobs. Weren't they watching him too closely just to be interested in his credit rating?

David felt watched by everyone. Even the fact that no one

accosted him seemed suspicious. Maybe they weren't closing in because they were waiting for him to lead them back to Randy. David stared all around him, didn't see anyone, and after that kept his head down. He headed back to the escalator, got off at the middle level this time, and hurried for the closest exit. He burst through the glass doors into the outdoors. The asphalt parking lot looked appealing to him: an urban man's idea of wide-open spaces. David walked quickly along the wall of the department store, looking for stairs down to the underground level. He heard footsteps but didn't look back.

He found stairs but waited a moment to see if he was being followed. If someone was, they hung back. David couldn't wait longer or be any more cunning than this, though. He had to find Randy. He bolted down the stairs, his feet only touching two or three of the steps, and ran through the underground parking. In the far corner of the underground garage he saw one of those security guards on a bicycle, coming slowly toward him. But David got to his car first. He looked in the back window, said, "Damn!" and unlocked the front door and wrenched it open.

The interior of the car sat empty.

David slammed his palm down on the roof of the car and said again, "Damn it!"

A hand grabbed his arm, a commanding voice said, "That's enough!"

Off balance, David felt himself spun around and pushed back against the car. He gasped, felt pressure in his chest as panic engulfed him, but at the same time a sense of hopelessness made him not even want to resist.

Then he released his pent-up breath so forcefully it sounded like a heavy sigh.

Helen Wills stood before him.

Her face was grim, making tight lines of her cheeks from her cheekbones to her chin. Authority made her look like the alpha prime version of an angry teacher. Helen raised her hand as if she would slap him.

David had never seen anyone so beautiful.

"Thank God," he breathed. Then he grew a little annoyed himself. "What were you doing, hiding from me?"

Exasperatedly, Helen explained, "I got there just as you bolted out of the men's department. You were going so fast I couldn't keep up with you. Then you were making such a spectacle of yourself I didn't *want* to get near you, I was afraid you'd get us both arrested. I stayed behind to make sure nobody was following you. What's your problem? What's the panic all about?"

David had begun to recover. "Gee, Helen, I can't imagine. Just mall phobia, I guess."

"Where's Randy? You didn't manage to get him, right?"

"As a matter of fact, I did. He was in this car ten minutes ago. But you didn't tell me that he can't be trusted. I was afraid he wouldn't stay put while I went to find you, and sure enough he didn't. Damn." David looked all around the underground parking garage and saw nothing like a small boy carrying a *Star Wars* toy.

"Check the trunk of the car," Helen said.

"What?"

"He does that sometimes, he thinks it's funny."

Staring at her as if she were trying to make a fool of him, David nevertheless walked to the back of the small blue car he was driving and opened its trunk.

Another empty space stared back at him.

Helen stood at his shoulder. "Huh," she said. "Well, he could've been there."

David slammed the trunk lid down. "Now what?"

Helen stared at him as if he were acting crazy. He might very well be. David felt as if events were driving him crazy. "Maybe you didn't get him at all," she said. "Maybe you're making up this story so you don't have to tell me how you screwed up."

"Right, Ms. Wills. I drove all the way to this damned mall to fool you with this idiot story, when you can very well check with the camp and find out the truth."

Casually, Helen said, "Actually, I've kind of burned my sources behind me, if you see what I mean. Come on, I want to go check on Mrs. McPherson. Drive us over there."

Helen walked around to the passenger side of the car, looked at David across the car's roof, and said loudly, "Randy, you'd better not be hiding under this car, because if you are you're about to get run over." She and David stared at each other with glimmers of hope. Then Helen suddenly dropped flat on the ground and looked under not only David's car but all the others nearby. She stood back up, looked ruefully at David, and shrugged.

He drove slowly away from the parking space, looking in the rearview mirror, hoping to see an eight-year-old boy come running after him, but saw nothing. Turning to Helen, he said, "So you did manage to get Mrs. McPherson."

"That's right," Helen said with a touch of smugness. "Kept her, too. Around that way."

She directed David through the underground parking area to a space as far from the department store as she could be, but not an isolated spot. He parked nearby, got out, and looked back. Far away, he could see the area where he'd parked, but still no sign of Randy.

David followed Helen to a dark green Ford Thunderbird. Helen glanced in the back window. "She's been sleeping a lot . . ." she began, then stopped.

"Now what? Don't tell me she's gone too." David hurried to look.

Helen opened the back door of the Thunderbird. Myra McPherson lay in the backseat, stretched full length, with a gentle, thoroughly contented smile on her face. Beside her, his mother's arm around him, lay Randy McPherson. The boy, explaining the intricacies of a new portal he had discovered in his Vibra-Wing spaceship, barely even glanced up at the other adults. He too looked content, in his busy, distracted way.

Helen turned to David, holding his arms. "You did get him," she said wonderingly. She stared at him searchingly but not in her glaring manner of the past. She seemed to be looking for something in him she hadn't expected to find.

"Didn't I say I did?"

She began a sentence and trailed off: "I was starting to wonder . . ."

"How you were going to pull all this off without a partner?"

"Yes."

David shrugged, to say, *Now you don't have to wonder.* Helen gave a small laugh. She turned back to Randy and asked casually, "How did you find Mommy, Randy?"

Equally casually, the boy said, "I watched out the window of my car while Mr. Owens went into the mall and a minute later I saw you going in after him, Ms. Wills. So I saw where you came from and I walked over here and found Mom. The hard part was getting her to unlock the car door. She seems kind of tired."

"Yes, she is, dear. Take care of her, okay?" Helen gently closed the car door so she could confer with David. "Now we just need to get quietly out of here. Maybe we should keep both cars for the time being. You could—"

"No," David said urgently. "I've been thinking about this. What we have to do now is go straight to the nearest television station and let Mrs. McPherson tell her story. That's the only way she'll be safe. Go public." David believed what he said, but fatigue also figured in his recommendation. He'd discovered in one day that he didn't like being a fugitive and had no talent for it. He wanted his life back, even the bizarre, twisted life that would result from being the First Lady's divorce lawyer.

Helen shook her head. "I want to get her someplace relatively safe first. This whole eastern seaboard area scares me. The White House has it too blanketed with their own connections. And even after she's had a press conference, if the Secret Service descends on her we won't get to her again."

David started to protest, but Helen continued. "Besides which, she's in no condition to talk to the press right now. She's still recovering from the drugs they pumped into her. If she goes public right now, she'll look crazy, and that's just what her husband would want. No, we have to stay in hiding for a few more days."

"Then we risk getting caught and never having the initiative again. I think—"

Helen said gently, "Until we get out of this, let me be the brains of the outfit, okay? You'll get your turn, I promise."

David acquiesced reluctantly. Helen saw his reluctance, but ignored it. "Come on, let's all go in this car, I've changed my mind."

David followed her to the deep green Thunderbird and settled deeply into its front passenger seat, which made the ride in the old clunker he'd bought seem like a night on the forest floor. "This is nice," he said admiringly. "How did you manage this?"

"Happened to come across it."

"Oh, my God, you're kidding."

"We're in my world now," Helen said grimly, settling behind the steering wheel. She glanced back at her peaceful charges and drove slowly out of the underground garage.

Helen didn't fear highways. She quickly found the interstate and headed south. "We're going to Washington?" David asked in some alarm. "I thought you said—"

"We're going to Texas. It's just a question of how to get there. They'll expect us to head west and then south, get away from this area as fast as possible. So I'm going the one direction they'd least expect, right into the jaws of the monster."

David didn't appreciate her metaphor, but kept quiet. He tried to take advantage of the fact that Helen was driving to relax, but couldn't. The past two days stayed with him in his shoulders and his neck and the slight tremble of his fingers. Helen seemed much more composed, as he would have expected. She appeared different than the other times he'd seen her. She wore a simple white blouse striped with blue, and navy blue slacks that didn't reach her ankles. White sandals left her feet oddly bare. David realized she was in disguise, dressed as a woman on a family trip. David still wore his suit pants and white shirt, looking as if he'd slept in them. He looked like the end of a terrible week at the office. David and Helen didn't match at all.

Quietly they told each other about their respective rescues. "Randy did most of the work," David said, glancing back at him. Randy still lay with his mother, the two of them murmuring together, Mrs. McPherson stroking her son's hair. Unselfconsciously, Randy touched his mother's cheek affectionately. They so obviously belonged together. Turning back to Helen, David continued, "If he'd been drugged like her when I found him I never would've gotten him out of there. I can't believe you managed it."

"It helped that most of them trusted me. Of course, they never will again."

David heard the loss in Helen's voice, and realized how much she had given up for this mission.

By the time they reached the Beltway around Washington dusk had fallen, turning quickly to full night. The city lit up.

"Look, Mom." In the backseat, Myra McPherson sat up for the first time. One arm around her, Randy pointed out landmarks. Helen drove closer to the part of the city Randy had always seen from his White House windows, as if deliberately taking a nostalgic farewell. The Capitol dome impressed David as always. No matter what anybody thought of the government or the present holders of political power, Washington's buildings were majestic.

David felt excluded as he realized the other three were saying silent good-byes. Their destination seemed obscure and distant, but at least David was headed toward home. The other three were leaving theirs.

Helen continued driving south, leaving the city behind.

They didn't stop until almost ten o'clock that night. When Helen did stop she chose a small, nonchain motel. "Wouldn't it be better to stay in some giant place where we'd stand out less?" David asked.

"Places like this are more likely to accept cash," Helen said. "Come on."

As they walked to the small office of the dozen-room motel, she asked, "How much cash do you have?"

"Well, I've got these." David showed a spread of credit cards.

"Forget those. We can't leave a trail. They'd be on us before morning. You remember I told you no cards?"

"Yes, but I had some unexpected expenses. I had to buy two cars and then abandon them. Didn't you take your own advice and bring cash?"

"There wasn't much time to prepare for this trip," Helen said shortly.

Between them they discovered they had less than three hundred dollars in cash. "Great," Helen said disgustedly. They would probably have gotten only one room anyway, but the shortness of money decided the issue. "Do you have a room with two double beds?" Helen asked the sleepy-looking young woman behind the desk inside the office.

"Of course," the clerk said, as if Helen had been trying to insult her establishment. The clerk didn't ask why a young couple needed two beds, or in fact even glance at Helen and David. In the motel business, clerkly curiosity quickly died. The young woman accepted forty dollars in cash for the room plus another fifty as a refundable deposit. The bills passing over the counter represented a sizable portion of their war fund. David and Helen looked at each other ruefully.

Back at the car, Helen said, "Let's get you two settled." She helped Mrs. McPherson out of the car and into the motel room, which turned out to be just that: a room. Not a particularly big room, either. It featured two double beds with worn-looking chenille bedspreads, a small nightstand with a lamp between the beds, and an old, scarred dresser on which a television rested. Randy turned it on and discovered to his disgust that it didn't have cable.

Helen had come better prepared than David, with a small suitcase containing clothes and pajamas for both Mrs. McPherson and

Randy. After a few minutes checking out the room, Helen said quietly to David, "Let's give them a little time alone."

Helen and David walked outside. The night air was very pleasant, especially after they'd spent all day in a car. Helen wanted to stretch her muscles as much as she wanted to give Myra and Randy some privacy. She lifted her arms toward the stars. Moving slowly so as not to startle her, David put his hands around her neck from behind and gave her a gentle massage. Helen accepted his touch for a minute before moving away. They walked to the motel's small pool and stood looking into it, both feeling the dislocation of life on the road.

They had been together for eight hours by this time, they had made a large variety of small talk, some plans for the near future, and had even talked a little about their own lives. Subconsciously, they had begun to feel the camaraderie of being pursued and on the same team.

Helen and David sat on lawn chairs that gave them a view of their room door.

"It seems like we might actually pull this off," David said.

"Maybe. There's still a long way to go, don't count out the White House." Helen thought she might have spoken too harshly and added, "If we make it, it'll be your turn. Do you feel up to it?"

"Sure. It won't be my first divorce."

Helen laughed shortly. "Oh, right. But there's never been one like this."

David shrugged. He stared thoughtfully at the motel room. "Randy's obviously real close to his mother. Sometimes you can see that so clearly, but getting it across to a jury is another story. Any picture you show them, any story you tell, you can see them thinking that maybe you concocted it just for the sake of the trial. It's a whole other world inside a courtroom." After a silent moment he added, "You know Randy didn't mention his father once yesterday or today? Didn't ask about him, didn't want to know if he was going to see him again."

"They're . . . not close."

David shook his head. "It's worse than that. It's like his father doesn't exist for Randy. You can tell a boy who hasn't been around his father much. I don't know how, but I can spot them."

Helen studied David in the starlight. His stare had lengthened, he seemed to be looking at something other than this tired little motel. "Can I ask you a question?"

David returned his attention to the conversation. "Sure, go ahead."

"Do you come from a broken home yourself?" Helen surprised herself by asking the question, especially in this old-fashioned phrase, but something in David's expression had prompted it. She felt curious.

David's face hardened. "Yeah."

"I'm sorry. So your parents got divorced?" Helen thought she had an insight into him.

"No. Cancer," David said abruptly. Then he stood up and walked away, around the pool.

Helen sat shaking her head at herself. Why did she want to get personal anyway? But now she felt responsible. She followed David and touched his shoulder. He stood looking off at nothing.

"I'm sorry for bringing it up."

"It's okay. It was a long time ago, I'm over it."

Helen had her own opinion about that, but didn't contradict. "Your father?" she asked gently.

David nodded. "He was only forty. He seemed old to me all my life, but now I realize he was young. And he really tried hard to leave me something. It must've been awful for him, but at the time I just resented him. He spent most of his time with me that last year. My father kept trying to pass on his learning to me. He'd give me all kinds of stupid advice like, 'If you beat an enemy, you've just made an even worse enemy. But if you turn your enemy into your friend, then you'll have a friend you can never really trust.' "

Helen burst out laughing.

Ruefully, David added, "He couldn't stay serious, even when he knew he was dying and was trying to leave me his wisdom." But his expression had softened. Helen realized he had just given away an important piece of himself, sharing his father's skewed wisdom that David had come to appreciate but had probably never passed on to anyone else, out of fear that it remained what he had called it: stupid. But he appeared to appreciate Helen's appreciation of the story. He no longer looked so bitter.

Helen remained amused. "Tell me another one."

David shrugged. "Once he told me, 'Son, I'd like to tell you I'll send you a message from the other side, but even if they've got a way to let you do that, I'll bet there's a pretty long waiting line.' "

Helen found this line much less funny and more poignant. She and David began to walk slowly around the pool, still watching the door of their motel room. David looked younger and younger as he talked, he almost began to resemble Randy McPherson. "My father knew he was dying for what seemed like a long time. So we had kind of a cram course in father-and-son. He spent as much time with me as he could, talking to me, giving me advice. It was a complete course in how to live, the condensed version. No time for recess. He never threw me a football."

Helen gripped his arm sympathetically. "How old were you?"

"When he started to die, or when he finished?"

"Jesus, don't be so tough. How old?"

In a softer voice, David said, "Twelve. Thirteen at the funeral."

After that he'd gone straight through school, college, and law school, on a very focused track that had only wandered aside when that first divorce case had come into his office.

David made a deliberate effort to rise from the somberness of the conversation. He hadn't talked about this in years, and hadn't intended to do so with this relative stranger. Being with Randy McPherson for two days had stirred the old memories. "Tomorrow night we'll delve into your childhood, okay? I realize you'll be hard put to top this, but make something up if you have to."

Helen remained caught in the implications of David's childhood trauma. "I guess now by contrast divorce doesn't seem all that bad to you."

David stared hard at her. "Man, you're good! You must've aced Psychology. Thank you, Helen Wills! Now I understand. Doctor, it's a miracle! I'm cured of being a divorce lawyer!"

"I didn't mean it like that." Deliberately and slowly, Helen gave him a hug. It seemed an awkward thing to do, and David didn't respond, but his anger did dissipate.

"Sorry. I'm not usually this sensitive."

"Yeah, you seemed pretty insensitive the first couple of times I saw you." Helen tried a joking tone.

"I'll try to get back there. Tomorrow it can be your turn to talk, okay?"

Helen replied with a sound that indicated the unlikelihood of her doing that. David had a sudden anxiety. "Don't tell me your father died young too," he said.

Helen walked on another step or two, then answered, "No, unfortunately." She said the last word so quietly David wasn't sure he'd heard right, and didn't want to pry. Helen obviously didn't want to discuss the subject.

They stayed outside another ten minutes, making the tiniest of small talk. With no one else stirring near the motel, the night began to seem very late.

They walked slowly back to their room, much more aware of each other than they'd been thirty minutes ago. Their shoulders brushed.

Inside the motel room, they found the TV on but both Myra McPherson and Randy asleep, huddled with their heads close together. Their obvious dependence on each other and affection gave both Helen and David a pang of loneliness. Then Helen turned off the television and David's eyes shifted to the empty double bed, noting its narrowness. Helen looked at him looking at the bed. David gave her a bright, blank smile that he tried to keep devoid of wiliness.

"I think a boy and his mother should stay together, don't you?"

"Dream on," Helen answered. Brushing past David, she picked up the sleeping boy and moved him to the other double bed. She straightened up and pointed down at the bed, assigning David his spot.

"You're so conventional," he said.

Helen went into the bathroom for several minutes. David didn't know what she wore when she emerged, because he was already in bed next to Randy, with the room lights off. Helen slipped into the other bed without a word. David lay on his back staring up into the darkness. He'd had very little sleep the night before, and a long day since, but he felt too edgy to sleep. Not a sound from Helen. Could she really drift off that easily?

David lay thinking about his father. For the first time in years he remembered earlier times, before that awful year and a half of enforced parenthood and impending death. He pictured his father as an ordinary man coming home from work looking tired but having time for a short game of catch. When David was Randy's age, eight years old, he'd had a good, ordinary life. His father had been special then not because he wasn't busy dying but because he wasn't home all that much, and he made sure to make time for David when he was. For the first time in a long time David remembered his father with unalloyed love. Which also meant he felt like crying, over everything he'd missed.

Randy had slowly but relentlessly burrowed closer to him. David felt the boy pressing into his side. He put his arm down around Randy. The boy had exasperated and alarmed David for the past two days, but he was a good kid, smart and quick and eager. Eager to make connections to other people, for one thing. Randy had spent a lot of time alone, even with lots of others close at hand. David imagined getting the President of the United States on the witness stand, and how he could take him apart. This boy deserved better than a President for a father.

★ The next morning they had a flat tire.

David woke to find that everyone else had preceded him into consciousness. Randy sat on the foot of the bed, dressed and watching *Sesame Street*. "The only other things on are news," he said over his shoulder.

Helen wore another touristlike outfit of white blouse and red shorts, and looked as if she'd been awake for hours. Even Myra McPherson moved around the room efficiently, apparently recovered from her drug treatments. "Good morning!" she said brightly to David, to which he mumbled a reply.

David wore only his underwear, which had seemed all right last night in the darkness but now made his passage from the bed to the bathroom very awkward. He scuttled out from under the covers, grabbed up his pants, and held them in front of him as he quickly crossed the room. But when he'd almost reached the bathroom door, Myra turned from the closet and stopped him with a big smile.

"Thank you so much," she said. "I couldn't appreciate before what you'd done, but now I find it simply amazing that you would do so much for us. Risking your life for strangers, really."

"Oh, you're welcome," David said inadequately, both flattered and cowed by her enthusiasm.

Myra opened her arms wide. "I have to," she said simply. She stepped toward David, then looked down and noticed for the first time that he was almost unclothed. "Oh." David felt himself beginning to blush. Then the First Lady smiled, shrugged, said, "Oh, well," and hugged him anyway. David stood with his body clenched, holding his pants between them.

"Thank you again," she murmured in his ear, arms around his back. She had a soft scent and smooth arms. David became aware that Myra McPherson was an attractive woman only a few years older than himself. Myra seemed aware of him too, in a way indicating more than gratitude. Behind the First Lady, Helen looked at David ironically. He finally escaped into the bathroom.

He emerged showered but still wearing his tired old suit pants. At least he had a fresh shirt he'd brought along on the rescue mission, but he felt far from his most presentable.

"Now let's get out of here," Helen said, as if launching a mission.

She had David stand by the window looking out while she opened the door with great caution. She poked her head out, looked over the entire uncluttered view of the motel parking lot, then motioned David to accompany her outside.

Everything seemed ordinary. The morning had not yet reached eight o'clock, and felt fresh and still cool. David breathed deeply.

He walked around the car feeling good, then lost that mood suddenly. "Oh, hell, we've got a flat tire."

Helen went on alert. She took an even harder look around the landscape, but nothing stirred. She bent over very suddenly to peer under the car. Apparently satisfied, she reached into her pocket and tossed the car keys to David. "Fix it, will you?"

"Great." David lay the suit jacket he'd been carrying on the roof of the car and went back to the trunk muttering angrily. He hadn't changed a tire in years and didn't like a day that started with such an omen.

Still talking under his breath, he opened the trunk of the car, already bending to find the tire compartment.

An enormous silver automatic pistol came toward his face.

David didn't react quietly, as if this were an ordinary part of his daily experience. He leaped back, screamed, and threw his hands up. The man holding the gun said commandingly, "Shut up!" David obeyed. The skinny gunman with stringy blond hair started to climb out of the trunk. "Where are they?" he said in the same tone of voice.

David involuntarily looked toward the motel room, then his vision was blocked by a shape hurtling toward him. The trunk lid slammed down on the gunman's back.

Helen had reacted much more quickly than David. As soon as David screamed she had jumped onto the hood of the car, then its roof, then leaped high and came down on the trunk just as the gunman was clambering out. For a moment the man's torso was caught in the closing trunk. He screamed fiercely.

David screamed again as well. As Helen slipped down from the trunk lid and the gunman twisted to try to get his gunhand free, David raised his foot and pushed it into the man's face. The thin gunman, already stunned by Helen, dropped the gun and fell back into the trunk. David triumphantly slammed the lid down.

Helen took the approved Secret Service gun style, knees bent and both hands on her own pistol that had abruptly appeared. "Open the trunk again, quick." But before David could reach for the keys again a shot sounded, a hole appeared in the trunk, and a bullet came zinging out between them. Obviously the gunman had carried a backup. David and Helen ran, around opposite sides of the car and back into the motel room.

Mrs. McPherson and Randy stood staring, having heard the commotion. "Out!" Helen yelled forcefully. "Not this way. Through the bathroom. Out the window."

She hurriedly locked the motel-room door, then rushed them through the room and into the small bathroom. The First Lady and first son didn't protest, as if they'd been drilled on this routine before. The sounds of more gunshots from the parking lot inspired them further. Helen unlocked and pushed open the small window above the commode, and boosted Randy up and through the window. The boy had only had time to grab up his toy spaceship, or maybe he had never let go of it.

"Now you," Helen snapped, pointing at David.

"I'll go—" He started to make a manly offer to stay behind, but Helen grabbed his arm and pushed him.

"Get out there and help her down!" she commanded. David obeyed, stepping up onto the toilet and wriggling through the narrow window. Half outside, he bent, fell, almost landed on his head, and scrambled to his feet. He found himself in an alley, the white motel units in front of him, a commercial area of warehouses behind. He turned quickly and found the First Lady already coming through the window. He caught her, she put her arms around his neck, and he lifted her out as gently as possible.

More gunfire. It sounded closer and louder, as if the gunman had escaped from the trunk of the car. Helen came out the bathroom window more athletically than any of them, first her legs, then her head, so that she jumped down to her feet, not needing David's help. "Come on!" she snapped, gesturing with the gun.

The four of them ran into the warehouse area, Helen bringing up the rear, continually looking back. David helped Randy along. Once they passed the corner of a building he felt safer, but far from safe. He pictured the gunman's face. Kind of a nerdy-looking guy, actually, but with the fiercest glare David had ever seen. David ran harder, holding the First Lady's elbow to keep her from stumbling. Randy in his big clunky tennis shoes stayed at the front of the small pack.

Within minutes they were lost, which was good. They hoped they were lost from view as well. The warehouses gave way to retail businesses, and they realized they were nearing the highway. Helen slowed and looked around more analytically. "Keep an eye out for him," she instructed David, making him feel complimented.

They came to a gas station. Helen looked longingly at an unattended car with its engine running, but the owner had only stepped inside the station to pay; he'd return in a moment. She led them on. David looked back constantly. In the distance he saw a narrow figure emerge from the warehouse distict and look both ways. "Hurry," David said, and led them around a corner out of sight.

"Was that him?"

"I'm not sure."

Myra McPherson and Randy hadn't spoken since Helen and David had burst into the motel room. They stood breathing hard and looking back and forth between their protectors. Again Helen glared around the whole area. "Wait here," she snapped, and hurried away.

"Where's she going?" Mrs. McPherson asked.

"We'll just wait. She knows what she's doing," David replied, hoping that was true. He looked around for shelter. They were behind the white stucco gas station, next to the men's and women's rooms. Behind them two stacks of old tires loomed. David decided they could hide behind there, or better yet put Mrs. McPherson and Randy behind the Dumpster while he stood behind the tires, so he could push them over on the gunman if he found them. "Back this way," he said.

They had only been in position two or three minutes when they heard a screech of tires. David braced himself.

"Damn!" said a familiar voice.

David looked out and saw Helen standing up from behind the wheel of a car, a dingy white foreign model, small and inefficient-looking. "What the hell are you doing?" she snarled. "I told you to wait here."

Myra and Randy emerged from behind the Dumpster. She waved them over and all three scrambled into the car. David didn't ask how she'd gotten it. Wires dangled from the steering column. Helen drove away quickly but without squealing tires. David watched carefully out the window but didn't see anyone who looked like the gunman. He felt everyone watching him watching. Only David had gotten a look at the man.

Helen reached the highway and headed back the way they'd come. "Where are we going?" David asked.

"Back to that airport we passed. This car is only a stopgap measure, we've got to get out of it before it gets reported stolen."

"Are we taking a plane?" David asked hopefully. Helen shook her head.

In the backseat, Randy said, "That was so cool." Myra McPherson smiled at them. She appeared barely ruffled. David felt like the only sufficiently alarmed person in the car. He glanced at Helen for sympathy but saw only steely determination as she glared out the windshield.

Helen drove straight to the nearest airport, in Greenville, South Carolina. By the time they arrived they felt more secure, but all remained jittery. Helen told David to park the white car someplace where it would be found eventually, and disappeared into the long-term parking.

Alone in the underground garage, Helen walked past a pay phone, hesitated, then quickly deposited coins and punched in a number from memory. When the White House operator answered she said authoritatively, "Secret Service office." She added an authorization number and was put through immediately.

"It's all right," Helen said when her call was answered. "I've got them. Yes, both of them. Just calm everybody down, okay? And who's this crazoid you've got following us? Look, Ben, I don't have time to talk. Just tell everybody to take it easy, okay? Yes, I will."

She hung up the phone and hurried down the car aisle, looking left and right.

A few minutes later she had picked up her party of fugitives, driving a much more appropriate vehicle, a long, dark Buick with leather seats. Helen's penchant for darkness showed in the car's midnight-blue exterior.

They hit the highway after that, but proceeding slowly, with Helen constantly watching the rearview mirror and taking several exits, where she would double back or just park somewhere and wait. The procedure would have been tedious if they hadn't all been in such a state of alarm. They peered out the windows intently and breathed shallowly. Even Randy had caught their tension. He hugged his spaceship. His mother put her arm around him.

It took an hour or more before Helen felt comfortably sure they weren't being followed. When she began to relax the rest did too.

"So long-term parking is where you do your car-shopping," David said conversationally.

"It's best," Helen said, glancing in the rearview mirror. "Especially if you switch plates with a similar-looking car. That way even if the owner comes back and reports it stolen, somebody else is driving around with those plates. The owner of the car I took the plates from doesn't notice he's got different plates—who ever looks at his own license plates?—so he just drives around. We should be okay for a couple of days."

David nodded admiringly.

After noon they drove through a Wendy's and had lunch in the car. "I have got to get out of this car soon," Mrs. McPherson protested mildly. She seemed to have recovered both from the drugs and the morning's scare, but David had noticed her long stare out the car window, trying to see the future.

They drove slowly through the streets of the small town back toward the interstate. As they approached an intersection he saw a skinny blond man in a gray van, stopped at the cross street and staring intently at all the cars that went by. David immediately dropped down out of sight and said loudly, "Duck down!"

He heard the First Lady and Randy obey. Helen, still driving toward the intersection, said, "What about me?"

"He never saw you," David said from the floorboard. "Just be a bored housewife."

Helen's face went immediately blank.

"Not a zombie," David said critically. "Never mind. Look mad. You're late for a meeting. Just don't stare around like a tourist. Look like you live in this town."

Looking angry seemed to come more naturally to Helen. She even glanced at her watch as she drove through the intersection. Once through the intersection, Helen sped up. Watching the van in the rearview mirror, she reported to the car's hiding occupants.

"He's not coming after us. Wait. Now I think he wants to, but he's in the wrong lane. He's making an illegal turn to come this way. Shit!"

"Ears," the First Lady said mildly, covering her son's.

"Sorry, ma'am." Helen accelerated, then down another street at random. As she drove she talked angrily.

"He did *not* follow us. I promise you that. I lost him. Even if there's a team of them, nobody followed us here. He's tracking us somehow. How?"

"Lodestone," Randy said from the backseat. Everyone ignored him except David. David sat up, risking exposure, to ask, "What?"

"Lodestone," Randy repeated.

Lodestone was a technology still in the development stage. Similar to the Northstar system installed in the latest high-model cars, that by use of satellites could locate the car on a map projected inside the vehicle, the Lodestone inventor aimed to be even more precise and yet smaller. He envisioned weaving the tiny tracking device into children's backpacks or clothing, so that a lost child could be located quickly.

The technology wasn't on the market, but Randy knew about it. He explained haltingly.

"Are these things for sale?" David asked.

Randy shook his head. "They don't have it—what's the word?—good enough yet. I think if you're tracing one you only get a general area, not exactly where the kid is or whatever."

"But you can't just set it to find a particular person, can you?" Mrs. McPherson asked.

"No, it's this little thingy that it follows." Randy held his thumb and finger an inch apart to demonstrate the tininess of the transmitter.

They all looked at themselves. "It's not in the car," Helen said. "We've switched cars. And we left almost everything in the motel except the clothes we're wearing . . ."

They began to feel itchy. "Stop somewhere," David said. "We've got to buy clothes."

"But he'll catch up to us."

"We'll never lose him unless we get rid of all this stuff."

Helen couldn't deny David's logic. She accelerated again, drove like hell to the outskirts of town, and turned into a large parking lot.

Meanwhile David turned to Randy again. "And you know about this Lodestone thing because . . . ?"

"I heard somebody say something about it at home"—meaning the White House—"and I wondered what it was, so I cruised the Internet until I found a Web site about it."

David nodded, wondering exactly where Randy had been when he'd heard this experimental technology mentioned in the White House. Not at a cocktail reception, certainly. Myra said carefully, "Randy, um, sometimes hears things when people don't realize he's nearby."

The boy smiled craftily. "I get around."

That's why we're here, David thought.

Then he looked up and saw that they'd arrived at a destination. "Wal-Mart. Perfect."

"Oh, yeah," Randy said, sounding excited. "I've seen their commercials." David stared at him. The boy had never seen a Wal-Mart before. Randy was in many ways an alien visitor to America. Even his mother looked at the cars and the store with curious eyes. She hadn't shopped outside of Washington in years.

Helen parked, then had a dilemma. "You two—No, you can't stay here. What now, what now? David, you just go in and get clothes for all of us. I'll drive around—"

"No. He might spot me here or you in the car. Come on. We'll all go in."

"How can we?" Helen inclined her head toward the First Lady of the United States.

"It'll be okay. Come on."

They all got out of the car and walked toward the store. Mrs. McPherson and Randy stared at the sign and the shoppers as if they approached the Emerald City of Oz. David said in an undertone to Helen, "Nobody would expect to see her here. Even if they notice her they'll just think there's a resemblance. Everybody knows the First Lady isn't going to be shopping in a Wal-Mart in wherever the hell we are."

Helen clearly didn't like it, but silently agreed. "All right, but let's split up so people don't see the two of them together. You take Randy. Get him everything. Socks, underwear. Don't keep any of the clothes he's got on now."

David replied, grinning, "And the same goes for you. You were in the White House, you might be the one carrying the Lodestone in your underwear."

A few minutes later, a faded gray van pulled into the Wal-Mart parking lot, Larsen at the wheel. He steered with one hand while staring at a small device the size of a laptop computer. His eyes followed he directions indicated and he found himself looking at the store. He parked poorly and hurried to the doors. Larsen wore a gray coverall that made him look more like an employee of an auto repair shop than like a customer. At Wal-Mart's front doors he stopped. The store was huge. He would look very conspicuous walking around with the Lodestone detector. He could wait here, just next to the doors, out of sight around the corner. If they'd gone in, they would come back as well. The screen would tell him when his quarry approached.

But Larsen didn't like waiting. He remembered waiting in the trunk of their car, and he remembered the lid of that trunk slamming down on him, clamping closed like the jaws of a huge metal beast. That Secret Service agent thought quickly and moved even faster. Coming out of the store, she'd be at her most alert. It would be better to track her through the store with the racks and shelves for cover.

Larsen began walking quickly, around to the back of the store. He didn't worry that his prey would slip out the front doors while he came in the back. He could always find them again. The boy was still carrying the Lodestone.

As David had predicted, the First Lady drew little attention from the hurrying shoppers in Wal-Mart. A couple of salesclerks did give her second looks, which made Helen draw her away. They picked out clothes quickly, only Helen looking at the price tags, and went into adjoining changing rooms with slatted doors that didn't go all the way to the floor. Helen listened to the rustling and shimmers of the First Lady changing clothes practically in public, and gritted her teeth. She dressed quickly in the white slacks and striped blouse she'd picked out, kicked her own clothes under the bench, and stepped out. "All right?" she called, and received an appreciative affirmation from behind the door of the First Lady's cubicle.

When Myra McPherson emerged from the changing cabinet it was clear she was enjoying herself. She beamed at her choice of outfits, a rather garish shorts-and-blouse combination featuring large orange flowers on a light blue background that made Helen want to put her sunglasses back on. The First Lady looked back over her shoulder at the reflection of her backside in the mirror inside the changing room and kept smiling.

"Very nice," Helen murmured.

She tried to hurry them out of there then, but Myra wanted to shop. In her new clothes people didn't even give her second glances. Not only would the First Lady of the United States not be in a Wal-Mart in South Carolina, but the staid Myra McPherson, known for her beige suits and sensible shoes, would *never* be seen in such an outfit. People's brains wouldn't entertain such a possibility, even if their eyes noted the resemblance.

Myra realized this effect and obviously enjoyed it. She sauntered through the aisles, looking over blouses and cooking utensils and gardening equipment, smiling at everyone. Helen stalked along in her wake, ready to shoot anyone who glanced at them.

The loading dock at the back of the store didn't hold much activity. Larsen hurried across the pavement and jumped up onto the dock, trying to look as if he belonged. He stared intently at the screen in his hands. The targets were still inside. He almost was, too.

"Hey, pal, what do you need?"

A burly man also wearing a coverall, a white one, with the sleeves rolled up to reveal his thick, heavy forearms, came strolling toward Larsen, burdened with a load of authority.

"Just checking on my shipment," Larsen mumbled, trying to edge past him.

"What shipment?" the man insisted. "What do you mean yours?"

"Just got to check the stock numbers, make sure the right things got shelved the right way, you know." Larsen held up the device in his hands as if technology would fend off this intruder. But the man stared at the device.

"Haven't seen a stock checker like that one," he grumbled. "Let's see your invoice."

"Invoice." Larsen said the word in an absolutely dead voice. The word meant nothing to him, and he had just run out of inventiveness.

The Wal-Mart employee waited for an answer, then took the skinny intruder's arm. "Let's just go check in the office."

"No, you know what? I'll just come back—"

The dock foreman shook his head, disagreeing.

"—when you're dead," Larsen finished. He stuck the barrel of his automatic pistol into the man's thick stomach, the barrel pressing in deeply. Before the employee could cry out or even register the intrusion of the barrel in his gut, the gun went off. It blasted Larsen's hand back a few inches, and the foreman away from him a step or two. The man looked down, saw blood beginning to rush out of his abdomen, and said, "Uh—"

Larsen hit him in the head and the man went down. Larsen looked around and didn't see that he'd attracted any attention. The man's fat had acted as a silencer on the gun. Leaving him dying, Larsen stepped over the man and hurried inside the store. When he entered the shopping area, his gun was out of sight again and his screen showed that his prey was still here.

Myra stopped to admire trinketlike jewelry. "Oh, look." She even drew a bored young sales assistant away from her conversation with a similarly underworked clerk to get her to open the case. As the assistant, a young woman still with a trace of acne and a huge fake sapphire on her left ring finger, stood watching this customer *ooh* and *ah* over the display, she began to study Myra's face more closely. The salesclerk frowned. She glanced at the customer's companion, the stern-looking blond woman, and began to grow even more curious. "Ma'am?" she said.

Myra McPherson looked up smiling. "Yes?"

"Ma'am, has anybody ever told you you look just like—"

"*There* you are!" boomed a hearty male voice, sounding both relieved and annoyed.

David, wearing a light blue knit shirt and white pants, came up beside Myra McPherson and took her arm. With a hand hidden behind his back, he waved Helen away. Reluctantly, she obeyed, looking around for Randy.

"Might have known I'd find you looking at the jewelry," David sighed, winking at the salesclerk.

"Just look at this one . . ."

In a more confidential tone that could still be easily overheard, David said, "Now I told you, honey, maybe when I get that Christmas bonus. But right now the budget's a little tight."

"Oh, but, darling, just this one."

"Come on, now, dear, we've got to go."

Reluctantly, Myra allowed herself to be led away, talking animatedly to her "husband." When they rounded the corner into another aisle, she laughed delightedly. So did David. Myra's enjoyment in living a normal life, even faked and just for a minute, infected him. She looked years younger in her silly outfit and giggling with Davd, clutching his arm.

But she quickly returned to reality. "Where's . . . ?"

"There. Helen's got him. Oh, damn," David said in a suddenly downbeat voice.

Myra grew instantly frightened. "Where? Is that man here? What does —"

"No," David said. He made a gesture at Randy, who had a new outfit of vertically striped top and blue jeans. He looked like an ordinary eight-year-old boy, but then, he had when they'd entered the store.

Randy's mother saw what David meant. They had all four changed from the skin outward, left behind anything that might be carrying the Lodestone taint, with one exception. Randy stood there staring around at the store, obviously as thrilled as his mother to be in a real live Wal-Mart. In his arms he clutched his beloved Vibra-Wing spaceship.

David and Mrs. McPherson both approached him cautiously and crouched in front of him, appearing remarkably like young parents talking to their child. Helen stayed a few feet away, looking around the store for trouble but also continuing to glance at the small family group.

A few aisles away, Larsen walked quickly, looking at his screen. He bumped into shoppers, glanced at them, saw they weren't the ones he wanted, and hurried on. He looked up, rising on his toes to stare over the racks of clothing. Voices from nearby. . . .

He bumped someone else. "Hey!" she shouted indignantly, then stood with hands balled on hips, waiting futilely for an apology.

Helen looked around. She'd heard the raised voice. She couldn't see any disturbance, but her skin prickled. "David," she said in a low, urgent voice.

"Randy," David said quietly, "we've gotten rid of everything that could let that man follow us . . ."

"I know. Neat clothes, Mom."

"Thank you, dear. There's just one thing that Mr. Owens is talking about."

"What? I got rid of everything." Randy looked down at himself, holding out his arms to do so. Then he caught sight of the Vibra-Wing in his hand. His mother nodded. Randy's whole face trembled. David waited for the outburst of wails.

"But Mr. Lucas gave it to me himself!"

"I know, darling, and I'm sure when we get out of here he'll give you another one even better."

Randy appeared on the verge of rebellion. Then abruptly his expression cleared up. He set the spaceship down on the display counter next to him.

"Anyway, everybody's got one now," he said bravely. "I saw a whole bunch of them in the toy section."

He marched away, the adults following. David wanted to hug him. Instead he impulsively picked up a spongy, undersized football from a display near the cash registers.

Helen walked behind David, bringing up the rear and continually looking back. She hadn't seen anyone. Glancing at David's intended purchase, she said in an undertone, "This is probably going to take all our cash."

"No, it's not." They went through a line, handing over all the tags from their new clothes along with the football, and David presented a Wal-Mart credit card for payment. The cheerful cashier swiped it through her register without looking at it, and handed it back to David with a smile. He smiled back.

As they walked out, Helen said, "Where did you get that?"

"I applied for it right now. It's only temporary. They'll be mailing the permanent one to John Armstrong."

"Who?"

"The fake ID you gave me, remember, Helen?"

"You idiot. They probably have that name by now. They might be able to find this purchase in the system."

"Then you'd better do like you suggested to me, Helen, and drive like hell."

As the little group exited the Wal-Mart, Larsen arrived at the counter where Randy had put down his Vibra-Wing. Larsen's gun rested in his waistband, just below his zipped-up coveralls. Several clerks risked death by looking at him. Larsen moved intently, glancing down at the screen in his hands, then around the store. The screen told him his prey was right in front of him. But there was no one, not a little boy, certainly not a group of four people including the First Lady. Larsen reached out to the counter and picked up the Vibra-Wing wonderingly. With a sudden curse, he hurled it across the store.

The image on his screen showed his target retreating, spinning through the air. Larsen cursed again and ran for the front door, knocking outraged customers out of his way.

Helen *did* drive like hell, or like a frightened bat *out* of hell, heading west now and using smaller state highways rather than the interstate. If they got stopped for speeding they'd be in a lot of trouble, but Helen seemed to have an instinct for where cops would lie in wait. The others trusted her and turned toward each other. Myra McPherson sat in the front seat, at first talking to Helen about their shopping adventure, but then beginning to listen to David and Randy in the backseat.

David asked about the Lodestone technology, trying to be subtle, wanting to know what other things Randy had overheard. The boy turned the toy football over in his hands, clearly not having held one before, but understanding David's questions easily.

Suddenly he said, "Once Dad can read everybody's E-mail and hear their phone calls, how can Mom and I stay hidden from him?"

"Oh, he can't do that, Randy. Nobody can. I know your dad's a pretty powerful man and you think he can do anything, but even he—"

"He can't *yet*," Randy explained earnestly. "But he's got people working on it. Pretty soon they will be able to."

David glanced over the seat at Myra, who nodded soberly. This was what she'd been trying to tell David Owens, divorce lawyer, what seemed like a long time ago in his office.

"How's he going to do that, Randy?"

Randy McPherson talked always in an odd but perfectly understandable combination of little-boy-speak and adult phrases, drawn from his short lifetime spent mostly with adults and television. "Well, the technology's pretty simple, really, just nobody's, you know, thought of applying it just this way before. For the E-mail, you just write kind of a shadow program into the program that sends the message to another address at the same time it sends it where you want the message to go. There's an invisible 'copy to' recipient hardwired into the system, see?"

Vaguely, David did. Also vaguely, he realized that he'd always suspected this possibility, as had millions of other unsophisticated technology-users, blandly sending their messages out into the void with no idea how they got where they were supposed to go.

"But to do that you'd have to have this invisible program written into all the hundreds of different networks that people use."

"Sure, networks," Randy replied easily. "But nearly everybody uses the same basic programming. That's why Mr. Boswell is in on this project with Dad."

"Wilson Boswell? TitanWorks?"

Randy nodded. He saw that he had explained enough, and sat watching David absorb the news and be startled by it. Randy enjoyed performing his own magic tricks.

The scheme sounded vast but possible, if Wilson Boswell and the President of the United States collaborated on it, but it also sounded like the product of a boyish imagination, fueled by science fiction and cartoons. "How do you know these things, Randy?"

Randy sat deciding how many of his secrets to give up in order to convince David. "Oh, I hear things. There are a couple of places in Dad's office or right by it where I can be and nobody notices me. And"—he lowered his voice and David leaned toward him confiden- tially—"Mom and Dad both write things in their electronic diaries and think they're secret because they've got passwords. *Ppsshh.*" He made a derisive sound at the suggestion that his aged parents could outwit him with technology.

David glanced up at Myra McPherson, who shook her head to indicate she hadn't heard. David shook his head in return with an expression that said, *Nothing important.* He leaned back and he and Randy exchanged smiles.

The long drive provided a good chance to talk, almost an ideal envi- ronment for a lawyer and his clients. After a rest stop they switched seats, Randy sat in the front and looked for radio stations. No one

suggested that anyone other than Helen should drive, so that left
David and his divorce client in the backseat. Myra McPherson
looked like the younger sister of the woman who'd come furtively to
his office that afternoon weeks ago. The flowered outfit did part of
that job, but so did her face and her gestures. Uncomfortable, a
fugitive, both her near and long-term future impossible to predict,
and possibly in mortal danger, the First Lady nonetheless visibly
relaxed more and more as they drew farther from Washington, as if
she'd been under a spell that emanated from the White House and
now grew more and more tenuous as they escaped its aura.

But she looked serious as she amplified what Randy had told David.
"You have to understand, before he went into politics John always
started businesses that failed. He could talk investors into them, he
was good at that, but then he never could quite carry through. So
after he went into politics and met Wilson Boswell, John wanted
more than anything to impress him. It was so important to John to
meet this enormously powerful business tycoon as an equal."

United States Senators are important, powerful people; meeting
one is quite an occasion. But by the same token, senators get to
meet all kinds of celebrities and must occasionally be impressed
themselves. Even becoming President wouldn't necessarily make a
man feel the equal of some of these famous, powerful celebrities,
not if a man had an inferiority complex to begin with.

"The way John could impress Wilson Boswell was on his own
playing field: technology. Especially since John's become President,
of course, he has access to all sorts of information about things
being developed. They began to see how they could use each other.
After a year or two of being President, John seemed to think about
these things more and more, even more than he thought about gov-
erning the country. John's always looked ahead, and now he's planning his post-retirement life, how he can be even more powerful
than any sitting President. This is what scares me so bad. Think of
all the implications. Think who might be using whom." She looked
into the front seat, over which they could just see the shaggy top of

her son's head. "And think what somebody might do if they knew how much Randy knows about their schemes."

David did think about that. It didn't take many miles down the highway before he realized the corollary of the First Lady's fear: any of the people pursuing them would have to assume that all four people in this car suspected their secrets as well.

By nightfall Helen had gotten them to Jackson, Tennessee. Small towns obviously made her feel safer than big cities. David wanted to ask her about that, about where she'd grown up. Helen got out and checked a phone book. David watched her long stride and was impressed by how little affected Helen looked by the fright and the long hours of driving. Her tourist outfit fit her becomingly, but her personality belied the frivolous clothing. Helen was on the job.

She drove them to a small bed-and-breakfast and they all got out of the car thankfully. The First Lady and Randy walked around the pleasant front yard of the cottage, admiring a gazebo. Helen kept an eye on them. David came up behind her and she turned to him.

"We have to watch her. She almost got us caught back in that Wal-Mart."

"No, Helen, *you* almost got us caught."

"Me? I was the only one paying attention, looking out for that maniac—"

"Yes, and quite obviously so. You were on duty. That salesclerk didn't get suspicious until she saw who Myra looked like and then looked at you. Myra wasn't acting like the First Lady, but you were damned obviously a Secret Service agent. *That's* what almost gave the game away."

"Well, excuse the hell out of me if I have a job—"

David stood close in front of her, looking into her eyes. "Look, Helen, we're role-playing here. You don't really have to stop working, but you have to look like you're not. Understand?"

Clearly she didn't. David sighed. Looking away from her, he said, "Now this is the part of the story where I should give you a playful little slap on the ass, to help you get mad and loosen up and also, frankly, copping a feel in the process"—Helen's eyes blazed at the suggestion; David continued without interruption—"but much as I'd enjoy it and it might help you, to tell you the truth I just don't have the nerve. Because I feel pretty sure that if I did the swat thing you'd do something to me that would hurt for a long time."

"Count on it."

"So you're on your own, Helen, you have to find a way to loosen up without any help from me."

Her eyes narrowed as she looked into his. "And what exactly about me would you like to loosen?"

"That's good, Helen, that's good. I think I detected a little hint of playfulness there. At least for a few seconds you were thinking about something other than your job."

"Listen, if you—Oh, damn."

"What?" David whirled around, thinking they'd been found again by the skinny psychotic. Instead he saw a laughing Randy, hanging backward by his knees from the gazebo railing. A pleasant-faced lady in her sixties, with tightly whorled hair, wearing a flowered dress and pearls, had emerged from the bed-and-breakfast and was talking to Myra McPherson. Helen hurried over to intervene. But the hostess didn't seem suspicious or curious. David realized he needed to give Helen the "relax" speech all over again.

A few minutes later he followed them down the hallway inside the old Victorian house. He wondered if it was only in his imagination that Helen's hips swayed more pronouncedly than they had before, and whether she deliberately stayed far enough ahead of him that he couldn't reach her with a playful hand. Then she turned and glanced back at him over her shoulder and David decided his imagination wasn't the only one at work. He wondered if they could get two rooms in this lovely bed-and-breakfast.

The hostess showed them into a large, sunny room. It featured a hardwood floor with a big oval rug, two comfortable-looking chairs grouped around a table, and a canopied double bed. David noted French doors to the outside that would make Helen very nervous. Maybe he could sleep on the floor there, blocking that entrance. The proprietor of the inn turned to them with a smile, proud of her fantasy room.

"I think you ladies will be comfortable here. And we can bring a rollaway bed in for your son. But of course only two adults can stay here. And other than this room I'm afraid we're booked up. It is one of our busy seasons."

She addressed these remarks to Myra, obviously having noticed her wedding ring. But she glanced curiously at David, wondering at his status, traveling with two attractive women and a little boy. David spoke up in his hearty voice.

"That's fine, that's fine, just want to get the ladies settled here and I'll be pushing on. Well, how does it look, honey?"

Helen looked at him curiously, but David walked over and put his arm around Myra. In the same tone of voice she'd used in Wal-Mart, the First Lady said, "It's lovely, dear," with obvious sincerity.

"Good, good. Well, just the one night," David said to the hostess. "That will be . . ."

"Eighty dollars a night."

David flinched slightly at the price, but he followed the hostess back to the living-room area and handed over most of their remaining money. The lady in the flowered dress had no apparent problem accepting cash, and didn't even ask for a cash deposit. David suspected that Myra and Randy had put her at ease. They both looked too nice to trash a hotel room, and Helen looked as if she probably slept standing up.

The others joined him in the front yard again. "But what about you, David?" Myra asked with evident concern, touching his arm. "After it gets dark we can slip you into the room, too." He appreciated her sympathy.

"I'll be all right. I'll take the car and stay in it or something. Don't worry, it's only one night."

"I want to go with David," Randy spoke up suddenly. The three adults looked at each other with surprise.

"But, Randy," his mother said, "Ms. Wills has to guard you, you know that."

"David could do that." Randy began to look sullen.

"Sure I could," David said, putting his arm around Randy's shoulders. He winked at the women over the boy's head. "Maybe if I come around to those French doors you can slip us a pillow or extra sheet or something."

They made a show of saying good night in the front yard, then David and Randy walked to the car, drove it half a block away, and returned. He found the side of the inn where the French doors of the First Lady's room opened onto the porch. Myra opened it, handed David the decorative pillows from the chairs and a blanket from the closet, then bent and hugged her son. "You take care of yourself, hear?"

Then she leaned close to David, putting her cheek against his. "Thank you again and again," she said quietly.

David looked over Myra's shoulder at Helen, who watched him curiously. In a soft whisper, David said, "I'll bring him back later if we don't find another place. Don't worry about us."

With Randy in the front seat beside him, David drove around aimlessly, just looking for a place to stop for a while until Randy got sleepy. He found a small city park and they got out, Randy carrying the football. "Can we play catch?"

"Sure."

In the soft summer night they tossed the small football back and forth. It became clear that Randy had never performed this boyish game before. He almost always dropped the ball, but laughed delightedly, and when he did catch it he beamed with pride and David applauded.

After a while he said, "Do you know how to play?"

"Play what?" Randy asked, probably not knowing the name of the ball in his hands.

David explained the most basic rules of football, backed away, and threw the ball high to Randy. David stood still until Randy picked up the ball, then advanced slowly, waving Randy forward. "Try to get past me. Remember, that's the goal back there. Come on."

Randy tucked the ball under his arm and ran surprisingly fast, but straight at David. David caught him and brought him down gently. "You're supposed to try to get past me," he instructed laughingly.

They tried again, with the same result. Randy ran right to David each time, slowing down to be tackled. He obviously wanted to be tackled, wanted the contact. After several tries they lay on the ground, David hugging Randy tight, the boy snuggling against him.

Later, he got Randy settled in the backseat of the car with a pillow under his head and the blanket over him. The small boy fit the seat perfectly. David sat in front, turned around to watch him. Randy smiled at him and reached out his hand. David held it. He talked quietly about all sorts of things, stories he remembered from his own early boyhood, and answered a hundred questions Randy conjured. The boy knew an amazing quantity of information, including some highly classified government secrets, but he also had significant gaps in his experience. Randy asked how many Wal-Marts there were in America, and David made up a number. Then David explained the idea of malls. Randy lay enthralled. "I want to go to one," he said, the way another kid would speak of Disney World. Randy had been to Disney World more than once, highly publicized trips with his father and a host of Secret Service agents, but before the last few days he had never seen anyone pump gas into a car.

Randy didn't seem to grow sleepy. He asked David about wildlife out here in the country. David kept watch out the car windows, more concerned with cops than with cougars. Randy watched him, still holding his hand.

David smiled down at the boy. It had been a long, long time since he had felt anything as good as the clasp of that small hand.

★

In their room in the Victorian house, Myra and Helen passed time slowly. While the First Lady read a book she'd found in the living room of the house, Helen sat and planned. After eleven P.M. it seemed that David and Randy would not return. The two women decided to go to bed. They had no clothes to change into, but found a pair of pajamas in a dresser drawer and a robe hanging in the closet. Helen insisted Myra take the pajamas. Helen simply undressed and got into the double bed beside her client, laying the robe across the bed so she could pull it on quickly if necessary. Helen imagined no other Secret Service agent in history had so zealously guarded a member of the first family.

They lay beside each other in the darkness. Myra didn't seem worried, but sensed Helen's unease. "They'll be all right," Myra said. "David seems very resourceful."

Helen didn't answer. The air hung very still with her unspoken reply.

"Don't you like him?" Myra asked. Her voice sounded very young.

"You chose him," Helen said noncommittally.

"Yes, and I think I chose well. Look at all he's done for us already." When Helen didn't answer Myra reached across and touched her arm. "Besides, I've seen you looking at him. You *do* like him, don't you? Helen, are you and my lawyer becoming an item?"

"Oh, please." Helen turned away. "This is so junior high."

"You're not going to tell me, are you? All right, I guess that answers the question."

Helen turned back, rising on her elbow to look at the First Lady, who lay placidly on her back, arms folded on top of the covers. "What difference does it make?" Helen asked.

Then it was Myra's turn to become coy. "I just want to know, Helen." She chuckled.

After that Myra McPherson went peacefully off to sleep. But Helen spent a bad night, lying beside the First Lady and waiting for David to return with Randy. When he didn't, Helen grew very worried, but she couldn't leave her primary client to go looking, and didn't have the car anyway. Myra obviously had more confidence in

David; she slept soundly, breathing lightly. Helen slept too, but not well.

Very early the next morning an exhausted-looking David tapped at the French doors. Helen sprang out of bed, pulled on the robe, and opened the door for him. "Where's Randy?"

"Asleep in the car. Would you watch him for a little while? Can I use your bathroom?"

David leaned against the door sill as if unable to stand upright. He didn't even seem to notice that Helen wore only a light robe. "Are you all right?" she asked.

"Sure, sure."

He stumbled past her and into the bathroom. Helen pulled on her Wal-Mart shorts and walked out to the car. She saw Randy asleep in the backseat, thought about moving him inside, but he looked very peaceful so she just left him. David had locked the car's doors. Helen hurried back inside.

She found the bathroom door ajar and pushed it open to find David standing at the sink trying to brush his teeth with his eyes closed. Helen couldn't help smiling.

"Do you know you're trying to brush your teeth with the back of the toothbrush?"

"What?" David opened his eyes. Helen gently turned the toothbrush for him. He stared at it as if he couldn't fathom what it did.

"Tired?"

David stared at her for a moment, then began recounting his night. "First we played Ten Thousand Questions. I explained everything on earth to him, except several things that he explained to me. Then when he started drifting off he made me promise to keep a lookout. I lay down in the front seat after that, but he sat up and gave a little scream. After that I was afraid to go to sleep, so I kept watch."

"For what?"

"Bears."

"Bears? Randy was worried about bears?"

David spoke to her in a deadened voice, as if she must be incredibly ignorant not to understand. "What state are we in, Ms. Wills?"

She had to think for a moment. "Tennessee."

David nodded. "And who's the most famous native of Tennessee ever?"

"Al Gore?"

He shook his head disgustedly. "Davy. Davy Crockett. King of the wild frontier. And Randy thinks it's still a wild frontier here. And what did ol' Davy kill when he was only three?"

Helen got it. "A b'ar."

David nodded, looking at her as if she were the prize pupil. "Randy thinks the place must still be crawling with them. He made me promise to keep a lookout. Also every once in a while I drove the car to a new location. That seemed to help him sleep, and I kept looking for a better place to stay parked all night. I'm a little tired."

Helen smiled at him sympathetically. She hurried outside to check on Randy again, found him waking up, and carried him inside. She put him in bed with his mother and they snuggled together. David had come out of the bathroom and dropped into one of the overstuffed armchairs. Helen stood behind him and gave him a shoulder-and-neck massage, which made him murmur gratefully. Helen kneaded his sore muscles, looking down at his tired face and then at the bed, where the First Lady and first son were giggling. Gradually a peaceful look came over Helen's face.

David woke up in the car. Randy leaned against him, pretending to sleep too, but he sat up alertly as soon as David did. "Us guys had a tough night, didn't we?" he asked proudly.

David gave him a one-armed hug, then leaned toward the front seat, where Myra McPherson smiled at him gratefully and Helen watched him in the rearview mirror.

"Where are we?"

"Coming up on Little Rock, which I'm going to circle around and head south. I think I'll just keep driving until we get there, because we don't have any money left for a hotel anyway."

They had obviously been making plans without him. But David had awakened with a new energy and purposefulness. He had come back to himself.

He shook his head at Helen. "No. Drive into Little Rock. Go to the airport."

"You think we need to switch cars? Maybe so."

David shook his head. "Just do it, please."

He wouldn't explain. Instead he and Randy chatted about football. Randy was trying to choose a favorite team, either the Cowboys from his native state or the Redskins from the only town he knew at all. He was distressed to learn that these two teams not only played against each other but in fact didn't like each other very much. David tried to help him choose an alternative.

And Helen, amazingly, did as she was asked. In thirty minutes she had them parked at Little Rock International Airport. They all turned to David for guidance.

"Let's go in. Bring all our stuff."

That amounted to a pathetically small amount of baggage, very little more than the clothes on their bodies. This group was down to their last resources, and hardly had any of those.

Inside, David marched straight to a Southwest Airlines ticket counter. "What the hell are you doing?" Helen asked.

"Trust me."

Helen didn't. She had come to trust David's good intentions, but she didn't like giving up control of her charges to anyone else. She let David go to the ticket counter with reluctance.

At the counter, David charged four tickets to San Antonio on one of his credit cards, using his own name for the first time in days. It felt very strange, and made an electric charge of fright run across his shoulders, but he marched back to the others confidently, holding up the tickets.

Helen stared. "What is this for, a decoy? They follow that flight while we—"

"No, this is us getting on an airplane. I'm tired of the car."

"Are you crazy, they'll trace those before we're halfway there. They may know about it already. There's going to be so many F.B.I. and Secret Service agents converging on that flight that—"

"That's okay." Still confidently, David found a pay phone, the others following closely behind him. David called his office, suddenly wondering if he still had a secretary. If Janice had quit in his absence, they were all in big trouble.

The phone rang four times, worrying him, his face worrying the rest of his group, then a voice he recognized answered. "Law office."

"Janice. Thank goodness. Listen."

"David! Where in the world are you? I didn't know if you were ever coming back. I've gotten a million calls, you missed a court hearing on the Silvestre case, I didn't know if you were dead or in prison. I kept coming in, but I—"

"Thanks, Janice. Hold on a minute."

David held the phone against his chest and gave Myra McPherson a look so serious that it held her attention tightly. Instinctively, she covered Randy's ears again.

"Mrs. McPherson, do you still want to get divorced? You can change your mind. I'm about to take an important step."

Myra looked nervous, but she nodded without hesitation. "Go ahead."

David accepted her orders. Into the phone he said, "Janice? Remember the instructions I gave you? The one special petition for divorce?"

On the phone, his secretary lowered her voice. "That one? I thought you were joking." Obviously, contrary to his instructions, she had read the petition, noticing the names on it.

"I'm not. File it. Right now. Take it over to the courthouse yourself. And don't be shy about it, Janice. File it with Raymond."

"All right. Yes, sir." It was the first time she had ever used that last word without irony.

David hung up.

"Who's Raymond?" Helen asked.

"A clerk who's the biggest gossip in the courthouse. The news that the First Lady of the United States has filed for divorce from her husband should hit the airwaves within an hour. Before we land the whole country will know about it."

"Are you insane?"

David gathered them all up and headed for the metal detectors. "The time for stealth is over, Helen. We need publicity. Secrecy got them kidnapped and us almost killed. Going public is the only protection she has now."

"But once it's started they'll—"

David gave her a confident look. He was wide awake now, and even in his horribly wrinkled Wal-Mart clothes, he had become a lawyer again. They could all see the change.

"Don't worry," David said. "We're in *my* world now."

★ President John McPherson felt a slight vibration against his upper thigh and stood up abruptly from the conference table in the Roosevelt Room.

"I have a headache," he said, touching his temple. Followed by expressions of sympathy, he walked quickly out of the room. To an aide, he said, "I'm going to the family quarters to lie down. Tell the chief of staff he's in charge."

"Yes, sir."

The President walked with his head down, not speaking to anyone, preceded and trailed by Secret Service agents. At the foot of the stairs to the private quarters he told them, "Thank you, that will be all."

"Sir—"

"That will be all."

McPherson ascended the stairs with a rapid stride. The private quarters were supposed to be private, that was their point. The President crossed the hall alone and opened the door to the long living room.

Angela Vortiz looked up from the sofa alertly and smiled. She had sent McPherson the signal that the meeting was ready.

Wilson Boswell rose slowly to his feet, smiling and extending his hand. Angela had smoothed his way through White House security and brought him to the family quarters, using her own top clearance. It was not possible to keep secrets entirely from the White House staff, but the fewest possible people knew that the TitanWorks tycoon was in the building, and Angela didn't think anyone knew he stood in the private quarters.

Burton Leemis, the President's lawyer, had found his way here more conventionally, the staff accustomed to his having private meetings with his client. Leemis, already on his feet, smiled and nodded and said formally, "Mr. President."

McPherson shook hands all around, smiling the grave smile he couldn't keep from his face on such occasions, even as he said, "This is a hell of a mess, isn't it?"

"I couldn't agree more," Wilson Boswell said. "May I ask, sir, how these four people could cross the country undetected for two days, with all the forces at your command?"

The rebuke hung in the air. The President looked angry. "I couldn't exactly call out the Marines and the National Guard. If I'd made a national, widespread alert and Myra were stopped by, say, some state trooper in Georgia, the first place she'd go would be on the national news. I frankly didn't want her having a press conference about her reasons for leaving here. Did you?"

Burt Leemis, the lawyer, cleared his throat and said, "Besides, she hasn't committed any crime. Anyone has the right to ask for a divorce. We can hardly ask to have the First Lady arrested."

Boswell addressed McPherson. "But surely, sir, there are private forces at your disposal."

"A few, but not enough to cover the country." McPherson's anger turned rueful. "The truth is, the only people I trust completely are in this room."

The smiles Boswell and Angela beamed on the President looked flattered and sincere. Boswell, resuming his seat on the couch, said, "Thank you, Mr. President. And may I say the feeling is mutual.

"But now to business. She'll be holding that press conference now. What's to prevent her telling the world what she knows"—he glanced at the lawyer—"or any wild speculations she might make?"

"How do we know we even have a problem?" Angela asked suddenly. "Why do we think she or Randy knows anything?"

McPherson looked shamefaced. "Myra's made little remarks about being afraid that I was involved in something dangerous. And that Randy could be caught in the middle of it. Plus once or twice I've been almost sure he was in eavesdropping distance when Angela and I—"

Burt Leemis coughed ostentatiously.

"—were talking," the President concluded, with a glare at his lawyer.

"But he doesn't necessarily know about—"

The lawyer coughed again. He did not want to know any of the secrets these people held, or even that there *were* secrets.

"I don't know." McPherson looked around the faces. He had obviously come here for advice.

Leemis took charge. "A petition for divorce has been filed, and we'll be served anytime now. But often petitions are filed and then dropped. Mrs. McPherson doesn't have to go through with this. Obviously she's been under a great deal of stress and has fallen into the hands of an unscrupulous attorney—"

"And a traitorous Secret Service agent," Angela interjected pointedly.

Leemis spoke man-to-man to John McPherson. "But she's still your wife, Mr. President. Don't you think you could reconcile with her?"

They all looked at John McPherson, and for once in his life he didn't like being the center of attention. He didn't want to disappoint Boswell, and feared being thought less of a man because he couldn't control his wife. Burt Leemis watched him with more open curiosity.

McPherson shot a guilty glance at Angela, but she looked on affectionately. Yes, Angela was part of the problem of a reconciliation idea.

The President studied the carpet for a long moment, considering how he could regain his closeness to his wife, and realized he knew nothing to recapture. A tender moment, an intimate conversation, a shared dream: offhand he couldn't recall any of these during his ten-year marriage. Perhaps immediately after the birth of their son? No, that had been when McPherson's political career had grown busiest and most promising. He couldn't think of a happy common ground he could ask Myra to share with him again.

"I don't think so," he said quietly.

The other three—practical people—dropped that idea immediately and went on planning. "What about Randy?" Boswell asked.

"What about him?"

Boswell directed a stern look at McPherson, reminding him that everyone here knew. That had been the reason for this meeting, after the President had hinted that Randy might know something, and they had all figured out much more than the hint.

"He's your son," Boswell said carefully. "Surely he loves you. You can—bring him back into the fold."

"He's very close to his mother," the President said listlessly.

"Good." Wilson Boswell had been acting deferential toward the President, but now he began to let his real authority show. Boswell was the oldest man in the room, and the smallest, but he had the strongest core of determination. His voice became quietly commanding as he turned to the lawyer, then to the President.

"Leemis, you said anyone has a right to a divorce. But that doesn't mean she automatically has a right to keep her son with her. Why shouldn't he be with his father instead? Doesn't he have equal rights as a father?"

"Yesss," Leemis said slowly, thinking.

"Mr. President, we must have Randy here." Boswell looked at McPherson pointedly: *You know why.* "I'd like to . . . question him. Boys get such crazy ideas. You need to have him close to you, sir. Obviously his mother cares a great deal about your son. Bringing him back here will bring her back as well. Or bring her . . ." *under control,* he didn't add, but the President understood. McPherson nodded thoughtfully.

The lawyer, probably sensing this conversation was approaching dangerously close to conspiracy and extortion, rose from the couch and stood close in front of his client. "There's more than one way to do this. Mr. President, he's your son. Believe me, he loves you. Your necessary absences on the most important business in the nation have probably only made him yearn more for your company."

He began instructing. "If the divorce does go ahead, temporary orders will be entered. Under those, you will have times of possession of Randy. No judge in America would deny you that. Even if it's only every other weekend, those will be *your* times, when you're the primary parent. Randy will be yours alone. Those times are when you have to cultivate him. Believe me, Mr. President, he'll long to be close to you. A boy needs his father. Close as he and his mother are, I'm not even sure she's a fit mother."

Leemis seemed to roll that idea around on his tongue, tasting it for possibilities. "Yes. She's been under a great strain, that she's obviously not strong enough to bear. She's behaved irrationally. This running away, not just from you but from their Secret Service protection, has put them both in jeopardy. Is that a sign of a good mother? A woman who can't take care of herself can't take care of her son, either. If she tells some crazy story about a conspiracy in the White House she'll sound deranged . . . especially after I get to the press first. Hmm." Leemis began to sound as if he were enjoying himself. He appeared to forget the others for a moment. "Yes. I like it. You may end up with primary custody of Randy. If that happened we wouldn't have any problem, would we?"

The others considered the possibility, not immediately taking to it, including McPherson. But Leemis seemed to grow in enthusiasm. He had a splendid relationship with his own four children; they remained distant but available, and, like his wife, didn't intrude on his time but seemed to appreciate him deeply. Leemis assumed his client enjoyed the same kind of bond with Randy, or could develop one. "What have you done to cultivate that relationship?" he asked.

The President said haltingly, "Well, I've always liked having him around, you know, and Randy seemed to like being near me, too."

"That's part of the problem," Boswell said darkly.

Leemis watched his client struggle for an answer, and began to discard this possibility. "Well, we have time to work on it."

"No, we don't have time," Boswell insisted. "We have to get Randy back here *now*. You said these temporary orders will be entered. But something has to be filed in court for that, doesn't it? And a hearing held? Those things take time. All courts do is chew up enormous amounts of time, that's what they're designed for. But until there are such orders, neither parent has more of a right to Randy than the other, do they?"

Leemis shook his head slowly. He didn't want to advise a legal kidnapping. But: "That's true," he said. "At this moment the President has as much right to have possession of his son as Mrs. McPherson does."

Wilson Boswell raised his eyebrow at the President and lifted his hand in a gesture of offering. A solution. McPherson looked even more thoughtful.

Burton Leemis remained expert at maintaining credible deniability, usually for his clients and always for himself. He began to take his departure. "I'll work on the legal aspects, and leave the rest of you to think of your own alternatives. Remember, Mr. President, Randy loves you. Be certain of that."

McPherson nodded unconvincingly. Leemis walked out quickly. They heard a door open and close.

Boswell immediately looked hard at John McPherson and dropped any pretense of deference. McPherson stared back. *It's not my fault*, he wanted to say, but knew it would come out sounding whiny.

Angela walked close to the President, gripped his arm, and rubbed his back. But McPherson ignored her. "I can take care of this," he snapped at Boswell.

"I certainly hope so."

McPherson, who understood people and sometimes had quick, penetrating insights, saw exactly what his mentor was thinking. His gaze hardened, but he didn't speak.

"The boy is absolutely the key," Boswell said quietly. "He must be brought back here at all costs. Any way possible."

"I said I'll handle it. It's not like he's been kidnapped by terrorists. There's only a lawyer standing in the way. He doesn't know what he's let himself in for."

McPherson turned and strode purposefully out of the room.

Angela immediately turned on her real boss. "What happened to *your* special private force? What happened to Larsen?"

Without apology, Boswell said, "He's only dealt with other computer geeks in the past, not with a Secret Service agent. But he learns. And he's relentless. They'll separate at some point. He's still out there."

"But you need to call him off now. The whole thing's gone way too public."

"No." As always, Boswell had thought further ahead. "I have to fire him. Authentically. I can't have any connection to him anymore."

"But what if he—?"

"What? Goes to the police? Tell them he's committed crimes for me? He would never do that."

"But there's no telling what he might do."

"That's true," Boswell said grimly. "A disgruntled employee . . . possibly psychotic . . . who knows what he might do?"

Angela looked more and more worried. She stood close to the older man. "But if they think he's still working for you, not just that he's gone crazy—"

"He's a game designer," Boswell snapped. "Who could tell the difference?"

"My God. He might come after you."

"If he does he won't get far. No, I'll make sure he knows the source of his problem."

It sounded to Angela as if someone else's voice spoke through Boswell. He had always appeared a quiet, even courtly man. She'd known there was another side to him, but this was one of the few times he'd let her see it. Angela noticed that as animated as Boswell seemed, his eyes had gone flat and dead.

Angela said haltingly, "But what if . . ."

"I am. This works either way. The boy is the key. And she's putting him in harm's way by running away from their protection. If the President regains custody of his son, everything will be fine. If not, what follows won't be anyone's fault but hers. They'll struggle over him, the President and the First Lady. That'll hook everyone's attention. If Myra wins him, tragedy will follow. It will be her fault."

That got Angela's attention. She stared at Boswell, who now seemed unaware of her as a person. He was planning a day of national mourning. Not for the first time, Angela felt afraid of him.

"It will be her fault," Boswell repeated. "That's what will take everyone's attention." His eyes gleamed harshly for a moment as he thought of a new implication. "And McPherson will be involved. He'll be in so close to the action he won't be able to deny me anything. There'll be nothing more to distract him from our business."

Angela wished she hadn't heard all this. She wanted to get away, but she was the most trapped person of all. She couldn't do anything but help the plan along. Frightened as she was, she was glad to be on Wilson Boswell's team. People who opposed him didn't understand the height of the stakes for which he always played.

The mob David had expected did indeed await the First Lady and her entourage when she landed in San Antonio. During the flight David and Myra had discussed what she should say, reaching the answer of *very little*. Myra seemed to appreciate that David actually turned to her for advice, didn't just impose a speech on her. Myra was used to taking orders, not being consulted. But when David and Helen and especially Randy looked at her expectantly, she found she had answers.

David expected on this occasion to act as a press secretary and little else, but in fact almost as soon as the plane touched down he had a legal problem to deal with: Helen's arrest.

The three adults had heard the whispers all through the passenger compartment during their short flight. They had tried to look like a family grouping, David and Randy on one side of the aisle, Helen and Myra on the other, but in order to come aboard armed Helen had been forced to show her Secret Service credentials, so the flight attendants stared at the First Lady from the beginning. Even though Myra kept her head down, it became clear she had been recognized. And someone on the plane must have been listening to the news, because after an hour or so the flight attendants looked at Myra with more alarm and wonder. News of her divorce filing had hit the airwaves.

The plane landed in San Antonio ahead of schedule. They came down quickly. Before the plane rolled to a stop, the pilot came on the intercom and gave sharply worded instructions to the passengers to stay in their seats. Amazingly, most of them did so. In a matter of moments the plane's exit door opened and men in black suits rushed in, looking like an overdressed S.W.A.T. team. Four of them hurried to where the small group sat. David looked up at them with some alarm, Myra and Randy with bored resignation, and Helen Wills with stoic wistfulness. This was her life, gone now forever.

"Ma'am, I'm Agent Ben Foster. If you could come with me, please." None of the team from the First Lady's sojourn in the medical center had come aboard. Undoubtedly they had all been reassigned, possibly to kitchen duties.

Myra McPherson stood as ordered, but David rose as well. "This lady is my client," he said in as authoritative a tone as he could muster. Agent Foster looked David in his rumpled tourist outfit up and down and didn't see any obstacle. "But she's my responsibility, under the Constitution. If you'll step aside, sir."

"Bullshit," David said distinctly. "Sorry, ma'am. But the Secret Service was created in 1865. The Constitution, you may know, was written some years before that. However, the Constitution *does* protect the attorney-client relationship, and you're not going to interfere with that."

The agent looked at him blankly for a moment, as if David had just spouted an impassioned speech in Lithuanian, then jerked his head and the whole Secret Service team moved as well as they could in the narrow aisle to form a square around Myra and Randy. David, deciding to pretend his speech had had some effect, tagged along, as did Helen.

The agents hustled the four of them down the portable stairs and into a waiting limousine. They didn't go near the terminal, but David got a glimpse of it, crowded with people staring out the windows, many of them holding cameras or notepads.

He didn't think to look for a skinny blond man with intense eyes in the crowd. David probably wouldn't have seen Larsen even if he had thought of it

Inside the limo, he said, "You know, we are going to hold a press conference. You can't keep us away from the press forever."

No one answered. In the third seat, Helen sat between two of her former colleagues and didn't even bother to glance at them. She knew if she did she would see no sign of recognition in their faces. She had become a nonperson.

They drove around the terminal building to a hangar that appeared to be empty of people, and the limo stopped. For a moment David felt very apprehensive. The huge, echoing hangar looked like a good place to stage a St. Valentine's Day style massacre. But Myra McPherson appeared unafraid. This seemed to be a standard procedure with which she was familiar. She held Randy close to her side.

The limo had parked next to a white car that also featured deeply tinted windows. "We'll change here," said Agent Foster.

Four more agents waited in the hangar. David felt surrounded. Also underdressed. A new agent, equally tall and blank-faced, held open a back door of the white car. David stayed close to Myra, but a hand gripped his arm suddenly.

"No, sir. Our instructions don't include you."

"You take your instructions from her," David said, looking to Myra for help.

"Not exactly," said the agent. "We're taking her home."

"No!"

"Her condo here in town," the agent said patiently. "We need to get them to a secure place. She'll be allowed to contact you."

"She'd better be." David leaned into the car, where Myra had taken her place with Randy beside her. She had begun to resume her resigned, deadened expression that David recognized. "Myra," he said sharply, but in an undertone. The first time he had used her first name obviously got her attention. "Call me right away. At my house. Here's the number. All right?" Quickly he wrote his home number on the palm of her hand. Myra smiled.

David reached to squeeze Randy's shoulder. The boy looked up at David with a frightening imitation of his mother's resignation. David straightened up and said to every Secret Service agent looking at him, which was none of them, "If I don't hear from her within forty-five minutes, I'm going to raise hell. I'll be on every network news show an hour later."

The agents managed to conceal their trembling. Still ignoring David, four of them got into the white car and took off.

That left four agents behind. One of them turned formally to Helen and said, "Helen Wills, you're under arrest. Come with me, please."

Helen nodded as if she had expected this. But David felt shocked. "What the hell—?" he said, stepping between Helen and the agent. "For what?"

"Criminal trespass, kidnapping, assault. I'm sure there will be other charges," the agent said in a flat, bored voice. The man had a very rectangular-shaped head, squared off at the jaw and his flat-topped head, and a way of speaking in which his face didn't appear to move at all. When cloning became available, the Secret Service would undoubtedly use this man as their model. "Come with me," he repeated to Helen.

"No." David stayed between them.

"Sir, if you interfere with a government employee in the exercise of his duties you'll be arrested too. I believe charges are already being contemplated against you, as soon as a positive identification can be made."

"You're not taking her."

"David," Helen began resignedly. He waved her to silence.

David stepped even closer to the tall agent and lowered his voice. "Do you know the real story behind that 'kidnapping'? Why don't you go and ask the 'victim,' the one who just rode away in the white car, if she thinks she was kidnapped or *rescued*. Do you want the true story of that hostage-taking to come out? Because if you arrest her it will, I promise you. At her bail hearing, at her arraignment, at trial, and in every newspaper and on every news show in America in the meantime. Starting now."

"We're taking her back to Washington," the agent responded. His voice had changed, lost its flatness. He seemed to be negotiating. "You won't be able to interfere there."

"You think I won't be able to get in touch with a lawyer there who *will* interfere? Any lawyer in the country would want to get involved in this case. You can't find a court where I couldn't find a small army of lawyers to intervene on her behalf. Besides, Ms. Wills is working for Mrs. McPherson now. The First Lady does have the right to hire her own staff, regardless of anything else."

The agent didn't respond. The mere fact that he no longer tried to push David aside showed his hesitation. David said even more quietly and firmly, "I think you'd better check with your superiors."

He tried not to sneer on the last word, but the agent looked at him sharply, as if insulted. Nonetheless, he recognized good advice when he heard it.

"I'll do that." Over David's shoulder he said to Helen, "Don't leave the jurisdiction."

"Where could I go where you couldn't get me?" she said in the same resigned voice. Better than David, she knew the necessity of appeasing a man like this agent. The only way a clash like this could end well was if no one felt like a victor.

But David clearly did. He took Helen's arm and walked quickly away. When they hit the twilit world outside the hangar he grinned. "You surprised me," Helen acknowledged. "You might be a good lawyer after all."

"So far I haven't done any legal work in this case. But I'll get my chance. Now it's back to secret-agenting, though. The Secret Service has her again."

"She's still their responsibility. But things are different now. They don't mean her any harm, David. I know those people. Most of them are very loyal to her."

"They helped hold her hostage."

"Because they were lied to. I think they know better now. I don't think anyone's going to be able to use the Service to get to her again. They'll have to find another way."

David started to object again, but Helen quieted him by turning to face him. "I'll go check on her right now. Make sure they did take her to the condo."

"Will you be all right there?"

Helen grinned suddenly, that mischievous grin he had seen only one time before, and loved. "If not, I know a good lawyer to call."

And to his complete surprise, she kissed him. She leaned in, tilting her head, and kissed his mouth, not in a slow, lingering way, but not hurriedly, either. Just as David was passing from shock to enjoyment, she drew back. "I'll call you," she said, turning away.

"That's what everyone says at the end of the first date."

He heard her quietly chuckle as she disappeared into the dusk, striding away confidently. David found himself standing on the asphalt of San Antonio International Airport, alone for the first time in days. He turned toward the terminal building and saw through its windows that the crowd of reporters had found him again. He walked slowly toward the building, feeling very strange. Of the small group of adventurers, he was the only one home again. But his life had changed completely, and David felt changed as well. His old worries—a shortage of clients and of money—seemed trivial. In a week his world had expanded enormously.

He walked to meet the press, reaching to straighten his tie and remembering that he hadn't worn one in days.

Ninety minutes later David got home to a house with overly long grass in the yard and a pile of mail inside the front door. The house was dark and muggy. David felt as if he'd been away for weeks. Nothing looked familiar. He took a long shower and changed into shorts and a T-shirt. When he walked back out into the spacious living room the house had regained its hominess. It felt expansive after the last few cramped days. David stretched out luxuriously on the couch, then frowned when a knock came at the door. Were the reporters so persistent?

But through the peephole he saw Helen, and the last of his weariness fell away. He opened the door quickly and pulled her inside.

"She's okay," Helen said at once. "Randy's fine too. The condo has a computer and a Nintendo game. I think they feel a little lost, but . . ."

"I know the feeling." And David could tell that Helen did too. Her eyes wandered around his living room.

"And I got my official discharge from the Service," she added listlessly.

"Oh, Helen." David put his arms around her. She accepted the hug, even raising her arms up his back, but David could feel Helen's sadness. Of course she had known this would happen, but the officialness of her firing today had obviously hit her. In being relieved of her duties, Helen had also been stripped of her identity. Secret Service agent wasn't just Helen's job. She was a Secret Service agent.

Now an ex-one. David wondered if the agent who had fired her had also said something insulting. Helen seemed to be questioning herself. She drew away and looked around David's living room again. It seemed hard for her to take in the reality of an ordinary home. She held up the shopping bag in her hand.

"I bought a few clothes, but now I don't know where to go. I don't want to go back to Washington. . . ."

"No. She still needs you."

"And I didn't quite feel safe in a hotel, although a room to myself does sound good after the last week."

David took her hand and led her across the room through the bedroom door. He turned on the light and waved at the room, and at its bathroom door. "Here," he said, "this is yours."

"I couldn't take your room."

"Sure you could. Just for tonight. I'll stay in the guest room."

"Well . . ."

"What I most wanted when I got here was a shower and a change of clothes."

Helen looked wistful, but kept making excuses, holding up her shopping bag. "I didn't get many new clothes, there wasn't much time to shop. . . ."

David pointed out the dresser and the closet.

"Wear anything of mine that might fit."

Helen's expression grew more lively. "None of it would, I hope."

"Hey, I've still got clothes from when I was fourteen."

David turned to leave the room, but Helen stopped him, with a hint of playfulness in her voice. "You wouldn't try to take advantage of a poor homeless girl, would you?"

"Not one with your training." He closed the door behind him.

Helen spent half an hour in the other room, and for most of that time David paced his house, sitting on the couch and popping up again. He turned the television on and off, then went to his stereo and looked over his collection of CDs, which now seemed pathetic. He didn't want to choose anything overtly romantic and certainly not something depressing, and almost gave up. Finally he picked something by Quartet West that was mostly instrumental jazz but with a few surprising vocals thrown in. He had just started it when Helen reappeared.

She wore an old, soft, long-sleeved light blue shirt of his, which fit her long enough that he could barely tell whether she wore anything underneath. But he recognized a pair of his running shorts that he hadn't worn in so long he'd forgotten he still had them. Helen couldn't resist striking a pose. His ill-fitting clothes became her, taking away her stiff formality. Her short blond hair was barely brushed, the ends still damp. Helen had rid herself of her lost look. She smiled.

"My," David said. He was afraid of making her mad with any more effusive compliment.

Helen raised the tail of the shirt to pull out the waistband of the shorts. "These do fit me big," she said commandingly.

"Oh, yeah, they're giant on you, they look like they might—they're about to—mm huh."

In lifting the shirt she had given him a glimpse of her taut stomach, contoured like the landscape of a strange and inviting land. David blinked. He decided to kiss her again, but found he lacked the nerve at this moment. Helen watched him, seeming to read his thoughts.

"Yes, I'd like a drink," she said. "Scotch if you have it."

"Yes, ma'am." David went to the kitchen and returned with two amber drinks. He found Helen still standing, looking around. The bareness of his living room suddenly embarrassed him. A couch, two armchairs, a coffee table. The furniture was all contemporary with the exception of a spindly, elaborately carved rocking chair off to the side. The chair had sat years ago on the porch of his grandmother's house. One summer he had spent a lot of time in it, sitting with his knees pulled up, his arms around them, barely rocking, and looking far away.

But Helen liked the room. He felt her approval. After their days in tiny motel rooms and the cramped car, this small house felt luxurious with only the two of them there.

Helen took a long swallow of her drink, then sat in the middle of the couch and put her head back. David sat at the end.

"Randy asked about you," she said quietly. "He misses you. It's like you're his only friend. What did you do to get close to him so fast?"

David looked at her to see if she seemed suspicious of his

motives, but Helen appeared to be asking an honest question.

"It wasn't hard. Anybody could do it. I played catch with him for half an hour, asked him a couple of questions, let him talk. He's dying just for somebody to show a little interest in him. Like every child."

"He snuggled up to you, in the backseat of the car. He's never done that with me."

David stared across the room, obviously invaded by memory. Helen watched him.

"Have you ever had a child in your charge? Been responsible for him?"

David sat with his elbows on his knees, fingers interlaced, and started to answer casually. "Sure, a few times. I've had . . ." He stopped. "No, not really."

"Randy is mine. More than he's hers, in some ways. I've been responsible for him." Helen spoke almost angrily, but no longer in her old flat voice. David heard emotion swelling beneath her words. He realized she had probably been close to getting in trouble over this. Bodyguards weren't supposed to get emotionally involved with their protectees. "Certainly he's more mine than he is his father's," she continued. "I won't let you hurt him."

"Helen, I may have to do some things in this case that—Never mind. I won't."

"If you mess with him I'll drop you like a target on the range."

"It's a deal."

Her eyes had gone moist. Helen swallowed the last of her drink and said, "You scare me."

"Me?"

"I brought her to you. Remember? It was her idea, but I took her to your office. That's why I had to be so suspicious of you, I felt responsible. I still do, even if I'm out of it. Now I'm starting to think you can be trusted, and that scares the hell out of me."

She stared at him some more, then laughed. "Stop trying to look innocent, you're no good at it."

They sat in companionable silence for a few minutes. Then Helen went to his bookshelves and looked over the spines of his books. David stood close by. Without looking at him, she said, "They're watching us, you know."

"What?" David looked toward his front windows at the far end of the room.

"Maybe not literally, not this second. But they know I'm here. They suspect the worst."

"What's the worst?"

"That we're just conspirators. That somehow we've been in on this all along." Helen moved closer to him. A pause held them in place for a long moment. Slowly, expression changing softly, Helen leaned close and kissed him, more lingeringly than at the airport. Her hands moved on his arms. When she drew back she said, "I've lost my job, but now I've got you to protect."

"I'm okay."

"You have no idea, David. They're going to come after you so hard. Are you ready?"

"This isn't my first case, Helen."

She laughed quietly, and held his arm again. "I'm going to stay right next to you."

"Not that I'm resisting the idea, but I don't think I need a bodyguard."

"Oh, no? Remember that guy who came after us in South Carolina?"

David said, "He was after Mrs. McPherson. Or Randy."

"Really? Are you sure?"

He looked toward the front windows again, and Helen started walking away, toward the bedroom. "So sleep well," she said. "I'll be on the job."

She walked slowly to the bedroom door. David decided her hips definitely moved more than when he'd first met her. Helen turned at the door, caught him watching, and gave him another curious stare, not flirtatious. "Are you really up to this?"

He knew she meant the case. "We should have a little breathing room for a while now."

"Don't count on it." She went into the bedroom. David moved around the house for a few minutes putting away their glasses, turning off lights, and washing up. The windows made him nervous. He should have an alarm system installed. From the second bedroom, which was furnished as an office, he got sheets from a closet. He spread them on the couch and lay down. The couch was thick and comfortable for lounging, but felt lumpy as a bed. Sleep might not come on this night anyway, with thoughts of Helen in his bed and possible malevolent strangers lurking outside.

Sometime later he thought he heard the click of the door latch. Thinking maybe the bedroom door had come open from a stray breeze, he sat up. Moonlight and streetlights filtered through the living room's windows, making the room brighter than dark but still dim.

Helen, coming out of the bedroom door, saw David's head over the back of the couch. "I thought you were in the guest room."

"This is the guest room. There's another so-called bedroom, but it doesn't have a bed in it. It's all right, I'm fine here."

She crossed the room to him. "I thought I heard something."

David lay where he was, unconsciously holding his breath. Helen now wore one of his T-shirts, a white one that made her look ghostly coming toward him. Her arms and legs looked very smooth in the dim light.

"I've been lying there worrying about you," she said quietly. "I want you next to me."

"Helen, are you—"

"It's a flimsy excuse, I know, but it happens to be true."

Helen put her leg over the back of the couch, her foot landing next to his leg, then she climbed over. Balancing above him, she leaned down and kissed him. David responded. Helen's hand landed on his chest and moved gently as he reached up inside her shirt. Her skin felt taut, expectant, waiting for caresses.

David thought she'd want him to say something. "Helen—"

"Shut up."

"Can't I say anything?"

"You can moan my name deliriously."

She sounded humorous but they didn't laugh. He caressed her arms and her back, marveling at the smooth polish of her skin, the strength underneath. Deftly, Helen tugged at the waistband of his briefs. Even in playfulness and in lovemaking, there remained an underlying seriousness to her. He felt her thinking, and trying to avoid thinking.

After a while the couch began to seem very narrow. They walked to the bedroom together, the short journey requiring a couple of stops for long kisses and embraces. Helen made a point of closing the bedroom door behind them, putting one more barrier between them and the outside world.

In bed, clothes gone, he kissed her shoulder while her hands continued to move on him, gently then more forcefully. He held her very close, their skin touching the full length of their bodies. Helen put her head on his shoulder, seeming to relax. But slowly her arms and legs moved, first touching then surrounding him, as if she would engulf him.

"Is this the approved Secret Service position for maximum protection?" he whispered.

"No. This is."

She kissed him softly as her body moved more forcefully. She took the lead for most of the time that followed, but David didn't mind at all. Finally, with a small sigh, she drew back from him. Helen wore a gentle smile he'd never seen on her face before. He touched her cheek and she covered his hand with hers.

They stayed close for a long time, drifting into sleepiness, waking again, stroking each other. No one would have taken them for two people exhausted from a long trip.

★

Outside, Larsen, dressed in black including a black stocking cap that enclosed his long blond hair, drew back from the position where he'd discovered the second Secret Service agent. The agents got up and walked around once in a while, as if on patrol. Larsen decided to withdraw for the night. The agents probably watched Helen Wills because she had been one of their own and they wanted to know just how far her treachery extended. Their protecting her at the same time was only incidental. They wouldn't be here every night. The agents would get bored with this stakeout.

Larsen wouldn't.

★ The next morning David and Helen walked into his office together, momentarily distracting the secretary Janice from her anger at being left to manage on her own for so long. Behind a pile of mail and faxes and messages, Janice looked mortally offended, but when her eyes fell on Helen she became obviously curious instead.

"Hello, Janice. I can't thank you enough for holding down the fort here. This is Helen Wills. You remember her, don't you?"

Helen was dressed rather casually this morning, in navy slacks and a white T-type blouse. She hadn't done much with her hair, wore little makeup, and looked beautiful, alert but not tense. She smiled at Janice.

"No," Janice said slowly. "I remember one time a robot came in here who must have been modeled on you."

"Yes, I was the prototype."

David tried to be businesslike. "Helen is no longer with the Secret Service. Mrs. McPherson has hired her, and Helen's going to be working with me on that case. She'll be working out of here some of the time. So how are we doing here, Janice? What's my most important message?"

Janice handed him a stack of a dozen. She continued to watch Helen, who smiled at her politely, giving nothing away. David retreated to his office and Helen followed.

"I'm going to go check on them," she said.

David nodded.

"You must have planning to do."

"Yes. I need to file a request for temporary orders. Make sure the President gets served. Probably set a hearing soon just to establish the jurisdiction. Schedule depositions . . ."

As he talked he began to smile. Helen looked at him with some concern.

"Are you all right?"

David laughed. For a moment he'd been thinking of this as a normal divorce, but much of his ordinary experience would no longer apply. He knew how serious this case was, how high the stakes not just for his client but for him. David risked looking like a weasel or a fool, but he couldn't help feeling exhilarated. This was the biggest divorce case of the century, and it was his.

Not much time passed before David had a visitor. Helen had gone to visit Myra McPherson and Randy at their condo, but before she'd had time to get there, after David had had only a few minutes to look through his pile of messages, Janice buzzed him.

"Someone to see you."

"I don't have time for any drop-ins this morning," David said irritably.

Janice lowered her voice on the phone. "I think you'll want to, David. His name is Burton Leemis. He says he's the President's lawyer."

David recognized the name, as almost any lawyer in America would. The President's private counsel. Here in San Antonio. In David's office. How bizarre.

David walked slowly out of his office, not wanting to look like a fan rushing for an autograph. In the small reception area Burton

Leemis stood waiting with apparent patience. He didn't carry a briefcase or have a cell phone in evidence. Leemis wore a dark gray suit that hung elegantly on his stout figure. His short brown hair lay unruffled, as did his face. His hand when he extended it to shake was dry and firm.

"Mr. Owens, a pleasure. I wanted to meet the lawyer who had the balls to take on this case."

David didn't match Leemis's smile. "As long as you're here, would you like to accept service of the petition on behalf of the President?"

Leemis chuckled. "We both know better than that, David." He put his hand on David's arm in a friendly, big-brotherly way and motioned toward the door. "Walk with me?"

"Where?"

"Just for the sake of privacy. We need to talk."

Leemis didn't glance at Janice. His eyes stayed on David's and the small smile stayed on his face.

"All right." David said to Janice, "We'll be walking in the neighborhood."

Janice didn't reply in words, but pushed his mobile phone toward him. David slipped it into his pocket, gave her a *who knows?* look, and followed Leemis out into the hall. David's office was on the seventh floor of the old building, so it didn't take them long to reach the ground. Outside, they strolled. This was not a particularly lovely part of San Antonio, featuring mostly parking lots, and the late July day was already hot and muggy this early in the morning. David felt his city wasn't putting forth its best showing for this distinguished visitor, but Leemis didn't seem to notice.

"Mrs. McPherson has to come home," he said without preamble.

"Mrs. McPherson would rather die."

"That's a possibility," Leemis replied without rancor. "As long as she stays outside the zone of White House security, she's putting both their lives in danger. Even worse in some ways. What if one of them is kidnapped?"

"She has Secret Service protection."

"But not the support facilities they need."

"Let's not be ridiculous," David said. "Lots of first families have spent significant time away from the White House. Lady Bird Johnson, Jackie Onassis—"

"—was not the wife of a sitting President when she lived in Manhattan. And Lady Bird lived on a ranch that was as easy to protect as Camp David, not in the middle of a city. But let's pass on from that. I just want to be able to say I've warned you. What about this case itself? You know it can't proceed. You've had your publicity from it, your client has made her point, and of course my client will gladly respond to her concerns in a quiet, private way. But this ridiculous divorce action—"

"It's not ridiculous," David said, growing angrier. "Anyone has the right to get divorced, even a First Lady. If this is your best argument—"

"You can't divorce a sitting President, Mr. Owens. It just can't be done. Your court here doesn't have jurisdiction, to begin with. No one lives here. The case should be in D.C. if anywhere."

"You mean the President's been lying to the whole country every two years when he makes a big show of flying back to San Antonio to cast his vote on election day? That's just been a fraud to keep himself connected to a state with a lot of electoral votes?"

Leemis smiled and shook his head as if in conversation with a child. "He did what every sitting President has done since the office existed. That doesn't create jurisdiction, and you can't use it to embarrass the President, either. You have no leverage there. Don't think you can blackmail us with threats to the President's image."

The case itself would do enough to ruin the President's image. David understood that underlying issue. The President wanted the case to go away completely, to have someone say it had been a mistake or a lie. David's client, on the other hand, wanted desperately to get away from the White House and her husband. This discussion couldn't come to any resolution.

"Look," he said, stopping on the sidewalk. "Just file your answer and we'll have a hearing. We're not going to reach agreement on this. A judge will have—"

"Please," Leemis said, smiling placatingly. "Just walk. We may not get another chance like this."

So David resumed walking. Leemis strolled very casually, like a tourist, and toned down the discussion, even asking David questions about his background and his practice, as if they were chatting at a cocktail party.

A sudden buzz sounded like the heat reverberating off the buildings, but then David realized it was his phone. Leemis frowned as David pulled the phone out of his pocket. Obviously the other lawyer hadn't noticed David slipping it into his pocket before he left the office.

"Let's not take any interruptions," Leemis began, but David had already clicked the button and immediately heard Janice screaming at him.

"DAVID! They're taking him! They're taking the little boy!"

"Who is? You mean Randy?" David wasn't sure he'd heard correctly, in spite of Janice's volume, so loud that Burton Leemis obviously heard her three feet away. The lawyer began edging away from David.

"Yes, Randy!" Janice shouted frantically. "Men from the White House. They showed up at the condo a few minutes ago. Helen called to tell you. She needs help!"

David grabbed Leemis's arm. "This is why you wanted to get me out of the office. You bastard."

Half a block down the street a white Continental pulled away from the curb and came toward them. The car moved so purposefully toward them that for a moment David feared they were both going to be victims of a drive-by shooting. But that wasn't the white car's purpose.

"You're coming with me," David said, tugging on the burly Leemis's arm. But the lawyer jerked away.

"The hell I am. This is your mess. I've taken care of mine."

He walked to the curb and the white Continental pulled to a stop next to him. Its back door came open.

"All right," David shouted. "But you're on notice. I'm asking you to come with me and you refuse."

Leemis laughed. "There's nothing you can do, Mr. Owens. You've already lost." He stepped into the car, which sped away even before the door closed. David stood alone on the sidewalk. He crossed the street, beginning to run. Janice was still screaming in his mobile phone. Panting, David said, "Janice, listen. Here's exactly what you have to do." As he gave her rapid, explicit instructions, he continued to run, as if he could catch up to the agents who had come to snatch Randy McPherson.

Helen Wills stood on the hot asphalt of the parking lot underneath Myra McPherson's condominium building, feeling glad to be wearing her relatively tight T-shirt and slacks, because if she'd had any suspicious bulges or even loose clothing she might have been shot by now. On the other hand, she felt fairly certain of being the only unarmed person in sight, and that didn't make her happy.

She stepped close to the black-suited Secret Service agent in front of her and said, "Ben, you need to ease off. This isn't in the client's best interest. He's going to hurt himself trying to get away from you, and then where will you be?"

Ben Foster, looking everywhere except at her, said, "Back away, Helen. You're not part of this."

This parking area filled the ground level of the condominium building, large enough to hold maybe four dozen cars. White brick walls enclosed the space almost completely. At the north and south sides, ornamental gates stood closed, a uniformed security guard inside each one. Other black-suited men also guarded the gates, while half a dozen more scoured the parking area. Upstairs, more agents and other men continued to go through the First Lady's

condo, looking for Randy McPherson. The boy had been alone in
his bedroom when a commotion had broken out at the front door of
the condo, as Myra McPherson asked what these intruders wanted.
By the time they'd opened the door of Randy's bedroom, the window
had stood open and Randy had been gone.

A drainage pipe on the wall beside that second-floor window led
down to this common area, so the men had come here. It seemed
clear Randy wouldn't have had a chance to reach the outside world.
Those security gates hadn't opened since the men had arrived. But
the parking area afforded a fair amount of hiding space: under cars,
inside storage closets and trash cans. Four doors led back into the
condo complex itself. So the agents searched methodically while
Helen tried to talk to them, which proved futile.

She walked away from Foster, hoping somehow Randy could see
her. But if he came out of hiding now and ran toward her, what could
she do? She looked around, trying to plan an escape route. She had
a rental car, but didn't think it could crash one of those gates. If she
did the car would be disabled and the agents would have her within
a block. On foot, on the other hand, dragging Randy . . .

"David, David," she muttered. "I told you you weren't ready."

A woman's scream froze everyone in the parking area. Helen
looked up. The second time Myra McPherson screamed, Helen recognized her voice.

"Randyyyyyyyyyyy!" the First Lady cried, a tragic wail that
stopped the listener's heart.

Helen ran toward the stairs. Before she could reach them, it
became clear the commotion and the reason for Myra's distress was
descending. A black-suited man came into view, carrying a struggling boy wearing black soccer shorts and a T-shirt. Randy tried to
dig into the man's ribs with his elbows, he flailed his head back
against the man's chest, but those small blows had no effect. The
man stoically carried him down into the parking area.

Behind him, Myra McPherson came too, half restrained by two
Secret Service agents who looked very stressed, trying to hold her
back and protect her at the same time.

"Give him here!" Myra shouted. "Give him back to me! Randy!"

Another man joined the one holding Randy. Together they got him on his feet and held in place with their hands on his shoulders. "We're just taking him to his father, ma'am. He wants to see him."

"Then let him come here!" Myra screamed.

But the men hadn't come to debate her. They began pulling Randy toward a black car with tinted windows. A door opened and Mrs. Phelan emerged, a kindly, grandmotherly woman who had sometimes served as Randy's nanny at the White House. Obviously she had been brought along to keep Randy calm on the flight home. She smiled at him affectionately.

Burton Leemis stood off to the side, not looking happy. But his client would be. Leemis came forward. "Where did you find him?"

"Up on the top shelf of the closet in his bedroom. He just opened that window to throw us off."

"Smart boy," Leemis said. "Come on, Randy, let's go home. Wouldn't you like to see your dad?"

"No," Randy said breathlessly, still struggling with his captors.

A screech of tires made everyone react. Agents' hands went inside their jackets. Helen jumped toward Myra McPherson, as did two other agents, who pulled her to the ground and blocked her. Two more grabbed Randy.

Outside the north security gate, a blue Toyota had come to a stop. David Owens jumped out of it, carrying a fistful of papers. He strode up to the gate and talked through it to the uniformed security guard. "Let me in."

The guard licked his lips. He was fifty-seven years old, twenty-five pounds overweight, a retired bus driver who still spent most of his days sitting. "Sir, this is a private residence—" he began his prepared speech.

"Yes, and I work for one of the residents, Mrs. McPherson. There she is over there, ask her."

"David!" Myra shouted, struggling to her feet. She reached toward him imploringly. The guard saw her obvious anguish.

But he continued nervously, "Sir, these men—"

"—have no authority over you," David said firmly. "What's more, they don't have a court order, and I do." He thrust a document through the bars. "Let me in," he repeated.

The guard barely glanced at the paper. It looked official, and that relieved him of responsibility. He pressed a button and the gates separated and began sliding open. As soon as David stepped through, the guard stopped the gates and closed them again. The whole crew remained locked inside the parking area: Myra and Randy McPherson, Helen, David, and the dozen or so men and women in black suits. David walked toward the biggest cluster of them.

Randy broke free and ran to him, throwing his arms around him. David bent to hug him and say, "It'll be all right."

"They want to take me away," Randy whimpered.

"I know. Listen to what I say to them and back me up, okay, Randy?"

Asking for Randy's help calmed the boy down, as David had thought it would. He straightened up and walked with Randy still clinging to him. Ben Foster, who appeared to be the agent-in-charge, waited, watching him warily.

"David," Myra said, struggling to her feet as well. "Why didn't you know this would happen?"

"It's all right," David said to his client. "Agent Foster, I have here a temporary restraining order that forbids removing Randy McPherson from this county. Helen, would you serve this on Mr. Foster, please?"

David handed one of the orders to Helen, who passed it on to Foster. Foster glanced over it quickly and didn't look impressed.

"This is directed at the President."

"As well as his agents, employees, and anyone acting on his behalf. I'm sure you fall into one of those categories," David said.

"And it's signed by a Texas state judge. He doesn't have any authority over me."

"He has authority over everyone in this state. If you want to assert some federal privilege, you'll have to come into court to do so. In the meantime, if you take this boy away from here you'll be in contempt of court, which is a criminal offense. I'll have you arrested."

Foster smiled tightly. "I don't think so."

"Yeah? You want to be involved in a standoff like that at the airport, in front of crowds? You think that's the best idea for your protectees?"

Foster stepped closer to David and lowered his voice. "Look, I'm not acting on anyone's orders except the directives of my own agency. I'm not trying to help snatch the boy. I'm just protecting him."

For the first time, David realized there was a distinction among the dark-suited people in the parking area. Most of them were Secret Service agents he recognized to one degree or another. Some few, though, four or five men, stood apart from the others. Tall, grim-looking men, they now stepped forward, led by Burton Leemis.

"That's right, Mr. Owens. These men are from the President's office, acting on his orders. He's not only the President, he's Randy's father. He has a right to possession of him. You have no right to interfere."

"This says I do. Helen, hand a copy of the order to the attorney, please."

Helen did so. Leemis looked for a moment as if he wouldn't take the document from her, but then he did. "The President has not hired me to represent him in this matter," he said formally. "I am not accepting service on his behalf. When he does respond officially, he will of course exert his executive privilege not to be dragged into any court in the land."

"Fine," David said. "Among other things, that order sets the case for a hearing on temporary orders. Two days from now. That's for your benefit, Mr. Leemis. Because you weren't there to present your side of the case to the judge half an hour ago. Now you can, if you want. If not, the temporary restraining order will be extended until we do have a hearing."

Leemis shrugged as if ignoring this explanation. "In the meantime," he said, "Randy's going to be with his father."

He motioned with his head, and two of the big men stepped forward and took Randy's arms. Randy squealed, David shouted, but before David could move he was knocked aside as Agent Foster and another Secret Service agent barreled forward and knocked the President's men back, yanking Randy away from them. Furious, Foster thrust Randy behind him and almost stuck his finger through the other man's nose. "Don't you EVER touch him again!" he shouted.

"Foster," Burton Leemis said placatingly. "He's sorry. These men have their job to do and so do you. They're going to obey the President's orders and you're going to come along to do your job. All right?"

Myra McPherson sobbed quietly. "Sir?" an agent called, and the group became aware of a murmur of noise. A light flashed.

The sound and the light came from the two security gates. David regained his feet. "Oh, and by the way," he said to Leemis, "I invited them."

Three or four reporters and cameramen of both the print and airwave variety stood at each gate. Cameras held on the people in the parking area, recording everything.

"Do you think your client will want this evening's newscasts to lead off with footage of his son being dragged away from his mother, screaming and crying? Do you think that will be a good launch for his custody case? Believe me, we'll see they get their footage, both here and again at the airport. That and the arrest scene, Texas state troopers against federal agents, with Randy in the middle thanks to his father. If that's what you want . . ."

Helen had grabbed Randy and held his face against her, protecting him from being photographed. On cue, Randy wailed, "Mom!" Myra McPherson went and covered him as well. Burton Leemis flinched slightly at the boy's cry and looked back and forth at the two exits blocked by reporters, and at the car with its dark-tinted windows.

But Agent Foster made the decision. "It's already set for a hearing. We'll let a judge decide."

He gestured to his people and they surrounded Myra and Randy and began leading them to the stairs. "David?" Myra called.

David gave Leemis a last look and then hurried to catch up to his client. "Oh, God," Myra said, clutching his hand. "Is every day going to be like this?"

She looked at the agents surrounding her. "I'm getting very mixed feelings about you people. But thank you."

"I'm sorry, ma'am," Foster said with strong traces of emotion. He and David exchanged a look, and David saw how conflicted the agent remained. Foster, too, wanted to be rescued.

David let the group go, and saw that Leemis and the President's men were already driving away. No telling what they would do next.

"Thank you," David said to Helen. "You held them off long enough for me to do something. I wouldn't have been able to—"

"Randy did it. I couldn't have. God, David."

She put her arms around him briefly. "I didn't know what you could do, but you were the only person I knew to call."

Ruefully, David said, "We need to get this case into court, where I at least vaguely know what I'm doing."

"I think you did pretty well just now." Helen smiled. They went upstairs with their clients.

Across the street from the condominium building a large vacant lot held enough trees to conceal one thin person. Larsen stood in the midst of them. He had watched the comings and goings of the dark-suited men without much curiosity, just resentment that they got in his way. He'd seen the arrivals of the woman and the lawyer, too, with more interest.

His mobile phone rang and he clicked it on without saying anything. Very, very few people would call him deliberately, and those who did knew his habits of minimal speech.

Wilson Boswell did. He verified his employee's identity and

began talking. "I'm afraid I have some bad news for you, Mr. Larsen. We're going to have to sever our connection."

Larsen seemed to pay little attention, still staring across the street. "You don't want me calling you?"

"I don't want you working for me. Your recent activity has been unacceptable. It could be an embarrassment or even a legal liability for TitanWorks Corporation. I'm afraid your employment with us is terminated, Mr. Larsen. Of course you'll receive a severance package and you may return once to collect your belongings."

Larsen listened more attentively, but couldn't understand what his boss said. He didn't for a moment take Boswell's words at face value. "Why?" he said.

"Because of this obsession of yours with Mrs. McPherson and her son. I don't know what you're doing there, but with that situation ongoing I can't have you working for me."

"Oh," Larsen said, beginning to comprehend.

"I am quite sincere," Boswell said fastidiously.

"You mean it? I'm really fired?" Larsen's face began to darken. He held the phone more tightly.

"Indeed." Boswell ended the call. In his office, he looked at his phone with satisfaction, thinking he'd managed to set just the right events in motion.

In the vacant lot, Larsen threw his phone on the ground. He didn't know whether he'd just received instructions or really been fired. Either way, he knew it was the fault of those people across the street.

He continued to watch the condo building, even more intently.

Two days later David stood in Presiding Court in the Bexar County Courthouse. San Antonio boasts an unusual system of docketing civil cases. Every case set for a hearing on a given morning is called in the large Presiding Court at the north end of the second floor,

then assigned by the Presiding Judge to whichever of a dozen or
more judges is available. Ten minutes before a hearing, the lawyers
have no idea what judge will be hearing the case that morning. It is
a system that encourages settlements.

That morning, by prearrangement, the Presiding Judge called
only the case number for David's case, not the names of the parties.
Nonetheless, other lawyers watched David with great interest,
knowing very well what client he represented.

"I'm here for the petitioner," David said, on his feet. He stood
rather casually, not expecting a response, not having seen Burton
Leemis or any Secret Service agents in the building that morning.

But from one of the two counsel tables a local attorney named
Brad Stinson stood too, looking at a piece of paper in his hand to be
sure of the case number. "I'm here for the respondent, Your Honor."

David should have expected this. Brad Stinson, who had a perpetually distracted air that disguised a very clever mind, was a well-
known San Antonio divorce lawyer. Obviously Burton Leemis, a
very careful lawyer representing a very important client, would
have given himself every possible advantage, including hiring local
counsel.

"Judge Shahan is available," the Presiding Judge said calmly, as if
there were nothing special about this case, and David and Brad
Stinson walked out into the hall. "So you're here to respond?" David
asked. "Do you have witnesses?"

"Not sure yet," Stinson said, as if he hadn't prepared for this at
all. David felt a slight tingle of alarm.

The two men separated on their way up to Judge Louise Shahan's
courtroom on the fourth floor, both pulling out phones. David took
the stairs. He used his phone to call Helen. "Bring her in," he said
shortly. "Judge Shahan's court, fourth floor." He gave rapid directions.

"What's happening?" Helen asked.

"I don't know yet, but something is."

The halls didn't hold many people, this end of the fourth floor of
the courthouse provided a good setting for a quiet hearing. David

reached the courtroom first, and went inside to tell the judge's clerk that a case had been sent. Judge Louise Shahan walked by and said casually, "Bringing me anything interesting, David?"

"Judge, you have no idea."

"Guess I'd better get into uniform then." The judge walked out into the large courtroom, leaving the door open, heading toward her office behind the bench. David followed slowly. The bailiff sitting at his desk inside the court railing waved in a friendly way. David felt at home. He could play this room, the scene of his triumph with Mary Smathers. Publicity over that case had brought the First Lady to him initially, and now she had brought him back. Today would play out differently, though. He knew that, he just didn't know how.

A clue came when the door from the hall opened and Burton Leemis walked in. He looked as well groomed and self-confident as he had when David had seen him two days earlier, but this time Leemis carried a large briefcase and appeared more lawyerly. He nodded curtly.

"I really didn't expect to see you here," David said.

Leemis spread his hands. "As you can see, you were wrong."

Behind Leemis, the courtroom door opened again and another man entered. Then a woman, then more people. David recognized Rose Phelan, the White House nanny, a couple of Secret Service agents, and Louis Roswall, the President's chief of staff. David felt confidence begin to empty out of him as the crowd of people brushed by him and followed Burt Leemis up the aisle, where they assembled around the lawyer inside the courtroom railing and listened to his instructions.

My God, they'd brought an army. Bringing up the rear, Brad Stinson gave David a half-embarrassed shrug and went up to join the throng.

A minute later David still stood at the back of the courtroom holding his briefcase when Helen and Myra McPherson entered, accompanied by three more Secret Service agents. Myra began to smile at David, then saw the group at the front of the courtroom and lost her smile completely.

"David," she said tremulously.

"It will be all right." David took her arm and drew her close to him. "Who are they all?"

"There's Louis, the chief of staff. His main quality is that he's fiercely loyal to John. Gloria Taylor, a secretary. That man is a foreign policy aide, I forget his name. Mrs. Phelan—Randy's never much liked her, I should have fired her a long time ago. My God, look at them all, David. Where are all our witnesses?"

"We don't need that many," he said, trying to sound confident. He led her up the aisle to the other counsel table. People from the President's group turned and looked at them. Two or three even greeted Myra courteously. Leemis stepped away from his crowd to shake her hand. "Good morning, Mrs. McPherson, I trust you've been well."

"Yes," Myra said stiffly, "except worried sick ever since you tried to kidnap my son."

Leemis smiled. "Even your own lawyer will tell you, I think, that what happened can't be characterized that way. At any rate, here we are to make our respective cases."

The bailiff suddenly stood and said, "All rise!"

Judge Shahan came out from her office and stood behind the high judge's bench. She looked out wonderingly on the crowd in front of her. "This is on temporary orders?" she asked.

Both David and Burton Leemis answered, "Yes, Your Honor," then Leemis stepped forward and introduced himself. "First," he said, "with all due respect to the court, we must challenge this court's authority to hear this case. Jurisdiction doesn't lie here, none of the parties lives in this state or county. Furthermore, the Respondent exerts his executive privilege as President of the United States, head of the executive branch, which is co-equal to the judicial, not to be brought before any tribunal against his will."

David heard this unperturbed. "We're not set for a hearing on jurisdiction this morning, Your Honor."

Judge Shahan opened the court's file in front of her. "That's true, Mr. Leemis. The only thing I have before me is the petitioner's temporary restraining order and request for temporary orders. If you're requesting a continuance, I could extend the temporary restraining order—"

"No, thank you, Your Honor. As long as this hearing and any orders are made subject to our plea to the jurisdiction."

"All right, Mr. Leemis, I'll grant that," Judge Shahan said quietly. "Then are we ready to begin? Mr. Owens, are you ready to proceed?"

"Yes, Your Honor." David turned quickly toward his client and spoke to her in a rapid undertone.

Judge Shahan waited a moment, waited for something to happen. Nothing did, and the judge realized that David Owens had just made his first mistake. Apparently flustered by the sight of all those witnesses for the other side, he had forgotten to invoke the rule that would exclude the witnesses from the courtroom during each other's testimony. Some judges would ask if either side wanted the rule enforced, but Louise Shahan was not one to do the lawyers' jobs for them. The moment passed.

Burton Leemis, realizing his adversary's absentminded lapse, quickly motioned his witnesses to seats in the spectator pews, urging them to silence. The witnesses sat filling two rows, like the most prominent mourners at a funeral.

David, apparently not noticing that crowd of witnesses at his back, said, "We'll call Myra McPherson."

He guided Myra to the witness stand. Judge Shahan instructed the First Lady to raise her right hand, and with an ironic glint in her eye, swore her in, then added graciously, "Welcome to our court-room, Mrs. McPherson."

"Thank you, Your Honor." Myra took her seat and gazed out at the large courtroom. The other side's witnesses watched her avidly. She glanced at Leemis, who sat casually toying with a pencil. He smiled at her, and Myra's shoulders hunched inward.

David quickly established his client's identity and the purpose of the hearing. "Mrs. McPherson, you had me file a petition for divorce on your behalf?"

"Yes."

"Do you want to be divorced from your husband?"

Myra shifted in her seat. She had never before made this declara-tion in public. "Yes."

"And are you asking that you have primary custody of your son?"

"Most definitely. That's what's most important to me."

"Why?"

Myra looked down at her hands. "I want to take Randy out of the White House. It's not a good atmosphere for him. I want him to have a more normal life."

"What about Randy's father? Do you want to take Randy away from him?"

"Oh, no." Myra looked up, and spoke rapidly and sincerely. "I want John to spend as much time with Randy as possible. I want him to spend more time than he does now. But I realize that won't happen. We live in the same building now, and John almost never has time for him."

"You realize your husband has important other work to do?"

"Of course. But that's hard to explain to an eight-year-old boy. Especially since things have been that way Randy's whole life. Maybe someday he'll understand his father was a very important man involved in weighty matters, that's why he didn't have time for Randy. But by that time his childhood will be over."

"Mrs. McPherson, do *you* have time for your son?"

"That's all I do, that's my most important job."

She looked at that crowd of witnesses again, all staring at her as if doubting every word she said. Myra looked abashed, but then straightened her shoulders and sat up. Judge Shahan watched her closely, not betraying any reaction to the testimony.

David had Myra describe a typical day with Randy, what cereal he liked, what clothes he always wanted to wear, driving him to school when she could, picking him up.

"Does he ever play with any of his schoolmates outside of school?"

"Once in a while." Myra frowned. "I try to arrange that, but it's hard. I'm sure the other parents are afraid to invite Randy over, they don't want to look like social climbers, and they know how difficult it would be to arrange." She glanced at her own Secret Service agents, one standing close beside her, another over by the door to the judge's office. That glance explained her meaning. "And if we invited another child to the White House, it's like a state occasion. Randy doesn't even ask for it."

David gestured back over his shoulder. So he hadn't forgotten the other side's witnesses. "Mrs. McPherson, do you know these people?"

"Yes. Most of them. Nearly all of them."

Those witnesses sat straight, staring somberly at the First Lady. They were an intimidating crowd, weighty in their numbers and their apparent solidarity.

"Who are they?"

"People who work in the White House or my husband's administration."

"Family friends?"

"Not really. Louis Roswall we've known a long time; he's an old friend of John's. Other than that, they're professional colleagues."

"Have they been in your home, the residence part of the White House?"

Myra looked them over. "Mrs. Phelan has been, of course. She takes care of Randy when I have to be away."

"Do you spend very many nights away from the White House?"

"No, I try not to."

"When you are away, is it accompanying your husband?"

"Usually. Maybe once a month I have to be gone myself overnight, appearing somewhere. But my staff know I don't like to do that and they try not to arrange those trips. Sometimes if I have to go I take Randy with me."

"Other than Mrs. Phelan, has any of these people spent much time with your son?"

"No. Very little. They see Randy once in a while on formal occasions. I suppose they may see him in the Oval Office occasionally, too. But not very often. He's usually in school or with me."

David hoped with that explanation he had managed to poison any testimony those strangers in the spectator seats might offer. He looked steadily at his client, willing her courage. "Mrs. McPherson, do you think it's in Randy's best interest that your son stay with you, during this temporary orders period?"

"Oh, yes. He has to. I'm the only parent he's ever known." She turned to look directly at the judge. Judge Shahan subtly shifted so she no longer looked directly at the First Lady, but Myra's obviously distressed voice came clearly to her from only a few feet away. "If Randy's ordered to go live with John, he won't have a family at all. He'll just be staying with Mrs. Phelan and wandering the White House like a ghost."

"Thank you, Mrs. McPherson. I pass the witness."

Brad Stinson, the local attorney, sat up straighter at the other counsel table. Burton Leemis slumped slightly in his chair, looking bemused as if he hadn't heard David. Once in a while during Myra's testimony the local lawyer had whispered to Leemis, but he seemed to pay no attention. But Leemis did the cross-examination, as David had felt sure he would. After Leemis looked up and his eyes fastened on Myra McPherson's face, he never let her go.

He began abruptly. "Mrs. McPherson, do you honestly believe your husband is such a bad, neglectful father?"

"Oh, no. Not deliberately. He just doesn't have the time. Everyone realizes that."

"Let's not presume what everyone thinks, since we have witnesses here to testify to that. Let me ask *you,* do you think Randy's father loves him?"

Myra hesitated. But David had instructed her that if she said no to a question like this she would look vindictive and unbelievable. "Yes," she said slowly.

The judge shot a sharp look at her. Leemis sat up and seized on the slowness of her answer. "You've heard your husband make references to his son in speeches, haven't you, Mrs. McPherson? Are you saying that's all feigned, the President's obvious love and concern for his son?"

"No, I don't think John's faking that. Not exactly. But it's easier to say things like that than to actually make time for your child day after day."

Leemis abruptly shifted subjects. "Mrs. McPherson, when you left your husband recently, you drove from the east coast to Little Rock, Arkansas, didn't you?"

"Yes."

"You and Randy? How many days and nights did you spend on the road?"

"Two nights. Most of three days."

"Who accompanied you?"

"Mr. Owens there. And Helen Wills."

"No Secret Service agents?"

"Ms. Wills is an agent."

"A former agent, isn't that correct, Mrs. McPherson?"

"Yes. Well, now it's correct."

"And Ms. Wills had to sleep some time during this trip, didn't she?"

"Yes, of course."

"Eat, go to the bathroom, just like other human beings?"

"Yes," Myra said, rather miserably. She saw the lawyer's intention.

"Had Randy ever traveled like that before, without a team of protection?"

"No. After what had just happened to both of us, we didn't know who we could—"

"Let me ask the question, please, Mrs. McPherson. At the end of your road trip, you boarded a commercial flight from Little Rock to San Antonio, is that correct?"

"Yes."

"Is that the way you and Randy usually travel?"

"No, in the last few years we've flown on Air Force One."

"When you had to fly on a commercial aircraft for some reason, do you know whether a Secret Service security team has checked out the plane to make sure it's safe?"

"Yes, they do." Myra saw where these questions led, but had no way to avoid the answers. She looked at her attorney for help. David stared back at her. Over his shoulder Myra saw that crowd of witnesses. They worried her and scared her, but also made her more resolved.

"Did that happen in this case?"

"No," she admitted.

"So you had your son boarded a flight that hadn't been checked for safety, amid more than a hundred other passengers you didn't know anything about, with no Secret Service team for protection. Does that describe the trip?"

"We had Helen with us."

"Is my description of the trip accurate?" Leemis insisted.

"Yes."

"And had you arranged for Secret Service protection at the San Antonio end of the trip?"

"We knew they'd catch up to us there."

"But you hadn't made definite plans for having Randy guarded?"

"I'm not sure I considered them guarding him," Myra said stonily. "But I knew they'd be there."

Again, Leemis abruptly shifted topics. "Mrs. McPherson, where is Randy in school now?"

"This is July, Mr. Leemis, he isn't in school."

"All right, then, what plans have you made for his starting back to school in a month or so?"

"I haven't yet. There's a public elementary school a few blocks from the condo where we're staying."

"Have you made inquiries there as to whether Randy could be admitted?"

"Not yet."

"Have you checked on any local private schools?"

"No." Myra saw Leemis's smug look and burst out, "We've only been here four days!"

"Was Randy doing well in school in Washington, ma'am?"

"Yes, very well. He was in the gifted program."

"Good school there?"

"Yes, we're very happy with it."

"How long has he been going there?"

"Since he started kindergarten a few months after John got elected."

"Mrs. McPherson, you said, 'the condo where we're staying.' 'Staying,' instead of 'living,' do you see the distinction I'm making? Do you plan to go on living there?"

"I'm not sure. I'd like to . . . move closer to my parents. But here is nice too. I'd like a house, though." Myra heard herself sounding uncertain, and her eyes allowed a little more fire. "I haven't had a real home since I married John."

"Most people would say you've got a pretty nice house now, Madame First Lady. Let me ask you one last thing. How do you plan to support yourself and Randy if you're divorced from your husband? It's been a few years since you earned a living, isn't it?"

"Yes. I'm not sure about that, either, but I've been giving it some thought." Myra looked steadily at the President's lawyer. "I think perhaps some writing. Perhaps serving as a consultant to certain magazines. I feel pretty confident someone would hire me for something that wouldn't take me away from Randy much of the time."

In her steady gaze, Burton Leemis saw the threat of publication, a notion he would definitely pass on to his client.

"Thank you, I have no more questions."

David said quickly, "On that subject, Mrs. McPherson, are you asking the court to order your husband to pay child support and temporary spousal support during this temporary orders period?"

"Yes, Randy and I will need money."

"How much do you think you'll need?"

Myra hesitated. "I think—maybe—ten thousand dollars a month." A very modest request, under the circumstances.

"Mrs. McPherson, don't you think during this temporary period it would be best for Randy to stay in the home he's used to and keep going to his same school?"

Myra shook her head sadly. "I wish that were possible. But no one there cares for him the way I do. He'd rather be with me than in that school, believe me." She turned to the judge. "Bring him in and ask him, Your Honor."

"We may do that," David said, a little threat to his opposing counsel. "No more questions."

Leemis stopped too. Myra stood hesitantly. David glanced back at the other side's witnesses. They watched the First Lady unsympathetically, as if she jeopardized all their jobs. Up at the front, Myra looked smaller under the weight of their stares. David hadn't forgotten to have these people excluded from the courtroom. He had made a last-second decision to leave them there, a pack of predators perched on the front rows, so that when Myra testified she would appear to be their prey, and look even more sympathetic. Because of the layout of the courtroom, the witnesses seemed opposed not only to Myra McPherson but to the judge, who sat beside her. During the testimony Judge Shahan's eyes had traveled from Myra to the pack, and David thought—hoped—Myra had come off well by comparison.

A small improvised lawyer's trick, but no one ever knew what would work.

"Call your next witness," the judge said in a noncommittal voice.

"We call Helen Wills, Your Honor."

That required a short recess, because Helen stood blocks away. David had decided that Randy should be nearby in case they needed him, but not actually in the courthouse. They hadn't wanted to keep him cooped up or in fact know that something important was going on nearby. David had suggested the nearby Hemisfair Park Playground. The Secret Service had balked at that idea at first, but after checking out the playground had said okay. The playground was fairly isolated, not visible from a street, and often sparsely populated.

Randy loved the place. It featured a large play fort full of walkways, slants, tunnels—a sort of three-dimensional maze—as well as swings and other equipment. About twenty kids played there this morning, enough not to crowd the playground. Helen stood on the sidelines and watched, surprised by how well Randy blended in. His parents had done a good job at one of their few areas of agreement: they had for the most part kept Randy's picture out of the media. And he looked so little-boy-generic—thick brown hair, skinny arms and legs—that he could go almost anywhere without being recognized. Helen watched him play with the other kids, laughing and shrieking and running and tumbling, with a sort of transferred longing. Randy should have this all the time, not just on very special occasions while his parents fought over him in a courtroom.

Helen prowled the perimeter of the playground, wearing white cotton shorts, a flowered top, and tennis shoes. She no longer carried a gun, but still unconsciously did the agent's job, scanning the crowd and the area. She spotted four other agents doing the same thing. The Secret Service's official party line was that every member of the first family got equal protection, but that was a fiction no one giving the idea much thought would believe. Of course the President came first, everyone else fell further down the list of priorities. The Service didn't skimp on Randy, but they didn't provide an army, either.

She walked past Agent Paul Herrera and they talked out of the sides of their mouths.

"I don't see him," Helen muttered.

"He's over there in that tunnel. Don't worry, Donna's right behind him."

"She's the one who looks like a teenager?"

"She practically is."

This was Helen's most pleasant conversation of the week. At first after her dismissal from the Service when she encountered other agents they ignored her, hostilely. But Helen remained in their presence a lot, because she guarded Randy too, unofficially. The agents began to tolerate her, then actually to speak to her occasionally. They could see that her loyalty to Randy and the First Lady remained real, and that counted for a lot with these people.

Helen looked suddenly over her shoulder and saw a man walking by, fifty yards away. He walked hurriedly, not glancing toward the children. "Who's over that way?" Helen asked.

"Henderson. Why?"

"This guy just spotted him."

Herrera turned and looked where Helen was looking, seeing a skinny man with black hair protruding from under a Spurs cap. The man also had a thick black mustache and sunglasses. Herrera watched him disappear around a building and shrugged. "It's a public park, Helen. People walk through."

"But why does somebody who doesn't care enough about children to even glance at them walk past the playground?"

Herrera glanced around again. The man had passed out of sight. "Relax, Helen, nobody's going to snatch him."

Helen gave him an ironic look. Herrera smiled tightly.

"Well, nobody except you," he said. After a pause he said, "Listen, Helen, I'm sorry about your job. What you did, well, I'm just glad I didn't face that choice. I don't blame you for what you did. . . . But of course, some people do."

They stood side by side, almost shoulder to shoulder, behind their sunglasses, both looking rigid and their eyes not on each other.

Helen said, "Thanks, Paul, that means a lot to me."

Luckily, at that moment Helen's phone rang, calling her away to the courthouse.

In a few minutes Helen came striding into the courtroom, having exchanged her shorts for white slacks that made her look a little more professional. She didn't need to wear a jacket because since she'd been defrocked she no longer carried a gun or radio.

The Secret Service agents in the room flicked glances at her that Helen didn't return. She quickly took her place in the witness stand, nodded respectfully to the judge, and fastened her eyes on David. David thought that to most observers in the courtroom, Helen still appeared the stiff, watchful woman who'd first come into his office. But David saw changes in her beyond the flowered blouse, particularly in the way she looked at him, alert but trusting. He also saw flickers of emotion cross her expression, as with the first questions he asked.

"Please state your name and occupation."

"Helen Wills. I'm on Mrs. McPherson's staff. I used to work for the United States Secret Service, assigned to the protection of the First Lady of the United States."

"In that capacity, Ms. Wills, did you spend much time with Mrs. McPherson?"

"Constantly."

"And her son Randy?"

"Yes. He was often nearby too."

"For how long?"

"Two and a half years. Since her husband took office."

"Have you seen Myra and Randy in private situations?"

"Yes. Well, not entirely private, of course, since I was there. But after a while they get used to us, we kind of fade away, and they act . . . in a private manner."

"Objection, Your Honor," Burton Leemis said. "What we've just heard is purest speculation."

"Sustained. I won't consider it."

David asked, "Did Myra McPherson seem happy to you in the White House?"

"Objection," Leemis said again, quickly. "Irrelevant to any issue in these proceedings."

Judge Shahan merely nodded, with a glance at David that told him to move on.

"At any rate, Ms. Wills, you actually helped Mrs. McPherson slip away from her protection team and come to see me the first time, didn't you?"

Helen hesitated. "Yes, I brought her to you."

David didn't understand her reluctance to answer. She had already been fired from the Secret Service. What worse repercussions did Helen fear?

"With only you accompanying her?" David clarified.

Before Helen could answer, Burton Leemis rose quickly and said, "Objection, Your Honor. Relevance?"

"Sustained. Let's get on with it, Mr. Owens."

David did, still feeling a vague itch about Helen's answers. "Ms. Wills, have you seen Myra McPherson and her son together on few or many occasions?"

"Many."

"And what kind of relationship have you observed?"

Helen smiled. "They're very close. I've never seen two people who loved being together more. Randy runs to her when he comes home."

"Have you observed anything that demonstrates Mrs. McPherson's feelings toward her son?"

"Yes. She talks about him when he's gone. About two, two-thirty in the afternoon she starts getting very antsy, waiting to go pick him up from school. When we travel, they sit together. She reads to him, that kind of thing. I've never seen a more devoted mother." Helen shrugged, not looking very happy herself. "Of course, I haven't watched many parents and children together."

"That's all right, Ms. Wills, just what you've seen. What about the President, have you seen Randy and his father together very many times?"

"Many fewer times. I'm assigned to Mrs. McPherson—was—so I wouldn't be there when only Randy and his father are together."

"But have you seen a few occasions?"

"Yes. We're not generally in the family quarters of the White House; that's supposed to be a private place for them. But once in a while Mrs. McPherson has asked me to help her with something there. Two times that I can remember I've been there with Mrs. McPherson and Randy when the President came in."

"Did you observe the same kind of enthusiasm, the two of them running together and so forth?"

"No. There was obvious affection. The President knelt and hugged his son and Randy seemed glad to see him. But there didn't seem to be the kind of closeness I've observed between Mrs. McPherson and Randy."

"Do you think it would be in Randy's best interest to stay primarily with his father in the White House?"

"Objection," Leemis said loudly. "Nothing has shown this woman's qualification to answer such a question. She's not a child psychologist, she hasn't questioned the boy, her testimony would be of absolutely no value on this subject."

"I'll hear it for what it's worth," the judge ruled casually.

"No, I don't think that would be in Randy's best interest. His father has very little time for him. With Mrs. McPherson, Randy has a full-time parent who cares for him very much."

"I pass the witness."

Burton Leemis said quickly, "That's very nice, isn't it, that the President has been able to provide this sheltered lifestyle for his wife and son, isn't it?"

"I guess it is."

"So now in exchange you think he should have his son taken from him?"

"I didn't say that, sir."

"On these two occasions in two and a half years when you saw the President and his son together, the President obviously knew you were in the room?"

"I'm sure he did."

"You come to attention or something when he walks into the room?"

"I stood up, yes."

"So maybe his display of affection toward his son was less effusive than it would have been if they'd been alone?"

"I have no way of knowing, sir."

"No, you don't, do you," Leemis said, and added dismissively, "no more questions of this witness, Your Honor."

Something else had occurred to David. "Ms. Willis, were you in the White House for two days or so earlier this summer when you didn't know where Mrs. McPherson was?"

"Yes. She kind of disappeared. I found her later in a private psychiatric hospital, undergoing—"

"Objection. I'm quite sure this witness isn't qualified to describe medical treatments."

"Sustained," said the judge, who seemed anxious to move on.

"At any rate," David asked, "during this time when Randy's mother was gone, did the President spend more time than usual with his son, that you could see?"

"No. Randy was sent to a summer camp a hundred miles away."

"No more questions."

Helen left the witness stand, walking past David closely enough that her hand brushed his. He wanted to hold her but didn't have time for more than this small private gesture. David felt confident that he'd wrapped up the issue of which parent should have custody of Randy during this temporary period. He wished he could have testified himself. Anyone who had seen Myra and Randy together could see the love and loneliness that bound them. But anything conveyed in testimony in a courtroom had a faked quality. Helen had been a pretty good witness but not great. She had qualified her testimony. He thought Myra's concern for her son had come across very clearly, but that wasn't the only issue. So he felt the usual lawyer's fear when he turned over the stage to Burton Leemis.

The President's attorney moved quickly. First he called the White House nanny, Mrs. Rose Phelan. Sixtyish, heavy but with a certain grace, Mrs. Phelan looked like everyone's Irish grandmother. She appeared so trustworthy the judge could have dispensed with swearing her in. But as the nanny began testifying, Myra leaned over and whispered, "She doesn't like me. Thinks I spend too much time with Randy. I should have fired her a year ago."

Wonderful time to tell me, David thought.

"They have a beautiful relationship," Mrs. Phelan said, describing John McPherson and his son. "The time they have together is so precious to them. Randy just lights up when his father comes in the room. And Mr. McPherson seems so pleased to see him."

"And what have you seen them do together, Mrs. Phelan?"

"Play games. Read. Talk. Mostly just walk and talk together, Mr. McPherson with his hand on Randy's shoulder. A boy needs his father. He needs to learn—"

"Object to the philosophical observations, Your Honor. It's not responsive."

"Sustained," said Judge Shahan.

Mrs. Phelan maintained her gentle smile, but for a moment her eyes fixed on David with a flash of Irish fire, as if a younger, quite different woman hid inside her. The nanny obviously didn't like the First Lady's lawyer. That was okay, David didn't need her affection.

"Mrs. Phelan, when his parents are gone overnight and he stays with you, does he seem content?"

"Oh, yes, sir. We have our routine. Homework, playtime, sometimes with boys whose fathers work in the building. Reading at bedtime. He's quite used to it, sir. Never cries or complains."

"Have you observed Randy with his mother?"

"Of course, sir."

"Do they have a close relationship?"

"Yes. Almost too close, if you don't mind my saying so."

"What do you mean by that?" Leemis asked, as if this claim by his witness surprised him.

The nanny spoke primly. "Mrs. McPherson doesn't seem to have any friends. She relies on Randy. She holds him too close, if you ask me. She seems to want him to be as isolated as she is. I don't think it's healthy for the boy. Shouldn't he have more people in his life than just his mother?"

Myra wrote on the legal pad in front of her, *I told you.*

Yes, a little belatedly, David thought. But the witness had been passed to him and he turned to the kindly nanny.

"Mrs. Phelan, how many times has it been that you've seen the President and his son do all these things together?"

"Many times, sir."

"And is Mrs. McPherson there too?"

"I'm talking about times when she's not, sir." She sniffed slightly. "I'm usually not there when Mrs. McPherson is there."

"I see. But sometimes the President has these long times alone with his son."

"Well, I don't know how long, sir, but very intimate."

"Let me ask you this, Mrs. Phelan, why have you been there to see these times?"

"What, sir?"

David explained patiently. "If the President's there with his son, why does he need you there?"

Mrs. Phelan blinked several times. "Well, the President could be called away anytime, sir. I'm there sort of on standby, if you see what I mean."

"Why couldn't you be on standby in another room, or in your own office in the White House?"

"Well, I suppose I could, but I like to be handy, sir."

"Yes, and the President wants you handy, too, does he? Even when he and Randy are supposedly 'alone' together, he has to have you there to help care for him, doesn't he?"

Mrs. Phelan's temper flared a bit. "No, sir, the President does very well on his own."

"How would you know that, Mrs. Phelan, since by definition you're not there when they're alone together?"

She couldn't answer, of course, but as the lady sat there attempting to come up with one, David thought her partisanship showed clearly. Judge Shahan didn't look at her, though. She looked past Burton Leemis at his crowd of witnesses, as if wondering which he would call forward next.

Leemis chose Paul Merton, a short, energetic man in his late forties who had once been mayor of Denver and now had an even more important job, which he identified in his first sentence of testimony:

"Paul Merton. I'm the Secretary of Housing and Urban Development."

Most people wouldn't recognize Merton, but certainly his name and title were familiar to everyone. He sat on the witness stand as if in his own living room, legs crossed and apparently at ease.

"Mr. Merton, you know why we're here? To decide among other things where Randy McPherson should live during this temporary period?"

"Yes, sir."

"Have you seen the President and his son together?"

"Yes, I have. Not a great many times, I'd say, but regularly."

"When would those occasions be?"

"When we're working in the West Wing. I've seen Randy in the Oval Office, and at least twice he's come into the room during cabinet meetings." Merton smiled at the memory. "His father seems to allow him the run of the place."

"Did he interrupt business?"

"No, not at all. During the cabinet meetings he kind of crept in and walked along close to the wall until he got to his father and they hugged each other and whispered something. It was very sweet. The President was obviously glad to see him."

"Did they seem affectionate?"

"Yes, very. You should see the boy's smile. And his father—Well, of course the President mentions his son often, so it's not surprising to see them so fond of each other. At the times in the Oval Office, the President just let Randy play on the carpet or by the window while we talked. They just seemed to enjoy being together."

Myra shook her head ever so slightly. David pushed a legal pad toward her, asking her to explain. He continued to watch the witness closely. Merton seemed quite sincere. Of course, he was a successful politician himself. Sincerity was one of his most important capacities.

Leemis frowned slightly. "Mr. Merton, have you been with the President in the last week, since his son has been gone from the White House?"

"Yes, I have. Just yesterday we had an emergency meeting over this situation in Chicago. That's all I can say about that—"

"But to the point," Leemis said a little irritably, "you have seen John McPherson at work very recently?"

"Yes, sir."

"Does he seem different?"

"Quite definitely."

"How so, sir?"

Merton looked at Myra McPherson as he talked, as if making a personal entreaty to her. "He seemed distracted. He had trouble concentrating on the problem at hand. This was very unlike the John McPherson I know. He's always been very quick and decisive. In the last few days, though, his mind is obviously elsewhere. I even asked him about it and he said he was worried about Randy, wondering where he was and what he was doing and whether he was safe."

Leemis leaned forward, a frown shaping his face into concern, as if he'd just heard this development. "In your opinion, Mr. Merton, and based on your observations, is his son's absence affecting the President's job performance?"

"Yes, sir, it obviously is. His distraction and worry are apparent to everyone." Merton turned then toward Myra McPherson and made his appeal to her overtly. "Ma'am, the country needs its First Lady in the White House. And the President needs his son."

This came out before David could think to object. Merton, even playing to a small crowd, gave a polished plea, looking very concerned and earnest. Myra didn't look at him.

Being careful not to sound overly satisfied with himself, Burton Leemis passed the witness to David. David sat staring at the cabinet secretary for a moment. Then he said, "This happened just yesterday, Mr. Merton, this occasion when the President said how much he missed his son?"

"Yes, sir."

"After this hearing had already been scheduled?"

"I wouldn't know that, sir."

"No. But would you know about building a case?"

"I'm not a lawyer, sir," Merton said this with a slight smile, as if boasting.

David glanced at the note Myra McPherson had written, but didn't respond to it. "Sir, if Randy weren't here in San Antonio with his mother, do you know where he would be? Where he was a week ago?"

"Yes, I do know. The President mentioned it. Randy was at a summer camp in Maryland."

"Yes. So the President's requirement of his son's constant presence isn't so great that it prevented him from shipping Randy off for the summer, is it?"

"The President mentioned that. The camp was close by, he planned to go visit Randy there, and could bring him—"

"Objection, objection," David said. "This is hearsay and nonresponsive."

"Sustained."

But Paul Merton had made his point. Leemis emphasized it with half a dozen other witnesses, including the chief of staff. In the last few days the President had been distracted and worried. His son's absence visibly affected him. Louis Roswall, the chief of staff, made the point most forcefully. "All I can say is it's a good thing we haven't had a crisis requiring military response in the last few days. When one comes, well . . ." He trailed off, looking very worried. David rolled his eyes.

He hadn't seen this coming at all. Burton Leemis had managed to turn this hearing on domestic issues and the life of a boy into a matter of national security. Let the President have his son or the country would go to hell. David watched Judge Shahan, who obviously paid close attention to these witnesses and also seemed surprised at this turn of events in her courtroom. By the end of the day she would be asked to make a ruling that would affect the safety of the nation. That was the obvious thrust of the testimony Leemis presented, and the witnesses came off as very believable.

But they didn't know Randy. The point and tone of the hearing had slipped away from David. At the end of presenting his case he had felt very confident of the judge's ruling that Randy should stay with his mother. Now the President's lawyer had managed to change that issue completely. It was what good lawyers did, and Leemis was one of the best.

Myra McPherson's hand had crept across the conference table until it clutched David's wrist, her knuckles white. Tears in her eyes, she whispered, "The judge is going to give Randy to him, isn't she? She doesn't have any choice."

David leaned over and whispered back, "I may have to bring Randy in to talk to the judge."

Myra shook her head. "Don't make him take a public stand against his father. I'd never forgive myself." She pointed at her note. But David didn't think her suggestion would change things.

The Leemis machine ground on, witness after witness. David managed to convey in cross-examination that these witnesses didn't know Randy at all, didn't know how he felt about his father, and couldn't say they'd seen Myra McPherson behave as anything other than a very devoted mother. But he feared Leemis had managed to make that beside the point.

Finally Leemis stood and said, after looking back over his shoulder, "That's all the witnesses I have in the courtroom at present, Your Honor. . . ."

Judge Shahan nodded. "A very impressive parade of witnesses, Mr. Leemis. Of course, I'd be even more impressed if your client had been present for this hearing, but I understand—"

"I'm here, Your Honor."

The deep voice carried easily from the back of the courtroom. David, turning, saw Burton Leemis smile ever so slightly.

President John McPherson stood at the back of the courtroom, the door from the court offices open behind him. McPherson looked very solemn. He stood tall and stern, then strode forward. No one else in the room made a sound. David just stared, as did the judge, who had unconsciously risen to her feet.

Passing through the gate in the railing, McPherson walked toward David, who suddenly thought the President was going to hit him. But he was wrong. The President ignored the lawyer and instead leaned over his wife. "Hello, Myra," he said softly, and kissed her temple. Myra McPherson shivered. She sat with her arms crossed, not looking at her husband.

McPherson walked toward the judge's bench. Judge Shahan said, "Are you going to testify, Mr. President?"

"With the court's permission," John McPherson said.

Judge Shahan nodded. "I think this hearing will be closed now," she said quietly. "Eddie?"

The bailiff moved to usher everyone out of the spectator seats. The room quickly emptied. At the back door the bailiff approached a Secret Service agent in his black suit, who barely glanced back at him. Eddie decided to pretend the man was invisible and therefore not subject to the judge's ruling.

Meanwhile the President took the oath as if he were being sworn into office again, and sat straight in the witness stand. Judge Shahan seemed surprised to find herself on her feet and quickly sat again. "Mr. Leemis?" she directed.

"Thank you, Your Honor." Leemis quickly established his witness's identity for the record and the purpose of the hearing and got to the point. "Mr. President, do you want your son to come back to live with you?"

"Yes, I do. Very much."

"You admit that over the years he's spent more time with his mother than with you?"

"Of course. I've tried hard to give them that time together."

"Don't you think Randy should be with her now?"

McPherson gazed across the room at his wife. He looked both compassionate and loving. "I'd like Myra to come back too. I want to talk to her about that. But failing that—Myra hasn't been herself lately. She's behaved erratically, like this taking off across the country with Randy with no one knowing where they were. I was frantic, I can tell you. If she needs some private time to work through some issues, that's fine, she should have that. But Randy should stay in his home. I'll take care of him."

David felt his client shake ever so slightly beside him at these words. David stared at the President, wondering what to ask him in cross-examination.

Burton Leemis continued, "How will you have the time to do that, Mr. President?"

"I'll take whatever time is necessary. I'll resign my office if necessary. Nothing is more important than my son."

McPherson spoke with such conviction he left David gaping. The bailiff and court reporter stared wide-eyed at McPherson, knowing they had just heard an announcement of national importance.

Burton Leemis knew when to pass his witness. David was left with nothing to ask. He hadn't realized how high John McPherson was willing to raise the stakes. McPherson turned his quiet attention to the lawyer.

Myra whispered, "You can't let him take Randy back. I'll never see him again."

David cleared his throat, beginning to think about Randy again. "Mr. President, in the past, how many minutes a day would you say you've spent with your son, on average?"

"There is no average," the President said emphatically. "Of course, on some very bad days I don't see him at all, when I have to be away. Other days I make deliberate holes in my schedule to spend time with Randy. For breakfast he likes Froot Loops. Sometimes he varies it with Cap'n Crunch, but he has an amazing capacity for eating the same thing every day. For lunch usually peanut butter and apple jelly sandwiches."

"Mr. President—"

McPherson bore down, staring at David. "His favorite game is called Space Blasters, which is sort of a board game but you also build devices beside the board, primarily a space station."

"Sir . . ."

"I know the rules, Mr. Owens. I've played it with him countless times."

John McPherson had obviously read about David's best cross-examination technique in his heretofore most famous case. When Rod Smathers had claimed to spend a lot of time with his children, David had asked him what was his son's favorite game and how it was played. Smathers hadn't even known how to begin the game of Yahtzee.

But the President knew. Burton Leemis had prepared him well. He would undoubtedly be able to answer in detail any question David might ask.

So David only asked, "Mr. McPherson, don't you think Randy would rather have his mother twenty-four hours a day than be with you in the White House and have only the few minutes a day you can spare him?"

McPherson answered without hesitation, "What Randy wants isn't necessarily what's best for him. I can protect him. I can keep his normal routine going. And I'll tell you, Mr. Owens, I can't concentrate with him gone. Missing him is killing me."

David couldn't let that go unchallenged. "Then why were you willing to send him to camp for the summer?"

"I knew he'd be safe. I knew where he'd be. I could see him at a couple of hours' notice. That was a very different thing."

David stared at the man. After a long pause he said quietly, "I have no more questions."

Neither did Burton Leemis. "We rest on the motion, Your Honor."

Judge Shahan, looking a tiny bit shell-shocked, said, "Rebuttal, Mr. Owens?"

David thought furiously. He looked again at his client's note. Then he said, "We'll call Paul Herrera, Your Honor."

"Who?"

"He's upstairs, Your Honor. I can have him here in one minute." Quickly David got on his cell phone and made a call. Helen answered. "Tell Agent Herrera he's wanted in the courtroom," David said quietly and urgently.

"What's going on, David?"

"Hurry, please."

They waited tensely. The President came down off the witness stand to sit beside his attorney. The courtroom staff smiled nervously at him, and he smiled back in a solemn, reassuring manner, as if giving a state of the union address.

In a few minutes a thirty-five-year-old man in a black suit entered the room. Secret Service Agent Paul Herrera was getting a bit heavy in the middle, but moved very gracefully. His expression gave away little, but he seemed surprised to find himself there. David quickly called him to the witness stand.

"Agent Herrera, what is your current duty assignment?"

"I guard Randy McPherson."

"Have you been doing that long?"

"Two years." The agent looked stonily at David Owens, and David realized why. This was one of the agents from whom he'd taken Randy at the summer camp.

"Agent Herrera, have you been present when Randy has gone and interrupted one of his father's cabinet meetings?"

"Where Randy goes, I'm nearly always present. Yes, I was."

Burton Leemis stood quickly and said, "Objection, Your Honor. This man can't testify to matters concerning his protectee. His duties—"

"I believe that issue has been ruled on previously in another court," David interjected.

"I remember that," Judge Shahan said. "Continue, Agent Herrera."

David asked, "Was it Randy's idea to go into those meetings?"

The agent looked uneasy, but said stoically, "No, sir."

"How do you know that?"

"One of the President's staff aides came and got him. He told Randy it was time."

"Did Randy seem eager to go?"

"No. He dragged his feet. He said, 'Do I have to?' The aide insisted."

"Was that aide acting on orders of the President?"

"What if he was?!" The angry voice responding didn't come from Burton Leemis, it came from his client. John McPherson was on his feet, saying loudly, "What if I just wanted to see my son during my workday? Is there anything wrong with that?"

David said, "Do you think it's right to use your own son to stage this little family scene when the truth is—" But the judge's banging gavel quieted him.

Testimony ended. The judge looked very troubled. David stood. "Your Honor? Shall we present argument?"

"Yes, yes," the judge said distractedly.

David hoped like hell he could return the hearing to his own issue. "Your Honor, they have brought you testimony that the President is distracted in his job because his son isn't there in the building. First of all, that seems untrue, since he's seldom spent time with his son and was willing to have him away at camp all summer. But more importantly, it's irrelevant. It's not what this hearing is all about. You are supposed to rule on what's in the best interest of this child. John McPherson's job performance, as important as it is to this country, isn't an issue here. If he's impaired in the performance of his duties, let him step down.

"You must agree that it is in Randy's best interest that he stay with the parent who has raised him almost single-handedly, who has the time to devote to his care, and the concern to do what's best for him, not just during little breaks in her day, but all day, every day.

"Your Honor, this is temporary orders. Let Randy stay where he is, with the mother who loves him, who knows him best. The person he loves most in the world, according to all the witnesses. Not the one who needs him for image value."

He had managed to get the judge's attention. Her eyes focused on him. She listened very attentively. But Burton Leemis had his turn.

"Your Honor, he is asking you to put this child into an unstable environment with a mother who has put him in danger. She has no plans for his schooling or a permanent place to live. Under Mrs. McPherson's 'care,' Randy may be enrolled in a new school in the fall, then another one when she decides to move again. Instead he could be sleeping every night in his own bed in his own room and going to the school where he's been doing very well, with other children he knows.

"Mr. Owens says the President's job performance isn't important here. Your Honor, I submit that there is no place on this planet where the way this man does his job isn't important. You must consider—"

Judge Shahan stood up abruptly. "I'll see the parties and attorneys in chambers." She turned quickly and stepped down from the bench, back through the door of her office behind the bench.

David found himself on his feet. Burton Leemis was stooped over, conferring with his local counsel, who shook his head. David thought he knew the question and answer. No, this was not standard procedure.

He took Myra's arm and helped her to her feet. She stayed close by him, keeping David between her and her husband. "What's she going to do?" she whispered, but David had no answer.

They followed Judge Shahan into her office, followed more slowly by Burton Leemis and his client. The Secret Service agents hesitated, then stayed outside the door, which closed in their faces.

The judge's office was not large, and shades were pulled down over the windows. The five people made the place seem cramped.

Judge Shahan had an elaborately carved, old-fashioned desk. She stayed behind it, but on her feet. Speaking very distinctly, she said, "You people have to reach agreement."

No one spoke for a moment. Then Leemis cleared his throat and said, "Well, Your Honor, we've just had a four-hour hearing in front of you because we *can't* reach agreement."

"Have you tried? I don't think so." Judge Shahan tapped her desk with her fingernail. "Understand what I'm saying. I'm not afraid to make a ruling in this case. I will do my job, if that's what you want. But have you thought about what that will mean? There will then be a public finding by a judge that one of these people is a better parent than the other. I don't think you want that, not at this point. Who knows how this case might end? Maybe in reconciliation, I don't know. It would be very difficult to work past having such an order in the public record."

"You could order the record sealed, Judge," said David, who still hoped for a ruling in his favor.

The judge shook her head. "There are three people out in that courtroom who aren't paid enough to keep a secret like that. I'm not sure I am. No, this case needs to have an agreement. There's another reason, too. This shouldn't be an adversarial process where a child is concerned. You both want what's best for your son, I know you do. Prove it by reaching agreement over this issue. I'll give the four of you ten minutes to confer. You can use my office."

Leemis said stiffly, "Your Honor, I must raise the issue of executive privilege. The President has a right not to be hauled into court without his own permission."

"Mr. Leemis, he is not here as the President, he is here as a father. He has no executive privilege over his own family. That's my ruling."

She walked toward the door. Leemis made one last appeal. "But, Your Honor, how can we reach agreement when we're so diametrically opposed? Can you give us some guidance?"

The judge turned. "I'll tell you this. If I were to rule, there is no way I would take that boy away from the mother who's raised him almost twenty-four hours a day. Not under temporary orders. I would order liberal times of possession and access for his father, but the boy would stay with his mother."

She turned to the President. "Sir, your testimony and that of your aides was very dramatic and compelling. But Mr. Owens is right. Your problems in office, even as hugely as they can affect the world, are not an issue for this court. I have to order what's in the best interest of this little boy, and right now, under temporary orders, that means staying with his mother." She looked ironically at Leemis. "Does that help?"

Leemis for the first time didn't have words. "Uh—"

The judge turned and walked swiftly out of the room.

★ Under those circumstances, they reached agreement quickly. Myra McPherson insisted on only one thing: "If Randy comes back to the White House, I'm going to be with him."

John McPherson said quietly, "You mean when he does. And I want you to be there. Gentlemen, could you excuse us for a minute, please?"

David looked at his client, who looked back at him anxiously. He whispered to her, "The Secret Service is right outside. I will be too."

He and Burton Leemis gave each other a look and left the room together.

John McPherson stood about eight feet from his wife and looked at her sorrowfully. "Myra," he said quietly.

She began shaking her head immediately. He waited for her to stop. "Myra, you have to come back to me."

"That is how you would put it," she said bitterly.

"I'm sorry. Will you please come back to me? I need you. I need Randy with us."

"Since when, John?"

He moved closer to her. "Always. Don't you know that? I have taken you for granted, I see that. But that was because I relied on you, I thought you knew how much I needed you."

"You just needed a First Lady, John. You'll find another. Or someone to fill the role."

"Don't talk that way, Myra. You're my wife. The only one I ever wanted."

Myra looked at him curiously. John McPherson sounded sincere, but he'd had a lot of practice at that. She'd succumbed to him in the past. This time she stared at him, looking for signs of the man behind the gentle smile. His eyes shifted slightly.

Still staring at him, she said, "John, did you ever love me? Or Randy?"

"Of course I do."

But this time Myra didn't believe him. "Which question are you answering?" Myra walked away from him, but stopped at the door. "You want us to come back to you? You'd do anything?"

He nodded, beginning to look eager.

"Then do what you said. Resign. Give it up."

Slowly, he shook his head. "That's too much to ask." As she reached for the doorknob, he said her name sharply. Then his face and voice changed. His anger began to show. Starting in a low voice, he said, "You'll never win this. You won't take Randy away from me."

"I just did win."

"Temporarily. That's what the judge said. Next time will be different. I'll do whatever it takes. I can't let there be a finding that I'm not a fit parent. He'll be with me, eventually."

That was the most frightening thing John McPherson could say to his wife, and he knew it. Myra suddenly looked vulnerable again. He took advantage, stepping toward her and softening his tone again. "Myra, come back. Think of the whole country. We need a first family in the White House."

But he had taken the wrong approach. Myra's back stiffened again. Opening the office door, she said, "God help the country, John, if we're a role model for marriage."

She walked out into the courtroom. David Owens stood up from the conference he'd been having with Burton Leemis. In a quiet voice he asked if she was all right. Myra nodded brightly.

David pointed at a legal pad on which he and Leemis had been writing. "We've pretty much got an agreement worked out, along the

lines the judge said. You have primary custody of Randy, his father
gets to see him occasionally—"

"Do we have to agree to that?"

"If we don't, the judge will order it."

Myra nodded again. Quickly she read the two pages and saw that
the order required her husband to pay her support and her attorney's
fees. The document became less specific about times when John
McPherson was to have possession of his son. The word "reason-
able" was used. "We have to accommodate his schedule," David
explained.

"Only if I go with Randy," Myra said.

David turned to the other lawyer, who shrugged acceptance.
David wrote in an addendum that both lawyers initialed. Myra,
seeming uninterested, signed the second page on her signature line.
The two pages, handwritten with cross-outs and additions, hardly
looked like a historical document. Leemis took it to his client and
conferred with him quietly.

"Look cheerful," David said. "You've got Randy."

"I know, David. Thank you. Thank you, thank you." She hugged
him briefly, but he saw her distraction. She didn't look like a victor.

The President came up beside them, having just signed the temporary orders. "May I see my son now?" he asked stiffly.

David nodded to his client, who said, "Of course, John. He's on
his way back to the condo right now."

McPherson nodded, still stiffly, and before turning away said
gruffly to David, "I want to talk to you."

Myra touched her lawyer's arm, looking anxious again. "What's
that about?"

"Maybe he wants to make us an offer." David smiled. "Are you
afraid I'm going to sell you out?"

He saw that that was what Myra feared. Her habit of trusting
people had been long damaged. "Don't worry," he said. "Go on back
and be with Randy. Or wait here. I'll only be a few minutes."

First David and Leemis obtained Judge Shahan's signature on the
temporary orders, after she had looked them over and nodded

approvingly. Then the three men walked up a flight of stairs to the fifth floor of the courthouse. Secret Service agents went ahead of them, clearing a path. At the top floor, in the reception area, Leemis said, "I'm told they have a copying machine here, so I can get copies of this order."

"Yes, through there." David pointed.

Leemis nodded. "And I believe they've set aside an office for us to talk."

Sure enough, an office belonging to a bar association staffer had been emptied of its occupant and a Secret Service team had checked the office. "I'll be with you in a moment, gentlemen," Leemis said, remaining outside the office as an agent shut the door, leaving David and the President alone.

It was a large office, bigger than the judge's office on the floor below, with windows looking out on the green-tiled roof of the old courthouse. John McPherson walked around the room and immediately seemed at home. Somewhere along the way he had picked up a large old-fashioned briefcase. He set it down on the desk, turned, and shook hands with David, which caught David off guard.

"You did very good work in there today, young man."

"Thank you, sir." David would have called the President "sir" in any event, but as it happened his mouth made the decision for him without conscious thought. The President continued to hold his hand in a long handshake, very firm on McPherson's part, at first with a tug as if he would pull David off his feet. Then he covered their hands with his left, apparently sealing a pact. He smiled in a warm, fatherly way, as if he had long looked forward to meeting this young man. David began to feel even more uncomfortable. Again, he realized the President was striving for this effect, but he did it so damned well that it worked in spite of David's awareness.

Still holding David's hand, the President said, "Do you know that the Joint Chiefs of Staff have put our troops worldwide on heightened alert status?"

"No, sir, I hadn't—"

"No, of course not. But we want the world to know. Who knows how many unbalanced dictators, hearing about what you've done, might think the President of the United States too distracted to do his job, and think this is a good time to attack? And some of them have the bomb."

David felt himself blushing. "Sir, I . . ."

The President released his hand. Still speaking in a cordial, fatherly tone, he said, "You didn't intend this, I know. You didn't consider the consequences. The international consequences, Mr. Owens, not just the stock market, which is taking a beating today, or important legislation we're trying to get through Congress and may not be able to do now, or national arms sales. How will you feel when American soldiers in Bosnia or the Mideast or Africa are attacked and killed because of the petition you've filed?"

David felt stunned. He hadn't expected this kind of attack at all, especially not in the calm, fatherly manner the President maintained. David stammered. "I'd feel horrible, of course. But I don't think—"

"These are the kinds of things I have to think about every single day. Often in the dead of night as well. If I trip going down the White House steps in public, will the Dow take a tumble? If I drop a fork at a state dinner, will some terrorist decide to drive a car full of bombs into the Capitol? Believe me, these are possibilities. And you, you go and throw a bomb right into the heart of the presidency." He smiled as if admiring David's audacity, then turned even more serious. He came around the desk and put his arm around David's shoulders. "Now, what can we do to prevent these repercussions? How can we demonstrate that America still stands strong in spite of your divorce petition?"

That quickly, John McPherson turned David into his ally. David thought hard. "Whatever you need, sir. As long as it doesn't harm my client's interests, we can join you in issuing any kind of statement you want. She'll hold a press conference . . ."

"These people don't read, David. And they don't believe prepared statements." He turned to face David, their heads close. David felt the President's cool breath on his face. "She has to come back to the

White House, David. We have to appear in public together, show that the First Lady is back at her husband's side. Whatever negotiations we conduct in private, we have to present a united front to the world."

David began to recover himself. He had already fallen back, far behind the fall-back positions he'd had in mind when he entered this room, but he scrambled to regain ground. "Sir, I don't think I can agree to that. My client's very clear wishes are to stay here, with her son. Your son. At least for a while."

The President turned abruptly away. David felt a pain of regret at having disappointed him.

The President resumed his discourse, beginning to sound angry. "So your nation's security means nothing to you? Do I need to explain to you why this can't go forward while I'm in office? The country can't tolerate the strain."

David thought of Myra McPherson coming back to live with this man, and could picture her trembling at the suggestion. The memory of her fright made him feel stronger. He stood firm. "Sir, with all due respect, yours is not the first family to suffer a crisis in office. England managed to survive the divorce of Prince Charles and Diana. I think—"

The President's face darkened with sudden fury. "Are you comparing me to Prince Charles? What armies answer to him? What buttons does he have his finger on?"

David went doggedly on. "And this country managed to keep going through President Clinton's impeachment. The bottom line is, I can't be concerned about anything except my client's wishes. I represent her. Your attorney will tell you what that means. I have to put her wishes first."

The President folded his arms and went quiet. David's mention of impeachment had been a mistake.

"I am *not* Bill Clinton. This is a *private* matter. We cannot have a public separation," he insisted. "Doesn't she know that? That would put her in actual physical danger. There are powers that might try to use her, and our son. In fact that may already be happening." He looked even more penetratingly at David.

"Sir, I don't think that's going to happen."

"And how would you know? What network of informants do you have who know more than the C.I.A. and the F.B.I. and the Secret Service?"

Of course that question had no answer. David stood shaking his head as if the conversation had gotten ridiculous. Oddly, it hadn't. It had grown grandiose, perhaps, but to speak of worldwide consequences in a case like this was not delusional. David still felt off balance, unused to thinking in such large terms.

The President grew quieter, his eyes more thoughtful. He sat again behind the desk and waved David to a chair as well. They sat staring at each other for a long moment. David wondered why Burton Leemis was taking so long to rejoin them. Leemis's deliberately taking himself out of the discussion seemed ominous.

"Let me make you a proposal," John McPherson said. He opened the briefcase he'd brought into the room, took out a manila clasp envelope, and pushed it across the desk at David. David opened it, expecting to see some kind of documents, perhaps a written offer. Instead he pulled out certificates. They were bearer bonds, representing value that could be gotten at any bank by anyone holding these bonds. As good as cash, in other words. There were ten of them, each in a face amount of one million dollars.

David gave a little cough and a very small joke. "This is more than you were ordered to pay in interim attorney's fees."

The envelope also held cash, banded stacks of hundred-dollar bills, at least twenty-five thousand dollars' worth. That was probably mad money, for him to have a big weekend with after he accepted the real bribe.

He put everything back in the envelope. "Is this for Mrs. McPherson and your son?"

The President shook his head. "That's for your withdrawal as her attorney. The thanks of a grateful nation."

David couldn't help hesitating. Ten million dollars could set him up in luxury for the rest of his life, just about anywhere he chose. He would be criticized in some circles, sure, but since he wouldn't have to practice law anymore or do any other kind of work, who gave a damn?

He put everything back in the envelope and closed its clasp.

"I know what you're worrying, what people will think of your withdrawing. Don't worry, we can put the proper spin on that. I have people who do that sort of thing," the President said ironically. He wore a small smile. He and David had become collaborators again.

David said quietly, "Sir, what good would it do if I withdrew? Your wife would just find another lawyer. There are thousands who'd love to have her as a client. Tens of thousands."

"Let me worry about that."

David thought of Myra after his departure. Yes, she'd be besieged by divorce lawyers and every other kind of lawyer eager to press her case. But how would she pick one? She had chosen David herself, she had come to him. She would never trust another lawyer the way she trusted the man who had rescued and befriended her son. And if her champion betrayed her, would she have the nerve to go forward again? David's departure would tell her clearly that her husband could get to anyone she chose to represent her. Myra McPherson didn't have a great deal of resolve. It would probably crumble if David withdrew as her attorney.

Or maybe he was just giving himself airs. At any rate, he pushed the envelope back across the desk toward the President. David's fingers trembled slightly. It would have been so nice just to take one of those stacks of hundred-dollar bills. He had earned it; he'd spent hundreds of billable hours on this case already. But taking any amount of the money would mean the same thing. He had come here as a lawyer and would be leaving a whore. Probably not the first time that had happened during a conversation with the President of the United States. But David wouldn't. He pushed the envelope away, out of his reach.

"I'm afraid not, sir."

David heard footsteps and Burton Leemis came through the

door, looming over David's shoulder. He had deliberately taken himself out of the picture during the bribe attempt. If necessary, he could truthfully testify that he hadn't seen anything go on between David and his client at that point. Now he returned to the negotiations conference with obvious relish.

"Well, we've gotten through the first step, the temporary orders," David began.

"Mr. Owens," Leemis interrupted, as if speaking to a student. "You don't understand that you still have to deal with some much larger issues. Jurisdiction, for example. The President doesn't live in Texas. He hasn't in years. Then there's the issue of whether any state court here has authority over the President. That issue alone can wind through the courts for years."

David knew that threat would frighten his client. Myra McPherson wanted as fast a resolution as possible. Leemis continued, "You're going to be so buried in discovery and motions you won't get this case into a court again in years. We'll move to have the case removed to federal court, to Washington. To have these temporary orders thrown out, and if they are, even for a day . . ."

Leemis stopped, having gone almost too far. David understood. If the court order was reversed or lapsed, the President's men would come again and take Randy. Perhaps Myra, too. Next time David might not be able to stop them. "I'll do whatever it takes to protect my client," he said stonily.

David saw the shot hit home with the President. McPherson fell into a momentary reverie, as if the ending of his marriage had become real to him for the first time. Then he abruptly ended the conversation. "I'm going to see my son," he said.

He picked up the briefcase and walked out of the room.

David walked downstairs slowly and found his client waiting for him in the courtroom. Myra looked at him with apprehension that David thought was also touched with suspicion. "What did he want?" Myra asked.

He took her aside and told her. "He offered me money to withdraw as your lawyer."

He had thought of not telling her about the bribe attempt, but if she found out later she might think he'd withheld the information from her because he was considering the offer.

Myra went very quiet. They left the courthouse without saying anything else. David, Helen, and Myra rode back to the condo together. The Secret Service agents had already taken Randy ahead.

"They tell me you were very good in court," Helen said, smiling at David.

He had almost forgotten the hearing already, thinking ahead. "Yes, he was," Myra said quietly, and patted his hand.

"Well, they've tried just to grab Randy and they've tried to take him legally," Helen said musingly. "What will they try next?"

By way of answer, David told his client, "Your husband wants you to come back to the White House."

Myra showed minimal reaction. "When?"

"To stay, Mrs. McPherson. He wants you to come back for good. He says we need to conduct our negotiations in private while you go on acting the part of the First Lady."

Myra shook her head slowly. "If Randy and I ever go back there . . . we'll never get out again."

David wasn't sure what she meant and didn't want to ask. He and Helen looked at each other past the First Lady. David said, "He says it's dangerous for you and Randy to be away from the White House."

"Dangerous for him," Myra muttered. But David thought something else, and watching Helen he thought she had the same thought: *How will John McPherson prove the danger to his wife and son is real?*

★

John McPherson walked quietly down the hallway of the condominium and opened the door to his son's bedroom almost silently. Randy sat at his computer, his back toward the bedroom door. For a moment the President stood there without speaking, looking at his son's computer screen. It showed a complicated schematic of full lines and dotted ones, some of which went into tubelike objects but didn't all emerge.

McPherson's face grew paler. He made a sound in his throat.

Randy immediately cleared his screen. As he turned toward the door, McPherson recovered himself and said, "Hello, son."

"Dad!" Randy cried enthusiastically, but he rose only slowly.

McPherson knelt and held out his arms and Randy walked into his embrace. "Boy, it's great to see you," John McPherson sighed.

"Me too, Dad."

The President held his son at arm's length. Randy gave a slight smile. "You look okay," McPherson said. "Are you bored here?"

"No, not really."

"No, I know you. Not as long as there's a computer and a Nintendo here. But don't you miss being home?"

Randy's eyes slid away from his father's face. "Sure," he said quietly.

"When are you and Mom coming back? Why don't you ask her?"

"Okay."

The President began to run short of conversation. "Let's go for a walk," he said suddenly. "What's that you've got? A football?"

He picked up the spongy football David had brought Randy during their cross-country run. The President had a hurried conversation with the Secret Service agent at the front door of the condo and he and Randy went out. McPherson walked with his hand on his son's shoulder. They made an attractive picture, though the President looked more like Randy's grandfather and someone walking with them would have noticed Randy's minimal responses to his father's overtures.

They left the condo, walking down the sidewalk toward the public elementary school and its playground two blocks away. Just as

McPherson and his son walked away, the car carrying David, Myra, and Helen arrived. "Wait," Myra McPherson ordered the driver, and the car pulled to the curb. By leaning forward, the three passengers could watch the progress of the President and his son. After a few catches and misses they gave up on the football, and within a few seconds the two had drifted apart, the President apparently lost in thought, Randy stooping to examine something on the ground.

David found the scene very bizarre. There was a boy—a boy David knew yearned for affection and companionship—with a chance to reach out and touch his father, and he didn't take it.

"Why doesn't Randy respond to his father?"

Myra gazed down the sidewalk at her husband and son, her face hard to read. "He's been pushed away too many times. He's finally learned deep down that his father doesn't care about him."

"Did you teach Randy that?"

"You don't believe that, David. All I ever wanted was for Randy to be happy, and I know he'd be happier if he had a real father. But neither of us could ever . . . break through. Look at him, he doesn't even realize Randy's not walking with him anymore." There was a catch in her voice. "Besides," she added, "Randy loves me."

David had to follow out the implications of that last sentence himself. Randy loved his mother and had seen how John McPherson treated her. And had probably heard his father with another woman. He glanced at Helen, who didn't say a word.

The President soon tired of playing father. He showed obvious relief when aides called him to take a phone call and he had a reason for hurrying back to Washington. David took his place playing catch with Randy as they walked back up the hill toward the condo. David took it slowly and patiently and Randy improved quickly. "If I get good at this, would Dad try playing with me again?" Randy asked. David couldn't come up with an answer.

As they walked back to the condo David's hand fell naturally on Randy's shoulder and Randy walked comfortably beside him, tossing the football up and catching it. Helen appeared on David's other side and whispered to him, "I know what your father left you."

David looked at her in surprise and didn't ask. Helen smiled at him. She reached past David to tousle Randy's hair. For a long moment her arm stayed across David's back. Randy accepted the hair-tousling placidly, until he looked up and saw that Helen had done it, which surprised him.

Helen walked away and they both watched her. "She's turning funny," Randy said. "She didn't use to touch me much."

"Is that so?" David said speculatively. Randy replied by socking him in the arm, then broke away from David and they raced back to the condo, the Secret Service agents startled and hurrying to keep up, Randy laughing delightedly.

The Secret Service agents were obviously glad when the first family went back indoors. The agents had cleared the area, including the vacant lot across the street. But Larsen had another vantage point by this time. He had watched the President and his son from a window in the third floor of the old brick elementary school. Larsen had a key to the building, and a legitimate reason for being there. He had been hired to spend the summer upgrading and rewiring the school's computer system. The contractor who'd originally had the job had been hit by a car while riding his bicycle and would be hospitalized for weeks. The school, scrambling around for a replacement, had found someone with the perfect qualifications literally standing on their doorstep. Larsen could doctor a résumé as well as anyone, and if he came across as a little strange in the job interview, well, he was a computer person, they expected that.

So now he stood at the hallway windows outside the third-floor computer lab where he had watched the President being reunited with his son. Larsen didn't know what the scene meant and didn't much care, except that he saw the lack of connection between John McPherson and his son. Larsen didn't have much insight into human emotion, but he recognized estrangement when he saw it. As he continued to watch, he forgot about the President and concentrated on the boy. He was the key. That's what Boswell had said.

Larsen didn't know whether he still had an employer, but he knew he had a job.

After the President's surprise appearance in San Antonio and quick return to the White House, life seemed to settle down. At least no more public events happened. But on both sides, in both cities, people operated at a higher, more anxious pitch.

Burton Leemis, true to his word, deluged David with discovery requests and motions that required response. David had other clients—the McPherson case's press coverage seemed to overcome any damage his old firm had done him—and had hired a legal assistant, but still spent most of his time on his most special client. Every time he went to see Myra, he had the feeling she'd had no other visitor since the last time he'd been with her. At first she'd just been happy to get away from the White House, but now she seemed restless. He had to make her sit down to go over the questions Leemis had sent.

"Yes, I wanted to bring up some of these," Myra said indignantly. "Why do I have to answer so many questions?"

"They're called interrogatories," David explained. "It's something both sides are entitled to. Believe me, I've sent your husband's lawyers questions, too, as well as requests to produce a lot of documents."

"But these questions I'm supposed to answer. They're so intrusive. Why do they have to get so personal? Will all this come out at trial?"

"Well, possibly," David said patiently. "If there are some questions that you think are just designed to harass you, we can object that they're not relevant. You won't have to answer, at least until a judge rules on our objections. Are there questions like that?"

"Well, of course," Myra said, sounding petulant. "Like whether I've ever hurt Randy. Of course not! List reasons why I think my husband isn't a good father!"

"Those are obviously relevant," David said quietly. "Are there any you think aren't?" He watched his client thoughtfully. Myra showed more spirit than usual. That was good. But why did she get worked up over these relatively minor intrusions? Maybe it was just cabin fever. She needed to get out of the house.

Myra scanned down a page, turned to the next one, stopped about halfway down. "This one, just for an example: 'Have you ever committed adultery?' Specify time and place. Have you ever had a man other than your husband stay overnight in your home?' I put, 'Yes, every head of state on earth plus a bunch of actors and businessmen.' "

David laughed. Myra's cheeks reddened as she showed obvious pleasure at entertaining him. In the short time he had known her, David had seen Myra McPherson blossom and show the possibility of having a life after all, if all this ever ended.

He answered, "Those are very standard questions; they obviously haven't tailored to this case. We can object that it asks for voluminous information. Don't worry about that."

He paused, then added, "You don't mind answering the adultery question, do you?"

"Yes, I do," Myra said, sounding petulant again.

"Why?"

"It's prying. It's personal. It's nobody's damned business. Do I have to have my whole life prodded and explored just because I want to do what's best for my son?"

Still speaking very calmly, David asked, "The answer is no, isn't it?"

"Well, of course it's no." Myra reddened. "But don't you see what I mean? Just being asked makes me feel dirty. And what does it matter to anything? If I had, would that make me an unfit mother? You could ask John the same question—"

"I have already."

"—and you know his answer would have to be yes, unless he lies. But I don't want to know, if you want the truth. I don't want it there on a page in black and white. That kind of confession should be made in a completely different way. Frankly it's not any of your business, either."

She had worked herself up into a small passion. Myra seemed to have thought out this answer rather extensively. A divorce case often came to this moment, though usually not so early, when the client realized that lawyers had come between her and her husband, and hated the idea. As much as she may have wanted to part from her husband, until now their marriage had been their own. Anyone would resent having it examined by strangers.

But David continued to stare thoughtfully at his client. "I'll see what I can do," he finally said.

Myra sighed as if shaking off the subject. "David, how can we go on like this? Trapped in this little condo, practically prisoners. I want . . . Especially for Randy. He's got to get out, he's got to see other children. That was the whole point of my leaving. If he's just going to be caged somewhere else, I might as well go back to the White House."

"I know," David said. "I've been thinking about Randy. And I can do something about that, I think, at least in the short term."

Helen jogged through the neighborhood around the condominium. She felt odd at being able to go and come at will, slipping out without guards and with no reports to make to supervisors. For the time being she enjoyed a freedom she hadn't felt in years. Of course, her freedom sprang partly from having lost forever the job she loved, and her current job remained only a stopgap, but for the moment she liked her life.

She still felt responsible, though. For Randy and the First Lady. In some variation of the Chinese curse, having freed them from their confinements she now felt responsible for their lives. In a way, thanks to Helen's maneuverings, they had become confined again. As much as anyone, Helen wanted to change that, but she didn't see any way.

She partially worked off this sense of responsibility by continuing to fulfill her old bodyguard duties. In fact, she could do things the Secret Service agents couldn't do, such as this jogging. She had studied the neighborhood. It was an affluent area, of course, the part of the city where the President kept a condo, but not grand. There were some large white plantation-style houses, but also some two-bedroom cottages where retired people or young adults lived. The higher standard of income showed mainly in leisure. At any time of the day women were out walking or working in their yards or driving down Broadway. Helen studied them, then blended in. Her blond hair already helped. She'd let it get longer, and now when she jogged pulled it back in a ponytail. She wore red nylon wind-shorts, running shoes, and a white T-shirt. In this outfit she'd quickly become such a normal denizen of the neighborhood that others waved to her when she walked or jogged.

But Helen was working. She jogged the streets, checked out alleys, went all through a nearby greensward that seemed to be a mini-thicket in the center of the neighborhood, where no development had been allowed. She looked for faces that she saw regularly. She looked for a surveillance camp. She looked.

A week earlier, Helen would have found Larsen. But now he had an apartment a mile away and his perfectly legitimate post in the elementary school. It was summer, no one disturbed him there. He waited, and watched out the windows.

David finished his conversation with Myra, squeezed her shoulder gently, and walked out. Just outside the doorway into the hall, the Secret Service agent who'd left him in privacy with his client stood alertly. David tried to ignore him as he walked down the hall to Randy's bedroom, but that was impossible. The agent walked in lockstep just behind him, like a malignant shadow in a cartoon. David thought of saying, *You know he can get away from you anytime he wants. He's done it lots of times.* But antagonizing the agent wouldn't do anybody any good.

He knocked and walked into the bedroom. It was a small room, with one twin bed, posters on the walls, a bookcase stuffed to over-flowing, and socks and jeans on the floor. It looked very much a nor-mal boy's room, which somehow made David sad. Randy should have a real room like this one, not one with a Secret Service agent just outside the door.

Randy lay on his stomach on the foot of the bed, holding the con-trol that connected by wires to the TV on top of his dresser. He had the sound off, working intently in silence. His face showed terrible concentration. Randy was used to people walking in on him all the time. He ignored intruders.

"Hey, kid. Still got our football?"

"David!" Randy jumped up off the bed, dropping the Nintendo controls, and hugged David. The boy's enthusiasm took David by surprise. He hugged back.

"Let's go for a walk or something, okay?"

Randy looked apprehensive, just like his mother. "Will they let us?"

"Sure."

But in fact the agent-in-charge resisted the idea. "I don't think so, sir. Not at this time."

The agent-in-charge had the regulation stiff black hair, but a browner face than the average agent, and his eyes were more lively. But he stood firmly inside the front door like a wall. David led Randy back a few steps, then returned to the agent. In a low voice, he said, "I'm tired of these confrontations all the time. I know you have your duty, but they have a right to lives, too. The First Lady has told you it's all right. That should be enough. And I don't want to threaten getting a court order, either. Let's just try to work together, okay? You know he's allowed to go out. So is she. They did it all the time, before. Or has something changed now?"

The agent didn't answer. David continued, "Are you protecting them, or are you holding them hostage . . . again?"

"We didn't do that, sir," the agent answered quickly. "Everything we do is for their safety. We would put ourselves in jeopardy—"

"I know you would. And I know you want what's best for them. So let them have lives while you're protecting their lives. Do you have a son? Would you want him to go for days without seeing sunlight?"

The men stood staring at each other for a moment, then the agent looked down at Randy, who looked back at him patiently but without hope. Randy held the undersized spongy football David had bought for him on their trip. The agent raised his eyes to no one. David put his hand on the doorknob and the agent stopped him. Then he took a walkie-talkie out of his pocket and said into it, "R2D2 coming out." He opened the door of the condo himself.

"Yay!" Randy yelled, and ran ahead.

A few minutes later he and David were walking through the late afternoon sunlight, still very strong in San Antonio in August. They tossed the ball back and forth, Randy dropping it half the time and scrambling around as it bounced on the sidewalk. He seemed to enjoy chasing it down as much as catching it.

Secret Service agents walked in front of them and behind them, but spaced far enough away to give David and Randy the illusion that they walked alone—if they had been very imaginative or very nearsighted. Randy was very well practiced at ignoring them, David less so, but he did his best.

"You know your dad wants you to come back and see him sometime," David said. He hadn't grown any better at preambles.

Randy didn't answer, though David could see him thinking about the idea. Before the silence became awkward, David changed his voice and said, "Go out for a long one."

"Oh, God," one of the Secret Service agents muttered.

Randy ran ahead, waving his arms. He stumbled on a crack in the sidewalk, making five grown men gasp, but he recovered himself and ran on. David lofted a high pass. Randy stopped, spread his arms wide, let the ball hit his chest as David had taught him, and caught it. Randy beamed, David cheered, and one of the agents quietly clapped his hands, until a glance from another agent stopped him.

They walked to the nearby school playground, nearly deserted at four-thirty, but the couple of parents and kids there did stare at the little entourage. The Secret Service agents spread out, stood close beside trees, tried to look relaxed, and blended in like crows in Antarctica. Randy and David tossed the football, then when Randy got tired of that he climbed on the tall wooden play fort. The agents gathered closer, looking as if they feared splinters as much as assassins. But Randy had a great time. He hung upside down from a bar, dropped down a pole, and hit his head on another bar as he climbed up to the high slide. He rubbed his head but didn't cry. At the top of the slide another boy sat, a blond boy a little younger than Randy. They exchanged a couple of sentences the adults couldn't hear, the boy gestured in the direction of Randy's companions and obviously asked a question. Randy shrugged dismissively and whispered in the other boy's ear, then they both slid down the slide together, laughing.

David stared significantly at the Hispanic agent he'd had to confront to get Randy out of the condo. Did the agent see this? How many times in Randy's life had he gotten to play with another boy?

The agent stared stoically across the street at the old brick elementary school as if it might pose a threat. David stood in the shade and watched Randy and the other boy throw sand on the slide. Randy laughed and laughed.

A blond woman jogged by. David admired her taut legs and— well, just about everything he saw—in the moment before he realized she was Helen. She came to a stop beside him, barely breathing hard.

"Did I see you checking me out? Do you ogle all the neighborhood women like that?"

David gestured innocently. "I'm watching Randy. You just happened to pass through my line of sight. And you looked like a suspicious character so I kept my eye on you." He folded his arms. "Just like the other agents."

Helen chuckled. She stood close beside him and unconsciously took up her old habit, surveying the landscape. Her eyes fell on the old elementary school and she scanned its windows, but the late afternoon sun had mirrored them.

"How's Myra?" she asked.

"Afraid. Why is she still afraid, Helen? We won the temporary orders hearing."

"How is she ever going to feel safe?" Helen asked rhetorically, by way of answer.

David nodded. The two of them watched Randy, having the time of his life. David said quietly, "How can this go on, Helen? They're still prisoners. They always will be. Myra wants them to have normal lives. How could I possibly accomplish that?"

Helen shrugged. "John McPherson won't be President forever."

"Maybe I should concentrate on trying to get him defeated for reelection."

Helen put a hand on his shoulder. "Don't worry, David, you'll think of something."

He didn't feel reassured.

"Let's go discuss possibilities," Helen said, her breath close to his ear.

David didn't even glance at his watch before deciding the work-day could be over and the Secret Service agents could take care of Randy without any further help from him.

The next day David placed a call to Burton Leemis. He called the White House, asked for the President's lawyer, and was told to leave a message. Two hours later he got a call back. The White House operator had tracked down Leemis, David didn't know how. Leemis could be sitting in a White House office with his client nearby, or he could be back home in Boston. Wherever he was calling from, Leemis sounded pleased with his surroundings. David, on the other hand, sat in a cramped, cluttered office with papers falling off his desk onto the floor. Burton Leemis sounded as if he realized that, too.

David said into the phone, "I think some of your interrogatories are overly intrusive."

"Thank you," Leemis answered in a self-satisfied way.

"Before I go over them with my client, I thought you and I should discuss a certain aspect of this case." Normally David would have said "we" in a conversation with opposing counsel like this, making it clear he expressed his client's desires as well as his own, but in this instance he wanted it to seem that this was strictly his own idea.

"Shoot," Leemis said.

David continued, "I need hardly point out to you that this is not an ordinary divorce case. Normally I would try to dig up whatever dirt I could on your client and you would do the same with mine. Because that might be useful in negotiation. In this case, though, whatever we learn is going to become public knowledge. You and I both know that we can have the record sealed, we can put it in a vault, but anything interesting to a tabloid will leak out. There are going to be too many eyes and hands on every document in the case."

"What's your point?"

"Your question about adultery, for example. I know it's a standard question, and I could just have my client make a standard denial. But I don't think we even want to go in that direction. Your just asking the question makes it sound as if her husband suspects her. Even that could be fodder for a tabloid story. 'Have the first couple been unfaithful?' It's not relevant. We haven't alleged adultery in our petition as a grounds for divorce. Of course, I can always amend and do that. Then I'll pose the same question to your client. And listen to me, Mr. Leemis, I know what his answer should be. I don't even have to ask him for names and dates. I know them."

Leemis went silent for a long ten seconds. "What's your suggestion?" he finally asked.

"That we both drop that line of inquiry. This is a couple with genuine problems, but we don't have to bring that issue up. Have it dragged through the press. Unless you want to."

"I'll consult with my client," Leemis said shortly, and hung up.

In the living room of the residence, John McPherson stood in earnest discussion with Wilson Boswell and Angela Vortiz. "I saw it, I tell you, on Randy's computer screen. It was the diagram you showed me of how the E-mail, uh, transfers happen." McPherson didn't want to call them "thefts." "Randy has it somehow."

"Sir, that's not possible." Boswell spoke patiently, but Angela glanced at him sharply, hearing the anger beneath his tone. "Forgive me, Mr. President, but I'm not sure you'd recognize that schematic. There are other patterns that look very similar, even a screen-saver image-builder that might resemble—"

"Damn it, I know what I saw! He has it. He has it on a disk or in his computer."

"How?"

"I don't know." The President suddenly looked shaken and nervous. "He could have gotten it off my laptop, I suppose, sometime when I'd had a crisis and laid it aside. He could have intercepted it—"

"That is not possible," Boswell repeated, his voice going flatter, his eyes deader.

"You keep saying that, but you don't know Randy's capabilities. He can—"

"Listen to me, sir. There is only one thing to do."

A knock at the door interrupted them. The President stared at the door in surprise. Almost no one knew he was here, and no one he could think of would dare disturb him.

The door opened and Burton Leemis entered briskly, with a self-important air. He smiled on everyone and said, "Mr. President, sir, I have to speak to you for just a second."

"I'll assume it's extremely important."

Leemis didn't bother to answer. He drew his client a few feet apart from the other two. Boswell began to speak quietly and sharply to Angela, but she waved him quiet. He stared at her, startled, and saw that she was eavesdropping on the President's low-voiced conversation with his lawyer. Boswell couldn't hear anything except an occasional word, such as "infidelity."

Leemis said quietly to McPherson, "I think in this case opposing counsel is right. I feel pretty confident that we're not going to gain anything from the question, and when we get asked it in turn we're going to be in a ticklish position." Leemis didn't even have to glance over his shoulder at Angela Vortiz, standing in a hip-cocked posture that emphasized her figure. The President did look her way.

"Why wouldn't Myra want to answer the question?" McPherson asked curiously.

"Her lawyer didn't say she didn't want to, just that he didn't want it asked. Besides, Mrs. McPherson has a certain . . . puritanism—I say that as a compliment—that would probably be offended just by being asked."

"Maybe she's still trying to protect me," McPherson said with a hopeful, almost wistful tone in his voice.

"Yes, sir. Perhaps there's a chance for reconciliation after all."

Burton Leemis didn't entertain that possibility, but if his client wanted to do so, let him.

"All right," the President said with sudden decisiveness. "Make the deal. Now if that's all . . ."

"Yes, sir. Unless you need me here?"

The President shook his head. Leemis made a graceful exit. McPherson rejoined the other conspirators. "Sorry. Just a little—"

Angela Vortiz shook her head at him scornfully. "Men!" she snapped, and turned and walked out of the room, walking very purposefully.

The President looked a question at his only remaining fellow conspirator. Boswell answered, "She has very good hearing."

"But what . . . ?"

"I don't know, John, but let's stay focused. As I was about to say when we got interrupted, there is only one thing to do. You must get your son back here. With his computer."

"Or maybe," John McPherson improvised, "if Randy comes back here, someone could slip into the condo in San Antonio and get a look at what's in his computer."

"Another good possibility," Boswell replied. "Except we don't want too many people in on this. And there's something else. You need to win Randy's loyalty."

The President frowned.

"Do you understand what's at risk?" Boswell said coldly. "Our technology is already in place. That means it will be used. What's essential is that it not be traced back to us. To me. If your son has a copy of the program made before it was used, that tells everyone that we were the source. You must get that back."

"I under—" McPherson began, but Boswell dropped the pretense of deference to him.

"Let's make sure you do. You must get Randy back here. He must be subject to your control. You cannot fail at this. Either you can go on being President for five more years, or you can spend the rest of your life in courtrooms or prison."

McPherson looked shocked. It had been a long time since anyone had spoken to him in a tone like this. But even as Wilson Boswell put McPherson in his place, Boswell's thoughts were elsewhere. As always, he had a contingency plan, which looked more than ever as if it would have to become the primary plan. Now that Randy had made a record of what he knew, Boswell risked having his scheme discovered or traced back to him. He no longer had much choice of what to do.

It seemed wiser than ever that he had set Larsen loose.

When Burton Leemis called David back, the President's lawyer had changed his tone. "All right," he said. "We think your implied condition of retaining their privacy a good one. We'll go along. You can strike my adultery question and I won't object."

"Thank you."

"I should thank you. I should have thought of it myself. An associate prepared the interrogatories, you know how it is." Leemis sounded almost chummy. He and David had become conspirators against the public.

"Now on to the next thing," Leemis said cheerfully. "When does my client get his first visitation?"

Angela Vortiz sat in the White House records room. In the White House someone kept a log of everything. Incoming and outgoing phone calls, visitors, the amount of flour the kitchen ordered in a week. And various employees kept track of the comings and goings of the staff and residents. Sometimes one had to sign a log just to pass from one wing to another.

Surveillance cameras cover much of the interior, as well. Angela checked logbooks, then went to corresponding videotapes. She wore a constant frown of concentration but with a happy light in her eyes.

She had other duties, so couldn't devote all her time to her search, and she had many days of tapes to investigate: days and nights when the President had been out of town and the First Lady had been at home in the White House. If what Angela suspected had happened out of town, she might be out of luck.

The exploration of the records and videotapes took her the better part of a week, but in the end Angela found what she sought. She went from a logbook to a videotape. The tape was from a fairly late night, after eleven. A wine steward arrived at the foot of the stairs that led up to the residence. The Secret Service agent on duty there checked the steward and allowed him to pass upstairs. Angela fast-forwarded. Time passed. The agent looked concerned. After a time he too went upstairs. When he returned his face had gone blank and stoical.

The residence held no cameras, but few people would know that. Angela smiled, a bright, happy smile only for herself. She put her evidence away and went about her duties humming, happily wondering exactly how to use what she'd learned. For the time being, she would keep the information to herself.

★ David found the first son lying on his stomach on the floor of his bedroom, drawing a diagram on a sheet of computer paper. He'd drawn several boxes, and lines connected them in a variety of ways, some of the lines unbroken and some of them dotted. David took his seat on the floor beside him and Randy continued his lecture from a previous day as if David had never left.

"See, when you send an E-mail," Randy explained patiently, "it goes from your computer to a server and then to another server, and if one's too busy it might go to a different one. It might go to three or four stops along the way before it gets where it's going."

"Can you tell afterward which way it went?" David interrupted.

"Usually. But this program tells it to leave a copy at one of these stops. Then it sends that copy somewhere else. So if you trace back the path of your E-mail it went the right places, and you can't tell that a copy got made. It just gets two different places instead of one."

"Huh," David said, staring at the diagrams. Randy looked pleased at holding his attention.

"The problem is processing," he said seriously. "You can collect all this information, but what do you do with it? Say you click on your E-mail in the morning and you've got ten million messages. Which one do you open first? Even if you knew one of them had some really important information, how would you know which one?"

"And it would be worse if you weren't even sure any of them was important," David said, sounding as if he were trying to keep up.

"Yeah. Or if message number seventeen and message number nine hundred eighty-five thousand were what you were looking for, but only if you put them together."

"Could you design a computer program that would search through them and find out?"

"Could I? Geez, I'm only eight years old, David."

"Could *someone?*" David asked exaggeratedly. Randy laughed.

The two sounded like old friends, of about the same age. Helen, passing in the hall, looked in on them and smiled ambiguously. Helen spent less time with Myra and Randy than she used to do. She had a small apartment nearby, in an effort to give the first family more privacy, and Helen as well. But she still occasionally spent the night here in the condo, more often with David. Today marked an unusually long separation between the two of them, a day and a half. She smiled at seeing him with Randy.

David turned and saw her. As much time as he had spent with Helen now, he still smiled at sight of her, especially when she wore something other than her black uniformlike suit, which these days stayed in her closet more often than not. Today Helen was dressed to go jogging, in her nylon wind-shorts and white T-shirt. "Has he explained this stuff to you?" David asked.

"He's tried. Hi, Randy. I'll see you guys later, I'm going for a run."

She waggled her fingers in farewell. After she walked away, both David and Randy continued to stare at the empty doorway where she had been. "Isn't that great?" Randy said longingly.

David nodded, then looked at the boy strangely. "What?"

"The way she can just walk out whenever she wants, all by herself."

David felt his heart turn over, the reaction Randy often gave him. "Come on," he said. "Let's go for a walk."

As they walked the few blocks to the school playground, Secret Service agents surrounded them at a slight distance. Today three of the agents were dressed appropriately for the weather, in khaki shorts and knit shirts, with the kind of sleeveless vests photographers wear covering their guns and radios. The fourth agent still wore his dark suit, but he seemed to look enviously at his colleagues.

David asked, "Are you looking forward to seeing your father next week?"

"Yeah," Randy said, but his answer sounded perfunctory.

"Has he been calling you?"

"Yep. Every day."

"Well, good."

"I guess." Randy didn't speak for a while, then said, "David?"

"Yes?"

"Have you ever seen my father give a speech on TV?"

"I sure have."

"Did you know that they have this thing right beside the TV camera, like a big Etch a Sketch, that has the speech words on it? He doesn't really have the whole speech memorized, he's just reading it. But he's pretty good at it, so people usually can't tell."

"Yeah, I know about that," David said. "Most people do by now."

Randy went silent again for several seconds, then said, "That's how he sounds when he talks to me on the phone."

David's step faltered. He put his hand on Randy's shoulder, then took it away. He wasn't applying for the job of substitute father. That wouldn't be fair to the President or to Randy. One of the Secret Service agents, obviously overhearing, glanced sympathetically at Randy, then soberly at David.

David said, "He probably can't help sounding that way, Randy. It's just a habit. Everything he says is so important, it's probably hard for him to, you know, lighten up."

Randy didn't answer. In a few more minutes they reached the playground. Randy brightened immediately. He waved and called, "Benjamin!" then ran across the field. Another boy of similar age looked up and ran toward him, calling Randy's name. They met in the middle of the playground and slapped hands, then did some more complicated greeting that involved bumping heads. David could almost hear the Secret Service agents groan. Two of them had run with Randy, keeping pace with him a few steps back. Another circled the field, looking at the streets. The fourth, Henry Perez, the one who had first let Randy come to this playground, stayed near David, also scanning the terrain.

"She's thinking of enrolling him in this school," the agent said without looking at David.

"Really?" David looked across the street at the tall old mound of yellow brick, an elementary school that looked more like a high school or even small college. It seemed big enough to hold three thousand kids or more. Randy had always attended small private schools. "And that would be okay with you?" David asked.

"We could make it work," the agent said. "It's not up to us."

David watched Randy run toward the play fort with his new friend and felt like a parent sending his child off on the first day of school. It wasn't up to him, either, what Randy's life would be like in the future. He wondered yet again if he had done the right thing. Would any reputable lawyer paid a surprise visit by the First Lady of the United States have gently talked her out of what she wanted to do? But her pain had been apparent. More so since he'd gotten to know her better. And Randy, as his mother had said, deserved better than the puny life he had in the White House.

Other boys arrived. Randy mingled and blended with them. This quickly, he had managed to make friends. The Secret Service agents, to their credit, had used this anxiety-producing situation to advantage. John and Myra McPherson had always tried to keep their son's life private, and for the most part the media had cooperated. Pictures of the President's son were relatively rare, and Randy was average-looking enough to fit in with these boys. The Secret Service had been very cooperative with this idea of keeping Randy out of the spotlight, which fit their own objectives perfectly. Here in San Antonio, they had even come up with a cunning new plan of their own. The agents had recruited a few of these local boys, with their parents' and Myra's approval, to come and spend time playing with Randy. The agents escorted these boys, of course, but let them be seen, so that the few photographers who did manage to hide near the condo's entrance had snapped photographs of several eight-year-old boys, none of them Randy McPherson. A few of these photos had appeared in print labeled as the first son, so that already the public's perception of what Randy McPherson looked like had begun to grow blurry.

David stood there watching him play for half an hour or more.

Larsen watched from his third-floor perch in the elementary school, taking in the whole scene: the kids on the playground, the agents watching alertly but seldom looking his way. He pictured the havoc he could create by raising this window, pointing a rifle, and firing it.

But too many kids ran wild down there. Too many agents would come rushing into this school, maybe trapping him. Larsen intended to win this game, not just cause brief panic. He had to get closer.

Larsen returned to the computer room and got on the Internet. Rapidly, he began assembling the materials he would need.

When Myra McPherson left the condo, she created an event. The agents insisted she ride in a car even though she only intended to go a few blocks. She obediently climbed into the back of the black

Lincoln, taking her place behind the tinted windows on the ground level of the complex, so that when the car emerged no one could be sure she rode in it. The car took her a few blocks to the elementary school, to her appointment with the school's principal. Consequently, she only managed a few moments in the open air. But halfway to the school's door Myra stopped, raised her head, and breathed. The humid air tasted marvelously fresh in her nostrils. She drew strength from the few deep breaths, and walked into the school smiling, imagining coming here for other conferences, school plays, lunches with Randy. The life she had always imagined for herself and had never had.

Helen, on the other hand, walked to the school from the condo ahead of time as the First Lady's advance person. By the time Mrs. McPherson arrived Helen's official work was done. She slipped away from the party in the principal's office and went for a look around the school.

Helen walked slowly and quietly along the old linoleum floors of the school. Schools had a peculiar air of their own, one Helen hadn't breathed in quite a while. A school in the summer felt creepy; all those empty rooms and closets. Every space seemed forbidden. She shouldn't be here. Schools have a way of turning everyone back into children, expecting to be reprimanded. Helen grew even quieter as she walked the corridors, looking into rooms. Most were empty, most locked. She wondered which room would hold Randy in the fall, in what seemed to her the unlikely event that his mother actually enrolled him here.

The school featured ramps rather than stairways. Helen went up one, circling the landing to continue toward the second floor. The stucco walls of the old school seemed terribly solid, which subliminally reassured her. No bugs, organic or otherwise, infiltrated these walls. The white stucco would show any scars, but they remained smooth. Helen began walking more forcefully, as if she belonged.

★

Larsen watched her come.

One task he had taken on in his work for the school had been to install surveillance cameras at key locations, such as the ramps and corridor junctions. He could tap into their coverage of the school at any of the computers in his computer lab. Larsen had done so this morning as soon as he'd heard visitors arrive. He'd seen the First Lady enter the school, but without her son. He'd seen the Secret Service agents spread out around the entrance. They didn't worry him. The agents had of course checked on all the school employees, but Larsen's job and past employment history made sense, and his appearance reassured the agents that he was what he seemed to be, a computer geek. In fact, he could drive them out of the room by starting to explain his job.

But Helen was different. He knew her, and with a little mental effort she might know him as well. They had seen each other very briefly at that highway intersection in South Carolina. The first time Larsen had seen her jog through the neighborhood and stop at the playground he hadn't been sure, but when he'd watched her talk to the lawyer, the one he'd seen much more closely, he had been. This woman's suspicions wouldn't be as easy to allay.

On his screen, she came to the ramp leading to the third floor. His computer lab was one of only five or six rooms up here, it wouldn't take her long. Larsen turned from the screen and reached for his equipment.

Something put Helen on alert as she came up the ramp to the third floor. She couldn't have said what caused this heightened sensitivity, but she had come to trust it. She moved slowly, her eyes barely coming over the wall around the rampway, then quickly the rest of the way up the ramp to the floor. Being unarmed made her even more cautious than in the past. That took a whole different mind-set. Her best weapon here might be to scream, to alert the agents below.

Probably, though, she was just going to alarm a teacher performing some summer chore, rearranging her room or writing a lesson plan. After all, the Service had checked out this school thoroughly.

Helen came around the doorway of the computer lab and stood stock-still. Slowly she raised her hands. A man stood with his feet widespread and planted, two hands gripping a pistol pointed at her. She didn't recognize him at all, he wore a sort of helmet that obscured his features and hair.

"Wait," Helen said softly, preparing to jump back out of the room, but the man moved quickly sideways to have a clearer angle at her, and also stepped toward her. "Back!" he suddenly screamed. And he fired the gun.

Helen gasped and jerked backward. The back of her heel caught on the doorsill and she went down backward. She couldn't feel the pain yet. When she hit the floor she rolled. But she was scrabbling like a crab, and the man was running. He caught up to her in a few steps and grabbed her shoulder. Helen tried to wrench away, but was backed up against the wall of the ramp.

"What are you doing?" the man yelled. He dropped his pistol. Helen scrambled toward it, but the man ignored her. He pulled off his helmet. Underneath he wore a baseball cap backward, all his hair tucked up inside. He had a thick black mustache, puffy cheeks, and a mumbling way of talking. "Don't mess with that!" he said sharply to Helen.

But she pointed the pistol at him. He took two rapid steps toward her, reaching for the gun. Helen fired. The man grimaced and took the pistol out of her hand.

"Sorry," he said calmly. He held up the gun so that Helen saw the wire trailing from it to the man's helmet. "Virtual reality," he said. "I didn't even know you were real."

Helen could have said the same to him. She gulped softly and regained control of her breath. "Don't tell me you're installing that in the school's computer system," she said, a little raggedly.

"Nah." The man smiled a strange, lopsided smile. "Just taking a little play break of my own."

He put out a hand toward her. "Wanta come in and see what I'm doing? I'm networking their computers. And creating hyperlinks that they can use either from here or anywhere else in—"

"Gee, I'd love to," Helen said. "But I've got to run."

She wanted to get downstairs and make sure the Service had checked this guy out, but they must have. They wouldn't have left him in place otherwise. This man had more right to be here than Helen did. She gave him a little wave and started back down.

"What grade?" he called softly. Helen looked up across the top of the wall. "What?"

"What grade is your child in?" the man asked in a friendly way.

Helen had to think for a second. "Third," she said, speaking of Randy.

The man nodded and smiled. "Be seeing you, then."

Helen mumbled a reply and hurried downstairs.

Larsen watched her depart all the way to the ground floor on the screens. He reached a finger inside his mouth and removed the inserts that had enlarged his cheeks and changed his speech. He had scared her off, but she would be back, he had a feeling about that.

He could have killed her here, but that would have ended his primary plan. Instead he put off that satisfaction. But he decided he needed to speed up his plans.

Helen appeared unannounced but not completely unexpected on David's doorstep that evening about nine. She stood straight, feet slightly apart, eyes bright, and she held a small brown bag in her hands. Wearing a casual summer outfit of navy slacks and a white, ribbed, sleeveless top, she seemed to present a picture, and after

David opened the door she just stood there for a moment, smiling at him. Then Helen thrust the bag toward him.

"I brought you a *good* bottle of scotch. Not that there's anything wrong with that stuff you have. But I wanted to get you a present."

"Thank you." David pulled a bottle from the bag, then held it more carefully as he saw that it was indeed a twelve-year-old single malt. He also noticed that the bottle had been opened. He glanced at Helen, who continued to smile brightly though not with her usual sharp focus. "Would you like one?"

"No, thanks." But Helen followed him to the kitchen, and when David put ice in a short glass Helen dumped all the cubes into the sink, picked out one and put it back in the glass, then poured the glass about half full. She swirled the glass for a moment, sipped, shook her head, said, "Wait for the ice to melt a little," then sipped again and smiled. "Perfect."

David reached for the glass but Helen held on to it and turned away without noticing his hand. He made himself a shorter one, surreptitiously added water, and followed her out to the living room. Helen stood surveying the room, looking toward the front windows, not with her old suspicious stare but in a surprised, curious way. When she heard David at her shoulder she said conversationally, "I almost killed a computer guy today."

"What?"

"Uh huh. Would have if I'd had a gun. Real gun." She nodded. "That's my training. That's my instincts. He seemed like a threat."

Her observations had the false detachment of someone who had puzzled over a problem until it grew unreal. David stood close enough to feel the warmth of her body. She swayed ever so slightly.

Helen turned and touched him. For the first time that David had known her, she seemed to need something, comforting or explanation. But when he reached to hold her she moved away again. "They tell me you were very good in court. Wish I could have seen it all."

"It wasn't that big a thing." But it had felt very good at the end.

Helen, on the other hand, hadn't had a chance to do her real job in some time.

Confirming his impression, she suddenly said, "David, what am I doing here, in San Antonio, Texas?" She looked toward the windows again, now with a small frown. "This is a surprise to me, to be here."

"At my house?"

She smiled at him, then looked more sly as she pushed his own glass toward him. "Drink up. Is this great scotch or what?"

"It is. Did you sample it before you got here?"

She looked momentarily offended. "Well, I can now, can't I? You know the last time I was drunk?"

"College?"

"Nineteen ninety . . . I'm not sure, but well back in the last millennium." She frowned down at her glass. "I don't miss it. But you need to drink up. Have I gotten you drunk yet?"

David took another sip. "Yes."

She smiled again, the broadest smile yet. "You're not thinking of trying something, are you?"

"Would that be all right?"

She moved close to him, realized she still held her glass, and set it down very carefully on a bookshelf. Then she pressed against him. The sleeveless top she wore proved very thin, and its ribbed texture complimented Helen's smooth skin as David reached under it to run his hands along her back. Helen kissed him, holding his cheeks in her hands. He thought he heard a catch in her breath.

"Don't worry," she murmured, soft as a lover's caress, "if I don't like it I'll break your arm."

The next morning David sat in his conference room going over the discovery materials forwarded by Burton Leemis. Leemis had nearly fulfilled his promise to bury David with discovery requests, and with his own answers. A truck had delivered the material.

The White House kept records of *every*thing. The President's schedule, phone calls in and out of the Oval Office, visitors, trips, decisions. David could almost reconstruct when the President had gone to the bathroom for the last three years. At first he pored over this material wondering what the President's lawyer had left out. Then he realized Leemis was too smart for that. He would include documents answering every request David had made, but he would bury the relevant information in so much obscurity it would take David years to find it.

David's interim attorney's fees had arrived from the White House; he no longer had to worry about money and had more time to devote to his major case. He had his paralegal and a temporary secretary helping him, but he had to do much of the reading himself. David spent so much time on it that after a while he drifted. He found himself looking at the phone logs, lists of numbers and times and dates. Some numbers included locations, others did not. David didn't see any sense to any of it at first. He began skimming.

Riffling through the logs, he found dates he remembered, the time earlier this summer when the First Lady had been held hostage in the medical facility, and then been on the run. There must have been frantic activity on John McPherson's part at that time, maybe he had consulted his secret partner. Probably he had used a cell phone or some more sophisticated means of communication, but in the first moment of panic he might have just picked up the phone. Or someone might have called in to the White House.

Someone had, in fact. Hundreds of someones. Some of the recorded phone numbers carried names, some just had the location called from. After the first two dozen pages David began to get blurry.

He cast back to that time, finding it hard to believe that he had taken such risks at the urging of a virtual stranger, Helen. He'd also been motivated by a desire to get close to Helen, and he'd accomplished that, but he hoped his emotions ran a little deeper than that. Now that the case had become a more conventional legal tangle, he looked back at that time on the road nostalgically. Playing catch with Randy, the shy First Lady beginning to blossom, her hugging him in the hotel room. Helen's competence guiding them throughout.

He continued to flip through pages as he reminisced, until he realized he'd come to a date when he and his entourage *had* been on the road, almost at the end of it, in fact. He tried to correlate the date to where they'd been, and just as he remembered he saw it on the page in front of him: Greenville, South Carolina, Airport. The phone log he held reported that the White House had received a call from the airport the same day the little group of fugitives had been there, apparently from a pay phone in the airport. The call had been very brief, only two minutes, and had been routed to the main office of the Secret Service. Even the time had been efficiently recorded—about the same time, as well as David could remember, that he, Myra, and Randy had waited for Helen to arrive with their new stolen car.

David stared at the page of the phone log until he had it memorized, then the pages fell from his fingers. Who had made that call?

It didn't take long to answer that question. Soon, he figured out why, as well.

Larsen had done his work overnight. The Secret Service had checked out the vicinity of the condominium complex, but they didn't have the personnel to patrol the entire neighborhood twenty-four hours a day. Their jobs had been made more difficult by Myra's growing assertiveness. In the good old days they knew weeks in advance exactly where she and Randy would be at any given minute. They could have a location secured shortly before the first family set foot in it.

Now, though, with the First Lady's insistence that Randy be allowed to have something like a normal life, the agents had to move much more quickly and secure a place almost spontaneously. They didn't have the numbers to do the job adequately. A small shift, three men, worked from midnight to eight A.M. The agent in charge had diverted most of his forces to daytime, when the first family might be on the move. The night shift didn't have the manpower to patrol the neighborhood very much.

Larsen had learned he could easily avoid the middle-of-the-night shift, as well as local police. For two nights, at three A.M., he did his work at the playground, planting his strange garden. He felt proud of the way he disguised the holes. When he walked away a few paces, then looked back, he couldn't tell where he'd just been working. Secret Service agents could find his equipment with a metal detector, but they didn't use one. Never enough time.

One day in August, more than three weeks after the First Lady's arrival in San Antonio, the agents accompanied Randy to the playground. Now the four agents all wore walking shorts and short-sleeved shirts, adorned with the necessary equipment-hiding vests. Their very dark sunglasses still marked them as official, but they blended in a little better with the occasional parents who appeared at the playground escorting their own children.

Randy ignored them, searching the playground for any of his friends. To Randy, the playground seemed a magical place. He couldn't decide what to do first: swing, run up the long ramp to the fort, or climb to the part of the fort that had a swaying rubber bridge to cross to the big slide. If Randy had had a normal childhood he would have been bored with playgrounds by the time he was eight years old. Instead, they still seemed novel to him. He chugged across the long empty lot toward the play area, scuffling his feet deliberately to kick up clouds of black dirt. He stopped to examine a blade of grass that held a spear point at its tip. Randy plucked it, tried tasting it, walked on carrying the grass stalk in his mouth. A boy he knew called his name. Randy waved and ran toward him. Just before they reached each other, each boy veered aside and kept running. "You're it!" yelled the other boy, a seven-year-old blond named Bobby. Suddenly they were playing tag, screaming and laughing.

Those screams shrilled along the nerves of the Secret Service agents, but they were growing used to them. Playing children screamed, they had learned. As often as they'd explained to Randy that screams should be reserved for real crisis situations, when he had a friend with him he forgot. So the agents watched stoically and did their jobs. Charles Rascoe, a stocky, balding man with thick hands, walked to the play fort and began methodically checking it, testing the wooden steps and the metal pipes to make sure nothing had been cut through or implanted with something.

Up on the third floor of the elementary school, Larsen saw Rascoe testing the play fort and knew the time had come. He checked the slide on his semiautomatic pistol one last time, stuck it behind his back under his belt, picked up his backpack, and hurried down the ramp.

"I need to talk to you very soon," Myra McPherson said to David Owens. She sounded tense, but in an angry way rather than the meek manner he'd seen too often.

"I could come over now," David said into the phone. At three-thirty in the afternoon he looked forward to getting out of the office, and he would always take an opportunity to see Randy. "I need to talk to you, too. Is Helen there?"

"She's out running. David, they want me to bring Randy to the White House. I got a call from John's chief of staff."

"That's something we agreed to do," David said slowly. He looked around his office, the stacks of papers and files everywhere, and thought how easy this job would be if it weren't for clients.

"Because I had to," Myra answered. "But now—Hurry over, let's talk. Randy's at the playground."

Helen jogged, then slowed down to walk rapidly through the San Antonio heat. It felt like slowly penetrating a thick barrier. She came to the playground, saw Randy well guarded by the agents and so preoccupied with his friends that he didn't see Helen wave. She smiled at that, and turned down a street that would bring her in a long circle back to the school.

Larsen saw her leaving as he emerged from the school, and watched her walk away with mixed feelings. He feared that one the most, for some reason, but also wanted her in on this climax to his scheme. He had not forgotten that she had slammed a trunk lid down on his head. In Larsen's world, vengeance wasn't a reward, it was one of the rules of the game. But maybe it would have to wait for another time. He shifted the backpack to his shoulder and started across the street toward the playground.

Agent Rascoe methodically and without much enthusiasm tugged on each of the five-foot-long metal pipes that formed steps up to one side of the play fort. He could see where they had been screwed into the wood, and it looked like a sturdy enough job. But when he looked more closely he saw from a faded indentation in the wood that the support had been moved just slightly. Maybe it hadn't been recent, maybe it had been done when the fort was first built. Rascoe thought it worth checking. He tapped the pipe with a fingernail.

"Anybody got a screwdriver?" he called across the playground.

Randy noticed the agent tinkering with the fort. Randy slowed down and Bobby, trying to tag him, plowed into Randy and they both fell over. Other kids had arrived at the playground, more than half a dozen boys and girls, drifting in and out of each other's games, circling close then running away. Randy saw a boy and girl only slightly older than he apparently engaged in a serious discussion. Randy found that odd, and watched them curiously for a long moment.

A boy named Jeremy, the same age as Randy and similar in appearance, ran by and yelled, "Come on." Bobby immediately followed him, running toward the fort, but Randy lingered behind, still taking in the details of the playground. Faintly Randy heard the creak of the swings, metal circle rubbing across metal circle where the swings connected to the crossbar at the top, the circles creaking in counterpoint. A happy sound, to Randy's ears. A few feet away Randy noticed a small hole in the ground, little more than an inch in diameter, like a snake hole. Randy noticed. His senses opened to everything.

Agent Rascoe went and consulted his fellow agents, but no one had any tools with them. Agent Jones gave Rascoe a small pocketknife and Rascoe returned to his task at the pipe. He began unscrewing the screws that held one end of the pipe in place.

Randy ran toward the play fort, climbed up to the first level, and ran across the swaying rubber bridge to the platform that led to a long metal slide. Jeremy and Bobby had already swooshed down its length. As Randy sat at the top of the slide, he looked across the street and saw a side door of the elementary school open. Randy watched as a vaguely familiar man emerged, carrying a backpack over one shoulder. The man wore a baseball cap and little could be seen of his face except a large black mustache, which seemed askew, as if the man were smirking broadly. Randy let go of the handles and slid down the slide, drawing the man's attention. The man in the cap waved in a friendly way, as if they knew each other. Randy just watched.

The Secret Service agents saw the man too, but recognized him as the computer nerd from the school. They didn't like people carrying backpacks, though. By mutual unspoken agreement, Jones left his post and started toward the man as the man crossed the street toward the playground.

Rascoe grunted with effort as the last screw came loose and dropped into the dirt. The agent squatted to retrieve it, couldn't find it. Above his head, the pipe slipped free from its side mooring. Something rattled inside.

Larsen didn't reach into his backpack. He knew that would bring instant action from the Secret Service agent approaching him. But Larsen saw the pipe come loose from the fort and knew the game had begun. He had the advantage of being the only one who knew that. As he passed through an opening in the fence and onto the playground, he lifted his right hand in a wave at the approaching agent. In Larsen's left hand he already held a small remote control. Larsen's upraised right hand acted like a magician's patter, a momentary distraction. As the agent glanced upward, Larsen pressed a button on the remote control.

Over at the play fort, Agent Rascoe gave up on his search for the missing screw and stood up again. As he did, he heard the rattle in the pipe. He grabbed the metal and pushed it farther down, so the object inside slid through the pipe and out the end. As the small black oblong object fell it exploded, set off by Larsen's remote control.

The explosion was small but powerful. If the bomb had stayed in the pipe it would have turned the pipe into metal shrapnel when it exploded, but falling through the air it just made a loud noise. As close as it fell to Rascoe, it sounded like much more to him. Instinctively he flinched and fell back.

Agent Jones, approaching Larsen, also turned to look in the direction of the noise. He hesitated, his eyes seeking Randy. The first son stood at the foot of the slide, looking around in a perplexed way. Jones saw that Rascoe was the closest agent to Randy, but Rascoe was distracted and might be injured. Jones turned and began running toward his protectee.

Which gave Larsen time to pull the pistol from his backpack and shoot the agent in the back. Jones went down with only a grunt, the force of the bullet knocking him over before he felt the pain.

At that moment thick smoke began pouring from the bomb that had fallen from the pipe. It rolled in clouds toward Agent Rascoe, quickly obscuring him. His coughing could be heard through the smoke.

Three other agents began running toward the fort and Randy, drawing guns. Larsen pushed other buttons on his remote control. From the small holes he had dug and loaded, other gas and smoke bombs shot out with exploding noises. Smoke spread thickly across the playground. Children screamed and ran haphazardly. Larsen stepped into his own fog and disappeared from view. The agent who had been drawing a bead on him stopped. He couldn't fire into that cloud, where children including Randy staggered and screamed.

The other two agents ran into the smoke in the direction of the slide, where they had last seen Randy. Rascoe also recovered and began groping through the thick smog toward his protectee. He bumped his forehead on the fort but kept going. "Randy," he called, but not very loudly. "Stay down, I'll find you." He had no idea whether anyone could hear him. In the smog children cried out and coughed, but he couldn't distinguish Randy's voice.

More explosions sounded through the fog. One agent began running. He hit his shin on a bench, cried out, but didn't fall. Then he noticed the acrid smell. He realized his eyes were running. This wasn't just smoke that covered the playground. Tear gas mixed through the darkness. The agent began coughing. He got out a handkerchief and covered his mouth.

Larsen moved confidently through the fog, a small mask covering his nose and mouth and eyes. The mask filtered out the tear gas and the spectacles helped his vision penetrate the murky gas. Larsen had practiced in such an environment. He moved across the playground like the only sighted person in a blind world. Coming upon a Secret Service agent with a handkerchief over his mouth, Larsen casually lifted his gun to the man's neck and pulled the trigger. Blood spurted. The man went down with no time for a scream. Larsen dropped to the ground and rolled quickly to the side before his gunfire could bring the other agents. He rose again and moved relentlessly toward the play fort.

In the fog agents ran, blundered, listened for the sounds of the first son, but couldn't pick his voice out of those of the other children. They had their guns drawn but had no target. And soon they were all choking and blind.

David Owens's car pulled up to the playground just as the first gas bombs went off and a man carrying a backpack walked into the playground. David sat stunned as the man drew a gun from his pack and shot Agent Jones. Fifty yards from the action, only David saw the man knock off his baseball cap as he stepped into the fog. Long blond hair fell out. David recognized their pursuer from the cross-country trip.

In the next few moments the playground became obscured by smoke and gas. David looked frantically and saw Randy standing frozen by the slide just before the gas engulfed him.

David leaped from his car. The Secret Service agents were closer and moved more quickly, running into the fog. But David doubted they could see anything. He started toward the fog himself, but then stopped. They needed reinforcements. The condo was only a few blocks away. David stood locked in place by uncertainty. He couldn't reach the condo and return with other agents in time. Even a phone call would be too late.

He ran again, but as he neared the gas he caught a whiff of it, a noxious, acrid odor. Faintly he could hear coughing. David skidded to a halt. The agents were in there. They could do more good than he could, if anyone could do anything in that fog. David ran in a wide circle instead, keeping out of the fog and the gas. The sound of a gunshot made his heart thud more heavily. He circled the playground to a spot closest to where he'd last seen Randy and yet still outside the gas. A slight breeze kept it away from him. David looked around and saw no one else to help. Drawing a deep breath, he jumped the fence and rolled on the ground toward the play fort and the slide.

Jogging around the far side of the school, Helen Wills thought she heard something. The sound could have been anything—a car starting, a kid hitting a baseball—but instinctively she thought of Randy. Picking up her pace, she continued to circle the school, back toward the playground. The closer she got, the more certain she became that something was badly wrong. She wished like hell she had a gun.

When David entered the fog he felt himself disappear. Everyone became bodiless and silent in that inky smoke, except, David knew, the killer. David rolled, came to a halt, tried to peer ahead of him, and called, "Randy!"

A small, frightened voice answered. David ran toward it, his eyes barely open to slits. In a moment he would have to breathe and his rescue attempt would be over. He moved quickly through the obscuring smog but didn't run. Twenty feet away he heard another gunshot. Groping with both hands, he felt the metal slide. His foot hit the upright support.

"Help," said a small voice below him.

David knelt quickly, his head almost hitting the slide. The boy sat underneath. A good hiding place, under the circumstances. David grabbed a skinny arm and pulled. A frightened scream answered him. "Don't worry, it's me," he whispered urgently. The boy came along.

David did run then. He picked up the first son and ran back in what he hoped was the direction of the fence. Either the smoke had spread or he was running the wrong direction, because it seemed to take too long to get back to where he'd started. David bumped into the fence, lifted the boy over, and then jumped it himself. He let out his breath explosively. The boy knelt on the ground gasping, only the shaggy brown top of his head visible to David.

After two deep breaths David said, "Come on, we've got to run. You're okay now."

"That's all right," said a voice behind him. "I'll take him from here."

The surprisingly deep voice came from the throat of the thin blond man. He stood a few feet behind David. David turned quickly, putting himself in front of the boy. That would be worthless, of course, as David was unarmed and Larsen held a large semiauto-matic pistol. He gestured with it for David to move out of the way. This close to the long sought object of his quest, Larsen felt reluc-tant to fire, which was silly, since the point of all this exercise was the boy's murder, anyway. But Larsen had a game player's instinct for not giving up a prize too quickly.

David looked at the gun and the man behind it and realized he couldn't defend Randy. Slowly, he moved aside. He had his hand on the boy's shoulder.

"All right," David said to the man with the gun. "You're his pro-tector now."

He pushed the boy toward Larsen, who glared at David. "What do you mean?"

David shrugged. "Why do you think everyone wants him? He knows the secrets. He has all the clues."

Larsen hesitated. Damned children. He hated children. In all the street slaughter and wizardry games he played, children represented the greatest prizes and also potentials for disaster. Many, many points to be won or lost.

Tears ran down the boy's face. As David pushed him toward the gunman, the boy stared at David with a helpless sense of betrayal.

David stared back. His eyes widened. "Oh, my God," he said. "I got the wrong kid!"

Without another word to Larsen, David leaped back over the low fence and disappeared into the fog. Larsen knelt, grabbed the boy, and turned him to face him. This was a trick. He had the right boy in his hands. A small brown-haired boy with thin limbs. Larsen had seen him for a week now. At a distance, though. And he had seen the boy's pictures in the newspaper. He'd noticed that the boy seemed to change appearance slightly in each picture, but all boys did that, didn't they?

"Who are you?" Larsen said angrily. "What's your father's name?"

The boy cried, from the effects of the gas and from fright. "P-P-Peter," he mumbled. "Scott Peterson."

"Shit!" Larsen snapped. Everybody lied. He couldn't trust anyone. But if Randy McPherson still stumbled through that fog on the playground, then all this had been for nothing and he wouldn't get another chance.

Larsen thought frantically. He had a car just across the street in the teacher parking lot of the school, but he couldn't lock this boy in it and have him stay put while Larsen went looking for another one. He was almost out of time already. The lawyer had delayed him. Maybe the trunk of the car?

No. He thought of a simpler answer. Knock this boy unconscious, leave him here, and make another quick scramble through the playground. If the lawyer had found the real first son, Larsen would snatch him. If it was a trick, he'd find out quickly and come back to this one.

He raised the gun. The boy cowered away from him. Larsen gripped him more tightly and swung the gun toward his head.

Helen Wills had just come around the school. She saw a man with a gun staring in puzzlement at Randy McPherson. Then the man pulled back his gun as if to swat the boy's head with it. Helen put on a last burst of speed across the street and threw herself at the gunman's legs.

At the same moment, David reappeared out of the fog and jumped back over the fence. His legs high in the air, using the fence for leverage, he kicked as hard as he could at Larsen's shoulder.

Neither of them aimed perfectly. Helen hit one of the man's legs and David struck him a glancing blow on the shoulder. But the combination of the two blows was enough to knock Larsen loose from the boy he held. Larsen fell back, the back of his head hitting the ground. Meanwhile David landed on Helen, lost his breath, and rolled off of her. They both rose to their feet. Not nearly quickly enough.

Larsen had recovered, and he hadn't lost his gun. Both David and Helen looked at him hesitantly. He pointed the gun at them.

Then Larsen cried "Ow!" and flinched, grabbing his cheek. David looked around. Randy was throwing rocks. He had picked up a handful and thrown them all at once, like a shotgun. One had connected.

Helen reacted much better. She didn't look for the source of the gunman's pain, she just tried to add to it. She took a very quick step toward him and kicked the gun out of his hand.

Larsen stood with his twin pains, glaring. The gun had flown backward from him, but he was still the closest person to it. He turned and scrambled for it. But before he reached the gun he heard the sound of tires screeching. Looking to his right, he saw the smoke on the playground dissipating and one agent stumbling out of it. Others were obviously arriving. Grabbing up the gun, Larsen kept moving, right across the street.

David started to chase him, but without a gun that seemed a fool-hardy thing to do. Instead he turned back to make sure Randy was okay. But again he had been too slow. Helen had covered Randy, so completely the boy could barely be seen under her body. David stared at the scene. He had risked his life, but he had never wit-nessed such an image of self-sacrifice as this. Only after a long moment had passed without gunfire did Helen look up to see what had happened. David gestured. Helen looked across the street and saw the gunman disappearing around a corner of the school. She stood and pointed. Black-suited Secret Service agents spilled out of a car that had just pulled up to the curb. Two ran in the direction Helen pointed. Two more hurried over to take their places around Randy.

Randy glared at David, but his glare was puzzled. "You gave me to him," he said accusingly, but as much a question as a statement.

David hugged him. "You know I'd never do that. I just had to con-fuse him."

Randy hugged him back. An agent gently pushed David away, and the two hustled Randy into the car. Helen turned to David, a strange gleam in her eyes. "*You* saved him? You? What happened to the agents?"

"I don't know, I just happened to be in the best place."

She looked at him ironically, then put her arms around him and held him tightly. She lifted her face, put her hand behind his head, and pulled him down to her.

Helen kissed him and held him with the urgency of gratitude and survival and sudden hunger. David returned her passion for a long moment feeling a strange mix of emotions that gradually resolved into one.

He turned away from her and saw that the door of the agents' car had closed. In the back seat David saw Randy staring out at him helplessly. That wasn't possible—the glass was too darkly tinted—but David saw the boy's face nonetheless. He grabbed the car's handle and tried to pull, but it had been locked from the inside. "Wait!" David called.

He couldn't be sure he had saved Randy. The first threat was over, but that put Randy back into the hands of these men. David had developed a small rapport with a couple of the Secret Service agents, but in a crisis they all became strangers. Who were these men, to whom did they answer? They could hold Randy in this car and drive him straight back to Washington.

David heard small sounds and then the back door of the car opened fractionally. "Let me in, I forgot to tell him something."

No one answered, but when David pulled harder on the door handle the door came open. He climbed over one agent and fell into the seat beside Randy, who sat huddled and small. He had an agent on either side of him on the long backseat, but it was their job to protect him, not comfort him. David put his arms around the boy and pulled him close. Looking out, he saw Helen looking in, and gestured to her. She too climbed into the car and sat on the jump seat across from them. The agent who had let them in gave an exasperated sigh and slammed the door. The car started up the street.

David held Randy and murmured meaningless whispers, to make Randy think they were ahead of the game, but mostly to reassure him. David drew reassurance too, from holding the boy and feeling his trembling cease. "We'll find your mom," he said. "It'll be all right."

Helen sat across from them and watched the man with the boy. David stole glances at her, too.

CHAPTER

fourteen

★ In a medium-sized White House conference room, John McPherson began to wrap up
a meeting with two western Senators and the
Secretary of Health and Human Resources,
along with various aides, advisers, and consult-
ants. The President's own staffers knew well
the signs that he had grown restless. Often he
betrayed those signs at the very beginning of a
meeting. This time McPherson had sat and listened patiently for fifteen minutes, asking only
an occasional pertinent question.

"Is there a cure for anthrax?" the Secretary
of Health asked.

Senator Pelham shook his bald head, the
noble dome that made him look like a states-
man. "It can't be cured, it has to be contained."

"Meaning kill every cow that has it," the
President said.

"That's right," said the other Senator, Margaret Waring. A rancher herself, she spoke
with authority. "Kill, bury immediately right
where they fall, quarantine the area. Along
with every animal that's come in contact with
them. It can't be helped. Every rancher dreads
it, but we know how it has to be dealt with."
Ten years in Washington hadn't deprived Senator Waring of her deep tan or made her look
like anything other than an outdoorswoman,
with her thin, deeply creased face and competent hands.

"When's the last time we had an outbreak of this?" asked the Secretary.

"That's the thing," Senator Waring continued. "It's been years. We thought it was wiped out, except in laboratories. These people may have had it, to use as poison, and were careless and managed to infect their own cattle."

"These survivalists," Senator Pelham said, "this is what makes it a federal issue. Why we need your help, Mr. President, to pull together the resources of more than one agency."

"And the survivalists who live right in the middle of this outbreak will never cooperate and in fact will say this is a government plot to wipe them out," observed the deputy press secretary sitting in on the meeting, a young man with a penchant for stating the obvious but saying it well. He stated this dilemma succinctly enough to bring them all silent for a moment, until Senator Pelham simply said, "Yes."

The President stood up, looking very stern but strangely relaxed. "This is a farm problem. Why isn't Agriculture here?"

"The Secretary's in Cuba, sir," said an aide. "But he's on his way back."

"Good. I want him in charge, along with Senator Waring, and of course coordinated with F.E.M.A. Let me say again, this is a farm problem. And a public health crisis. This is not a raid. When people see this on television, they will see men in cowboy boots and hats and yellow dusters. There will be F.B.I. agents to protect them, but not many, and damned sure no A.T.F. people. We're not there to arrest anybody. If these survivalists interfere or refuse to cooperate they will be endangering their neighbors and everyone else in America. If they do cooperate they are simply good Americans with a tragedy on their range. We will leave it up to them. This is not going to be Waco or Ruby Ridge.

"Start the operation with someone else's ranch, someone who will cooperate. Senator, you know the people, you can guide us."

Margaret Waring nodded. She began to look less senatorial, as if she had already pulled on her jeans. Her eyes clouded with the thought of all that livestock soon to be dead and wasted.

"We'll want local police in on the roundup too. And the press will be informed every step of the way," President McPherson concluded. "Secrecy is the enemy of this project. We have nothing to hide. Clear?"

Everyone in the room nodded or said, "Yes, sir," with no irony at all. The President wielded his authority so comfortably it seemed hereditary. He said, "Thank you, Senators, for bringing this problem to my attention. You'll have all the federal resources you need."

"Thank you, Mr. President," the Senators said in unison. Only one of them shared the President's political party, but an observer couldn't have told which one from their respectful nods to the Chief Executive.

The President strode out of the conference room. Just outside the door, another aide waited. The aide drew him aside and whispered in an undertone. The President's face turned stricken. "Oh, my God!" he cried, loudly enough for all the dozen or so people in the hallway to hear. Then in a quieter voice: "Is Randy all right?"

"Yes, sir, absolutely. No harm to him at all. A little effect from the tear gas, that's all. We can have you on the phone with him in two minutes."

"Yes, do." The President looked around as if figuring the shortest route out of the building. His small audience, including the two Senators, looked on very concerned. "But I want better than that. I want to go down and see him."

The thirty-two-year-old aide had been chosen by the rest of the staff to break the news to the President because the aide had the most soothing voice and manner of anyone on the team. He tried to use both to best effect now. "We knew that would be your response, sir. But your meeting scheduled this afternoon—"

"Fuck the meeting!" John McPherson said loudly. Senator Margaret Waring, who had four children and seven grandchildren of her own, nodded as if echoing the words. Her senatorial colleague obviously agreed as well. "He can follow me down to Texas for his meeting, or even come on Air Force One. I'm going to my son!"

He strode away without a backward glance. Senator Pelham, not yet knowing what crisis had taken place, but recognizing fatherly devotion when he saw it, murmured, "Good luck, sir," and left quickly.

The President nearly ran through the corridors of the West Wing toward the Oval Office, concerned expressions following him everywhere. McPherson's eyes jerked frantically.

Just outside the Oval Office, Angela Vortiz sat waiting patiently, a small smile on her face. She was dressed more conservatively than usual, in a forest-green business suit and severe black high heels. When the President appeared in the anteroom, trailed by his retinue, Angela looked up at him for a long moment before she stood.

McPherson appeared to recognize her only as a White House employee. "Ms. Vortiz, did you need to see me? I'm afraid I don't have any time, I'm leaving for San Antonio immediately."

"Certainly, sir." Angela hesitated for just a moment. "In fact, perhaps I could accompany you."

"That would be fine," the President said, and hurried into the Oval Office, not glancing at her again as he brushed by Angela. She stood there after the parade had passed, but didn't lose her smile. Angela looked at the videocassette tape she held in her hand, and touched it fondly.

Angela Vortiz believed in piling on. What better time to kick an enemy than when he or she was down? What kind of idiot kicked an enemy who was up? News had broken quickly of the apparent attempt on Randy McPherson's life. Already public opinion had begun to shift away from the First Lady. Meanwhile John McPherson continued to appear both presidential and a concerned father. His game went well. But this videotape would shift the balance of power totally. There could be no comeback from this defeat, for Myra or her friends.

Angela sauntered away with joy evident in the movement of her hips.

"Oh, Randy," Myra McPherson almost screamed, and pulled her son to her chest. The boy said something reassuring in a muffled tone. Myra continued to hold him tightly. Over his head she stared at David and Helen.

"What happened?"

Agent Paul Herrera gave her a swift report, standing stiffly and speaking almost formally. Two of his colleagues lay dead on the playground. The agent's face barely moved as he talked.

"Have you caught the man?" Myra asked.

"Not yet. We will."

They wouldn't. Helen walked away, across the room. The Service wouldn't find this gunman. He obviously had accomplices, and an escape ready. The gunman might already be dead himself, for that matter. If they did find him, it would prove to be a dead end. After all, the Secret Service had already investigated his background and found nothing unusual.

Helen's mind raced even faster than the First Lady's, because Helen wasn't distracted by terror for Randy. She loved the boy, and was frightened for him, but he had also been her job. She still felt that way.

Across the room, David watched Helen, a blank expression on his face. His attention didn't return to the small meeting in the living room of the condo until the First Lady put her arm around him. "You saved him," she said thankfully.

"With a lot of help, ma'am."

Myra nodded, her forehead moving on his cheek. Then her voice hardened. "We have to talk," she said quietly.

It was David's turn to nod.

While Myra took Randy to his room and stayed with him, Helen crossed the room to David, took his hand, and led him to the empty kitchen, where she put her arms around him and kissed him more thoroughly than she had on the playground. "You're good at this work," she murmured. "Everyone seems to forget about you and then you . . ." She drew back, eyes half-lidded, but suddenly lost her smile. "What is it?"

Without stalling, David said, "While we were on the road you reported to the White House."

Helen sighed.

"I'll bet you did it other times too, didn't you? Myra wasn't really sneaking away from her Secret Service protection, was she? Because you were with her."

Helen let go of his neck but took his hands. "David, when you and I rescued them from those places, it wasn't a fraud at all. It ruined my career. But once that madman was chasing us on the road, I had to use my resources. I had to report to the Service office so they'd know she was safe. Yes, I made that one call from the airport. How do you know about that, by the way?"

"It's the White House, Helen, they keep records of everything. And I've got some of them now."

"So now—?"

"I figured that's what it was," David said quietly, looking straight at her. "I understand you still felt an obligation to your job. You were trying to protect her."

He had convinced himself of that, that Helen hadn't betrayed them. When he'd seen her covering Randy on the playground this afternoon, there'd been no question of Helen's devotion. She harbored odd, inconsistent loyalties, but he didn't doubt her heart.

She couldn't be sure of his feelings, though. She released his hands and stepped back. "So what are you going to do?"

"I'm not going to tell her, Helen. If you want to, you can. But you know what? Maybe the White House still trusts you. Maybe we can use that."

David moved closer to her, looking straight into her eyes, and repeated, "I believe you."

She searched his face, obviously wondering whether she believed him. "You should," she said quietly, and kissed him again.

The First Lady came upon them like that. She coughed discreetly, which didn't work, so she busied herself making a cup of tea, and when she turned back David and Helen had separated and assumed professional expressions. Myra smiled to herself. As dusk fell, Randy rested in his room to recover from the effects of the gas he'd inhaled, and David and Myra and Helen sat at the kitchen table, their heads close together. The agents stayed out of that room, but the First Lady always felt observed. She hadn't truly believed in her own privacy in some time. Helen watched David attentively as he talked, looking for all kinds of signs. She only joined the conversation gradually.

Myra began. "He's coming. John. He must be on his way right now."

Helen nodded. David said, "Probably."

"No probably about it, he's coming here. He'll be here tonight."

David said slowly, "He has a right to see his son."

Myra laughed humorlessly. "He'll want a lot more than that."

David agreed. He could imagine Burton Leemis gloating over the news of this tragedy. "They'll say Randy isn't safe in your custody. You can't protect him."

"The Secret *Service* couldn't protect him," Myra said fiercely.

Helen spoke up. "Because you took him away from the White House, where all their security arrangements are in place." The other two frowned at her. "I'm only telling you what their response will be."

David foresaw another response: a motion to modify temporary orders from the President's lawyer, asking that Randy remain with his father in the White House at least while the divorce was pending, so they could be assured of his safety. And what judge wouldn't grant that? At the very least temporary orders should ensure that the child remains alive. Here, Randy seemed in perpetual jeopardy.

"They arranged this, you know," Myra said suddenly, darkly. "They arranged this attempt on my son's life so I'd look like an unfit mother."

"I don't think the President would ever—"

"I told you, it's not John in charge anymore. These people he's in business with . . . they'll do anything. They don't care about Randy or anything else. What will they do next? What will they do when they have him in the White House?"

David didn't think they would have to do anything. Once the conspirators had Randy, they would also have Myra McPherson's complete cooperation and silence.

"What can we do?" Myra asked.

"I'm not sure," David said slowly, rising and turning away from the table. "I need some time to think."

"There isn't any, David." Myra moved right in front of him and held his arm. She seemed suddenly inspired. "Why don't we run again? Get our Wal-Mart clothes and be a family. I can—"

"What? Get a job as a waitress? What would we live on, and how, and where? You'd be looking over your shoulder for the rest of your life. No, not that long, because they'd find you. They'd never stop looking. Last time you ran you had a place to run to. We had a plan. We have to stick with the plan, Myra. We have to depend on the law."

Even as David said it, he didn't quite convince himself. He wasn't so sure the legal system could be trusted to reach the right result. Not with all the power on the other side. But he tried to sound forceful and certain for the sake of his client.

Helen stood back from the conversation, as if they conspired against her.

Myra looked at her lawyer uncertainly. "I won't let him take Randy," she said.

"Neither will I, Myra. Neither will any of us."

She remembered how he had saved her son that afternoon, and her hand moved down his arm to his hand. For both of them, the human contact felt comforting but brief. Then Myra McPherson left the room quickly, to stay with her son.

Helen walked close to David and put her arms around him briefly. He held her more tightly.

Air Force One flew swiftly toward San Antonio. Whenever it approached a population center, traffic parted for the plane. Night fell as the President's jet hurtled southwest. On board, a small staff read briefing books and made phone calls. John McPherson sat alone, gazing pensively out a window. He hadn't allowed press aboard; he didn't feel like entertaining anyone. After an hour of trying to brief the President or get his position on various issues, staffers had left him alone. Angela Vortiz finally saw her chance.

"Head in the clouds?" she said lightly. McPherson looked up to see her standing beside him in the aisle. His face showed no reaction to her, not even recognition for a moment. Angela registered that lack, but her charming smile didn't falter. "If you have a few minutes, I have something you'd want to see."

"Thank you, Angela, but not now."

She held up the videotape cassette. "I assure you, Mr. President, you will."

She had stirred his curiosity. Without a word, he rose and led her to his private office. On a credenza behind the desk sat a television with built-in VCR. Angela turned it on and put her tape in. For a minute or two neither said anything. "What are we watching?" John McPherson finally asked.

"The White House has surveillance cameras in strategic places," Angela said. "Not in the residence, but at access points to it. In case there's ever an intruder—"

"I recognize the stairs to the residence," McPherson said dryly.

"This is a tape I found of a certain night at the residence. Watch: one of the White House wine stewards goes up to the residence at about eleven o'clock one night. Here he is now. This was a night when you were in California and Mrs. McPherson was in the White House. Now we're watching time pass. The steward remains upstairs. The Secret Service agent goes to check and comes back looking as if he'd seen or heard something he didn't want to witness." Angela began to fast-forward the tape. "Finally, an hour later, the steward comes down. The agent won't look at him."

The President watched without comment. On the tape now the steward, a dark young man with delicate hands, looked a little disheveled. He and the agent didn't exchange a word or a glance as the steward logged out. The clock on the screen showed ten minutes past midnight.

"How did you find this?" McPherson asked. His voice sounded hollow, as if he'd been struck in the stomach.

"Because I looked for it," Angela said sharply. "Women aren't squeamish. Her lawyer objected to the interrogatory about adultery because of some silly public relations argument that all of you bought. But I didn't. When a woman says she doesn't want to be asked a question, it's because she doesn't want to answer it, not because just being asked offends her. We can say 'no' quite easily. Even the prissy ones like your wife. Maybe especially that kind. They've had a lot of practice at saying no."

The President looked at Angela's sneer. Something had shifted between them, perhaps the balance of power. As the tape had rolled, Angela had lost any deference she had toward John McPherson.

"Doesn't prove anything," he said gruffly.

"This does." Angela produced a one-page document with a notary's seal at the bottom. A sworn affidavit. McPherson read it in a few seconds. In that brief time his expression changed more than once. He looked shocked, saddened, angry. Looking up, he had emerged completely from his deadened daze.

"Why on earth would anybody admit to this?"

Angela didn't smile. "Because he was accused of raping the First Lady of the United States. He thought that there might be an indictment pending against him and that we had certain evidence."

McPherson asked a question with an eyebrow. Angela did allow herself a small smile then. "He may have been misled. I'm not a cop. There aren't any rules about what I have to tell a suspect. The young man thought he was defending himself when he gave this statement. I thought we could use it."

John McPherson spoke wonderingly. "Angela, we . . . Coming from you, this is a little—" He stopped abruptly, his face going blank again. "What is that?"

He reached for her, but her fingers beat his to the target, a thin pink line on her neck, close to the front of her throat. "Nothing. I scratched myself somehow. It doesn't hurt. Barely a tickle."

McPherson looked at the straight, thin scar, so tiny it would disappear in a few more days. His eyes rose to Angela's. She stared back at him without a sign of a secret message. McPherson turned away. "Thank you, Ms. Vortiz. I know you did this in an attempt to help me. I appreciate that. I'll hang on to both of these, if you don't mind."

Angela frowned at his back, not understanding. After a moment, realizing she'd been dismissed, her face turned red. "You can't just tell me to go away," she said. "This is my evidence, I found it. And you haven't asked what I want in return."

McPherson looked at her in surprise. "Angela—"

"Don't worry, you'll find out soon enough."

Avoiding his hand, she turned on her heel and left.

Behind her in the otherwise empty office, the President stood lost in thought. He had never considered Angela as having her own agenda. Of course he should have. But he needn't worry about her now. It looked as if her employer had already taken care of her.

McPherson dropped Angela from his thoughts. His face reddened as he reread the short affidavit from the wine steward. He felt sick at heart, guilty himself, and finally angry. The anger prevailed. It kept him going the rest of the trip.

Myra McPherson sat on the edge of Randy's twin bed reading him another chapter in a book about three friends, two boys and a girl, who find their way into an alternate universe through an old abandoned well at a house in the woods. To hold Randy's interest, a book had to resemble the fantasy worlds of his games and TV shows. Myra wished she could get him interested instead in the classics she remembered so fondly from her girlhood, but in fact this *Lost Well World* wasn't all that dissimilar from *Alice in Wonderland*. She read on, getting a little caught up in the story herself. Randy's hand crept into hers that lay on the bed-spread.

No one knocked at the outer door. Myra heard a stir, feet coming swiftly down the hall. She barely had time to look up, but her instincts flared swiftly. Her husband entered the room.

The sight didn't calm Myra's nerves. Her heart beat even faster. She stood up, book in hand. John McPherson wore suit pants and a white shirt. He looked tanned, tired, but filled with nervous energy. He gave her a quick, blank-faced stare, as if wondering who she was, then turned quickly toward the bed.

"Randy!"

The boy jumped a bit at his father's voice, even though Randy had been looking right at him. Randy didn't move from the bed. John McPherson rushed to him and put his arms around his son. His head bent over Randy's. Randy sat stiffly, then put his arms tentatively around his father, his arms looking very small and thin against McPherson's back.

The President drew back and held his son's face. "Are you all right?"

Randy nodded. "A doctor came. He said I'm fine."

"Good." John McPherson sniffed.

Across the room, Myra still stood where she had when her husband had entered the room. She saw his eyes gleam as he looked into his son's. *Who is this performance for?* she wondered. There was nobody else in the room.

The President's voice became firmer. "Come on, Randy, you're going with me."

"No!" Myra blurted.

McPherson looked at her coldly. "I think I'm entitled to some time. With me at least I know he'll be safe."

"That's not fair, John."

His dead eyes frightened her. They barely held recognition of her, let alone affection. "I'll keep him tonight. Besides, there's something you need to look at."

Randy still sat, barely breathing as if he could become invisible. But his father took his hand. "Come on, son."

Randy stood up from the bed. Myra came toward them, reaching for her husband. "John, you'll bring him back?"

McPherson forced warmth into his voice, for his son's ears. But his eyes remained black and lifeless. "Of course, dear. We'll be fine, won't we, Randy?"

Then, with exaggerated movements, he removed a legal-sized envelope from his back pocket and set it on the desk. "This is for your good night reading."

He led Randy out without looking back at her. Myra hurriedly threw shoes and a change of clothes into an overnight bag and followed them out, glancing fearfully at the envelope. She found the living room empty. A Secret Service agent stood by the condo's front door and gestured with his head. Myra rushed down the stairs. When she reached the parking level a long black Lincoln was just pulling away. She couldn't see through the car's tinted windows. She held up the overnight bag but the car didn't slow. The gate to the outdoors glided open and the car sailed through. Myra waved, feeling certain Randy watched her through the car's back window. But she couldn't see him.

Tears stood in her eyes. Another agent gently turned her away, back toward the door. Myra went, her steps dragging. She didn't know where her son was and she didn't know what waited for her in that envelope upstairs. But she knew they were connected.

David Owens turned restlessly in bed. He sat up, giving up on the idea of sleep. The First Lady's case worried him; he wondered what was happening with her, but his thoughts were on Helen as he lay in bed. She had left the condo early without saying where she'd be. As much as David trusted her when he'd been with her, alone in the night with his thoughts he found it much more difficult to believe in anyone. When his phone rang, he reached for it gratefully.

"David?"

The voice was a woman's, but not Helen's. He stood up, almost at attention. A moment later he said, "I'll be right there."

Ten minutes later he drove through the muggy San Antonio night. Clouds obscured the stars. David lived only a few miles from the First Lady's condo, and he drove them very quickly. There was no need for speed, except in his own blood. The car moved no faster than his heart.

The condominium seemed very quiet and dark. Only one standing lamp burned in the living room. Only one Secret Service agent stood outside the front door, and others must be nearby, but there was none inside. The disaster seemed already to have happened, so they had nothing to guard against.

Myra McPherson had re-created a tiny piece of her girlhood home in the condo, with a large, heavily padded white couch that had a scratchy, textured fabric that would leave a pattern on the backs of a woman's legs or a napper's face. A piano stood against the wall next to the window, family pictures on top of it. Myra sat at the piano bench, touching keys in a random pattern, as her lawyer read the one-page affidavit and then reread it. He looked puzzled, then disgusted as he lifted his eyes from the simple document.

"These people are uncanny, they can get anyone to say anything, can't they?"

The First Lady looked back at him with shamed eyes and her cheeks growing red. David stared at her. "Oh, my God."

"David . . ."

He let the affidavit fall from his hand to the coffee table and paced away from her, eyes lifted and mind racing.

"Tell me you can fix this," Myra said in a small voice.

"I can fix this," David said hollowly. Then: "Tell me how."

He calmed himself and turned to her. She could still barely meet his eyes. "It's all right," he said. "It doesn't matter. It doesn't make you a less fit mother. You've still been Randy's primary caregiver. He'd still be better off with you."

"After today? After he was almost killed in my custody?"

David rolled his eyes skyward. She was right, the combination of disclosures was crushing. If the other side had planned this, they were beyond smart. They had sold their souls for a good price.

"I have to ask something," he said to his client. He didn't even feel like her lawyer. But it did seem as if he knew her as well as anyone did. "Was this your real reason for wanting a divorce all along? Because you wanted to be with someone else?"

Myra coughed, a choking sound that turned into a sob. She started crying anew. He'd broken through her thin shell. "No!" she said loudly. They stood alone in the living room; she could talk. "It was Randy. It was all for Randy, I swear. I didn't want him growing up in a loveless marriage, either."

David found that "either" devastating. So Myra McPherson did have a selfish motive for wanting a divorce. She wanted out to have a chance of happiness for herself.

So what? he argued to himself, as if composing a jury argument. *So she wants to find happiness. Is that evil? Her husband has denied her happiness for years, the whole duration of their marriage. Who is the villain in this picture?* But he knew it was possible now that a jury would award custody of Randy to the President. In spite of what he'd told her and the fact that a new century had arrived, a double standard still prevailed. Average jurors expected a mother to be more pure than a father. Boys grew up with a father's sins, but a woman's somehow appalled people more. Especially if she was the First Lady of the United States.

But while David's mind raced with possibilities, schemes of how to absorb this latest development, Myra's posture showed that she had already given up. David might tell her fervently that they still had a good chance, but she couldn't face even the remote possibility of losing her son.

"He's right, David. I can't get away. I was crazy to think I could. I have to do whatever they want."

"And what if you don't believe that's best for Randy? Remember, Myra? You told me that growing up in the White House would ruin him. You've got to give me some time. Let me negotiate."

He didn't sound sincere even to himself. He hadn't convinced her, either. After a long moment of silence, David looked down at the couch. "I could stay here tonight if you want. We could keep talking."

Myra smiled faintly. "Just what I need, the agents finding a man in my apartment in the morning."

The phone's ringing broke an awkward moment. Myra leaped for it. As David watched closely, she said, "Really? They did? Thank you, I appreciate it. You know I do. Would you like . . . ? All right. Good night, then."

She put down the phone with a strange expression. "That was Helen. She followed John when they left here. She wanted me to know that they were still in town, that they didn't drive to the airport. They're staying at a house on the edge of town. A place called the Dominion?"

David nodded. A gated community where some of San Antonio's wealthiest people lived. Myra looked at him. "I asked her if she wanted to talk to you, but she had to run."

A thought that David couldn't stop crossed his mind, that perhaps Helen was in fact with the President, part of his team. A lawyer's thought, analytical. He decided not to share his brief doubt with the First Lady. There couldn't be any point in adding to her worries.

In the borrowed mansion in the Dominion community just outside San Antonio, the President looked in on his son. The people who lived here didn't have young children; Randy slept in a guest room furnished rather lavishly, but not for a child. He looked tiny in the queen-sized bed, his head barely emerging from the covers. The long car ride had seemed to lull the boy. He had barely stumbled into the house when they'd arrived and had asked to go straight to bed. McPherson had sat with him for a few minutes, but Randy hadn't moved or spoken again. Relieved, McPherson stood up, looked at the boy tenderly from the doorway, and went to make a call.

He didn't use a phone. He used the micro-thin screen to which he still hadn't accustomed himself. It seemed that Wilson Boswell appeared in the room with him. John McPherson didn't like the effect.

The two men exchanged no greetings. Quickly the President filled his advisor in on what had happened. "I gave her the message." McPherson assumed—no, knew for a certainty—that Boswell would have known about the affidavit and videotape from Angela.

"That doesn't matter," Boswell said brusquely. On the screen he sat at a desk, wearing a suit jacket and black tie. Maybe in his home study, or perhaps Boswell was still at the office, in spite of the lateness of the hour. Maybe Boswell didn't have a fleshly life at all, maybe he only existed in these electronic images. In that strange night, nothing seemed too fanciful to McPherson.

"Now that you've got him, you've got to bring him back here," Boswell said.

"I will soon. For now I've got to get close to him again, as we—"

"That doesn't matter," Boswell repeated more harshly. "Listen to me, John. My program is ready to send. It cannot wait. The more delay, the more chance for discovery. Bring him back now. Tonight. The legality doesn't matter. We can—"

"No. I can't be defying a court order. I need to save my reputation. I, we, have an election to think of after this."

Boswell glared. It seemed to McPherson they were in the same room. But he glared back.

"Do I need to remind you—?"

"No, you don't," the President snapped. "But I can win this now, legally. You've given me the ammunition. Thank you for that."

Boswell might not have heard the irony. He stared through the screen for a long moment, then reached a hand out of the picture and snapped off the transmission. John McPherson suddenly sat alone in a dark room. Boswell hadn't acquiesced. He might be launching his own new plan. Most assuredly he sat somewhere still thinking.

But McPherson had to assert himself at some point. He was, after all, the President of the United States. And soon he would have his family restored.

He went to check on his son.

Once again Randy heard his father's footsteps, and once again feigned sleep. He was afraid that if he really fell asleep he would be carried onto an airplane. He was prepared to run, or worse, if that happened.

The boy lay in the dark with his eyes closed and trembled.

That night Myra sat alone, curled up on the sofa in the condo, guilt a physical pain in her chest as she tried to picture her son. Her thoughts roamed the world for him, and she hoped he felt them. This was her fault. Her punishment seemed too harsh, the God who hated her too puritan.

At the age of forty, after years of marriage to a cold, other-directed man, Myra McPherson had discovered her sexuality, something she had never expected. It could have been a physical change or psychological: a shift in her hormones as she neared the end of

her child-bearing years, or just a change in perception, the beginning of a self-awareness she should have had much sooner in life:
she didn't try to analyze the reasons. She just realized that she began
noticing men in a way she never had before. Their eyes, their hands,
the shift of muscles in their forearms.

Ironically, by the time this change in perception came upon her,
she was living like a fairy-tale heroine in a castle, but discovering
that "happily ever after" didn't include the traditional aspects of
marriage such as love and desire. As her marriage worsened and she
grew more and more lonely, her observations of other men had a
stronger effect on her. But the prisoner of the White House had
almost no opportunities to make her fantasies real. The President
did have such chances, in his travels and his work, but Myra never
found herself alone with a man.

Occasionally she knew a man noticed. The wine steward, Paul,
had always returned her glances and smiles. On more than one
lonely night she had sent for a bottle of wine and they had talked as
the wine breathed. Finally a time had come when she'd acted on her
desires, as so many men and women do. So why should her life be
ruined by this?

Because she had married a man who loved power and not her.
And she had tried to defy him. She wasn't being punished for sin,
she was being crushed for wanting to be happy.

Now he would take Randy from her. Myra squirmed and paced
and had a glass of wine. As the night deepened her thoughts grew
wilder. Somehow she would get Randy back and they would run
together. But David had been right about that. Where could she go
where the President of the United States couldn't find her? She had
no money of her own, they couldn't get far. Even if they did, what
kind of life could Randy have, always on the run? That would be
worse than the alternative.

Myra began to understand those people who killed their children
and then themselves. It wasn't out of hate, it was an act of love. A
journey together to a better world.

Finally she fell asleep on the couch, her posture and restlessness remarkably like her son's, far across town.

The next morning David arrived early at his office, his eyes grainy and his tie askew. He sat at his desk and tried unsuccessfully to work. Shortly after nine, he heard what he'd been expecting and dreading: the fax machine.

He went to the outer office and watched the paper crank out of the machine. Yes, a motion to modify temporary orders in Myra McPherson's divorce case. Circumstances had changed significantly, said the motion. The life of the child the subject of the suit was in danger in his current placement. David read listlessly, finding nothing unexpected except the timing on the last page. The motion was set for a hearing the following week, only five days away.

Then the machine surprised him again. The motion to modify temporary orders was followed by another simple motion. He read it and closed his eyes.

A little later the First Lady of the United States found him at his desk, the papers in front of him. She sailed in without announcement or entourage. Her Secret Service agents waited in the reception room. David scrambled to his feet at sight of her.

"Mrs. McPherson! I would have come to you, you didn't need —"

Myra didn't look at him, she looked around the office. It suddenly seemed very shabby to David, and must to her as well. She probably hadn't seen a chair in need of reupholstering in years.

"This reminds me of my father's old office," she said in a dreamy sort of voice. "He was a boat mechanic and later he had his own marina. He had a little office where he hardly ever sat, it was just a storage place. Like this."

True, David did have papers or files on every flat surface. But that was a sign of how good he was, he wanted to tell her, how much new business had come in lately that he hadn't quite had time to organize.

But Myra smiled reminiscently, not criticizing. "I'm sure you could lay your hands right away on whatever you wanted. That's how Daddy was. It looked like a rat's nest, but he had it all organized in his own mind."

"Let's not test your theory," David said, moving one stack of pages to the floor so he'd have room to fold his arms on the desk when he sat there. "Would you like to sit down?"

Myra shook her head. Something had happened to her. Her eyes were red, she'd obviously spent as poor a night as David, but it had left her energized. She looked younger than he had ever seen her. David didn't expect this appearance from his client. Myra tended to look worried, if not hopeless. He remembered the first time she'd appeared in his office, so quiet and mysterious. This did not remind him of that occasion at all. Now she seemed to have a plan, and the resolution to carry it through. He hated to give her more bad news.

"I was about to call you. I received these this morning. I was expecting the first, but not the second. It's a motion setting the case for final hearing in less than two months. They seem to think they're going to win now, and want this over with quickly."

"So do I," Myra said. She barely glanced at the motions, as if they didn't surprise her. "Do me a favor, David. Call John's lawyer. Ask what they really want. Exactly what they want."

David obeyed his client's wishes, and to his surprise got through to Burton Leemis in his Boston office in only a few minutes. David pictured Leemis standing talking into the speaker phone, rocking back and forth from his heels to the balls of his feet, the picture of self-satisfaction. But oddly, Leemis sounded sympathetic. "You received my motions, I suppose. And listen, I don't want to surprise you. There's new evidence."

"I've seen the affidavit," David said.

"Ah, good. The man's own wording. Could be better, I grant you. The next statement will be. And the testimony he'll give at our final setting. For the temporary orders hearing we'll just need the evidence of the attempt on young Randy's life, I think."

"My client and I would like to know whether we can reach agreement on something," David said.

"Such as?"

"You tell me," David answered. There was no use pretending that Leemis wasn't in a position to dictate the terms of any agreement.

He heard the sound of a shrug in Leemis's voice. "My client wants what he's always wanted. Reconciliation. For her to withdraw her divorce petition and come back home, to be a happy family again."

Leemis didn't even sound ironic. David glanced up at Myra, who looked at him expectantly. He knew what this request—no, demand—would do to her.

Myra said, "Tell him to have John call me."

"They need to talk this morning," David said into the phone.

"I'll see what I can do. Where's she going to be?"

A minute later David hung up. He didn't want to pass on the gist of the conversation, but Myra demanded it. "Well?"

"Your husband wants you back," David said wearily. "He wants you to give up the divorce action and come back to the White House to live."

Myra raised her eyes heavenward. "Thank God," she said. "I still have something he wants."

David stared at her wonderingly. He began to fear she had genuinely lost her mind.

Myra leaned across the desk toward him. "I want you to make a deal for me."

"Well, of course. That's my job. I'll negotiate, take charge, try to get the very best—"

Myra shook her head again. "I mean the terms of my return. Don't negotiate. Tell them how it has to be."

"You'll go back? Mrs. McPherson, you need to think about this. I still think we have a good chance—"

"No, David. John knows I won't take any chance of losing Randy.

I can't. If Randy had to go back there to live without me . . ." She shrugged, almost a shudder, clearing her head of that image. "No. I'll go back. But I need certain conditions."

David knew what her life would be like if she returned to the White House. What a prisoner she'd be. He had seen her blossom in the last few weeks into a woman with a zest for life, long-stifled but still there. Her reckless affair with the wine steward had proven that Myra still had all the normal yearnings. David knew what a sacrifice she was suggesting. In their conversations he had continued to try to assure her that they could win the case, but in fact he had come to believe as Myra had once suggested that this case could only end in death. Her extraordinary case gave him a sense of tragedy.

But Myra didn't look resigned. Her eyes were bright. Her fingers tapped on his desk. She turned away and walked a few brisk paces around his office. David studied her with a worried expression.

"What are you planning?"

"To go back."

"Myra."

She looked at him sharply, as if to put him in his place. But David just stared back at her. He'd earned the right to act as if he knew her. He came around his desk and stood close in front of her. "If you can't trust your lawyer, who can you trust?"

She wore a small smile, like the Mona Lisa's. It scared David anew.

"Let's go someplace private so I can give you the details."

She laughed, perhaps at the suggestion of privacy, but he followed her out of the office. The Secret Service agents accompanied them, but at a respectful distance once they were outside, and David led his client toward a little-used stretch of the Riverwalk where they could talk. He was almost afraid to hear her plans.

By the next day they'd had a call from the house where the President was staying with Randy. Secret Service agents drove Myra McPherson to the house, and her lawyer followed. David didn't like the message he carried, but he'd be glad when this case was over one way or the other, when he could shrink back into his life.

The cars pulled up in front of a wide brown stucco house with accents in gold and glass, such as the lamps on either side of the front door. They found Helen standing outside, which seemed odd. David smiled at her. "Have they offered you your old job back?"

"As a matter of fact they have," Helen said without embellishment. She looked, in fact, as if she were working again. She wore black, stood with her arms folded, and looked past David at the terrain around the house. But as she felt him looking at her she slipped him a little wink.

"Aren't you coming in with us?" he asked.

"No, I'll stay out here. We'll talk afterward."

"Yes, we will." They exchanged a long glance.

A butler many years older than the house admitted them. "Where's my son?" Myra asked him immediately.

"He's out with the nanny," said a deep voice from across the room.

David's eyes flicked back and forth between his client and the President of the United States as Myra turned to her husband. John McPherson stared at her, not exactly hostilely. He wore an expression that was hard to read. A small gesture with his head brought his wife toward him, and he held out a hand to stop her lawyer. Myra walked into a small sitting room off the entry hall and John McPherson followed her in and closed the door behind him.

Myra kept walking, across the room, and stood with her back to him.

"Why did you do it, Myra? Right in the White House, our home. Right under my nose."

She whirled. "Don't take the high moral ground with me, John. How many years has it been since you've been faithful to me? I know very well you don't have that damned woman on your staff, that Angela person, because she's good at public relations. It's the private kind that she has a talent for. How many others have there been? You don't have any right—"

"That's not true," John McPherson said stiffly. His voice and his face seemed disconnected. In his expression, the slant of his eyes, he acknowledged the truth of what she said, but his voice went woodenly on denying. "Besides, I have proof of your infidelity. Your lover confessed. And it happened just a few rooms away from where your son lay in bed."

Even now John McPherson spoke in a well-rehearsed voice, as if for posterity. This was one of the things she hated about him and about their marriage, Myra suddenly realized. Even in their most private moments he chose his words carefully, for an invisible audience. They had no intimate life of their own, and never would.

"Tell me what you want," she said flatly.

"I want this divorce business ended. If you insist on going through with it now, I'll take Randy. You know I can't let there be a public judgment that you're a better parent than I am. Don't you know I'll do everything in my power to prevent that? I'll get custody. I'll take him from you. With that affidavit I can do it."

"This is the twenty-first century, John. No one is going to award you custody just because you can prove a woman committed one act of—" She couldn't bring herself to say the word.

"You think not? When that woman is the First Lady of the United States? Who's supposed to be the most sacrosanct individual in this country? Do you want to be smeared with that dirt for the rest of your life? Have Randy know about it?"

That shot hurt. Myra looked away from him, unable to keep up the eye duel any longer. McPherson continued relentlessly. "You had two jobs and you've abandoned them both. You had your little fling with him under the same roof. Well, you can go off and have your midlife crisis, but Randy won't be part of it. He'll stay with me."

John McPherson was so angry, he threatened her with torture. That's what taking her son away would be. But not just for Myra. She thought of Randy in his father's custody, left alone most of his life, with John McPherson hating his former wife and with no object for that hatred available except the boy who so resembled her. Randy a prisoner of the White House and of his father's rage. She pictured her son alone and lonely, deprived of her, having no one close. Changing in the rapid way children do, so that one day she would come to visit Randy and not know him. Tears came to her eyes.

"Just let us go," she said quietly, pleading.

"No. I can't do that. To remain President I need my family back with me. Withdraw your divorce petition. You had an aberration, some brief problems. Come back to the White House. Be the First Lady. Do your duty to me and the country. Maybe years from now, after my second term, you can have what you want. But not now. Not while I'm President. Put an end to this, Myra."

He didn't say, *Come back to me.* His voice sounded triumphant, but still bitterly cold. Myra looked at him again. He didn't hold out his hand to her, he didn't offer the tiniest smile of enticement. Restoring their marriage wasn't part of what he asked or offered. Just for her to take up her public functions again. Smile and be interviewed. Hold his hand in public. Walk and sit and stand beside him on all those public occasions that called for a wife. And nothing more. She understood that in the private quarters, behind the scenes, her life would be hellish. There would be no more slightest pretense of marriage. And he would keep her completely isolated, untouchable, for the next five years. John McPherson would go on his way, his presidential travels, his private meetings, while she would remain locked up like a fairy-tale maiden in a tower. That was what he offered. Demanded.

But she would have her son.

"All right."

"What's that?" the President said sharply. She had spoken so softly. Myra raised her head. "I said I will. I'll come back. You know I can't fight this."

McPherson stared at her, unsure of his victory. "Work out the details with my lawyer," Myra said. She walked toward him and past him to the door. The President heard a catch in her throat like a sob as she passed, and that convinced him he'd won.

By the time he emerged Myra had disappeared. David Owens still stood in the entry hall with his briefcase. John McPherson waved him toward another room. In this one, a large study, David was surprised to find Burton Leemis standing to the side, beside a window. The Boston lawyer turned and smiled at him.

"For important clients I travel," he said, very pleased with himself and his surprise appearance. "Besides, I like to conclude a case in person."

David knew that Leemis meant he liked to see his opponent's face when they both knew that Leemis had won. David looked resigned, unhappy, and that put the other two men in the room at ease: the First Lady's lawyer was obviously here to offer terms of surrender.

The President walked past David and leaned back against the desk, folding his arms. "My wife has already told me she'll drop her divorce action and come home. Now we're just working out the details, I presume."

David put his briefcase on the table, tried to smooth out his suit with his hands.

"Yes, sir." He drew his briefcase toward him, but it was just a prop. He wouldn't have committed any of this to paper. "I'm here to negotiate a reconciliation."

John McPherson only nodded impatiently. David's announcement didn't come as a bombshell.

"These are Mrs. McPherson's terms," David said. "And all of them have to be met. None is up for deal-making. First, she wants separate bedrooms. From my historical research, this won't be a first for the White House."

The President didn't answer, but his expression darkened. He obviously didn't like having his private life discussed or bargained over.

"She wants to be able to take extensive vacations with Randy. To Texas sometimes. Spend time with her family, more than she's had in the past. And she would like you to arrange a private retreat somewhere for significant mother-son time together." David directed this at Burton Loomis. The President had access to every rich person in the country, any number of whom should be willing to loan out their vacation homes.

The President scowled. "Never with me?"

"Certainly with you, sir, whenever your schedule permits The point is that Mrs. McPherson wants to be able to get away from the White House at times, with her son. If you can join them, that would be great."

In fact, it sounded like a test. How much time away from the seat of power would John McPherson be willing to give for his family? Again, he didn't reply directly, but his expression grew less angry. "I'll make time for them," he said.

He sounded sincere, but David had often heard parents, mostly men, make promises like that and then forget them in day-to-day life. That really didn't matter to this negotiation, though.

"Anything else?" Burt Leemis asked ironically.

David gazed at him with a slight smile. "Ten million dollars."

"What?!" both the other men said angrily. The President jumped upright. Leemis sneered at David. "This was your suggestion, wasn't it, Counselor? What's your cut of that going to be?"

David said calmly, "The cash is so that you'll know that my client has resources of her own and can get away when she chooses. It'll be her own private security blanket."

The President looked angry again. David dropped his smile and spoke quietly to McPherson. "You win, sir. That's the underlying fact of this discussion. You get what you demand. Your wife returns to the White House, she lives there, she takes up her duties. She will be your First Lady for the rest of your public life. These other things, frankly, are sops to her, to make this look less like a total capitulation on her part. Because it is, and I've told her so. But she insists on the main issue. The separation is over as soon as you say so."

The President took a deep breath. He still didn't look remotely happy, but David's speech had obviously mollified him.

"Then it ends now," he said. "I'm taking Randy back to Washington today. Myra can come with us."

"I'm afraid not, sir." This was the most important part of the negotiation, so David spoke casually. "My client has to get what she's asking for first."

The President stared flatly at the young lawyer, as if he were a small pothole in the road in front of the presidential limousine. "All right. Randy and I will go back. She can follow after we've worked out the details."

"Sir, I don't think that's the best way. It would look, frankly, as if you were holding your son hostage to force her to come back. We don't want that appearance, do we? We all need to make this reconciliation work, sir, not only in reality but in public perception. Just imagine what makes a better picture? You holding Randy in the White House until she comes to you—or the two of them coming up the steps of the White House freely and by their own choice, coming back to you together?" David spoke earnestly, like a member of the team. "We all have to sell this, sir. For all your sakes." John McPherson didn't answer. But as he turned away, he and his lawyer exchanged a look. Then McPherson left the room without a backward glance, leaving the two lawyers alone. David had to turn to Burton Leemis for an answer.

The eminent lawyer seemed to have accepted David's speech at face value, too. This occasion was victory for him and his client, regardless of the conditions. After all, in Leemis's world the things David had asked for were rather petty.

"That's all doable," he said. Which is a smart, subtle lawyer's way of saying, *You should have asked for more.*

★ Myra McPherson strolled with Randy in a park near their house. The Secret Service gave them faux privacy, standing yards away, watching alertly for passing cars or picnickers. Myra felt like a leper, as always. Randy walked close beside her and held her hand, apparently oblivious to the agents. Myra suddenly gripped his hand more tightly as her heart filled with love for Randy. If only she could arrange an escape for him. She couldn't do what everyone told her she had to do: take him back to that place.

But she couldn't let him go, either.

Most of the agents had dressed in khaki today, but they stood close by like prison guards. They had hardly demurred when Myra had insisted on taking a walk with her son. Instead of the playground in the neighborhood they had driven and picked a park at random, which seemed safe enough. At ten in the morning the park was barely inhabited. Myra had wanted to get out of the condo to tell Randy that they would be returning to the White House. He had taken the news very quietly.

"Why do we have to go back?" Randy asked now, in a dispirited voice.

"It's for the best, Randy. We belong with your father, we're the President's family."

"But I didn't ask to be. And he doesn't want us."

Myra knelt in front of him and put her hands on his cheeks. "Oh, that's not true, Randy. He wants us very much. He's been talking to me every day, wanting us to come back."

Randy stared at her. She saw his thought: *Now you're going to start lying to me, too.* Myra hugged him hard. No, she wouldn't lose his trust. But she couldn't tell him the truth, either. "We'll take care of each other. Like always, right, darling?"

"Can David come?"

Myra stared at the trees within her view, twisted mesquites and oaks, and thought. Could David help? Her attorney continued to reassure her that they could win the divorce and custody case, but Myra didn't believe him and David knew it.

She returned her gaze to her son's face, that very young, thin, unlined face. She noticed he had dark smudges under his eyes, though. His face remained unformed—it could change drastically in a year's time—but sometimes he looked distressingly like a little old man dressed as a boy. Randy had too many worries; he thought too much.

"I'll never leave you," Myra assured him. "That's what counts. We'll always be together."

Randy nodded. He didn't smile.

Myra smiled. She knew she had tears in her eyes and her smile must look kind of pathetic, but for a moment she felt a fresh sense of purpose. "Let's go back," she said, "and stop making the agents nervous."

"Let's run away from them," Randy said, grinning.

She would love to do just that. But Randy's life might still be in jeopardy. In her mind Myra had managed to resolve this twin dilemma, that she hated the life they would live in the White House, but Randy wouldn't be safe anywhere else. For a moment, though, she doubted herself. At that moment Randy took her hand, and she suddenly felt much stronger. She could do what was necessary.

She said quietly, "Promise me, darling, you'll do whatever I tell you." She could feel Randy nodding in reply.

In the living room of the condominium Myra McPherson kept start-ing to talk and then stopping herself. David and Helen listened attentively. After another hesitation on the First Lady's part, David interrupted his client.

"I think we should let Helen be our point person on this. Have her contact the White House to make this plan."

"Why?" Myra asked. She didn't sound suspicious, she just ques-tioned everything, including her own plan. Helen looked curiously at David too.

He watched her as he explained. "Because they'll trust her. She used to be on their team and they want her back. This can be her beginning, planning your return."

Helen gave David an odd, shy smile as if he were teasing her. Myra shrugged and said, "Fine."

"I'll go make a call now," Helen said, and to her employer, "we'll talk soon."

She didn't have to elaborate. Randy sat in a corner of the room, pretending to play on his Game Boy, but in fact listening intently to their discussion.

Helen stopped for a second beside David and squeezed his shoulder. A moment later she had walked out.

Myra continued talking to her lawyer. "Tell him I want to be already halfway there when I get the money. Somewhere on the east coast. On the water. I think I know the place he'll pick, but I want him to choose it himself, so it's his choice."

"Yes, ma'am."

"Then we'll make our final plans."

The First Lady walked back and forth across her living room. She burned with purpose as with a fever. She had already steeled herself for this, David saw, and she couldn't let herself waver. She impressed him. He had seen flashes of this resolution in her before, but never sustained like this. Myra McPherson had found a mission.

Of course, she might also have lost her mind.

Randy sat in the corner watching them both. His mother included him in the discussions. She intended this to reassure the boy. It could equally have frightened him, but not Randy. He grinned at David. David didn't smile back. The First Lady's madness had infected her son.

But maybe they both needed this, he thought, this high resolution. They couldn't just return to the White House, slinking in like chastised puppies.

So the plans went ahead. David conveyed the message to Burton Leemis, who got back to him two days later. He named a stretch of coastline in North Carolina that meant nothing to David, but when he passed on the name to his client it made Myra smile. "That's what I thought. There's a resort there, and John has an old friend with a house nearby he let us use for vacations a couple of times. It's beautiful but isolated. That's the kind of place I thought he'd choose."

The word "isolated" struck David. A desolate location suited the First Lady's plans, but why had John McPherson chosen such a place? Maybe the President had plans of his own.

In the Oval Office, the President sat at his desk. Angela Vortiz stood in front of it. He had just told her the name of the location where he'd agreed to send a representative to meet his wife and pay her what she'd demanded. Angela had to be told because Wilson Boswell would provide the ten million dollars.

"Thank you," Angela said sweetly. "We'll have the money there. And of course, you won't want to have the place swarming with Secret Service agents. We don't want to call attention to the fact that you're paying your wife to come back to you."

"That's why I picked the place. Good roads, but not very populated, especially this time of year. I have an old friend who lives near there."

Angela and McPherson stared at each other. Angela seemed very happy and very sure of herself. Their positions had changed. McPherson felt the loss. Without smiling, and in a voice that he tried to keep firm, the President suddenly said, "Could you do that leg thing again? Just for old times' sake?"

Angela beamed at him. She came around the desk, exaggerating her old gliding walk, stopped beside his chair, and put her foot up on the edge of the seat, her knee almost as high as the President's face, her short green skirt sliding up her thigh. She leaned forward until her face was only a foot or so from his, then slowly shook her head. "Teach it to your wife when she comes back," she said.

Angela put her foot down on the floor again and turned and walked out of the room.

Thirty minutes later Wilson Boswell played a tape of the conversation for Larsen. Boswell didn't tell him the location of the transmitter. No point burdening someone like Larsen with extra details. "North Carolina," he mused. "Empty beach, not many Secret Service agents. Think you can find the place?"

Larsen didn't answer. He might have felt insulted by the question, if he ever had such feelings.

Boswell had had to bring Larsen back in from the cold. Larsen had become too dangerous and unpredictable as a free agent. Better to give him an assignment, Wilson Boswell thought, and then give him help to carry it out.

"I'd like to be there myself," Boswell said. "But no, probably better to be far away. And in some public place, surrounded by people. Maybe there's a convention somewhere."

"Be sure to look shocked when they bring you the news," Larsen said.

Boswell was startled. Larsen had made a joke. Boswell stared at the man who had once worked for him.

Later Wilson Boswell made contact with the White House. These days when he wanted the President's ear he called him directly, no longer working through Angela Vortiz. John McPherson seemed to have noticed.

"Angela has designs of her own," he said.

Boswell smiled. No one ever had news for him. He was on top of every piece of information in the world. "Don't worry about her, John. I've had the transmitter modified. If she ever gets troublesome . . ."

He let the sentence trail off. "Don't worry about a thing," he concluded. "We've got everything under control now."

Boswell ended the call, leaving the President of the United States looking at a blank screen with a rather blank expression on his own face. He realized that Boswell had never once called him "sir" or "Mr. President" during the brief conversation. These were marks of respect to which John McPherson had become accustomed. He missed them when they weren't offered.

Boswell had also subtly threatened the murder of Angela Vortiz. He could end her life at any time, from any remote location. Her body could be found on the floor of this office, in the President's private quarters, anywhere.

John McPherson rubbed his own throat and stared into space.

"I'm thinking of coming back," Helen Wills said to her old boss. She had hoped to startle him, appearing suddenly in the doorway of her old office, but Jack Peters didn't startle.

"I know," he said. "The President already called to ask for you."

"What?"

"Actually, Ms. Vortiz called for him. Conveying his orders, she said." Jack sat casually at his desk and tried to keep his voice uninflected.

"Glad you can spare me," Helen said.

"Well, when the President calls . . . When can I expect you back here, Helen?"

She looked distracted, gazing off into an unpredictable future. "I have no idea."

Helen flew to North Carolina. She carried very little luggage but a load of thoughts. *Angela* had asked for her. Angela wanted Helen in on this. That couldn't be good. But Helen couldn't back out now. She was on the President's team, even if she didn't like her associates.

She left the airport in a rental car and drove to a beauty supply house where she bought a blond wig. It was ready-made, nothing special, but it would do. From there she went to survey the beach location where Myra was to receive her money, give it to her lawyer, and then travel on to the White House to resume her old life. She wanted the money in advance, the First Lady had said, before she ever set foot in D.C. That had seemed a small concession, and the President had made it. He was in the appeasement business, now that he had won.

The wind blew cold from the Atlantic Ocean in September. Helen didn't look strange in her long dark overcoat. No one saw her, anyway. In the afternoon of a weekday the week after Labor Day, the beach was almost deserted. The water looked freezing, its whitecaps like ice crystals. Helen shivered. But she walked the whole location. It was as Myra McPherson had described it, beautiful but desolate. A good place for the exchange, where the agents could see for a good distance and be reassured. There wouldn't be very many agents, anyway, the President would see to that. He wanted this business kept very quiet. So did everyone involved.

From the beach location Helen drove only a couple of miles to the beach house owned by the President's friend. She found a key under the porch, where she'd been told it would be. No elaborate security system here. It was a nice house, but a cottage by the standards of the wealthy. Perhaps two thousand square feet, three bedrooms, the closets almost empty. Helen passed through the house and walked across the backyard to the boathouse. The boathouse was very elaborate, almost as big as the main house. It also had a bedroom, and a living room with huge windows giving ocean views.

Two boats hung suspended in the bays under the boathouse, a small speedboat and a larger cabin cruiser. Helen started the engine of the winch and carefully lowered the cruiser into the water. It hadn't been drained and stored for winter yet. She made sure it was full of gas, and went inside the boat to check it over very thoroughly. Half an hour later, satisfied, she got back into her car and went looking for a location she knew from F.B.I. files but hadn't ever seen. Either there or somewhere else, she needed to pick up some things she hadn't been able to bring on the airplane.

A day later, Myra McPherson, her son, and her attorney boarded an airplane in San Antonio. An American Airlines flight this time, not Air Force One. Myra had insisted on that. Along with three Secret Service agents, they had the first-class section to themselves on the flight to Raleigh-Durham Airport. The agents sat one behind them, one in front, one across the aisle. For most of the flight Myra had Randy sitting beside her in the wide first-class seat. A flight attendant started to say something to her about seat belt regulations, but Myra gave her a long look and the attendant decided not to finish her sentence.

David, pretending to read some papers he'd brought, noticed this nearly silent exchange, one that would never have happened a year ago. Myra McPherson had begun to shed her gentle, accommodat-

ing personality. The process had started on the road this summer
and had accelerated rapidly in the past week or two. He knew she
was steeling herself for the ordeal ahead, doing what she thought
she had to do but not liking it. She had become a different woman.
Myra had always had a withdrawn quality, but now she had added a
hard-edged component to her remoteness. Strangers were reluctant
to intrude on her. David wanted to warn her that there was no point
to making this deal if it cost Myra her personality. Whenever the
President saw his wife again, he might not like the bargain he'd
made.

Myra hugged Randy hard against her side and David relaxed a little. As long as she didn't lose Randy she'd be okay, she wouldn't lose
touch with her softer side. But for the remainder of this adventure,
Myra would do whatever she had to do. David put his hand over
hers. Without looking at him, Myra turned her hand and squeezed
his, hard. She wasn't as tough as she looked, which reassured him.
But she hurt his hand.

Randy suddenly said, "Did you know they have a computer now
that's about the size of a fingernail?"

"Where'd you hear that?" David asked.

"Internet. Regular news service," Randy said contemptuously, as
if that were both cheating and unreliable. "The man who invented it
had a press conference. It's tiny."

"What can it do?"

"Not all that much, but you design it to do just one thing. But it's
a computer, David. And you could hide it anywhere. In a shoe heel.
In a belt buckle. I could hide one in my room and nobody would
ever find it. Even'"—he glanced up at David with a sly look—"put it
under a person's skin. Like under a false patch of skin that looks just
like the real thing."

"You've seen too much James Bond," David said.

"Who?"

David was often unsure whether Randy had really heard about
these things through regular news, had more unusual sources, or
was making it up. He could fool David, and Randy had begun to

realize that. He smiled at David. His grin seemed to say, *I can't catch a football every time, but you can't imagine the uses of a computer under the skin.* David had for a moment the feeling common to parents, that not only would this child outlive him, but was already living in a future that remained mysterious to David.

"You keep thinking, Butch, that's what you're good at."

"What?"

David enjoyed his own moment of triumph. Randy held a host of arcane technological information, but he could never match David's storehouse of memories.

"He's saying a line from a movie," Myra explained to her son, and David looked at her with renewed appreciation.

"Oh." That satisfied Randy. He didn't even ask which movie. A moment later he returned to his Game Boy. Myra and David smiled at each other over his head. The Secret Service agent across the aisle glanced at them.

They couldn't talk on the plane. But they had already made their plans. For the rest, Myra relied on Helen. David's thoughts stayed on Helen as well.

Two limousines and a cluster of Secret Service agents met the First Lady's party on the runway in North Caolina. Beyond them, apart from the other agents, Helen Wills slouched against a baggage truck, arms folded, wearing a dark overcoat. David smiled unconsciously at sight of her. Randy waved. Helen smiled back, but in spite of her relaxed posture she seemed tensed, waiting for confrontation.

It came quickly. As soon as Myra saw the limos and other agents she stopped dead still and shook her head.

"What's the matter, Mrs. McPherson?" asked the agent in charge, a medium-tall, stocky man named Ben Warren.

"I want my own car, a normal car, preferably American-made. My attorney can drive it. My son will come with us, and Ms. Wills. Two of you can follow us in one of these monsters." She indicated the limousines disdainfully.

"Ma'am, I'm afraid we can't accommodate—"

Myra turned her back on him. "David, would you please check to see how soon we can get a return flight to Texas? We'll wait for you in the lounge."

She started walking toward the terminal, holding Randy's hand. The seven Secret Service agents near her looked panicked. All tried to surround her. The agent-in-charge called, "Wait, wait."

David stood still. Helen was the only Secret Service agent to continue completely doing the job, going into alert mode, turning her head to scan the runways, the passengers departing from planes, the airport terminal building. David saw her hand go inside her overcoat.

Ben Warren caught up to the First Lady, took her arm, and said, "Please, ma'am, we have a duty—"

"I believe you have orders. I said very few agents. If you think the number eight falls into the range of 'few,' then you need to return to elementary school."

"There are only seven of us, ma'am."

"I believe Ms. Wills is back on duty as an agent, and she is as well trained and, believe me, as dedicated as any of you. She can come with us. And two of you following. I want my own car because I need to confer privately with my attorney. Randy and I will wait in the public hallways until you find one."

She started walking again. Helen spoke up for the first time. To no one in particular she said, "I've got a rental car outside the terminal."

Myra McPherson appeared not to have heard. Ben Warren chewed his lip for a moment, then called after her again. "Wait, ma'am, wait. We've got you a car."

"We do?" another agent said to him.

"Go get it!" Warren snapped at him, obviously glad he could give orders to someone. Helen took keys from her pocket and tossed them to the second agent. "Blue Toyota Camry," she said. "Parked illegally right in front of the baggage claim doors." The agent hurried away. Myra took the opportunity for a reunion with Helen, putting her arms around her. Helen held the First Lady, too, but loosely, and continued her surveillance over Myra's shoulder. David knew how those distracted hugs of Helen's felt. Helen's eyes passed over him for a moment, looking at him only as another potential suspect, then her gaze snapped back to him. Her expression changed, but very subtly. She gave David a long look of recognition but no other greeting. He nodded at her.

In a matter of minutes Helen's rental car pulled up. The agent who'd fetched it jumped out hurriedly.

"Remember, only two of you follow," Myra said to Warren, then to her own party, "let's go."

Helen brushed by David, putting her lips close to his ear. "I'm glad to see you David," she whispered, and her arm went around his neck very briefly. David touched her briefly as he followed her into the car, noting how glad he felt to see her even in the middle of this unhappy occasion. He got into the front passenger seat, Helen behind the wheel, Myra and Randy in back. Myra turned to look out the back window, making sure her instructions were being obeyed. The agents on the tarmac argued briefly, then two of them jumped into one of the limos and quickly began following Helen, who was already driving forty miles an hour to the road out of the airport. She acted as if she knew the terrain intimately. "When did she turn into the steel magnolia?" she asked.

David answered, "It's been kind of gradual and then speeded up here just recently."

Myra turned around and smiled both to show that she'd overheard them and that she could still smile.

"Here we are," Randy said contentedly, "on the road again. Why don't we just keep driving?"

Myra put her arm around him. "Because, darling, we have to get the money first."

The two cars, the blue Toyota and the black limousine, looked odd driving down the road, like a very small funeral procession in reverse. But there were few other cars on the road to notice. Helen drove straight to the beach road, then to a particular stretch of it. When she stopped the car they all looked around in surprise, because they didn't seem to be anywhere. But Helen knew what she was doing. She pointed down the beach to where two men in overcoats waited.

"The President's men. I met them here this morning."

Myra nodded. She had sobered quickly. She stared down the beach as at her fate approaching. Once again she hugged Randy. "Go slowly, darling."

They would have liked to leave Randy behind at the cars, but if they did one of the Secret Service agents would stay with him, and they couldn't have that. The limo had stopped too, the two agents quickly emerging. They followed, hands in their overcoat pockets, looking all around, as the First Lady's small party made its way down the beach to the two waiting men. One of them carried an overnight bag.

The wind still blew hard off the ocean. It was an overcast day, gray clouds merging into the gray water at the horizon. The sand blew across the agents' black dress shoes. The two waiting men hunched their shoulders inside their overcoats. They were hard-looking men, with an official appearance even in their civilian clothes. They might have been F.B.I. agents. They could have worked for Wilson Boswell. David thought they looked exactly like those soldiers who would do whatever they were told, the kind of private reserve army everyone suspected the President of the United States must have available to him.

The two groups didn't exchange many words. Helen had already made the last arrangements earlier today. As Myra McPherson stopped on the beach one of the men held out the overnight bag to her. David stepped forward and took it. It was oversized for such a bag, made of leather, and had no lock. Heavier than he'd expected. David opened it, looked inside, then reached in and pulled out a handful of bills. "You'd think it would take up more space than this, wouldn't you?" he said to no one in particular.

Apparently satisfied, he nodded at his client and zipped the bag closed again, transferring it to his left hand. With his right he reached behind his back as if for his wallet, as if he were going to give the President's men a receipt.

"Now if you'll come with us, Mrs. McPherson, you and your son, we have a car waiting just over there."

One of the two men held out his hand to take her arm. Myra shook her head and stepped back.

"No, we'll be going another way," David said, pulling out the .38 automatic from behind his back, the one he'd taken from the glove compartment of Helen's car.

The Secret Service agents' hands moved quickly, but Helen's voice stopped them. "Don't move. Now, very slowly, take your guns out and drop them on the sand. The one around your ankle, too, Ben, and the one at the back of your belt, Simmons."

"You guys too," David said to the President's two men as the Secret Service agents obeyed reluctantly. Helen, her own gun in hand, waved the agents back, picked up their guns, and threw them into the ocean. She also took their phones from their overcoat pockets and did the same thing. In the process she was careful not to get between David and the President's men.

"Hurry," David said, and Myra turned and walked quickly back up the beach toward the cars, holding Randy's hand. Randy turned and looked back over his shoulder curiously.

"Everybody down on the sand," Helen said. "On your faces. Now."

When the men had obeyed, Helen and David looked at each other. They heard the sound of the Toyota's engine starting. "Don't get up until we're gone," Helen said authoritatively, then she and David turned and ran.

Up at the Toyota, Helen took careful aim at the agents' limousine and shot three holes in the radiator, low. Water and antifreeze spurted out. If they'd been in D.C. the agents would have had one of the Service's bulletproof cars, but this was just a local rental, unprotected.

They drove a short distance down the road, found the car in which the President's men had come parked there, and similarly disabled it. Down the beach where they had all stood, they could see the agents already running up to their car.

"This won't hold them for long," Helen said. "Hurry."

They jumped into the car, Helen driving again, and roared away.

Before the blue Toyota had disappeared from sight, the Secret Service agents reached their disabled car. Ben Warren popped open the trunk and found his backup digital phone. Quickly he made a call, while Simmons, the other agent, opened a locked case in the trunk and took out two more pistols. He handed one to his boss.

The President's two men stood and watched, hands in their overcoat pockets.

Simmons stared down the two-lane blacktop road at the Toyota. "What the hell do they think they're doing? Do they really think they can get away from us? We'll have the interstate blocked off before they can get near it."

One of the President's men said, "There's a house down that road. Belongs to a friend of the President's. I think that Wills woman stayed there last night."

"So what?" Warren said. "Does it have a helicopter?"

"No, but it's got a boathouse."

The two Secret Service agents exchanged a look. Behind them, the second limousine appeared over a hill. In a moment it stopped. The four men piled into it and the limo took off, the heavy car picking up speed quickly, giving chase to the Toyota that had a head start of only two or three miles on the road that led only one place, with no turnoffs.

"What are we going to do when we catch them?" Simmons asked. "Make her come back to the White House with us?"

One of the President's men answered. "That's the deal she made. Don't worry, we'll take care of it."

Within five minutes the agents' limousine reached the beach house that belonged to the President's friend. The car came to a stop. The Toyota wasn't in sight, but the agents had already radioed ahead and had a roadblock established at the next intersection, five miles farther up the road. They knew the Toyota hadn't reached it.

Off to their right was a small wooded area, the trees looking bare and shabby in the early fall. The road at this point was on a slight rise, so they looked down to the beach house and over it to the boathouse in back.

"Let us out here," Warren said. "Simmons and I'll check this place while you—"

"Look!" shouted Simmons, pointing.

They looked to the boathouse and the cabin cruiser that was now tied to the dock. Myra McPherson and her lawyer hurried along that dock, the lawyer carrying the overnight bag.

Faintly, the agents heard Mrs. McPherson call, "Randy! Stay down inside!" So Randy must have already been inside the cabin. Myra McPherson jumped aboard and disappeared from sight inside the boat as well.

David Owens looked back, saw the agents, and his movements turned panicky. As the agents began running, the lawyer untied the boat and jumped aboard it. He tossed the overnight bag into the cabin and went forward. The agents heard the engines shift into gear. They ran hard, around the house, toward the boathouse, all six of the men bunching up together. But they knew they were too late. The boat began to move.

One player had gotten there well ahead of the agents, though. A thin blond man suddenly appeared out of the shadows of the boat-house. He ran down the dock and jumped aboard as the boat pulled away. Up at the front, guiding the boat into open water, David Owens obviously didn't hear him over the sound of the engines.

Ben Warren pulled up in his pursuit. Looking at the thin figure now skulking up the side of the boat, he said, "Who the hell is that? Is he one of ours?"

The President's two men, who actually worked for Wilson Boswell, glanced at each other knowingly and didn't answer.

David wasn't much of a boatsman, but he didn't have to go far. He steered cautiously and pulled back the throttle, going unsteady on his feet as the boat changed speed. He looked back over his shoulder and saw the Secret Service agents on the dock, too far back to catch him. They were yelling something at him and waving their guns, but he couldn't hear.

Then he caught motion out of the corner of his eye. A thin blond man, the same one he'd seen in the trunk of Helen's car outside the motel this past summer, was struggling to open the door into the cabin. The man gave the door a yank and it came open.

"No!" David screamed. "Myra! Look out!"

Larsen looked over the roof of the cabin at him. There was no hatred in his eyes. There was nothing. David had caught his attention, but Larsen had a primary mission. He pulled a gun from his jacket pocket and stuck his head through the doorway of the cabin.

"No!" David screamed again. He pulled back hard on the boat's throttle. The boat lurched forward in the water and Larsen stumbled back out of the cabin, pushed by the force of the boat's sudden forward thrust. He fell on his back against the railing.

David saw this and yelled in triumph. He turned the steering wheel hard right and then left again, trying to shake the intruder off. But a boat isn't a car, it doesn't respond that quickly. David's attempted rapid course changes only made the boat shudder like a nervous horse. It curved to the left, still gaining speed. David saw a buoy coming up directly in the boat's path. He eased back on the throttle and turned the wheel.

When he had it back under control he turned to see what had become of the blond man. Too slowly. Something came whizzing at his head. David ducked, but the club hit his shoulder. David felt his left arm go numb. He fell away from the steering wheel.

Larsen dropped the boat hook he'd used for an improvised club and took out his gun again. He pointed, but the boat, turning, caused him to lose his balance. Larsen was even more of a landlubber than David. As he hesitated to shoot, David kicked out, hitting Larsen's gunhand. The gun flew away, onto the roof of the cabin.

On shore, sheltered in the small stand of trees across the road from the house, Helen Wills stood watching the struggle on the boat through binoculars. "Come on, come on," she muttered under her breath. In her left hand she held a small transmitter, the size of a television remote control. She continued to mutter aloud as she watched the fight.

David felt a moment of triumph when he kicked the gun out of the killer's hand, but the movement also made him fall backward, and when he tried to put out his hands to brace himself he realized his left arm had gone numb from the blow it had been struck with the boat hook. He tumbled sideways.

The intruder, seeing his advantage, jumped down to the narrow path beside the cabin where David clung precariously.

Larsen had wanted to bring a sword on this adventure, preferably a flame sword. But the weapons that always lay readily to hand in the violent computer games he designed and played had proven hard to find in a small North Carolina beach town. He'd settled for a gun, but still preferred swinging something. That's why he'd used the boat hook. Larsen looked slow and stupid, he knew that, but he could actually move very quickly when motivated. He felt motivated today. He wanted inside that cabin, to accomplish his goal and get away. His escape route was all planned.

David held on to a handrail with his one good arm, the right, and tried to pull himself upright as the intruder approached. But suddenly the man leaped forward, catching David by surprise. The man grabbed David's jacket and pulled him forward with surprising strength. David reached for the other man's jacket or arm or head, but that meant he released his hold on the handrail.

And Larsen simply let him go, with a gentle push. David fell backward, flailing for purchase, but there was nothing to grab. The backs of his calves hit the boat's railing and he fell overboard. A moment later his back hit the water and he went under.

The water felt bitingly cold. David resurfaced quickly. The cold water revived his left arm. He thought he could swim. He knew he had only a few moments.

But the intruder had gone forward, to the controls, and increased the boat's speed. It had already pulled away, hopelessly out of David's reach. He saw the blond man leave the steering wheel and start back toward the door into the boat's cabin. He had recovered his gun.

"No!!" David screamed urgently.

The killer turned, looked at him with very little curiosity, saw that David posed no threat, and ignored him.

The boat continued to speed away toward the open ocean. It was already a hundred yards away from David when the man disappeared into the cabin's interior.

Back on the dock, the Secret Service agents watched, equally helpless but even more frantic than David. One talked into a phone, on the line to the Coast Guard. Two others had gone into the boathouse and were trying to get the other boat started. "Hurry up!" Ben Warren called down to them.

The President's two men—Boswell's men—had faded out of sight. They were walking quickly down the road, also talking on phones, trying to arrange a rendezvous.

On the dock, Ben Warren saw the cabin cruiser pulling farther away. He could see the lawyer in the water, flailing his arms futilely.

The speedboat emerged from the boathouse. No question, they could catch the cruiser now, one way or another. But who was that bastard on the boat with the First Lady and her son, and why had he gone into the cabin with a gun?

The next moment all sound vanished—the speedboat's engine, the agents' voices urging each other on, the crackle on Warren's phone—except the one huge sound that obliterated all others. The agents, all military veterans, most with combat experience, immediately recognized the sound of explosion. The wind from off the ocean seemed to grow stronger, blowing back their hair, as a small shock wave passed over them.

The cabin cruiser was gone. Pieces of it slapped down in the water. Where it had sat in the water, only a thick oil slick and debris marked its grave. The smoke from the explosion, black and roiling, rose from the spot.

"Oh, my God," Ben Warren mouthed. He stared dully. The First Lady and her boat had been obliterated. And the President's son. In front of Warren's eyes. He looked for movement in the water but there was none, except for the pieces of boat continuing to splash down, and the First Lady's lawyer still treading water a hundred yards from where the boat had exploded.

The speedboat took off. The two agents aboard it quickly reached David Owens. One agent reached over the side and hauled him aboard. David fought them for a second, obviously not realizing what was going on. He was crying and raging, seeming out of his mind.

"The money bag!" he sobbed. "It must have been rigged!"

The agents stared around the water. All that remained of the boat was debris and a few bills floating.

"Get divers!" the First Lady's lawyer begged them. "Call the Coast Guard! Maybe—"

But the agents, floating in the remains of the cabin cruiser, knew no one could have survived this. David Owens must have realized it, too. He put his head down and sobbed harder.

Up above the house, across the road in the grove of trees, Helen released the button of the small transmitter that had set off the bomb she'd planted aboard the boat the day before. At her feet was a shallow hole she had dug earlier. She quickly disassembled the transmitter, dropped the pieces into the hole, and covered it up. It really didn't matter if someone found it.

She turned away from the sight of the house and the water and David Owens crying in the speedboat, and began walking quickly to the car.

CHAPTER

sixteen

★ President John McPherson stood in the Oval Office with his closest advisor behind him. Burton Leemis talked, but McPherson didn't hear him. He stared out the tall windows at the city of Washington, white and beautiful in the morning sun of a crisp September day. McPherson wondered if someone in this city had had a hand in murdering his wife and son. But he thought—he was afraid— he knew who had planned and executed that tragedy. Someone who didn't want the President distracted from more important business.

If it had been Wilson Boswell, John McPherson thought he would never be able to prove it, and if he did he would be proving his own complicity. Boswell would have arranged things that cleverly. So the President didn't even want the investigation to go in the right direction.

Most of all, he just didn't have the energy to give a damn about anything.

Leemis continued summarizing the evidence, his voice almost a monotone as if he were reading from a report. "The currents in that part of the ocean are very strong and very tricky. We'll never find . . . everything. Certainly not the money, which would be the first thing to drift away. Just as well, probably. That would have been hard to explain, why the First Lady was carrying such a huge chunk of cash."

Divers had found pieces of the wreckage and traces of blood and flesh, but not enough to identify. They would never find enough of the first wife and son for a burial. Leemis left that part out, the most human thoughtfulness he showed that morning.

"As for the perpetrators, I'm sure you have your own thorough reports on that. The Secret Service agents were so busy in the first few minutes trying to see if they could rescue anyone that they failed to get a couple of small roads closed off. Someone could have gotten away in the confusion. In fact, of course, whoever did it might not even have been there. The bomb might have been on a timer. Or that person who jumped on the boat might have had it on him."

The President didn't even nod. Leemis clearly didn't have his client's attention. The intercom beeped, and the President's secretary said, "Your ten o'clock is here, sir."

"Let him in."

"That San Antonio lawyer?" Leemis said contemptuously. "He's keeping the appointment? Does he think there's still a case here? This smacks of desperation, if you ask me."

The President didn't ask him.

David Owens entered the room. He wore a black suit and an expression of bitter mourning. David looked grim and worn and much older. He walked up to the desk without a word.

It galled Burton Leemis to see the late First Lady's lawyer walking around free, let alone standing in the Oval Office. Leemis had brainstormed with Justice Department officials over what crime David Owens should be charged with in the wake of the disaster in North Carolina, but they hadn't been able to come up with anything worth pursuing. What had he been doing but attempting to aid and abet the escape of a woman who had every right to leave if she wanted? He certainly hadn't been in on the murder plot. Every witness at the scene swore David had done his best to prevent it.

The President had clearly not wanted that investigation pursued, so it had been quietly dropped. David Owens's worst punishment was losing his famous client and only big case.

Leemis noticed that the man didn't even carry a briefcase. "Do we have some wrapping-up business? Surely there's nothing more. It would be gracious of you to non-suit your divorce case, instead of letting it linger on the docket. Other than that, I don't see—"

David stared at the President, who stood with his back to him, shoulders slumped and hands behind his back. Without glancing at the lawyer, David said, "I want to speak to your client alone."

Leemis drew himself up. "Absolutely out of the ques—"

"Permission granted," said the client in a deep rumble. No one moved until the President turned and gave his private counsel a penetrating glare. Leemis harrumphed, started to speak, looked at his client's face, and changed his mind. He gathered up papers and began reading them as he walked out of the room, as if he had more important business elsewhere.

After the door closed behind him, John McPherson turned his flat stare on David. McPherson's eyes were sunken and listless. Even as he stared at David, his attention seemed to wander. Then he came back into focus, saw the lawyer's angry expression, and the President said wearily, "I didn't have my wife and son killed."

"I believe that. If I thought you had, you'd be dead right now. I admired your wife a lot, and I loved your son. I'll never stop trying to find their killer."

The President showed no interest, even letting pass the threat on his life that could have landed David Owens in jail. "That's great," he said flatly. "Is that what you came to tell me?"

"No, sir."

"Then why come?"

David leaned forward onto the desk and spoke in a tone of quiet authority. "Because you're the President of the United States."

This obvious remark got John McPherson's attention. He looked more closely as David continued.

"This tragedy will get you reelected, no question about it. Then you can have any First Lady you want. You can pick Angela Vortiz if you like."

"That will never happen."

"I don't really give a damn. But I do care what you do, because you're the President. Everything you do matters. Even your mood matters. You could have five more years in office. An incredibly long time. You can spend those years plotting your retirement and wondering when your 'friends' will betray you. Or you can be the President you're capable of being. You could be one of the best we've ever had. You could leave a legacy. First you can show a nation how to mourn, then how to recover. You can achieve greatness." David looked at John McPherson with a mixture of admiration and contempt. "You can redeem your soul."

McPherson began to stand straighter as David spoke. His eyes moved, examining possibilities.

"Also, you're the only one who can stop him." David didn't have to say the name. "He needs your help. If you oppose him instead, he can't make it happen. That would be risky, of course."

"Very." McPherson tried to sound skeptical. "So why should I?"

"So your son would be proud of you."

The two men stared at each other. There was a question in the President's eyes, and a longing. But when David Owens left the Oval Office a minute later, John McPherson no longer returned to staring out the window. He spoke to his secretary on the intercom to ask about his day's appointments, then strode briskly out of the office to find his chief of staff.

The President was going to work.

★

Two months later, toward the end of November, David Owens finished a court hearing and stood beside his client for the judge's ruling. Afterward his client hugged him. It was only temporary orders, but as a result of the hearing and the judge's ruling, David's client would be getting to see his six-year-old daughter for the first time since summer. David smiled at him, clapped the man on the shoulder, helped arrange the pickup of the little girl, and then left the courthouse, walking slowly down the outside steps. The day was gloomy, appropriate to the season, but not cold. David didn't wear an overcoat.

A dark car glided by on the street behind the courthouse. David watched it pass. The driver found a parking space at a meter and got out. Just a lawyer, a well-off one from the looks of his big black car. But he wasn't a Secret Service agent or an industrial spy. No such people showed any interest in David Owens anymore. He had become once again nothing more than a divorce lawyer in San Antonio. A prominent one, one of the best, but just a lawyer.

He walked the few blocks to his office, still in the old Milam Building. David could afford more elegant quarters now, but he remained in his old office out of sentiment and inertia. But he would have to move into a larger suite of offices soon. David would soon have to take on an associate, due to the quantity of new cases that came calling on him every week, many of them with pending crises and tangled relationships.

Today, though, he checked his messages, promised to return a couple of calls from his mobile phone, took a small suitcase from his office, and walked back out to his car. He dropped the suitcase, his suit coat, and tie in the backseat and drove slowly away from his building, taking the evasive maneuvers that had become second nature to him. When he was quite certain no one followed him, he turned onto the highway and drove south.

The hundred-twenty-mile trip to the smaller coastal city of Corpus Christi convinced him even more that he was not the object of anyone's scrutiny. The land was flat, the highway straight, and for much of the trip no other car was in sight. Corpus Christi was a beach town, and November was not its big month. But the sun shone on the city as David arrived. He drove into downtown, located next to Corpus Christi Bay, and saw the waves sparkling.

He drove out Ocean Drive, past beautiful large homes, until the houses grew smaller and farther apart. David rolled down his window. There was a breeze off the water, but the temperature must have been seventy degrees. He felt himself beginning to relax.

He parked in the driveway of a small seaside bungalow, noting the freshly planted flowers in a bed around a tree, and the wicker swing on the front porch, perfectly positioned for watching sunsets. The yellow house with white trim looked cozy and safe, but it didn't exactly invite the outside world in, with its shuttered windows.

There was a long pause after David knocked on the front door. He felt himself observed. Then Myra McPherson opened the door and held it wide. She looked very young and fresh in a shorts outfit bought at Kmart. It took David a moment to recognize her; he almost thought he'd knocked at the wrong door. The changes in Myra's appearance were hard to pinpoint—a lighter shade of hair, less angular face, a couple of extra pounds on the hips—but added up to a substantial alteration. Mainly her expression and appearance shrugged off the fleeting perception of resemblance to her former self. Myra looked much too much the young homemaker to be mistaken for the late First Lady. She said David's name and gave him a big hug.

"Oh, it's great to see you."

"You look wonderful, Myra." He put his hands in his pockets, feeling suddenly shy, like a suitor. "Is it lonely for you here?"

"Oh, a little, right now. I have to keep kind of a low profile, but it's not bad. I'm so much freer than in the White House. I drive a car!"

She almost yelped in satisfaction, smiling a big grin.

They had apparently pulled off her escape. It is possible for a live person to walk away from a scene where authorities are frantically searching for dead or very injured people. The little party had dropped Helen and Randy in the woods before the Secret Service agents caught up to them, then David and Myra had let themselves be seen running to the boat. Myra, as planned, had slipped overboard and back into the boathouse, where she'd hidden and donned a blond wig, so that if she were seen running from the scene afterward she'd be mistaken for Helen.

Then it had just been David's job to drive the boat away, get off it himself, and let Helen blow it up. They hadn't counted on the appearance of Larsen, but once he'd knocked David off the boat and gone into the cabin, Helen, who had been watching from the woods, hadn't thought they could afford for him to emerge again, screaming, "Where are they?" So she'd pulled the trigger on Wilson Boswell's assassin.

In the ensuing confusion Helen, Myra, and Randy had driven away, losing themselves in America with most of the ten million dollars—all except the hundred thousand or so David had scattered on the boat for authenticity's sake. David hadn't spoken to any of them since. He had stayed at the scene, playing the victim and trying to throw searchers off the track if they showed any signs of not believing the First Lady and first son had died in the boat explosion.

He had assumed Myra had made good her escape, but hadn't known for certain until he'd received an unsigned note in the mail giving him this address—not by E-mail or cell phone, but good old-fashioned U.S. Postal Service.

They stayed on the porch, feeling the breeze from the ocean. Myra McPherson's hair blew back. Her expression was part of her disguise. She looked genuinely happy. Walking along the porch, her body moved more easily than in the past. She acted a different person than the prisoner of the White House and so looked different.

"Where's Randy?"

"He'll be home soon," she answered. "The school bus stops right across the street over there."

"You let him ride the bus?"

Moving her gaze from the ocean to her lawyer, Myra said seriously, "This wouldn't have been worth doing if Randy couldn't have a normal life. One thing John and I accomplished, we kept his picture out of the newspapers. Even those last few weeks when we were separated, half the time a newspaper printed some other little boy's picture and called it Randy, remember? But mainly nobody expects to see him here. I got my sister to register him in school so they didn't see my resemblance and his at the same time. If somebody thinks he looks like the President's lost son, well, so do a lot of boys. He's just a normal little boy now, growing all the time. Soon people won't even think there's a resemblance. The same goes for me. Nobody expects to see the dead First Lady in the grocery store. In a couple of years my face will change enough that I won't have to wear those dumb hats in public all the time. We'll be fine."

"Rumors will probably start. . . ."

"Don't you know they've started already, David? I'm hiding out in Paris. I'm living on that Caribbean island with John F. Kennedy and Marilyn Monroe." She stretched her arms around at her new life. "This is just as unlikely. I've met people, I've talked to people. I can get by, believe me. There's even a nice man I met at Randy's school, a single father . . ."

David gave her a sharp look. "As your lawyer, I should tell you   "

She laughed. "I'm not talking about bigamy, David, just dating."

They talked for another hour. Myra seemed glad of the company. She gave him a tour of the little two-bedroom house, a perfect size for her and her son. Randy's room had a red-and-blue coverlet on the bed and two sports posters on the walls, tacked up with thumbtacks that looked as if he'd pushed them in himself. The room also had a computer.

"I miss him," David said quietly.

Myra put her arm around him. "He misses you too, David. Stay and see him. But he's making friends at school. For the first time in his life. He's . . ."

She became suddenly tearful, and covered it with another smile.

"Happy?" David said, and she nodded.

Later, hearing the school bus pull up across the street, he said, "Is this worth it, Myra? Giving up everything?"

She nodded. "I haven't given up anything."

"What about your husband? You're still married to him, you know. Will you ever let him know?"

Myra looked troubled. "Let's see how he does, David. What he seems to want. A boy should see his father, if the father wants. You know, if he really wants to find us, he can. He's the President. He just has to want it bad enough."

Gesturing around the cottage, David asked, "Then what would all this have been?"

"A vacation. Or I think I may have amnesia. Or Randy and I have been hiding from a threatened kidnapping, with the President's help. Don't you know you can always explain anything, David?"

David nodded soberly. He heard the running footsteps of tennis-shoe-clad feet. Just before the front door of the cottage burst open David felt suddenly very anxious, as if he shouldn't be there. He should just back out of these people's lives completely. But then the door opened and Randy ran in calling, "Mom!"

"I'm here, darling."

Randy saw David standing in the gloomy interior. His face lit up. "David!"

David went down on one knee and the boy threw himself unashamedly into David's arms, almost knocking him down in his enthusiasm.

"Whoa. Man. You're strong. What have you been doing, working out? Good grief, Randy, you're as tall as I am. What are you, twelve years old? Is it the sea air?"

Randy had changed, as his mother said, even in just two months' time, with the rapid mutability of children. He seemed more outgoing, less withdrawn. He showed David around all his new possessions, including the swing in the backyard. Randy had more color in his face, as if he spent time outdoors here in the mild coastal climate.

"Hey, Mom, I almost forgot. Jeffrey asked if I can come over to play at his house. Can I? Please?"

"Don't you want to stay and see David?"

"I've got to go anyway," David said quickly. "I'll see you soon, Randy. You go play with your friend."

"All right." But Randy looked torn.

David bent to him again. "I'll come see you all the time, Randy, now that it's safe. It's only two hours from where I live. We can take a trip sometime this summer if you want. Or you could come stay with me for a while."

Randy looked shy, or disbelieving. "Aren't you busy?"

"Yes. But I'd rather see you."

Randy smiled.

"Write to me, okay? Send me a school picture."

Randy nodded and hugged him. David wanted to hold him very tightly. He wanted not to leave, to stay here forever. But he had to give this little family a chance to make a new life.

Walking him out, Myra took his hand and said, "If people see you coming around here all the time, it'll kill my dating prospects."

"You can use me to make them jealous."

"I already am," she answered. As he took his leave Myra turned a bit kittenish. "Meeting someone?" she asked slyly.

He nodded.

Myra kissed his cheek. "Give her my love."

As David climbed into his car he looked back at the two of them standing in the doorway, Randy tugging at his mother's hand to get her to make the phone call so he could go play at his friend's house. Myra waved. She and her son both looked young and happy and utterly ordinary. David waved back and drove away, feeling a sense of loss he hoped they didn't share. But he'd be back.

This drive was a short one, half an hour or so from Corpus Christi to Mustang Island, a small, narrow island that hugged the coastline and featured only one town, Port Aransas. David didn't go into the town, he followed his instructions and drove out a Gulf Beach Access Road, parked in the parking lot of a hotel, and walked north on the beach, away from the more populated areas. Even in winter the vacation island wasn't deserted, in fact some "winter Texans" made their homes there during this time of year, but very few people strolled the beach. Most of those who did were older than David and showed little interest in him.

Here on the beach the air was blustery, the wind off the ocean chilly. It raised gooseflesh on David's arms. White and gray clouds scudded around the big sky, letting the sunlight come down in visible beams.

He saw her coming toward him, her blond hair catching the sunlight the same way the sparkling waves did. Wearing a thigh-length lightweight green beach jacket, she looked better prepared for this place than David, or as if she'd been here longer.

He felt a great relief, or something more, at the sight of her. He saw her eyes move, scanning the terrain around him, a trait that seemed to be genetic in Helen. Her eyes finally landed on David.

And she smiled. Helen took her hands from her pockets, spread her arms, and walked faster. They closed the last gap between them and threw their arms around each other.

"God, it's good to see you," she breathed, just as he was about to say the same. Holding Helen, David realized how lonely he'd been. He had his work, and a couple of friends, but no plans for the future, no reason to go home at night.

Helen held him tightly, then stepped back. He saw her eyes were moist. "I didn't think I'd been thinking about you much. . . ." she said with a little stammer.

"Until you see me, and then you realize how empty your life has been, and how much you already hate the thought of driving away from here without me?"

She laughed. "God, you really take an idea and run . . ."

"I'm describing how I feel, Helen."

She stopped talking, looked at him with an attempt at irony but didn't pull it off. She laughed again and took his arm. They walked along the beach.

"So how's Dallas?" he asked.

"It's Dallas."

"That's how I've always felt about it."

"It's just a place to be. Biding my time. I've got a good job, big insurance company, they loved my Secret Service background. Think I can find out anything. I'm just waiting to become anonymous again. I don't think anybody's checking up on me anymore. They buy this new career, I think. I don't know. I'll wait a while longer."

"You could wait in San Antonio." When she didn't respond he added, "Somebody has other things to worry about. That computer virus had some limited release, but the F.B.I. caught it early and tracked it back to TitanWorks. Wilson Boswell's probably going to be in court for the rest of his life."

Helen smiled. "Yes, I read about that. Interesting how they traced it."

"Makes you wish you knew the inside story," David agreed, then returned to the subject of Helen's life. "Did you have to resign from the Service? If you were still in the White House maybe you'd hear . . ."

"After the First Lady and her son were killed on my watch? No way I could have stayed, David. People wondered why I wasn't on the boat ahead of them, they looked askance at the idea that I was still checking out the boathouse."

"Pulling a gun on other agents probably didn't look good in your permanent record, either."

"No, even after I explained I was just trying to stay close to a conspiracy she would have pulled off without me. No, I had to resign. Besides, they would never have told me anything again. In the week I spent there after it happened there'd be a silence every time I came through a doorway. It was an ugly place to work, anyway. I didn't want to be there without . . . them."

"Have you seen them?" David asked.

"Just from a distance. I didn't want—you know. They seem happy."

"I think they are. I miss him, though. I wish—" He changed the subject. "What about you? I know you're not going to be happy working in an insurance company in Dallas for long. How about San Antonio? I know lots of lawyers who could use a good investigator. It's interesting work. Don't you miss . . ." *Feeling important,* he meant to say, but stopped. Helen knew what he meant, anyway.

"It's not that," she said. "But I do miss my job. Being Myra's protector, and her only contact to the outside world. And Randy's friend. I know—" She spoke slowly, looking down at the sand. "I'll never again be that important to anyone."

They walked on a few feet. David cleared his throat but didn't speak.

Still looking down, Helen said, "You just can't bring yourself to say it, can you?"

David laughed, stopped walking, turned to face her. "I'm sorry, Helen, I can't. It's just too obvious an opening. Here, say it again, give me another chance."

She shook her head in mock disgust. "As a boyfriend, you need a lot of work."

David fell silent, and Helen read his mind. "Yes," she said, "I want to work on you."

"That sounds—"

Helen tripped him. He pulled her down with him, and they fell onto the sand together. He held her waist, she put her arms around his neck.

"How much longer do we have to wait?" he asked softly.

"No time at all," she said, and kissed him.